ABOUT THE AUTHORS

Mary Balogh was born in Swansea, South Wales. She now lives in Saskatchewan, where she taught for twenty years. She won the *Romantic Times* Award for Best New Regency Writer in 1985 and has since become the genre's most popular and best-selling author. Recently she has begun to write historicals, which have received critical acclaim as well. Her most recent Regency is *Christmas Belle*, and *Longing* (Signet), her new historical, will be published in December.

Sandra Heath, the daughter of an officer in the Royal Air Force, spent most of her life traveling to various European posts. She now resides in Gloucester, England, together with her husband and daughter. Her most recent Regency is *A Halloween Husband* (Signet).

Emily Hendrickson lives in Reno, Nevada, with her retired airline pilot husband. Of all the many places she has traveled, England is her favorite and most natural choice as the setting for her novels. Her most recent Regency is *Althea's Grand Tour* (Signet).

Emma Lange is a graduate of the University of California at Berkeley, where she studied European history. She and her husband live in Benton, Kentucky, and pursue interests in traveling and sailing. Her most recent Regency is *A Heart in Peril* (Signet).

Sheila Walsh lives with her husband in Southport, Lancashire, England, and is the mother of two daughters. She began to think seriously about writing when a local writers' club was formed. After experimenting with short stories and plays, she completed her first Regency novel, *The Golden Songbird* (Signet), which subsequently won her an award presented by the Romantic Novelists' Association. Her most recent Regency is *A Perfect Bride* (Signet).

SIGNET REGENCY ROMANCE
COMING IN DECEMBER 1994

Gayle Buck
Lord Rathbone's Flirt

June Calvin
The Jilting of Baron Pelham

Carla Kelly
Miss Drew Plays Her Hand

A Regency Christmas

Mary Balogh

Sandra Heath

Emily Hendrickson

Emma Lange

Sheila Walsh

A SIGNET BOOK

SIGNET
Published by the Penguin Group
Penguin Books USA Inc., 375 Hudson Street,
New York, New York 10014, U.S.A.
Penguin Books Ltd, 27 Wrights Lane,
London W8 5TZ, England
Penguin Books Australia Ltd, Ringwood,
Victoria, Australia
Penguin Books Canada Ltd, 10 Alcorn Avenue,
Toronto, Ontario, Canada M4V 3B2
Penguin Books (N.Z.) Ltd, 182–190 Wairau Road,
Auckland 10, New Zealand

Penguin Books Ltd, Registered Offices:
Harmondsworth, Middlesex, England

First published by Signet, an imprint of Dutton Signet,
a division of Penguin Books USA Inc.

First Printing, November, 1994
10 9 8 7 6 5 4 3 2 1

 REGISTERED TRADEMARK—MARCA REGISTRADA

Printed in the United States of America

Contents

Christmas Magic

❦

Emma Lange

1

The air was sharp with cold. Lady Rebecca Trevor breathed deeply, concentrating on the nip of it in her lungs, as she again reminded herself that she had had excellent reason for accepting Lord and Lady Hargrove's invitation to celebrate Christmas with them in the Palladian mansion looming so dauntingly before her. She had already passed one Christmas with no one for company but servants, and she did not want to be so lonely again.

"Shall I take the babe for ye, m'lady?"

Rebecca shook her head at Smithy, her nanny. Katie's warm, familiar weight eased some of the tension coiled in her stomach. She wished it weren't there, wished she could trip lightly after the young liveried footman leading the way up the gleaming marble steps ahead, but if she yearned for companionship, it was because she had not been in company in a long while and never without Bernard's unswerving support to bolster her. She liked what she knew of Lord and Lady Hargrove, but she did not know them well. Would their friends be gossips, she wondered, her step growing heavier. Would she be obliged to endure all the old, pitying whispers about Bernard's age? Would there be gossip about her drunken lout of a father? Would the other guests whisper sotto voce about how origins will tell in the end and wager slyly on how soon it would be before Katie's mother became the courtesan her father would have sold her for, had not Bernard . . .

"Rebecca! Oh, I am so glad you could come!" Lady Olivia Hargrove rushed out to wrap a friendly arm about Rebecca's waist and sweep her into the relative warmth of a splendid, marble entry hall. "Welcome to Haddon Hall, my dear, and you, too, little Katie." Lady Hargrove transferred her vivid, welcoming smile from Rebecca to Katie and back again.

Rebecca smiled, too. She'd forgotten her hostess's warmth. "We are both pleased to be here. You were exceedingly kind to invite us, Lady Hargrove."

"The pleasure is entirely mine, my dear! And you must call me, Livy, please. I want us to be the best of friends—that is, if you haven't taken me into the greatest dislike because you half froze to death on the way. Lud, what a cold snap! I've tried to make amends by having tea brought to us in the gold saloon, but if you would rather go up to your rooms first—"

"No, no. I should like some tea very much," Rebecca replied, handing Katie, still blissfully asleep, to Smithy and then divesting herself of her heavy, sable-trimmed cloak and her velvet bonnet. When the butler had taken it, Livy wrapped her arm through Rebecca's.

"Come, Stevens will show your nurse to your rooms, while we have our coze. La, I can enjoy myself to the full now that everyone has arrived and is safe and warm! At least they will be the latter," Livy continued with a laugh, "when they've returned from their various activities. My dratted husband cannot simply sit savoring a good fire, you see; he must be active every minute and has taken more than half our little party out to the woods to scout for the perfect Yule log! As if that could not as easily be done on Christmas Eve, when it will be cut! The curse of a restless man, my dear, and it does not stop there. The rest of the group, doubt-less believing they must do something or be scorned, faced the cold to go into Millsbury village, for a look at the three shops there. What they be-lieve they will find in them that they could not find in the rudest shop in London, I cannot imagine, but at least, thanks to you, my dear, I was not obliged to go and pretend to an enthusiasm that would have strained me so I'd have become sour as a lemon before a quarter of an hour passed."

Rebecca chuckled, the last of her tension evapo-rating before the gay, bubbly warmth of the most unsour woman bustling her along in the direction of a fire. Lady Hargrove grinned delightedly. "I am glad to hear you laugh, my dear! Christmas is a time for laughter and nonsense, don't you think?" The question was entirely rhetorical. Her face glow-ing with a warmth that rendered her rather plain face exceedingly attractive, Livy patted Rebecca's arm. "Merciful heaven, I am glad you came! It would have quite ruined my Christmas to think of you all alone again at Penhurst. But shall I tell you who is here?"

A dry twinkle in her eye, Rebecca answered wryly, "Only if there are not so many people that I feel inclined to turn tail and run."

"Goose! If I had your looks, I should delight in having mobs of men about to dance slavish atten-tion upon me, but that is a discussion for another time. Now, I shall hasten to assure you that we are all family but for a pair of exotic Russians, whom

Prinny himself asked my brother-in-law, Peter Barlow—a luminary at the Foreign Office, if I do say
so myself—to entertain for Christmas. As it was the
year Peter and Anne were to come to the Hall, we
insisted they bring Count and Countess Oblonsky
along with them. What a procession their group
made, for Mary and Jane, Anne and Peter's daughters, came too, of course, and my brother Adrian
Ashe, whom you met in London, I believe?"

Rebecca nodded. Adrian Ashe had been one of
the many gentlemen who had paid her court the
Season her husband had taken her to London.
After two years, she recalled indistinctly an amiable
man with pleasant if not striking looks. When she
tried for more exactness, however, her mind played
a cruel trick, conjuring in precise detail the face of
another who had paid her court. But Rebecca was
practiced at deflecting thoughts of him. Instantly,
almost before she marked what she did, she turned
her thoughts away from London and its rakes, and
back to her hostess.

"Then, last but certainly not least," Livy was saying, "we are delighted to have Gerry's closest friend
and cousin—"

But she never finished, for when the footman
threw open the doors of the room before them,
Lady Hargrove was interrupted by a shrill squeal
of dismay.

The cry came from a young maid who held a
feather duster limply in one hand. The other hand
she snatched from the shoulder of the gentleman
who still held her loosely about her waist.

The gentleman was standing with his back to the
door, but even so, Rebecca realized the impeccably
dressed man was not Adrian Ashe. Mr. Ashe, as
she recalled, had been slender, of medium height,
and dark haired. This man was tall and well built

and his light brown hair was streaked through with warmer, tawnier tints ...

Suddenly, the bottom of Rebecca's stomach seemed to fall away. Instinctively, she lifted a hand to it, but no other movement was possible. Her limbs feeling heavy as lead, she could only stare helplessly, all the color drained from her face, and wait for the Earl of Bedford to turn around.

He did just after the maid squealed, and Rebecca marked with a dazed lack of surprise the incorrigible laughter that gleamed in his unexpectedly dark brown eyes.

"Rob!" Livy cried, and Rebecca noted as well the unabashedly indulgent tone her hostess used to say the earl's pet name. "And I thought you had gone scouting yule logs with Gerry! But here you are—"

"I am, of course, whatever you say, Livy," the earl interrupted, in the lazily amused tones that Rebecca had thought never to hear again. "But in my defense, I think it only fair to remind you of the tragic curse laid upon any gentleman who stands beneath a sprig of mistletoe and does not kiss a pretty ..." The dancing light in Robert St. Edmund's eyes stilled suddenly, for finally, he saw the other woman standing behind Livy in the doorway.

Reality seemed to unravel for Rebecca when the earl's eyes locked on hers. Livy and the maid ceased to exist even as shadows. Nothing existed, but Rob and all that lay between them. What was he thinking? A million times she had imagined that moment; imagined what might be in his eyes. But now, face to face with him and in utter tumult, she could not have read a single word in a child's book much less Rob St. Edmund's richly dark eyes. If she could not guess his thoughts, she did learn he was not so shaken as she. He retained the power of speech, for example.

"Lady Trevor," the Earl of Bedford said quietly and then, inclining his head in formal greeting, "Your servant, ma'am."

For a man as famous as the Earl of Bedford was for his ease with women, the greeting was remarkably brief and even stiff, but Rob allowed no one time to mark his unusual manner. Already he was looking down at the maid at his side. "Off with you, girl," he said, giving the small of her back a light push. "And don't look so distraught. Your mistress means to read me the scold."

"I do, indeed, Rob!" Livy stepped briskly into the room, discreetly ignoring the beet-red young maid scuttling by her. "You are incorrigible, and it is I who shall pay the price, for now Annie will moon over you to the neglect of her work for weeks on end."

"Nay, she'll come around sooner than that, Livy. Downstairs maids are fashioned of stern stuff. It's the chambermaids who take weeks to recover from me."

Rob's wryly amused riposte was entirely in form. Livy giggled and never noticed either the enigmatic glance Rob flicked to Rebecca or the little satisfaction he appeared to derive from Rebecca's flawless, but determinedly averted, profile.

Thoroughly caught in her own play with her rake of a cousin-in-law, Livy gave him a cuff upon the arm, though the censorious nature of the gesture was mitigated considerably by the mock despairing tone in which she cried, "Wretch! Behave yourself, please, or Rebecca will form the wrong notion entirely of you."

"Having been to town, Lady Trevor cannot but

be acquainted with my reputation, Livy, and doubt-less has her opinion of me already formed."

Rebecca felt his eyes upon her. Did he mock her? Dared he? Indignation pricking through her shock, Rebecca flung Rob a sharp glance, but the look in his eyes was as carefully neutral as the tone in which he remarked when their eyes met, "It has been some time, Lady Trevor. I own I am surprised to see you. I did not know you were acquainted with Livy and Gerry, much less that you would be a guest at Haddon Hall this Christmas."

That answered one question. He hadn't known she was to come. Another, whether Rebecca could respond with any degree at all of normalcy, was to remain unanswered. Livy spoke first. "Of course, we know Rebecca! Mama and Papa's estate marches with Penhurst. But where did you meet one another? Ah! I know! It must have been in London when Lord Trevor took Rebecca up for the Season I missed because Phoebe was so ill."

Rob answered in the affirmative, but Livy lis-tened only absently. Given that Rob was Rob, she was struck by a sudden, unhappy concern that ought to have occurred to her before. Was it not possible her two guests had exchanged more than names in London? Rob would have taken note of Rebecca. She was too beautiful to miss. And her husband had been old, while Rob was ... irresistible.

Yet, no scandal had touched upon them. Livy was certain of it, for if she had not gone to London that year, all her friends had, and they had kept her informed of all the prize *on-dits*. Nor was either of them casting meaningful glances at the other just then. Indeed, Rebecca wasn't looking at Rob at all. She had gone to warm her hands at the fire, be-cause she was cold and her hostess so remiss that she had not even offered her a seat! Making her way to the couch, Livy all but rolled her eyes as she castigated herself for having been an old biddy grown too nosy to be gracious.

"When you are warm, Rebecca, come and sit by me." Livy patted the place beside her. "And I shall tell Rob just how it was we met."

In truth, Rebecca had grown almost hot before the bright fire, but she had to make herself turn around. She knew instinctively where Rob was, though, and therefore, where not to look, and mercifully, Livy had introduced a topic that had nothing at all to do with the man hovering at the edge of her vision. "I have been meaning to ask after Alex," she said, forcing her lips into a smile as she crossed to the couch.

Rob's eyes closed briefly as the sound of her voice washed over him. It was the same, even to the slightly husky timbre that had made her seem so much older than her years. She had been seventeen then, so young to be so composed. And so desirable.

His eyes came open, and while Livy rattled on about the difficulties her scamp of a son had gotten into in the last few months, Rob studied Rebecca from beneath discreetly lazy eyelids. She was nineteen now, and every inch as collected as she had been when he met her. More so, perhaps, for now that the fire had restored the color the sight of him had leached from her face, she betrayed nothing of the extraordinary shock he'd unwittingly given her.

Yet, it had not been her self-possessed manner that had brought him across a crowded ballroom to her, a girl of only seventeen. To a rake, character mattered little beside beauty, particularly seductive beauty.

And she was still so very beautiful in that same

misleading way. A little puritan she was, with a willowy waist no thicker than a man's hand span setting off the soft, flaring curves of her hips and breasts; skin so creamy it begged to be caressed; and a face a courtesan would make a pact with the devil to have. He'd not forgotten the unexpectedly saucy tilt just at the end of her slender nose, or the fine line of her jaw, but Rob stared at Rebecca's mouth, caught because he had almost forgotten just how full and unknowingly provocative it was.

He couldn't compare her eyes with his memory of them. She kept them steadfastly averted. But Rob was confident there. He had seen her eyes too often in his dreams not to remember exactly their honey-gold color. It was only a little darker than the glorious gold of her hair. Its beauty had not dimmed in the two years since he had run wondering fingers through it. Still gleaming and thick as he remembered, it was pinned in a coil atop her head. She had ruffled it when she had removed her bonnet, and Rob amused himself a moment by imagining Rebecca's reaction should he reach out to smooth into place the little tendrils that had risen to form a halo about her face.

"Thanks to you, my dear, Alex is quite the scamp Gerry assures me a five-year-old boy should be." Lady Hargrove turned to smile at Rob, putting an end to his covert study of Rebecca. "Did you know that Rebecca saved Alex from certain harm, Rob?"

"I think I have already said, Livy, that I was unaware you were even acquainted with Lady Trevor."

Livy wrinkled her nose at him. "Well, I forgot! Pray excuse me, and now, for being so excessively dry, I shall make you listen to the long version of Rebecca's heroism."

At the same moment Rob said with every evidence of sincerity, "I should be delighted to hear it," Rebecca exclaimed in her throaty voice that made Rob think of warmed honey, "Oh, no, Livy! Please."

Livy patted Rebecca's hand. "As you are the lady, your desire shall prevail. Rob will have only the abbreviated version, but yes, of course, he must hear the story! It is not every day my child escapes from his nanny and trots directly to a stream that has been swollen by a recent rain, and promptly jumps in after a flock of intriguing ducks, though he cannot swim. What a nose for trouble that child has!" Livy shook her head, turning to Rob, who was attending to her with gratifying interest. "Had Rebecca not happened to be riding nearby when Alex began to scream and had she not had the daring to jump into the stream after him, Alex would have drowned."

"You give me too much credit, Livy—"

"Too much credit! I could never give you enough, my dear. You saved my child, and what is worse, when I could have repaid at least a portion of my debt by lending you my presence at a time you needed it desperately, I was nowhere to be found."

"That is a most unfair charge to level against yourself, Livy," Rebecca insisted with a firmness that made her seem older in age than Livy at twenty-eight. "You live a full day's journey from Penhurst and could not know of my circumstances."

"I could have written to ask who would be with you for your lying-in! But I did not and so you were all alone. Alone!" Livy repeated, turning to glare indignantly at Rob, as if he were somehow at fault. "Can you imagine how difficult it would be for a woman even to approach her lying-in knowing she would be alone but for a country midwife? But of course you cannot. You are only a man."

"I am that, Livy, but nonetheless, I think I can guess something of the difficulty." Rob defended himself with unusual quietness, before he transferred his dark, steady gaze to Rebecca. "You have had a child, Lady Trevor? I did not know."

"Yes." Despite the difficulty Rebecca had looking at Rob, the expression in the amber-gold eyes she flicked briefly in his general direction was soft. "Katie was born in July."

"It is a pity Lord Trevor never knew her!" Livy remarked with a sentimental sigh. "Still, at least he did know he was to be a father."

"Yes, he was very pleased."

She seemed pleased for Trevor, too. Rob's expression never changed, but he experienced a sudden, raw desire to cram a fist down the old man's throat. He told himself that the cause of his temper was the thought that Trevor had left her to face the dangers of childbirth alone, and it was, in fact, enough the cause that Rob could believe himself.

Livy's butler rolled in the tea trolley then, and with its arrival, the conversation changed to the Christmas festivities Livy and her husband had planned. Rebecca said little as she sipped her tea and listened to Livy rattle on in her lively way about a dance that evening, a possible skating party the next day, a traditional afternoon fete at their neighbors after that, and so on. Rob spoke occasionally, mostly teasingly. Once or twice Rebecca glanced at him through her lashes, but she never looked at him directly. She couldn't trust what she might betray to Livy, who was no longer distracted by discovering him with the maid.

He had been kissing the girl. Rebecca tightened her hold upon her teacup until she realized she was in danger of cracking it. Carefully she relinquished the fragile cup altogether and hoped Livy would take the hint. Great God, but she needed time to order her thoughts! Then, surely, pray to heaven, with the fierce storm of her emotions calmed, she would be able to treat him as the distant acquaintance he ought to be.

2

As Livy took Rebecca up to her rooms, they encountered Alex, now five and showing no ill effects from his near drowning the year before as he danced about describing the size of the tree they had found for the yule log. With him was his sister, Phoebe, four; as well as the children's governess, a pretty young woman named Pamela Richardson; Livy's eldest sister, Mrs. Barton; and her two girls, Mary, nineteen, and Jane, seventeen. It was Phoebe who explained the little group's purpose, piping excitedly, "We are to have tea with Uncle Wob!" at which laughter bubbled from her elder cousins, Mary and Jane.

The little girl was charming, but Rebecca thought the instantaneous trills of laughter, not to mention the deep flush on the rounded cheeks of both of the girls, had a different source. The Barton girls were less amused by Phoebe than they were excited at the prospect of being in the company of the Earl of Bedford.

Despite herself, Rebecca felt a pang of envy. Mary and Jane were so much what they should be, young girls free to be giddily excited at the prospect of speaking to a strikingly handsome nobleman of dangerous reputation. They'd no need to hide their interest. Nor reason to fear it.

As she did. Rebecca laid her forehead against the bedroom door she at last closed behind Livy. Why?

Why of all the country homes in England was he here at this one? Was he some trial sent by God to test her? But surely God knew already how weak she was! She needed someone—not a husband, oh no, a husband had not been enough—to act as her guardian. The Barton girls had that protection, and they were the same age as she. It wasn't fair that they could be so giddy and innocent, while she must be on guard. But on guard against whom? Aye, there was the question. Rob? Or herself?

"My lady? Is aught amiss?"

"Smithy." Rebecca straightened, swallowing the dismal sob aching at the back of her throat. "No, no, nothing is amiss. I'm only tired. How is Katie?"

Smithy, a middle-aged country woman as warm and commensensical as she was stout, gave her mistress a shrewd look, but she delved no further into the cause of the strain so clearly reflected on Rebecca's beautiful face. She reported that little Katie was awakening and hungry.

Rebecca was not sorry, though she ached with weariness. She wanted her daughter's soft little body in her arms, wanted to feel her at her breast, for she needed to be reminded what was important in life. She knew too well what was dangerous.

Settled in a wing chair before the fire, Katie enthusiastically seeking out a breast, Rebecca traced the child's smooth, downy head with a gentle finger. Would she be blond when she grew up, or auburn-haired like Bernard? It didn't really matter, of course. More important that Katie be gentle and kind, as Bernard had been.

He needn't have married her. Her father, staggering drunk and vile-tempered as usual, had told her that. "I've rid myself of you and your cursed glares at last, witch! Aye and for a goodly sum!" She had defied him, crying she was no cow to be sold at his whim. For answer, he'd cuffed her hard enough to make her ears ring and shouted, "You'll go to him, and be grateful! Though I can't think why he'd want to shackle himself to your impudence, he's set on marrying you. Mayhap, he wants an heir, though he'll have to work quick, if he does!" At that, her father had laughed so raucously Rebecca had known the worst was yet to come. And it had. "Quicker than the reaper he'll have to be, for he's a decade older than me. Ha! Ha! But he's rich. That should suit you. And a baron. You'll be a lady, Miss."

Marrying a rich baron, she'd be free, finally, of the struggle to hold onto the appearance of being gentry while the few hundred acres her father had inherited and the rents that came with them disappeared down the bottles her father and brothers seemed to believe it their duty to guzzle. Nonetheless, Rebecca would have fled from the baron and his riches had she had anywhere to go or the money to get there. She had known few men other than those in her family, and assumed this one, though older, would be much the same as they: good for little but drinking and gaming and clouting his wife with the back of his hand if she failed to keep sufficient claret on hand.

Rebecca smiled drowsily to herself. She could not have been more wrong, except that Bernard had been old. From the first, he had treated her with the greatest respect. When she flinched at the marriage bed, he had not insisted on his husbandly rights. Instead, he had waited patiently until she was ready and then had tried very hard to please her. She hoped he thought he had. He deserved to think it, for all he had done for her.

Even now, after his death, he protected her from her father. She did not know the particulars of the arrangement Bernard had made with him; she only knew that if her father came to Penhurst for any reason, or her brothers, they'd never see another penny of the quarterly allowance Bernard had settled upon them.

But Bernard had not only protected her and shown her respectful consideration. He'd showered her with so many beautiful and costly things, she had begged him to stop. His reply had been that it was the greatest pleasure in the world for him to see her have what she deserved, and to that end Bernard had insisted upon taking her to London for a Season. She, who had had to scrimp unmercifully merely to buy something so lacking in utilitarian value as a book, had made her bow at court, had gone to the opera, the theater, art galleries, balls and soirees.

Ever indulgent, Bernard had not expected her to keep to his slower pace. He claimed the first dance of each evening, but when he retired to the sidelines to discuss old times with his cronies, he had sent Rebecca off to enjoy herself with the younger men thronging about, begging a turn. She had enjoyed their attentions and flattery as Bernard had intended her to do, but none of them had meant more to her than a laugh or an interesting conversation and she had easily held each one at arm's length . . . until the Earl of Bedford.

Katie came up for air and a change of sides, interrupting Rebecca's memories, but they were too strong to be routed long. Even as she settled Katie, she was remembering the first time she had seen Rob. Of good height, with shoulders that needed no padding and a waist that would never cry out for a corset, he might have drawn her interest for his build alone, but in truth, it was the way he had stood looking over Lady Ainsley's ballroom with

lazy, almost indifferent assurance that had caught
Rebecca's eye. Intrigued, for the glittering assembly
awed her, she had looked back to study him and
realized how handsome he was with those tawny
streaks in his hair and his well-cut yet strong
features.

Then suddenly he had turned and pinned her
with unexpectedly dark, gleaming eyes that were
not indifferent at all.

Despite all the self-control she'd learned beneath
her father's fist, Rebecca had not been able to tear
her gaze away, and so not only had she plainly seen
the interest that flared in his eyes, but she had been
shaken by the answering thrill that shot through
her.

He had come to her slowly, taking his time, stopping to talk here, to request a dance there, but all
the while she had watched him from the corner of
her eye. And when at last she had turned to find
him there before her awaiting an introduction, she
had trembled as much with relief that the waiting
was done as with excitement at the prospect of the
dance she'd have with him.

Yet not everything between them had had to do
with the desire that had blazed so intensely between
them from the first. In the course of time, they had
laughed and teased and even discussed seriously
one thing or another. But always, underlying every
encounter, there had been the hot, fierce tension
that sprang from the fact that she wanted him and
he her and that what they wanted was forbidden.

At first, their only close physical contact had
come when they danced, but even so little was in-
cendiary. When they waltzed, Rebecca could rarely
manage to force a smile, she was so acutely aware
of Rob, and as to normal, polite small talk, there
had been times neither of them could summon a

word. Soon, they couldn't bear the exquisite torture of dancing and, having to have more, snatched stolen moments in dark gardens, hands entwined, thighs brushing, lips aching and finally, finally touching, only to set off a fierce, hotter need.

Rebecca had tried to resist that growing need. By fits and starts, she had avoided Rob or ignored him when they chanced to meet, but her efforts had been short lived in every instance. Rob had only had to look at her, his expression set but for the volatile light that might have been anger or desire or both, even, flaring in his eyes, for her breath to catch in her throat and her resistance to crumble.

Then had come the night Bernard had had to cry off from an engagement to go with a large party to Vauxhall. He had not been seriously ill, only had a cough he wanted to nurse, and he had insisted that Rebecca go on without him. She had, and felt like a schoolgirl on holiday, free from rules and watchful eyes. It had been the merest child's play to slip away from the loud, gay party in the rotunda to meet Rob on a deserted walk. Her blood rushing like quicksilver through her veins, she had run into his arms, and when he had whispered all those husky, loving endearments in her ear, she'd groaned and yearned to give him every part of her. She would have, too, but for some revelers whose drunken shouts had intruded upon them in their secret nook, shocking them into remembering they trysted in a public place.

Rob had jerked his hand from the breast whose peak was rising greedily for his pleasure and hers, and, disgust for himself evident in his unsteady voice, he'd growled that Vauxhall was no place for him to love her, that she must meet him in the Park the next day, early in the morning. He would arrange a place for them to go from there, an excuse even, everything, for he must have her or go mad, and she, nearly faint with longing, had said, yes, yes, she would come to him, would come to his bed.

When she had returned home that night, Rebecca had not expected to find Bernard awake, but tired though he was, he had waited up to be certain she was safe, to ask after her evening, to tell her how incomparably beautiful she was, and how proud she made him. Sitting on the side of his bed, gowned in the sumptuous evening dress he had bought her, the diamonds and amethysts he thought right for her gleaming at her throat, Rebecca had felt as contemptible as it was possible to feel.

Yet even so, remembering the feel of Rob's firm, warm skin as she held Bernard's wrinkled hand, she realized that even if she resisted Rob the next morning, she did not possess the strength to resist him forever, and so she acted on sudden, desperate impulse. She told Bernard that though she enjoyed London, she was weary of its social round, and longed so for the quiet and peace of Penhurst she wanted to leave the next day. Bernard had never denied her anything, and did not then, rousing himself to take her home, far out of temptation's way.

She had done what was right. She had preserved her self-respect, honoring the vows she had made before God, but at a cost. Each day at Penhurst had seemed to drag by more gray and tedious than the day before, yet the nights had been the worst, for they had been filled with shocking, shameful dreams of Rob from which she had awakened to cry out in frustration and shame.

Frantic, Rebecca had prayed that time would prove a balm, and gradually, it had—time and the ready gossip of Livy's mother. A chatterbox like her daughter, Mrs. Rutherstone had thought the latest *on dits* from London would entertain the young neighbor for whom she could not but feel sorry, and if the well-intentioned woman had failed to entertain, she had at least instructed. Having a particular interest in Rob, as Livy was married to his cousin, Mrs. Rutherstone had avidly reported on the opera dancer with whom he had taken up; the actress after her; the subsequent demi-rep of great beauty; and on and on.

He was a rake. If Rebecca had loved him, he had not, she realized after Mrs. Rutherstone's revelations, loved her. He'd only desired her, and would have had her betray her husband only to discard her when he tired of her and found a new interest. It was a bitter truth, but it helped to know it.

And by heaven, Rebecca swore, holding Katie the more tightly, she did not mean to forget that hard-earned truth now. His charm, his searing looks, all were practiced. He'd use them as readily on a maid as upon her. A bedmate was all he wanted, and so little would not do for Katie's mother. Never would she have her child grow up to hear ugly rumors of a weak, corrupt mother. She would be strong, and if she had the least suspicion she might succumb, then she would do what she had done before. She would turn tail and run.

3

The Earl of Bedford glanced down the hallway and seeing no one, knocked softly on the door before him. Though he received no answer, he did not doubt the countess was within, for she had made the assignation. After tea, when her husband had left the drawing room for a game of billiards with Gerry, Natasha had drawn him aside to whisper in a breathless voice that she simply must see him.

She had not said why, but he could guess easily enough the reason for her invitation. As for her urgency, he knew from a brief experience with her the year before that she was dramatic by nature.

Stepping soundlessly into the room, Rob closed the door carefully behind him. "Tasha?" he called quietly. When still no one answered, he searched the shadowy room. He wanted to see the countess. He wanted to clarify any misconception she might have about the origin of her invitation to the Hall. It had been Prinny's doing and for purely diplomatic reasons, not his for less laudable ones. Glancing about, puzzled by the silence, he finally caught sight of a pair of feet resting upon a footstool placed before a large wing chair near the fire.

A wry smile quirked his mouth. He had been deplorably vain, it seemed. The prospect of receiving him had put the flamboyant countess to sleep. So much the better, he thought, still smiling to himself as he walked around the wing chair, calling her name quietly so as not to startle her.

"Tasha? Tash—"

Rob broke off abruptly, Countess Oblonsky entirely forgotten, for it was Rebecca who sat dozing, her golden head resting against a wing of the chair. He had mistaken the room and should go, leaving as quietly as he'd come. He knew it, and yet he stood staring. She was not only lovely, her golden beauty softened by the fire's light, but she nursed her child at her breast. Despite his experience with women, Rob had never seen a woman nursing her child, and perhaps that was why something tightened in his chest with such fierceness that he hurt. And did not move.

With Katie in her arms, Rebecca dozed only lightly. She thought she dreamed the man's voice saying a name she did not recognize, and when her eyes drifted open, she believed at first that she still dreamed. Then Rob lifted his gaze from Katie at her breast, and their eyes locked. What exactly he was thinking she could not have said. It seemed in the past two years she had lost the ability to read his expression, but whatever emotion it was that gleamed in his dark eyes, it was powerful enough that she straightened in her seat and pulled her loosened robe tighter, covering the top of Katie's head and all of herself.

"What are you doing here?" Rebecca had meant to add "uninvited" but her voice was too unsteady, and she stopped short.

Rob did not make her an immediate answer. His gaze dropped back to Katie, nursing peacefully despite her mother's sudden tension.

"How old is she?"

The softness in Rob's voice caught at Rebecca. She glanced away from him to Katie and ran a slender finger along the rosy cheek that was still exposed. "Six months," she said.

"She seems to be thriving."

Rob meant his comment as a compliment. For a child to thrive, the mother must be a good one, but Rebecca was reminded how different their backgrounds were. He was a nobleman, had inhabited the highest circles from birth, and doubtless considered it common for a woman to suckle her own child.

"If you are offended, my lord, you may—"

"No!" Rob cut her off with such force Rebecca knew with certainty she had mistaken him. "Good God, Becca, it is . . . beautiful to see."

Anguish twisted in her. She wanted to believe him, believe his words, his roughened voice. Dear God, so much did she want to believe she thought she might scream. Instead Rebecca opened her

mouth to demand again why he had come to her
room, but Katie diverted her. The child had fallen
asleep in the sudden way of a baby, and equally
suddenly released her mother with a slurp, causing
the robe to fall open and fully expose Rebecca's
breast. Hot color surged into Rebecca's cheeks, as
Rob, after a moment of frozen stillness, spun on
his heel and strode to the fire.

She had no cause for embarrassment, Rebecca
lectured herself. Nursing was a perfectly natural act,
and besides, she added heatedly as she laid Katie
down in the handsomely carved cradle that stood
near her bed, Rob had surely seen nothing he had
not seen a hundred, nay, likely a thousand times
before. Even ... but she closed off the memory of
that night at Vauxhall when he had touched her.

She could not so easily deny her acute awareness
of Rob, however. He stared still into the dancing
flames of the fire, his hands braced on the mantle
and his coat stretched tautly across his shoulders.
She watched him from the corner of her eye as she
straightened away from the cradle, but he had no
indication that he marked her movements, until he
spoke into the stillness of the room.

"Why did you leave, Becca?"

Rebecca jerked, then sank slowly down onto the
edge of the wing chair. She had not prepared for
the question, though now, too late, she realized that
its coming had been inevitable from the moment
she had seen him in the gold saloon.

"Bernard was ill," she replied, so softly she didn't
know if Rob had heard her, until he turned to
pierce her with hard, dark eyes. "That was why
Trevor did not escort you to Vauxhall that night. I
asked why it was you left London so precipitously
that you could not even send around a note of

warning. I cooled my heels for three hours waiting for you in the Park."

Rebecca flinched, thinking of him striding restlessly about their meeting place and to no avail. "I am sorry for that. I should have warned you, but I had no one I could trust with a note."

"You can surely devise a better excuse than that," he said, his eyes narrowing as he watched her closely. "There are boys waiting on nearly every street corner in London to run errands for a ha'penny or two."

Rebecca's mouth tightened. If he was within his rights expressing displeasure at having been made to wait futilely she did not accept that he had the right to belabor the point and in such a cutting tone. Were they ranking degree of wrongdoing, surely Rob would hold a position above hers, for he had nearly persuaded her, with the charm he'd honed on countless women, to do something she would have regretted all of her life.

Rob did not suffer Rebecca's mutinous silence gallantly. "Did it please you to leave me hanging like that?" he demanded, his eyes heating.

"No! Of course not!" She glared at him, angry, too, now. "How can you think such a thing of me? It simply was not possible to get a note to you."

"I worried about you, damn it!" Guilty heat surged into Rebecca's cheeks and her eyes dropped away from his so abruptly she stared at the floor without knowing it. But Rob had little sympathy for her distress. "I thought Trevor had found out there was something between us. Great God! I worried endlessly, imagining he had wrenched you from London to keep you from me and fearing that when he got you to Penhurst he might do anything to you, even beat you!"

"Oh, Rob!" All the color that had risen in Rebecca's cheeks receded, leaving them pale as porcelain. "I am sorry. It never occurred to me you would think Bernard capable of such a thing. Under no circumstances, even had he discovered something, would he ever have beaten me. But, in truth, he suspected nothing. When I came home from Vauxhall that evening, he was as kind as ever. He said. . . ." Her throat seemed to close, and Rebecca had to swallow past the tightness before she could speak again. "He said how glad he was that I had gone, and how he wanted me to enjoy London to the utmost." Tears swam into her eyes and she looked down quickly again, curling her hand into a fist as she struggled to control herself. She failed and a harsh sound, half sob, half bitter laugh, escaped her. "The utmost! Poor old man! He had no notion that the utmost was to be betrayal for all his goodness to me."

There was a long moment of silence broken only by the sound of a log cracking and falling in the fire. Then Rob said, "So you did not leave London because Trevor was ill. You fled from me."

However Rob may have meant it, to Rebecca it sounded like a rebuke, and she flung up her head, not caring if he saw the tears clouding her eyes, and certainly not aware they made her eyes shimmer like jewels. "You may characterize my leaving any way you like, my lord, but I would say I found in the end that I had not the stomach to deceive Bernard with a rake who likely recovered from the disappointment of my disappearance in the arms of the next woman to stroll across his line of vision."

The lines bracketing the corners of Rob's mouth went white. "I should say your opinion of me has deteriorated remarkably, Becca. You did not think so harshly of me in London, or was I wrong about that as well?"

"I was a naive girl when I went up to London! Since, I have had two years with little to do but think about the nature of rakes in general, and specifically one who would urge a young woman, woefully ignorant of men with charm as well developed as his, to deceive her own husband and break the vows she had made before God. But tell me, my lord, do I malign you? Are you no longer a rake? Just now, when you came into the room, did you come for this conversation or did you come murmuring quite another woman's name?"

Rebecca was only guessing. She was not positive she had heard Rob calling a woman's name as she dozed. She might have dreamed it, but the sharp jerk of Rob's chin told her she'd landed a direct hit. He had come to her by mistake.

Katie stirred in her cradle, and Rebecca shot angrily to her feet. "We will wake Katie if we continue this pointless discussion. If you will excuse me, my lord?"

Without another word, Rob turned on his heel and left the room.

4

Rebecca paused in the shadows outside the drawing room to scan the small, festive group within. She did not see Rob, and she relaxed fractionally, slowly, pleasurably taking in all the trappings of the Christmas season, from the fragrant green boughs and heavy red satin bows with which the room had been dressed, to the soft glow of the candles lit against the dark of the long winter's night.

Yet despite the pleasure she took in those marks of Christmas, it was upon the people in the room that her eyes lingered longest. There was a small group standing around the piano where Miss Richardson accompanied them in an enthusiastic attempt at Christmas carols. The others in the room ignored the singers for the most part, though occasionally someone or other would turn and good-humoredly shout out a line the singers had forgotten. Everyone, singers and talkers alike, held a bubbling glass of champagne or a darker glass of punch, and everyone was either singing or chattering all at once, their eyes sparkling and their faces wreathed in cheerful smiles.

Once, when she was a little girl and her mother was alive, Rebecca had asked her mother what people meant when they said they believed in Christmas. A thoughtful woman, her mother had not replied until she had considered awhile, then she had said that though Christmas was a magical time, the magic of Christmas was not ordinary magic. It could not work its power on people by itself. Christmas magic, her mother had said, was a tenuous magic that required belief to become real. And what happened then? she had asked, to which her mother had replied with a faint smile, "Why, everyone who believes in Christmas is full of good cheer towards others, is merry and warm and giving, and for the time of the Christmas season at least, feels as if all is right with the world."

Watching the merry group in the drawing room, everyone so obviously full of good cheer toward each other and the world, Rebecca smiled to herself. She had all but forgotten her mother's wisdom, though it must have lingered in some corner of her mind, for surely it was what had given her the courage to come and spend Christmas with near-strangers. And, Rob notwithstanding, she was glad she had believed in the magic of Christmas, for by believing, she had found the warmth and camaraderie that was to her the essence of the season.

Almost before Rebecca had completed the thought, Livy gave a cry of welcome and bustled forward, hands outstretched in welcome. With her came her husband, Gerald, who welcomed the rescuer of his son with such undeniable warmth and congeniality, Rebecca began to feel she really belonged at Haddon Hall at Christmastime. Adrian Ashe made haste to welcome her, too, bowing over her hand with a broad smile that prompted Rebecca to remember how unfailingly pleasant he had been in London. Peter Barlow, Livy's brother-in-law, broke away from the group by the piano to pay his respects. He reminded Rebecca they had danced together once at Carleton House, whereupon Mrs. Barlow, displaying some of the vivacity of her younger sister, said with mock seriousness that she imagined she remembered the dance far better than Rebecca, for she had danced the following set with her husband, and it had been a most unusual one, as he had been floating an inconvenient three feet off the floor. They all laughed, including Rebecca, who, hearing the sound that had been all too rare in the past two years, felt a deep flow of warmth for these people who had included her, a virtual stranger, in their celebrations.

All too soon, however, Rebecca discovered that whatever its origins, the power of Christmas magic was nothing to the power a flesh-and-blood man had over her. It happened when Livy exclaimed that Count and Countess Oblonsky had come. Rebecca turned to see them, but in the end scarcely noticed the Russian couple whom Livy greeted and drew toward the fire. She forgot Christmas even, for in the doorway stood Rob, and it was as if she were catapulted back in time to that first evening

she'd seen him. As then, the black evening coat he
wore elegantly set off the well-made width of his
shoulders, while at his throat, the graceful folds of
his ivory-white cravat played counterpoint to his
entirely masculine good looks. Again, he appeared
indifferent to the effect he created. Disregarding
the eyes turning to him, he looked about as if he
searched for someone. Rebecca whipped her gaze
away from the door. Perhaps he was not looking
for her; likely he wasn't, but whatever the case,
she would not have Rob find her staring mindlessly
at him.

Just how intently she had been staring at Rob
Rebecca discovered when she turned and found
that not only had a newcomer joined the chattering
group around her but that he was examining her
openly, a monocle affixed to his eye.

When he saw he had her attention, the gentleman
gave her a deep bow, though his eye, magnified
absurdly by the monocle, never left her, and there
was a gleam in its depths that made Rebecca stiffen
slightly. "Lady Trevor, I believe?" he said in heavily accented English.

Before Rebecca could respond, Anne Barton
gave a self-deprecating cry. "Lud, you'll think we
English lose our manners when we reach the country, Count Oblonsky! I beg your pardon. I did not
realize you had not met Lady Trevor, and yes, this
lovely girl is Lady Trevor. Lady Trevor, Count
Oblonsky."

The Russian moved quickly, possessing himself
of Rebecca's hand and raising it to his fleshy lips.
"My deepest pleasure, Lady Trevor. I did not know
it was the English custom to keep the greatest
beauties in the land hidden in the country, but now
I know, I shall be certain to accept every invitation
to a country home that I receive."

The others chuckled with good humor, and Rebecca murmured the expected, "You are too kind, my lord," but she did so with little warmth. Despite every desire to find the foreigner interesting, she did not care for the way his eyes trailed down over her.

Repossessing herself of the hand he seemed inclined to hold, she meant to turn away to strike up a conversation with Mr. Ashe standing near her, but Mrs. Barton, thinking to make up for her earlier lapse, mentioned that Rebecca could not have met Countess Oblonsky either. At once the count exclaimed, "Ah, no, but it is an oversight easily remedied. Come, my lady, I will do the honors myself."

As she could scarcely refuse to meet the man's wife, Rebecca placed her hand on the arm the Russian held out to her and allowed him to lead her across the room. She told herself that she had nothing to fear from the count, that she was being overly sensitive because she was not accustomed to going out in public without a husband. But her urge to resist the count's lead became almost irresistible when Rebecca saw that not only were Livy and Gerald among those near the fire, but Rob, too.

"Tasha!" The count called out to the small but opulently curved and costumed woman sitting on the couch nearest the fire.

Tasha. Rebecca recognized the name. It was the one Rob had called out in her room when he had come to her by mistake. The last of the warm, merry Christmas spirit she had enjoyed when she first entered the drawing room drained entirely away. She wished herself away from the Hall. She didn't want to meet the woman who was Rob's mistress or soon would be; didn't want to observe that she was beautiful in a heavily sensual way with full breasts that gleamed temptingly above a daringly low decolletage; a lush, red, pouty mouth that begged for attention; and dark eyes that were exotically, intriguingly slanted.

The look in those eyes was not friendly. Rebecca had seen softer agates, but she made herself return the abrupt, almost disdainful greeting the countess gave her with one as pleasant and gracious as she could make it. She might have taken as immediate a dislike to the countess as it seemed the countess had taken to her, but no one was going to know it, and most particularly not the man lounging so negligently by the fireplace, looking tall and loose limbed and desirable despite everything.

"I think you have met nearly everyone gathered for our Christmas, now, Rebecca." It was Gerald who gave her a friendly smile. "At least Livy gave me to understand that there is no need to present you to my reprobate cousin."

"Indeed not," Rebecca murmured quietly. "My lord," she acknowledged Rob with a nod.

"My lady."

Rob's greeting was as politely distant as hers. If there was a suspicion of rue gleaming in his dark eyes, it disappeared before it could become more than a suspicion, leaving his expression neutral, even distant. Certainly he didn't smile. Even the creases at the corners of his mouth remained uninvitingly straight. Well, Rebecca told herself with a tightening of her own mouth, that reserve was precisely what she wanted. Rob was welcome to his voluptuously bosomed countess, she of the exotic, heavy-lidded eyes and smoldering sensuality. He deserved the creature. She was obviously as capable of faithfulness as he.

Rebecca did not linger to make polite conversation with the little group by the fire. She left immediately after greeting Rob, seizing upon the excuse provided by a new round of singing at the piano, but if she avoided Rob's immediate presence, she remained wretchedly aware of him.

At dinner, she marked his low, lazy voice every time he spoke, and given the sudden acuteness of her hearing, she had little difficulty distinguishing the laughs of both his partners. Mary Barton giggled breathlessly, while the countess's amusement had a high, rippling ring to it. The women seemed to laugh often, and Rob to speak constantly, but whether he entertained the women out of politeness or real interest in them Rebecca could not tell. She would not look to see. She had forbidden herself even to glance across the table and down to where the three sat, and so she could only analyze the intonations of his voice as it drifted down to her, until she caught herself. Then she clenched her hands beneath the table and forcibly concentrated her thoughts upon her own dinner partners, where they should have been all along.

After the fraught meal, Rebecca received some distraction from Rob in the form of the Christmas ball that Gerald and Livy gave. It was not a large affair by London standards, with only the guests they had staying at the Hall and their nearest neighbors attending, but there were enough people that Rebecca could lose herself in the crowd.

Sometime in the middle of the first dance, a girl's high, tittering laugh resounded throughout the ball room, and Mr. Ashe, who had secured the honor of partnering Rebecca at dinner, conjectured with a twinkle in his eye that one of the young men must have noticed the several sprigs of mistletoe Mary and Jane Barton had hung about the ballroom that afternoon. As the other gentlemen present were not slow to arrive at the same conclusion, the rest of the evening was punctuated by the breathless giggles of flattered females, young and old.

Rebecca was herself kissed. One of the young men with whom she danced, a Mr. Barrett, gave her a light, if endearingly earnest, salute, and Mr. Ashe made a show of gallantly kissing her cheek. Then Count Oblonsky requested the honor of a dance, and though Rebecca had little wish to dance with the Russian, she'd less desire to offend a man with whom she'd be in company for the next fortnight, until he maneuvered them beneath a sprig of mistletoe. Even then she'd not have begrudged him a brief kiss. It was a gay, festive night with women on all sides receiving merry buzzes, but the count gave Rebecca far more than a buzz. He caught her head with a thick hand and held her captive while he forced upon her a wet, hot kiss more suitable to a bedroom than a ballroom. Guest or not, he'd have received a kick on the shin had not Mr. Barton appeared to claim the next dance.

Mr. Barton had seen the count's offensive salute, and the moment he led Rebecca out of Oblonsky's earshot declared earnestly that he hoped she had not been offended. "As a foreigner, of course, Oblonsky does not understand all the nuances of our customs, but it is also my experience that Russian noblemen are often rather more ... demonstrative than we consider seemly. But whatever the reasons for it, you shall not have to endure such attentions in future, Lady Trevor. No matter Oblonsky's connection to Prinny, I mean to explain carefully to him the limits of the custom of kissing beneath a sprig of mistletoe, I promise you."

Rebecca was very relieved to have a champion, and putting aside any concern that the Russian might not heed a man as diplomatic as Mr. Barton, she expressed her thanks, then politely turned the subject. They were still discussing the various countries Mr. Barton had visited when he led her from the floor and a man spoke from just behind her.

"Lady Trevor? I wonder if I might have the honor of this dance?"

Because Rob took her by surprise, Rebecca was looking into his dark eyes before she knew what she did. Shocked that he was so close, that he had even approached her, and worst of all, that she should feel a sudden heat fly through her, she stared into his handsome face, her mind scoured clean of any reason to refuse him that would not sound odd to Mr. Barton, standing at her side.

To Rebecca's dismay, her hand trembled as she put it in Rob's. At once, his fingers tightened about hers, and she looked swiftly away, appalled that she should have betrayed how greatly he affected her. But he did, whether she wanted to admit it or not. Though she stared forward intently, she marked nothing that she saw. She could not. Her mind pulsed with no other thought but that he held her hand ... until she realized the dance was to be a waltz. Then Rebecca nearly groaned aloud. She could manage one of the country dances with relative ease, but to dance a waltz, feel his arms around her ...

"If you remain this tense, Becca, everyone will wonder why you were able to dance so easily with every man but me."

Rebecca studied Rob's starched cravat as if it were the eighth wonder of the world. Not for anything could she have looked up to see if there was the same softness in his eyes as in his voice. If there were, she was afraid she would melt into him. She wanted to even while staring blindly at his white linen. He smelled good, painfully good. His scent triggered vivid memories of the two of them in

London: the nearly unbearably exciting tension; the fiery longing she'd felt when she had rushed into his arms; the low, husky groan he had given before catching her trembling lips with his ...

No! Rebecca bit her lip hard. She could not allow so little as his scent and his lightest touch to do this to her.

"You are stiffer than ever, Becca," Rob whispered, the very quiet of his voice making it seem as if they were the only two people in the world. "I swear I don't intend to lead you to the mistletoe, if that is your worry."

Rebecca hadn't thought of the mistletoe. But now she did. Though she had not let herself watch him outright, she knew from stray sidelong glances she'd not been able to control that he had lightly, laughingly kissed several of his partners, including the Russian countess. But he would not kiss her. And she did not want him to!

"Well, if that is not your worry," Rob went on, when Rebecca still stubbornly refused to glance up from the graceful folds of his cravat, "then the cause of your stiffness must be all that eating you did at dinner."

"What?" Startled, she flung back her head and her eyes collided with his.

Rob nodded gravely down at her. "Two helpings of peas, a bit extra of the pheasant, and, I believe, just a taste more of the sole, not to mention, of course, the single helpings of everything else. I do wonder," he went on, a half smile just beginning to tug at his mouth, "where it is you put it all."

"In Katie," Rebecca retorted quickly, fighting a sudden, too-warm awareness of her body when he flicked a light but comprehensive glance over her. Before she could dwell on her responsiveness or upon how carefully he must have observed her at dinner, she began to explain, "Nursing makes me—"

"Ravenous?" he supplied, before she could finish.

"Well, I am sorry to have offended you," she snapped indignantly, but the moment she spoke, Rebecca could have bitten her tongue, for she saw laughter flash suddenly in Rob's dark eyes, and realized that he had been teasing her all along.

Rod held her gaze, smiling down at her while she tried to fume, and failing that, at least to steel herself against him. He was a rake. He knew what to say to charm. Even knew when to change tack, as he did then, becoming so suddenly sober and intent that she found it impossible not to hang on his every word.

"Actually, I don't think you could offend me, even should you try, Becca, but in truth I admire a woman of appetite, particularly one who has the reason for her appetite that you have. I do not, however, admire a man of appetite, at least when he cannot control it. Shall I speak to Oblonsky?"

It took Rebecca a moment to think why he would ask her permission to speak to the count, then she shook her head quickly. "No, no, R—ah, Lord Bedford." She colored, embarrassed to have stumbled so obviously, but she forced herself to be firm when she continued. "I thank you for your concern, but Mr. Barton intends to clarify the limitations of the custom the count could not, as a foreigner, be expected to understand."

Rob swore, and not beneath his breath. "Damnation he didn't understand! Oblonsky understands very well that a gentleman doesn't maul a gentlewoman. He kissed you as if he had you alone in his bedroom, because you are the most desirable woman he's ever seen and because he'd the mistaken impression that you haven't anyone to defend you. Someone must clarify his confusion before he attempts more."

"Mr. Barton will!" The sharpness of Rebecca's tone had less to do with Rob's argument than with the sudden, treacherous leaping of her heart. It was the most worn of ploys, backhandedly telling a woman she was desirable, even the most desirable woman ever seen. She knew that! The extent to which Rob had been speaking for himself, and whether, therefore, he found her more desirable than the countess was impossible to know and irrelevant besides. "If you speak to him, the count will inevitably assume that you—that we—that there is something between us! And I'll not have that said of me, of Katie's mother. I won't have her tarnished by such a shadow! The proper person to act as my protector, if you will, is my host."

Rob regarded her a very long time without reply. In the face of the unfathomable look he gave her, Rebecca's heart began to pound. She did not know quite what she feared, but in the end, he did not argue further. He said only, with a cool emphasis that seemed to mock her, "As you will, Lady Trevor."

5

"But you cannot go so soon, mon chèr!" Countess Oblonsky protested, pouting as Rob rose from the breakfast table. "I have only just come down, and my night was so very lonely!"

Genuinely amused, Rob smiled into the slanted eyes regarding him with such soulful reproach. He'd thought more than once that were she forced to it, Tasha would do very well upon the stage. "I am sorry to hear that Paul was not attentive, Tasha. Perhaps you might try that seductive pout to bring him around. As for me, I thought I made it clear yesterday evening that I've no intention of carrying on an affair in my cousin's home at Christmastime. It simply isn't done."

"Pah!" The countess's eyes flashed as her mood changed in an instant. "You are what the English call a rake, n'est-ce pas? And you are an earl. A nobleman! Alors, you may do what you wish! You have found another woman to amuse you! It cannot be the one whose father sold her to cover his—how do you say—gaming debts? Ah, yes, I heard of that. So sordid, n'est-ce pas? So un-English! But Paul's intrigued with her and did not sleep in his own bed last night, so you cannot have been with her. Still, there is the mouse of a governess! I watched her at the ball. Her eyes promised you any—"

"That is quite enough, Natasha." Rob regarded the Russian countess with a cold steeliness that made her straighten in surprise. "You sound like a jealous fishwife, a most unpleasant sound, I assure you. Now, I shall take my leave, as I began to do a few moments ago, and when we meet later, my dear countess, I trust I shall hear no more of either Lady Trevor or Miss Richardson."

Rob sketched a cool bow before striding from the room, not caring that he left the countess with her mouth gaping. She was a malicious witch. Rebecca would not have welcomed Oblonsky to her bed! She had gone rigid when the boor had mauled her beneath the mistletoe! And she wasn't that kind of woman anyway. Great God, it had taken him weeks just to win a kiss from her. She'd been married to old Trevor then, of course, and ruled by those quaint, old-fashioned notions of honor and loyalty he'd almost persuaded her to betray . . .

"Rob!" Livy panted, trying to catch her breath. "Lud, I have been trying to catch your attention for several minutes. Your thoughts must have been serious, indeed."

"Never more," Rob replied, then couldn't help but smile when Livy's eyes flared wide with interest. "But my thoughts are not for publication so you may as well not quiz me, a course I know you well enough to know you are considering, my dearest and most curious Livy."

Rob's smile was strong and white and powerful, but Livy had long held it was the teasing gleam in those brown eyes of his that made his smile potent enough to affect the breathing of even a happily married woman. To cover her breathlessness, Livy grinned fetchingly. "You know me too well, Rob! But it was not to delve into your intriguingly serious thoughts that I stopped you. Gerry has just informed me that the lake is frozen hard enough for a skating party, and so we shall most definitely go this afternoon."

"Excellent! I shall tell the children. I was on my way to the nursery."

"Oh? Anne's girls are there, you know."

"Are they? In fact, I did not know, Livy."

At Rob's even, patient tone, Livy gave a rueful smile. "Have I pushed them at you? I am sorry, Rob, Anne is so hopeful, and they are both good girls and attractive, I think."

"Quite," Rob agreed readily. "They are also charming, well-mannered, and entirely amiable."

"But not for you?"

Rob shook his head. "No, Livy, not for me."

"Ah, well." Livy shrugged her shoulders philosophically. "I did not really think they would interest you. They are so very young, or seem so, though Mary is the same age as Rebecca. She is lovely isn't she? Rebecca, I mean. And not merely on the outside. She's survived the trials she's met in her as yet short life with a dignity and grace few I know could equal." Livy paused, looking down to flick a piece of lint from the skirt of her dress. "I am waxing on absurdly, I know, but I, ah, did chance to see you watching her last night, Rob. I don't fault you for taking an interest in her. I imagine I would, if I were a man, but I am only a woman, and I like her so well, you see, and I do not want to see her suffer more."

Livy did not see Rob's expression change, but she sensed the sudden stiffening of his body. In all the years they had known one another she had never spoken a word of criticism to him, and her eyes flew up to his as softening words tumbled from her lips. "I did not mean that you would hurt her purposefully, Rob! Truly! I meant—"

"I know what you meant, Livy," Rob assured her in a carefully neutral tone, when she faltered. "And you needn't fear that I will carelessly strip Lady Trevor of her heart. I assure you that I've no more desire to see harm come to her than do you. Truly, Livy. Now, erase that bemused expression from your brow. Lady Trevor is safe, and I am unoffended." Rob's words did not assure Livy so much as the crooked smile he gave her. Immediately she returned him a bright, relieved grin, whereupon he chucked her affectionately under the chin. "That's better. And now with your leave, I shall take myself off to advise everyone in the nursery of the good time we are to have this afternoon."

Rob's reassuring smile faded rapidly as he took the stairs to the nursery two at a time, but it was not at Livy he frowned. She couldn't know her plea that he spare Rebecca hurt came too late. All Livy knew was the danger he presented, for he was a

rake, even a rogue. Though he had never de-
bauched anyone unwilling or innocent, he was an
excellent persuader, and he had broken hearts. Not
on purpose. He had never collected hearts like tro-
phies, but women came to him, had done since he
was a boy, and though he had not ever sworn to
devotion that was not real, neither had he taken
care to see that the woman was not deluding herself
as to the depth of his feelings. Women often believed what they wanted to believe in order to jus-
tify succumbing to their own desires, and he had,
he admitted, been more inclined than not to take
advantage of that characteristic.

Only one had resisted both her own budding desires and his play upon them. Only one, and given
his heedlessness with women in the past, perhaps it
was justice that she, the only one to have resisted
him in the end, was the only one he wanted.

And was it not more of that same justice that
she'd had her bad opinion of him confirmed upon
their first meeting in two years? Rob winced, thinking of the maid, Annie, who had sidled up to him,
plague take her; then of Tasha. Rebecca had recognized the countess's name. Watching for it, he'd
seen the flare of recognition in her eyes. And seen,
when the flare died, how dark those glorious eyes
had gone.

Rob frowned, oblivious to the several august
busts housed in niches along the staircase. In his
mind, he saw Rebecca. Surely it was not a bad sign
she'd responded so to Tasha. Had she displayed no
reaction, had she not cared ... but she meant to
resist caring. And she could be so determined.

Well, so could he, and if the fates had not been
entirely kind to him, neither had they been entirely
unkind, either. They had thrown Rebecca with him
here at the Hall, giving him time with her. His own

plan to stop at Penhurst on his return to London would have failed precisely because he'd not have had time. She'd have turned him away, damning him for a rake, denying him the opportunity to persuade her that he could also be as loyal and faithful as she, if he had the right woman.

Just as Rob reached the third floor, a woman's laugh wafted down the hallway from the nursery, and his grim expression eased at once. It seemed the fates smiled upon him still. He had hoped Rebecca would be in the nursery with her daughter.

And she was laughing. He had not forgotten the rich, throaty gurgle that was Rebecca's laugh. More times than he cared to remember, he had heard it echo in his mind, remembering what an honest, genuine sound it was, and how invariably it had made him smile, too. But remembering was nothing to hearing it again.

Wanting to see her laugh, Rob strode up quietly to the nursery door only to find he need not have been so careful. Rebecca was sitting on the floor with her back partially to him, her legs stretched wide to accommodate Katie between them and her skirts carelessly arranged so that Rob was afforded a clear view of one trim ankle and a slender, well-shaped calf. It was absurd that he should be so enchanted by so little. He had seen a great deal more of a great many other women. Still, his gaze lingered there until Phoebe gave a loud shriek.

Phoebe had, it seemed, just caught a ball Alex had bounced to her. Pleased for the child, Rebecca laughed her throaty laugh and urged her to try to bounce the gaily colored ball to Katie, who was clapping excitedly, though she couldn't have understood exactly what treat was in store for her.

For a long moment, Rob studied the profile of the little girl in Rebecca's lap. Trevor had had the same sunny, pleasant countenance, and had been as good a man as his countenance had suggested. True, at almost sixty he had taken a girl nearly a third his age to wife, but had he not, the drunken lout who was her father would have offered her to the next man he lost to at cards, and it made Rob go cold to think who might have gotten Rebecca. At least Trevor had had the honor to marry her. And to dote on her.

But how could he not have? She was beautiful. So beautiful, most of the Ton had applauded Trevor for protecting her, even as they winked knowingly about the number of men hoping to cuckold the good baron. She was that beautiful, with those tawny eyes and golden hair; and Trevor had been that old. Had Rebecca been a wanton, few would have blamed her overmuch. They'd have said it was only natural that such a young, desirable girl tied to a man who could have been her grandfather sought her pleasures where she could. But she hadn't been a wanton. Her sensuous beauty had been tempered by reserve. She had enjoyed herself, had let anyone who wished to play the gallant do so, but she had drawn a firm line around herself, and any man who had attempted to cross it had found himself resolutely if quietly dismissed. The Ton had taken note and accorded her an even rarer honor than admiration. She'd earned the respect of her husband's peers, which was saying a very great deal, given her background.

"Lord Bedford!"

Rob started. He'd entirely forgotten Mary and Jane and had not looked to see them sitting to his far left by the window, cutting out something with Pamela Richardson, the governess Tasha would have had him seducing.

"My lord!"

"Uncle Wob!"

"Uncle Rob!"

A chorus of different voices hailed him, but none the voice Rob wished to hear. She acknowledged his presence with a startled look and a hurried twitching of her skirt into place.

Too late, my lady, Rob thought, grinning incorrigibly to himself as he pushed away from the door frame against which he'd propped himself. He moved not a moment too soon, for Phoebe hurled herself headlong into his arms.

"Did you bwing us candy, Uncle Wob?"

"Phoebe!" Miss Richardson scolded, aghast. "That is no way to greet Lord Bedford. You must curtsy politely and say how glad you are to see him."

Rather sourly, Rebecca thought Miss Richardson was only giving voice to what she would have liked to do herself, though the governess did not really need to say how glad she was to see the earl. Her shining eyes spoke for her.

And she was quick to reverse her own stand, when Rob sought to excuse young Phoebe by smilingly remarking that he and the child were acquaintances of such long standing that they had long since dispensed with ceremony. "Of course, of course, my lord!" Miss Richardson simpered, or so Rebecca termed her manner, as the young governess went on to exclaim about what a lucky child Phoebe was.

To Rob's credit, and Rebecca remarked it, if grudgingly, he did not allow Phoebe to defy her governess entirely. Half-smile still charmingly in place, he inquired of the child if Miss Richardson really had taught her to curtsy. "I cannot believe you are old enough," he said, and with so little incited Phoebe to wiggle from his arms and do the very thing he had scowled at Miss Richardson for suggesting. For good measure, she even informed his lordship in her piping voice how glad she was to see him. Rob applauded, as did the Barton girls, both of whom were flushed in a way they had not been before the earl's appearance. As for Miss Richardson, she turned red when Rob complimented her abilities as a teacher.

Rebecca would have liked to dismiss all four females, from Phoebe to Miss Richardson as idiotish, but she was too honest. The sight of him had caused her own heart to give an odd lurch, and yet he looked much as he always did, though perhaps the gold streaks in his hair were in unusual evidence, as the nursery was positioned to catch the morning sun. Still, he needed the gilding as little as the lily. He was handsome as the devil.

And she would soon be gazing at him as raptly as the Barton girls and Miss Richardson, if she were not careful! At the appalling thought, Rebecca wrenched her attention from Rob and tried to rise from the floor. With Katie in her lap, however, she found getting to her feet awkward.

"May I help?" Before Rebecca realized Rob was even approaching, he dropped down before her, blocking everyone else in the room with his large body—or reducing them to such a level of insignificance they became invisible—and held out his arms. "I'll take Katie. I would be pleased to make her acquaintance."

He was so close, almost as close as he had been the night before when she had lost her composure and lashed out at him. He did not seem to be harboring resentment for that, though it was difficult to read his expression as he had his back to the light. All Rebecca could say for certain was that his dark, liquid gaze held hers without wavering.

"Thank you, my lord. I could use the assistance," she said, feeling wildly grateful when her voice emerged sounding as crisp as she wanted. "Katie, this is Lord Bedford." Rebecca looked down at her child to find Katie already staring at the tall man sitting so easily on his heels in front of her. "He is going to pick you up."

Katie went without protest into Rob's arms, but she observed him too solemnly. He wanted a smile and lifted her high in the air as he had often done with Alex and Phoebe. He got the same response: Her eyes went wide as saucers, then she gave an ecstatic gurgle. Laughing, Rob repeated the maneuver, eliciting another squeal, and then to end the game, he lowered her and gently bumped her forehead with his, causing her to giggle and grab his nose.

"Katie likes you, Uncle Wob!"

Rob tucked the little girl into the crook of his arm and looked down at Phoebe. "I think she would like to fly," he teased, acutely aware that Rebecca had risen and was watching him, but too cowardly to look to see whether she approved or disapproved of his antics with her child.

There was no question what Miss Richardson thought. Her hands pressed tightly together, she exclaimed raptly, "You are very good with children, my lord! Unusually so!"

Both of the Barton girls were moved to agree and to add wonderingly that Katie had gone to no one else but her mother that morning. Rob knew the pleasure he felt was out of all proportion. The child had gone to him for reasons that likely had nothing to do with him. Still, he shot a glance at Rebecca. He wanted to find an approving smile on her face, but she looked as grave and composed as a statue of the Madonna he had once seen in Rome. And she was not looking at him but at Katie.

"Well, if she likes flying, perhaps she would like skating," Rob said, turning fully to Rebecca and forcing her attention to him. "May she go out with us to the lake this afternoon, my lady?"

Rebecca was taken by surprise until she saw the smugness edging his smile, and realized he had wanted to discompose her for some reason. As cool as a lily on an April morning, she returned pleasantly, "She may certainly go, my lord, if you have skates in her size. Have you?"

Rebecca regretted teasing Rob the moment he grinned and her heart tripped in its beat. "I will be her skates. As you can see, she does not seem averse to me."

"Hmm." Rebecca glanced down at Katie who was, indeed, sitting as trustingly in the curve of Rob's arm as if he were her—Rebecca cut off the thought even as she felt a stab of yearning so intense it made her flush. "Well, ah ..." Rebecca sucked in a breath when she heard her voice waver. "Well," she began again, almost brusquely, "comfortable as she seems now, in the cold she would begin to fuss. I'm afraid she'll have to wait another year or so to skate."

"And you, my lady, will you join us?"

It did not seem an idle question, he regarded her so intently, and it crossed Rebecca's mind to wonder whether Rob's primary purpose in coming to the nursery had been to ask her, and her alone, to go skating. The sharp surge of emotion the thought caused scared her out of her wits. Instantly she pulled her eyes from his and made the first excuse she could think of. "I shall have to wait and see whether Katie is hungry then, I'm afraid. And to that end, my lord, I had best take her back."

Rebecca held out her arms, her gaze firmly fixed upon her daughter. And in part because she refused to look at him again, Rob could not resist murmuring, as he returned the child, "Even if it keeps you from us, I wish Katie joy of her luncheon."

Rebecca did not need to look into those brown eyes of his to see the devilish light dancing in them, but somehow she could not resist doing so. *Wretch!* she said with her eyes, prompting him, as she settled Katie in her arms, to grin outright.

Rob flicked his gaze over the blush coloring her cheeks too, but he made no other provoking remark, now he had her complete attention. Instead he urged her to make effort to join them at the lake. "This may be our last opportunity to skate for a while. Though we've sun today, old Jepson, Gerry's coachman and a renowned weatherman, predicts a heavy snow will fall tomorrow."

"Thank you, my lord. I shall keep that in mind."

Rob looked as if he might press her further, but if he was tempted, he resisted, inclining his head with lazy grace instead, then turning to the others to make a formal announcement of the particulars of the skating party.

6

Rebecca's temporizing with Rob proved more prophetic than she had expected. Katie did demand a second luncheon just as the skating party left for the lake, but Gerald put a trap and a groom at her disposal, and soon enough, she was wrapped warmly in her cape, bouncing toward a large ice-covered lake where thirty people or more from the Hall and the neighborhood had gathered for the viscount's impromptu skating party.

Rebecca saw Livy warming her hands at a bonfire the servants had built at one end of the lake. On the ice she saw Gerald skating with Alex, and then her roaming eye caught on a lighter head.

Rob was not skating alone. He partnered Miss Richardson. The governess did not look very steady, and that may have been why Rob had an arm wrapped about her waist. As Rebecca watched, the governess stumbled, and when Rob righted her, she looked up, her cheeks flushed, her eyes shining, to smile her gratitude. He was looking down already, and returned her his strong, white, appealing smile.

The moment was over almost as soon as it began. The pair turned the corner at the end of the lake and skated away, their backs to Rebecca, but she saw them even when she fastened her gaze upon the merry bells tied to the harness of the horse pulling the trap. Miss Richardson was pressed close against Rob, looking pretty and adoring, while he, holding her to him, was irresistible and attentive.

Rebecca clenched her hands together tightly. She had expected no less. She had known Rob would not be languishing for the lack of her, however much his look in the nursery had implied he wanted only her to come skating. He had a gift for making a woman believe she was the sole object of his interest. She knew that, and she would not feel bereft. It was absurd to feel abandoned. She had never had him in the first place, and in the second, she had not come skating to see Rob.

To prove that she had not, when Mr. Ashe hurried forward to help her down from the trap, Rebecca gave him a bright smile and, determinedly ignoring a heavy feeling in her chest, accepted his invitation to skate. He was the essence of amiability, amusing her with harmless stories about Livy's neighbors, but still, Rebecca was not sorry when Mr. Barrett, the young man who had given her the light, earnest kiss beneath the mistletoe the night before, skated up to ask if he might have the honor of a turn around the lake with her. Mr. Barrett was younger and more vigorous than Mr. Ashe. If she were to keep up with him, she would have to concentrate, and, concentrating, would be less tempted to look about and so catch a stray glimpse of Rob and whomever he partnered then.

Mr. Barrett did indeed like to speed, but it was Count Oblonsky Rebecca did not see approaching until he skated in front of her and Mr. Barrett to request the pleasure of Rebecca's company. She would have made an excuse to avoid him, but Mr. Barrett, well-mannered to the tips of his young toes, never thought to deny the distinguished, older man. Before Rebecca could form a polite rejection, the young man was lifting her gloved hand for a gallant kiss and then skating swiftly away.

Left standing alone with the Russian, Rebecca reluctantly placed her hand in his. She wanted to avoid an unpleasant scene, and though she did not care for him, she reasoned that surely he could do her no harm in one turn about the lake. When the Russian encircled her waist with his arm and directed her away from the bonfire toward the less-crowded end of the lake, she reconsidered and gave him a flashing look, but the count only complimented her skating, saying she was supremely graceful, even an angel on ice. Rebecca knew he was giving her Spanish coin, but false flattery she could bear easily enough until they came around to the bonfire, and so she relaxed slightly. Too soon. Almost in the next moment, she felt the thick, gloved hand on her waist drift up to brush the side of her breast.

Stopping so suddenly she took Oblonsky by surprise, Rebecca spun out of the arm he'd circled about her waist. "I find that I would prefer to continue alone, sir," she informed him tightly, pulling on the hand he yet held to free herself entirely.

"But my dear beauty, what do you mean?" With his tone Oblonsky cajoled, but the grip he had on her hand tightened. "I was only guiding—"

"I am not your dear beauty, sir," Rebecca interrupted, enunciating each syllable clearly, her low voice rough with indignation. "And I wish to go now. Good day."

She pulled again, but the Russian smiled as if she were a charming child who did not know her own mind. "I cannot let you go, my beauty. You are too entrancing. Come, come. We both know you are a courtesan, no more. My man had it all from the servants. Your father sold you like a serf to an old man. Whom do you serve now, cherie? Hargrove or Bedford? I can give you more than either man. In Russia I've vast estates—"

"Excuse me, but is there some difficulty? Count? Lady Trevor?"

The hard, not at all lazy voice was Rob's. The count bristled and spun sharply, his face reddening, to glare at the intruder. In his annoyance, he forgot to hold tight to Rebecca, and the instant she felt his grip loosen, she skated free of him.

And went straight to Rob. The earl's nostrils were flared like an angry stallion's, and his eyes were narrowed so ominously, Rebecca did not need to see his hands fisted tightly at his sides to know the situation was explosive. "There is no difficulty at all, my lord," she said in a low but determined voice. "I merely found I was more tired than I had realized and was taking my leave of the count. Will you escort me to the bonfire, please?"

It seemed an eternity before Rob finally looked from the count to her, and even then he did not seem to have heard her. He stared at her unmoving but for a muscle that flexed in his set jaw. Rebecca impulsively laid her hand on his arm. Beneath her fingers, his muscles felt alarmingly tense. "My lord?" she said, her voice rising slightly in pitch. "Please?"

Rob flung a taut, narrowed look at the count, but when Rebecca's fingers tightened upon his arm, he finally responded to her pleas, and settling a hand on the small of her back, escorted her away.

Rebecca released a long breath as they left the count behind. She had not known what would happen, for she had never seen Rob look dangerous. But nothing had happened, except that she had been spared any further unpleasantness with the Russian. Thanks to Rob.

She glanced up at him. His jaw still appeared to be hard as granite. He'd have done battle for her if need be. Rebecca did not delude herself into believing she was the only woman he'd have sought to protect, but nonetheless, she could not help but be grateful.

Feeling her gaze, Rob glanced down, and she blinked to see how fierce his expression was still. Rake though he was, he would never force his touch upon any woman, and it obviously infuriated him that another man would.

He was gallant, along with everything else, good and bad. Rebecca smiled a little at the thought. "Thank you," she said quietly.

Perhaps it was the softness of her voice, perhaps the tenderness of her smile, but some of the tension left Rob's body and his voice was more gruff than hard when he said bluntly, "The devil offended you."

"Yes," she allowed, her head drooping so that her neck was exposed above the fur of her pelisse. It looked very slender and somehow vulnerable to Rob, and he was only the more frustrated when she added, "But Oblonsky is an unpleasant man, and I do not want to speak of him anymore."

I want to skate with you. The thought came from nowhere, and Rebecca buried it almost before she registered it herself. Certainly she did not give Rob the opportunity to guess at it, though even had he, he might still have argued.

"I do not want to cause you upset, Becca," he said and circled in front of her, halting her and taking both her hands. "Truly, that is the last thing I want to do, but neither do I want this man to ruin your stay at the Hall. You deserve a merry, festive time for Christmas, not Oblonsky's insult."

Rebecca realized that Rob meant what he said. She knew by the sternness of his frown and the tension in his hands. And Rob's caring, his wish that she have a merry Christmas without any reference to himself, sapped at the strength of the barrier she had flung up hard and cold against him. She even felt an impulse to confess the insult Oblonsky had given her. She wanted Rob to soothe away the humiliation of having been called little better than a harlot and treated accordingly. He would do it, she believed. He had wanted her like the count did, true, but he had never, ever degraded her.

Tears threatened Rebecca suddenly. As did, again, the thought that all she wanted to do was skate quietly in the circle of Rob's arm. It came so strongly she could not deny it, or the knowledge that it was not skating she wanted as much as the feel of his arm around her, his warmth, his strength. Him.

Had the ice beneath them started to crack, Rebecca could not have felt any more threatened than she did then. She wanted Rob to hold her; wanted it very much. She had learned nothing. He was genuinely concerned, true, and she could be grateful. But dear God, she should feel no more than gratitude.

Dismayed, she wanted only to get away from Rob and quickly shook her head at him. "I will speak to Mr. Barton. He will know what to say in a diplomatic way. I am grateful you intervened. Thank you, but I do not wish you to do anything more. And now, I am certain you have far better things to do than to attend to me, when I've no need of you. Miss Richardson, at the least, must be languishing without your attentions."

Rebecca could have cried out in vexation the moment she uttered the words. The very last thing she had intended to do was to make mention of Miss Richardson. Rob would believe she was jealous. She hadn't the least doubt of it, and refusing to meet the knowing, triumphant gleam she believed would be glinting in his eyes, she tried to pull free of him, but Rob did not relinquish his hold on her hands. Furious at being held against her will a second time in one afternoon, Rebecca flung up her chin only to find Rob regarding her not with triumph at all, but with such serious, even grim determination that she stared.

"I was only teaching Miss Richardson to skate, Becca, and that at little Phoebe's request. There was nothing more to my skating with her than that. Nothing. Most certainly, I was not attempting to seduce her."

"Nor even hoping to make her fall in love with you?" Rebecca heard the bitterness in her voice but could not still her tongue. "She is besotted with you, as you must know."

"I do not concede that I know any such thing, Becca," Rob said, his dark eyes urgent and compelling. "But I *do* know that if Pamela Richardson is infatuated with me, I have done nothing to encourage her attachment, and I will not be blamed for it. In the first place, I am an earl, and in the second, at the risk of sounding vain, I know I am not physically unattractive. The combination is appealing to a good many women, whatever I will. And it would be as fair to hold me to account for Miss Richardson's presumed interest as it would be to hold you accountable, Rebecca, for the interest you stir in every man you meet."

"Me! I have not been the recipient of the languishing looks Miss Richardson or the Barton girls or the countess give you every time you are near!"

Rob arched an uncompromising eyebrow down at her. "The Barton chits have been set upon me by their mother, and I can scarcely tell them apart. I did have an affair with the countess, but it lasted all of a week and occurred when you were still married. I went to her room that night only to tell her that I neither invited her to the Hall, nor wanted to resume our quite cold relations. As to the looks you do not receive, however," he continued in the same unrelenting tone. "Did you not see Barrett after he skated with you? The pup returned to his fellows with his arms flung wide and his face split in a triumphant grin, and just to make certain the world knew how you'd affected him, he announced in a near shout that he was madly in love, that you are the most beautiful and," Rob added with hard emphasis, "the most desirable woman he has ever beheld. And what of Adrian? Have you not noticed that his face lights up brighter than a yule log when you enter a room? Great God! At the first opportunity, he'll declare himself. And then, as you *do* know, there is Oblonsky. The Russian may not be madly in love, but he would happily eat you for dinner. Ah, Becca, Becca. You needn't blush quite so hotly. I know full well you did not try to snare any of them. I only wish you to give me the same benefit of the doubt as I give you. Now, what exactly did Oblonsky say and do to you?"

But Rebecca was too unsettled to give thought to the Russian. Had she been unfair? Was Rob as guiltless in relation to Miss Richardson, say, as she was in relation to any of the men he had named? She had certainly done nothing to encourage Count Oblonsky, and had merely enjoyed herself with Mr. Barrett and Mr. Ashe. Had Rob only been himself with Miss Richardson? Was he really not to blame if a pretty, unmarried girl with a good deal of time on her hands found him irresistible? Was he to blame if a lonely girl married to a man older than her father should have fallen in love with him?

"Damn it, Becca! Trust me!" Rob shook her hands impatiently, sending her thoughts scattering. "The man cannot insult you with impunity because you are widowed and without any visible protector. He offended you, and I've no intention of letting you go until I know the particulars."

However guiltless Rob might be in relation to Miss Richardson and the others, he was unmistakably guilty of disregarding her wishes in regard to the count. "I do not want you to speak to him! And if you have any regard for me you will not, for talk will inevitably arise if you have some altercation with him over me!"

She was angry. Her golden eyes flashed with the emotion, but it was fear that darkened them, and

Rob understood. She had been the subject of gossip before and knew its ugly sting. "There will be no talk, Becca. I assure you of that."

Precisely because she had been the subject of gossip before, Rebecca knew how little could incite it and was not the least reassured despite the firmness of Rob's tone. "Please, Rob!" she begged. "Please think of Katie, if you will not think of me! She will suffer most if there is any scandal."

"There will not be any scandal if I speak to him. The scandal would be in allowing him to maul you at will. You came to enjoy yourself, and by the devil, you shall. I mean to warn him off you, Becca!"

"And what will happen then?" Rebecca cried, throwing off Rob's hands. "Oblonsky will assume that you are guarding your latest conquest, because you have no legitimate responsibility for me!"

She told herself she was inflamed by a sense of helplessness, but in her heart Rebecca knew something far worse caused most of her distress. She wished he did have the right to speak for her. Spinning away, angry with herself far more than Rob or even Oblonsky, she didn't look where she skated. Unprepared when her skate caught on a rut in the ice, she went down hard, hitting her hip first and then her head.

7

The world tilted crazily. Rebecca closed her eyes against the dizziness but she felt Rob's arms go around her and heard his voice and the urgency in it. "Becca? Dear God, Becca, can you hear me?"

She forced her eyes open and saw Rob looked as worried as he sounded. "Yes," she managed to get out, then winced when she tried to nod. He swore and she tried to smile an assurance at him, only to have her effort fade when a wall of people surged up to encircle them, their cries of concern making Rebecca intensely aware of a sharp, insistent throbbing in her head. When she turned her face into Rob's chest, he miraculously understood, calling out, "Stand back," in a quiet but sufficiently authoritative voice to send everyone scuttling back several paces. "Lady Trevor has hit her head and noise is painful for her." Continuing in the same quiet voice that rumbled in his chest, soothing Rebecca rather than disturbing her, Rob arranged for Livy to send a servant for a doctor, for Gerald to have a carriage readied, and for someone to bring him his boots. When he was ready, Rob leaned down to whisper that he was going to lift her and that she should tell him if he caused her any sharp pain. Rebecca managed a muffled, "All right," before Rob lifted her into his arms and stood. The movement did cause her head to throb unmercifully. She winced and felt rather than saw Rob glance down sharply at her, but she'd hadn't the strength to do more than lay her head against his shoulder and close her eyes. "It's only a little further now," he murmured, and soon indeed, Rob was settling himself on a carriage seat, holding her all the while.

Rebecca made no move to rise. Had it been Mr. Ashe who held her, or any other man, she would not have remained curled up on him, her cheek buried inside the warmth of his great coat, listening to the steady, soothing beat of his heart, but she did not question what she did. The aching in her head, the lingering dizziness, and even the lesser but still painful throbbing in her hip, sapped her

will. Closing her eyes, she simply gave herself up
to the soothing feel of his strong arms around her.

Taking advantage of her own lassitude, Rebecca
didn't open her eyes again until Rob settled her on
her bed in her room and straightened away from
her. Then, feeling the chill of his absence, she
opened her eyes. His face was very close, for he
was leaning down over her, and she could see the
concern that filled his dark eyes. She tried to smile.
"I'm—"

He cupped her cheek with his hand, cutting her
off. "Don't talk, my love. Rest until the doctor
comes. I'll be by the window if you need anything."

Love. Rob had called her his love. She wanted
to be, Rebecca thought dreamily, and she wanted
him to remain as he was, touching her with sweet
tenderness. He did not, though he did brush her
forehead with his lips before he left her.

As her eyelids drifted shut, Rebecca smiled to
herself. He cared about her, at least at that moment, and she was glad. Later, when she did not
hurt so, she would worry about that gladness, but
not then, when it comforted her even to hear him
arranging a chair for himself over by the windows.

She dozed until the doctor came to tell her what
she already knew, that she had a bump on her head
and a bruise on her hip, but had sustained no major
injury. Her nap had refreshed her, and she could
receive an anxious Livy, as well as take some broth
after the viscountess had gone. Fortified and rested,
her headache duller now and her hip only paining
her when she moved, Rebecca had regained enough
strength to begin to think and therefore to worry.

She was falling hopelessly in love with Rob again,
if she had ever been out of it. Even then, she
wanted him to come to her again. It was not just
that he soothed her. She did not feel dizzy or cold

now. She wanted him in the bed by her. She wanted to feel his touch, his hands, his lips; to look at him; to marvel at how sleek and smooth he was; to surprise that tender light in his eyes. Oh, yes, she was most certainly fallen.

Rebecca bit her lip and stared hard into the shadows above her bed. She had to go, and quickly. It was a cowardly thing to do, to run away again, and she would upset both Livy and Gerald if she deserted their Christmas party, but like the rabbit staring fascinated at the fox, she'd an ungovernable urge to flee before she became entirely mesmerized and yielded without battle.

But would yielding be so dreadful, an insidious voice whispered in her mind, and for a half-moment Rebecca imagined what it would be like to sit in Rob's lap, held against his chest, if she were well. She caught her breath at what she thought of doing to him and him to her. She must go at once! She could scarcely shut off the passionate, shameful images. And, she would not lose her self-respect, not ever have herself dubbed a wanton widow.

She never entertained the illusion that Rob's interest, however real then, would prove more than passing in the long run. If she openly gave him her heart, he would treat it like a Christmas toy, cherishing it for a little, until another, newer heart came along to interest him. And just the thought of seeing Rob with another woman, bending low to smile lazily, teasingly at her, say, gave Rebecca such pain she understood her choice had little to do with avoiding hurt. She would suffer whatever she did, but if she left, at least she would retain her dignity.

Having decided, Rebecca turned her mind to the details of leaving, but when she tried to think what possible excuse she could give Livy for leaving so abruptly, she shrank from lying. Livy had become a friend, which was why, when she came to visit Rebecca later that morning, the viscountess found her guest fully dressed, gathering together a few items with which to entertain Katie in the carriage, and frowning to herself as she considered what exactly she would say.

"You are up!" Livy cried in surprise. "And dressed. But it looks as if you are packing!"

Rebecca looked about at the trunks her maid, Hutchins, had packed and nodded slowly. "I am packing. Livy, I must go." The viscountess's cry of dismay was no less upsetting for having been expected. Rebecca caught Livy's hand and held it tightly. "More than anything else, I regret distressing you. You have been so good to me, but . . . oh, I do not like admitting this!"

Livy firmly squeezed Rebecca's hand in return. "You may tell me anything, my dear. I would never think the less of you."

"Even if I admit to allowing you to believe an untruth? I did, you see, when I allowed you to believe that R—that Lord Bedford and I scarcely knew one another. The opposite is the truth. I knew him too well in London. I fell in love with him." Livy's second cry of distress, Rebecca smiled bleakly. "An oft-told tale, is it not? Another foolish girl falling in love with the infamous Lord Bedford, but at least I did not become his lover. I left town, or more accurately fled, before I could betray my wedding vows. I should have learned once and for all then, but Livy, he exerts such a power over me that even now, when I've my daughter's name to think of as well as my own, I can feel myself falling back under his spell. I must go!"

"Come and sit down," Livy said, dismayed by Rebecca's obvious distress. "And you most assuredly need not worry that I think ill of you, my dear. I've my own secrets in regards to Rob. Oh, it was years ago, when I made my come-out. He was as handsome then as now, and had almost every ounce of that same effortless charm. Unlike you, I threw myself at him, I am ashamed to admit, and would have gladly betrayed my betrothal vows, but Rob, ever so gently, resisted me. He said he cared too much for Gerald to take advantage of what he assured me was only a fleeting impulse on my part." Livy smiled ruefully. "It was, but only because Rob's rejection was like a cold bucket of water. I awoke to realize what a dear and desirable man I was betrothed to, while you were married—well, be assured that I admire you, Rebecca, very, very much for resisting the attraction Rob must have been. But as for leaving us, you have just suffered a bruising fall. Do you really wish to travel? I promise I will do my best to keep Rob at a distance from you."

Rebecca shook her head. "I thank you, Livy, but you could not keep Rob away. I interest him, I suppose because he enjoys the novelty of the chase. The difficulty is that I know I'll not deny him forever! I must go and soon!"

"Then you shall, my dear." Livy gave Rebecca's hands another comforting squeeze. "If you must, you must. Let me see, we are to go to the Barncastles' this evening. That should give you a time to leave without fuss, and I will make your excuses—say something about an emergency at Penhurst, perhaps—when we return and find you are gone."

It seemed almost impossible that Livy should be so understanding and helpful. Tears pricked Rebecca's eyelids and she returned the embrace in which the viscountess enveloped her with a fierce gratitude that left Livy as dewy eyed as she.

In her carriage at last late that afternoon, Katie

in her lap and Smithy and Hutchins seated across from her with a thousand questions in their eyes if not on their lips, Rebecca laid her head back on the cushion and forced her mind to her immediate future. The party from the Hall had departed late for the Barncastles' fete, and so there was no possibility she could reach Penhurst that day, but she did hope she would arrive in time the next day, Christmas eve, to light the traditional yule log. The thought reminded her of the festivities Gerald had planned at the Hall and a wave of loneliness nearly overwhelmed her. Fighting it, Rebecca bit her lip. She had done the right thing. She loved him, but he would never return her a love that did not bring her dishonor.

"Ach, look there, m'lady, 'tis snowin' now!"

The lugubrious announcement came from Hutchins, who had not been pleased to have to pack her mistress's bags and set forth from a warm hearth late on a cold winter's afternoon. Rebecca glanced out into the gathering gloom, prepared to see a few desultory flakes. But the snow was whirling down so she could not see beyond the edge of the road.

Soon, only a few hours after they had left Haddon Hall, Rebecca's coachman advised her they must stop at an inn just ahead. It was not a large hostelry, but it was clean and there was one last private room for Rebecca and Katie, as well as beds for Hutchins and Smithy and the coachman.

As Rebecca hurried Katie to the warmth of the fire in their room, the wind gusted around the eaves of the inn, and her host, Mr. Cummins, observing that it promised to be a killing storm, said she was lucky to have found shelter. Rebecca agreed and shivered as she thought of the disaster that might have befallen had they not found the inn. She could not have borne it had Katie had to pay for her weakness where Rob was concerned.

Rob. In that inn, far from friends and home, Rebecca could hardly allow herself to think of him. She wanted him more then, alone and with Christmas so close, than she had ever wanted him. Yearning for what could not be, even questioning her impulse to flee him, Rebecca slept so poorly, she came fully awake at the sound of bustling in the entryway below later in the night.

"Heavens above!" Rebecca distinctly heard the innkeeper's wife exclaim. "Ye're frozen half to death, m'lord. Ach, I do wish we had a bed for ye!"

Rebecca heard the man's low, weary response only because she had gone very still. "There's no room at all in the inn?" he asked, wry despite his fatigue.

"We'll not be puttin' ye in the stables, if that's what ye mean, m'lord, but ye'll have to make do with a pallet on the floor in the private parlor, though it'll not be as warm as ye need."

"It will do, but tell me is—"

"Rob!" Rebecca burst out of her room, pulling her robe tightly about her, and stared in disbelief, but it was he, in a greatcoat covered with snow and ice and a wool scarf wrapped around his neck. At the sound of her voice, he looked up. His face was gray and drawn, and he swayed suddenly as if he had no strength left. "Rob!" she cried again, and though she could not seem to find fluent speech, she communicated volumes to Mr. Cummins and his wife, both of whom had surged to catch Rob before he collapsed.

"'Tis yer husband come then, m'lady!" Mr. Cummins's tone oozed with satisfaction, for he had been thinking he should give up his own cozy bed to the tall, imposing, nearly frozen man who was so obviously a member of the Quality.

His wife's sigh was one of pure romantic pleasure. "Yer lordship's risked a great deal to be with ye for Christmas, m'lady! He must love ye very much!"

8

"Any longer in the storm and it might've gone bad for him," the innkeeper said, looking down gravely at Rob, who seemed to have fallen asleep the instant his head touched Rebecca's pillow. " 'Twas a lucky thing he kept a hold on his horse's mane. Had he fallen off ..." The man shrugged his broad shoulders.

Finishing the phrase for herself, Rebecca shuddered uncontrollably, prompting Mrs. Cummins to pat her arm. "Nay, now, ye needn't worry, m'lady. He's a strong 'un, and young." She nodded sagely toward Rob, whom Mr. Cummins had dressed in one of his own voluminous nightshirts and put to bed, while Rebecca stoked the fire as hot as it would go. "All he needs is rest and yer warmth, m'lady."

When Rob shivered convulsively in his sleep, Rebecca never hesitated. The moment the Cumminses left, she crawled into the bed beside him. He felt so cold, she wrapped her arms around his shoulders and held him to her. Ever so gradually, her warmth and that provided by several bedpans prevailed. His shivering stopped and his breathing became the deep, even breathing of real sleep.

If Rob slept, however, Rebecca did not, at least not for a long while. He had forsaken his family and friends at Christmas; had risked his toes and fingers at the least, his life at the most, to follow her. Tears wet her cheeks, and she kissed the top of his head. Surely only love could have prompted him to do such a thing, but Rebecca hardly dared to let herself think the thought aloud. It seemed too utterly impossible.

Though Rebecca fell asleep holding Rob, when she awoke, she found they had reversed positions in the night. Now her head lay upon his chest, and his arm was around her shoulder, holding her to him. For a moment she simply lay there, savoring the feel of him, trying not to think how she wanted to wake every morning just like that. Even Mr. Cummins's coarse nightshirt felt wonderful beneath her cheek, warmed as it was by Rob's body. Moving carefully, not wanting to wake him, she lifted her head to steal a look at him, but he awakened despite her precautions, his dark eyes opening as she watched. They were heavy with sleep, but even so, they widened abruptly in surprise.

Rebecca couldn't help smiling. "You don't recall being half-carried to my room?"

"No." An endearing sleepy smile curled his lips. "Nor being put into your bed. Surely I am dreaming?"

He was not. They were in the same bed, and Rebecca was suddenly aware of every part of Rob that touched her. She flushed, and her lashes swept down over her eyes. "There was no other bed left in the inn and so I said you were my husband."

Rebecca darted Rob a look from beneath her lashes. His eyelids were still heavy with sleep, but there was an arrested gleam in his eyes that lifted her head. She was not so caught by that look, though, that she did not remember why she had wanted him to have a bed, and in voice gone hoarse with remembered fear, she cried half angrily, "Rob, you could have died last night! Why on earth did you not wait to leave the Hall until after the storm?"

She had lifted herself up on one elbow, the better to see him, but Rob pulled her down against him again and wrapped his arms around her. "I couldn't lose you again, Becca," he said into the silky gold of her hair. "I couldn't have borne it a second time, and as to the storm, I would ride through a thousand winter storms to prove myself to you."

"Oh, Rob!" Rebecca buried her head in the hollow of his neck, breathing in the scent of him. "It was I who ran away again."

"From me," he said grimly.

She shook her head, for she had done some thinking in the night. "From myself more than you—"

Rob cut Rebecca off, lifting himself abruptly to a half-sitting position and pulling her up with him. His light hair was tousled from sleep but there was nothing sleepy or boyish about his expression. "You will not blame yourself for anything. I'm the one must beg forgiveness. When I met you in London, I set out to seduce you without a second thought, but treating you like all the others is not my greatest shame, Becca. I knew then only that you were the most beautiful and desirable woman I'd ever seen. It was later that I came to understand you are nothing like all the other women I've known; that you are loyal and honest and steadfast and true; that if I persisted with my selfish designs I would have you betray the very qualities that make you so rare, that make you the woman I love." Rebecca gave a wondering cry, but Rob hadn't done. "Still, I persisted, Becca. That is my shame. I could not make myself give you up. I kept saying that in another day I would go to the continent, rusticate in the country, take a mistress, anything, but I did not. The thought of never seeing you again made me wild."

"As it did me," Rebecca admitted in a small voice as she laid her forehead on his chest and held him again.

Rob kissed the silky top of her head. "I do have one consolation, and that is that I did not invite myself to stay with Livy's parents any of the thousands of times I considered pursuing you. You were strong, Becca. And you were right."

"I knew Trevor better than you," she whispered simply, then after a moment looked up, the amber gold of her eyes darkened. "Rob, I'm afraid. I don't know if I deserve to be so happy as I am in your arms."

Rob cupped her lovely face with his hands. "You cared for Trevor beyond his wildest expectations, Becca. Do you believe he would begrudge you this happiness because we met while you were married to him?"

He had guessed her concern exactly and, made to think of Lord Trevor, Rebecca remembered how, as he lay dying, the good man had gripped her hand with the last of his strength and said, "Promise me you will live your life to the fullest, my dear. You are young and lovely and made to love. Open yourself to it. Promise!"

Remembering, she began to smile. "No, of course, Trevor wouldn't begrudge me this. He would be glad."

Rob nodded, but it wasn't of the baron he spoke. "Can you believe in me, Becca? In my love?"

"How could I not?" She thought of him in the snow and driving wind and the tears already in her eyes spilled onto her cheeks. "Oh, Rob! I do believe!" Trying to smile, she added softly, "I know your love's no tenuous magic."

Rob's response was to sweep Rebecca up and hold her fiercely against him. "Ah, Becca! I feared you would never say that. But what are these tears, then?" He leaned back just far enough to kiss her wet cheeks. "And what is this tenuous magic?"

"The tears are tears of joy," she said with a tremulous laugh. "And the tenuous magic is a notion of my mother's. She told me once Christmas has a magic, but a tenuous magic that must be believed in to become real."

"No," Rob said, kissing her cheeks again, then her nose, then the corners of her eyes. "There is nothing tenuous about my love." As if to prove it, he kissed her full and hard upon the mouth. And, passion rising suddenly, kissed her until they were both flushed and out of breath. Then, Rob lifted his mouth just inches from Rebecca's to ask, "Will you make my Christmas magical, Becca? Will you give me your hand?"

"Oh, yes." She kissed his cheeks and nose and eyes as he'd kissed hers, then whispered huskily in his ear, "I will give you my hand and my heart, forever, my love."

A stirring sound interrupted the kiss she meant to press upon Rob's lips, and Rebecca glanced to Katie's cradle instead. "And I give you my daughter, too," she murmured, turning to smile up at him.

If there was a hint of question in her eyes, Rob answered it with the broad smile he gave her. "A daughter who has enchanted me already," he said. Kissing her softly, he added, "You have made it a magical Christmas, indeed, my own love."

Dinner at Grillion's

❦

Sandra Heath

1

It was the last day of September, and Christmas was still three months away. Another thunderstorm made its way along the Thames valley, enveloping the fashionable town of Richmond in a haze of cloud and rain. At Lanham House, high on Richmond Hill, the celebrated view from the library was obscured by the constant sluicing of the rain, but the weather was of no consequence to Guy Fitzallen, fourth Lord Lanham, as he struggled to write the most difficult letter of his life.

He was in his early thirties, tall and athletic, with thick fair hair and singular green eyes that could freeze in an instant toward someone he found disagreeable, or warm with such caressing invitation that many a lady had fallen victim to his charm. Sought after for being excellent company, and admired for his immaculate sartorial style, he was reckoned to be one of London's more fortunate gentlemen, but for the past year he'd been wretchedly unhappy. And all because of the beautiful but faithless woman he'd married.

A flash of lightning split the lowering skies outside, and the short-lived light illuminated the incomplete letter, causing one word to leap from the vellum. Fleur. He gazed at the name. Dear God, he'd never have thought it would come to this. Their love should have endured until death did them part, but he was writing to inform her of his intention to seek a divorce because of her desertion. It had to be by letter, for she was across the Atlantic in her home city of Philadelphia and had made it very plain indeed she never intended to return.

How far away now that wonderful July evening two years ago when a chance decision took him to dinner at Monsieur Grillion's exclusive Mayfair hotel? Fleur Barrymore had been staying there with her uncle, Gerard. Wealthy Pennsylvanians with a fine estate just outside Philadelphia, they were on a long visit to Europe. Fleur caught his attention from the outset. Enchanting in strawberry silk, with eyes as blue as forget-me-nots and chestnut curls cascading from a knot at the back of her head, she seemed to shine with happiness and spirit. Her figure was delightful, her smiles and laughter infectious, and her American accent engaging. He thought her the most fascinating creature in the world, and before the evening was over he'd known she was the only one for him.

Over the following weeks he'd laid siege to her, and to his joy she seemed to return his love. Neither she nor Gerard mentioned the real reason they were in Europe. It hadn't anything to do with a desire to see the sights, but everything to do with Gerard's insistence that his niece put a disastrous liaison behind her. What Guy knew now, but hadn't known then, was that Fleur had fallen hopelessly in love with a certain Richard Ashwood, a planter from Georgia. The affair ended when Ashwood lost interest, but there was so much talk in Philadelphia that Gerard felt obliged to take her away for a while.

Fleur obeyed her uncle, but remained secretly in love with Ashwood, and while basking in the flattering attentions of her lordly English suitor, it was of the Georgian she dreamed. She'd gone so far as to become Lady Lanham, pretending for a whole year to love her husband, but when the planter changed his mind and beckoned, she'd gone to him without so much as a letter to explain her departure. There'd been no word from her since. It was almost as if she'd never existed at all, except for the terrible void she'd left in her husband's life.

Even now, twelve months later, he was tormented by the hurt she'd inflicted. Fleur Barrymore had missed her vocation, for she was a gifted actress, feigning love so well he'd really believed his devotion was reciprocated. Now he could hardly bear to recall his joy on their wedding day or the consuming fire of their first night together, for while he'd been duped into thinking he was the happiest of men, she'd been yearning for Ashwood.

Guy got up and went to the window. The rain dashed audibly against the panes, and more lightning illuminated the countryside. It was appropriate weather for his mood, he thought, but then drew himself up sharply. He was a fool to dwell on the past, and must look only to the future. Two months ago he'd unexpectedly become heir to an earldom, and his friends had discreetly pointed out that unless he had a son he would be the last holder of the title. It was very simple. To have a son he must remarry, but to remarry he must first divorce Fleur. Now he saw the futility of clinging to a wife who felt nothing for him, and he had Imogen to thank for opening his eyes.

He smiled a little. How could he have been so

foolish for so long? He'd been so filled with self-pity that he hadn't seen the prize right under his nose. Imogen Wakefield was the poor relation of the family, a widow who'd been his aunt's companion here at Lanham House since before he'd met Fleur. She was the angel his wife had never been, and she understood the pain of betrayal, for her first husband had humiliated her with numerous infidelities and on his death left her impoverished by mountainous gambling debts.

Guy stared down toward the gray Thames. He wished it were not so, but what he felt for Imogen was a pale shadow of the love he'd had for Fleur. It seemed so wrong to still feel so much for his present wife when his future wife confessed to having adored him to distraction from the moment she came to the house, but part of him would always belong to Fleur. Nothing could end that. What could be ended, however, was the marriage itself. He needed to sever the link, and then marry Imogen.

As yet no one knew about his new love, not even his Aunt Patience, but soon it would become public knowledge because he'd promised Imogen divorce proceedings would be under way by Christmas. It was a promise he meant to keep.

He pondered the stir the announcement would cause. The *monde* was going to throw up its hands in outrage at the prospect of a mere companion becoming Lady Lanham and eventually the Countess of Danchester. There'd also be shocked whispers as to the propriety of her presence here at Lanham House, even if she were in his aunt's employ. Scandal of one sort or another was inevitable, but he and Imogen would weather it all in their quest for happiness. Hopefully, by this time next year their little *cause célèbre* would be forgotten.

His green eyes became troubled as he considered the immediate problem of breaking the news to his aunt. Patience Fitzallen was a middle-aged maiden lady who adhered to the old values. Proud and reclusive because a childhood illness had left her with a limp of which she was immensely self-conscious, she spent all her time in isolation here in Richmond and never took part in the social whirl of London. She thoroughly disapproved of divorce, no matter what the grounds, and in spite of his unhappiness had remained stubbornly fond of Fleur. Guy sighed. He wasn't relishing the task of informing his aunt of his plans; running the gauntlet of society gossip was infinitely preferable!

Someone came into the room behind him, and he turned to see Imogen. She closed the door and leaned back against it to gaze at him for a moment. She was slender and graceful, with her shining brunette hair in a French plait. Her lace-collared amber woolen gown was demure, but there was nothing demure about the smile on her lips as she paused to place her large black velvet reticule on a nearby table before hurrying to him.

It briefly crossed his mind to wonder why she always carried the cumbersome handbag wherever she went, but then she was in his arms and her lips were raised yearningly to meet his. Her body moved sensuously against him, and he held her closer. When he was with her like this he could forget Fleur. Except the ecstasy was never quite the same. Emotion didn't pound needfully through him with Imogen as it had with Fleur. He could always draw back from the brink of desire. Always resist.

It was like that now. He unlinked her arms, smiling in her lustrous eyes. "Aren't you supposed to be with my aunt?"

"She wishes to sleep for a while." Imogen

searched his face intently. He wasn't hers completely. Not yet. But he would be, oh, yes, he would be, and in the meantime she would continue to play her hand with infinite care. She hadn't schemed and lied her way to this point only to toss it carelessly away. And so she smiled now. "Have you written the letter yet?"

"It's almost done."

"You do still mean to send it, don't you?" For a split second she couldn't keep her vulnerability entirely hidden.

"Of course. I've given you my word. By Christmas everyone will know I intend to marry you."

"I do love you so," she whispered. It was one of the few truths she'd ever uttered, for lie usually followed lie with amazing facility, but in this one declaration she was completely honest. Everything she'd done had been for him. She'd plotted, been deceitful, forged and stolen letters, and all to one end—getting rid of Fleur and then winning him for herself.

She linked her arms around his neck again, arching her lissom body against him so they were hip to hip and she could feel his masculinity. "Make love to me now," she whispered provocatively.

But an astounded voice interrupted them from the door. "So this is what's been going on! I should have guessed!"

They leapt guiltily apart, for Guy's aunt stood there, her green Fitzallen eyes bright with indignation and disbelief. She was small and slight, her gray hair coiled up beneath a neat day bonnet. Her fine-boned face still bore traces of her former loveliness, but it was pale with anger as she limped awkwardly toward them.

She halted, her icy gaze resting accusingly on Imogen. "I've begun to wonder greatly about you, madam. To wonder and suspect."

Imogen lowered her eyes quickly.

Patience looked at Guy then. "Well? What do you have to say for yourself?"

There was nothing for it but to tell the truth. "Aunt Patience, I intend to divorce Fleur and marry Imogen, as all London will know come Christmas," he said bluntly.

Patience was thunderstruck. "Divorce Fleur?" she repeated faintly.

"Yes."

Her glance fluttered coldly toward Imogen, of whom she'd become so belatedly suspicious. Now it was clear the companion had successfully set her cap at Guy. One was irresistibly reminded of a viper, beautiful but deadly. It was interesting to ponder what she'd say if she realized her employer knew about the secret diary she carried everywhere in that large velvet reticule. Oh, to be able to read those hidden pages, for only a very important and intimate journal required such constant conceal-ment. What might the creature have written about? Had she maybe confessed to having deliberately and calculatedly intrigued to drive Fleur away? It was an interesting possibility, one that seemed more probable the more Patience thought about it.

Her long silence made Guy feel uncomfortable. "Aunt Patience, I didn't want to tell you like this."

She looked coldly at Imogen. "Leave us," she commanded.

Gathering her skirts, Imogen hurried to the door. For a moment Patience thought she'd forgotten the all-important reticule, but then the young woman turned to snatch it up before going out. The older woman's lips pressed together disappointedly. One day the designing madam would slip up where the diary was concerned, and when she did its secrets would fall into unfriendly hands.

Outside the library door, Imogen clutched the handbag to her breast as she prepared to eavesdrop. Her eyes glittered with anticipation. The old tabby was Fleur's champion, but she wouldn't win this battle.

Patience faced her nephew. "I've had a feeling for some time now that Imogen wasn't quite what she should be to you, and so today I tested her by saying I wanted to sleep. Instead of returning to her own room she came straight here to you, and her purpose was demonstrably improper."

He colored. "You misinterpreted," he said, thinking of Imogen's reputation.

Patience raised an eyebrow. "I think not."

"Aunt Patience, I know you insist on defending Fleur, but she can't be defended. Now that I will one day be the Earl of Danchester, I can't afford to leave things as they are. I'm therefore in the process of writing to Fleur, informing her of my intention to seek a divorce on the grounds of her desertion. I could cite her affair with Ashwood, but I'll spare her that, even though God knows I've grounds to name him. The whole business is to be well in hand by Christmas, at which time I'll enlighten the whole world as to my plans."

"I can't believe you're doing this," Patience replied, shaking her head sadly.

"See for yourself." He gestured toward the desk.

Thunder rumbled outside as she read the few lines he'd written and then looked accusingly at him. "Marrying Imogen will be a monumental mistake because you still love Fleur."

"My mind is made up."

"I've been wondering about Imogen's part in the scheme of things, and with hindsight it's clear she's been oddly involved from the outset. In whom did Fleur confide? Imogen. Who claims to have been the unwilling accomplice in the secret flight? Imogen. Who then found the supposed letter from the fellow in Georgia? Imogen. And who subsequently made herself indispensible to you? Why, Imogen. What an amazing string of coincidences, to be sure."

"There was nothing 'supposed' about that letter from Ashwood, and you wrong Imogen greatly by hinting she did anything untoward."

"Oh, Guy! How can you be so blind to the truth and so trusting of lies? Yes, lies. The more I think about it, the more convinced I become that Mr. Ashwood of Georgia never existed, and therefore any communication purporting to be from him could only be a forgery. And since Imogen now appears to be the beneficiary, I must conclude that in all probability hers was the hand that wrote it."

"That's enough, Aunt."

"Look me in the eyes and tell me you love Imogen Wakefield."

"With all due respect, Aunt, what would you know of love?"

Her green eyes sharpened angrily. "How dare you, sir! Don't damn me as naive simply because I've never married, for I know about matters of the heart. It may interest you to know you weren't the only Fitzallen to fall in love with a Barrymore."

She caught him unawares. "I—I beg your pardon?" he responded.

"When you gave your heart to Fleur, I gave mine to her uncle," Patience said candidly.

Gerard Barrymore? Guy thought of the tall, distinguished American with the charming smile and twinkling blue eyes. "I—I had no idea," he murmured, marveling that his passion for Fleur had blinded him to all else.

"Of course you had no idea, sir, for we were discreet at all times."

Outside the door, Imogen's eyes had widened. Not such an old maid after all, it seemed!

Guy ran his fingers awkwardly through his hair. "Why haven't you mentioned this before?"

"Because I was foolish enough to turn him down." Patience looked away, fighting back a bitter smile. "I feared that in the end he'd be embarrassed by my lameness, which I couldn't face, but now I wish I'd followed my heart." She looked urgently at her nephew. "You should follow your heart, too, Guy. If you turn your back on Fleur, you'll regret it for the rest of your empty life."

Her words found an exposed nerve. "Aunt Patience, as I recall it, Fleur was the one who turned her back. She left me, remember?"

"What I remember is how everything was done through Imogen. One cannot help wondering how many tall tales Fleur was told. It simply wasn't like her to leave without warning, and on the very day after your first wedding anniversary ..." Patience paused in dismay as she suddenly realized the significance of today's date.

Guy nodded. "Yes, Aunt, it's my second wedding anniversary today. At least, it would have been," he said quietly.

"It still is," she countered. "Fleur may be in Philadelphia, but she's still your wife, still Lady Lanham, and still the future Countess of Danchester."

"Not for much longer," he replied with an edge to his voice.

She went to the window and looked out through the rain-distorted glass. "Don't do this, Guy. Ask Fleur to come back to you."

"No."

"Guy—"

"No! Fleur hasn't once seen fit to contact me. Her wishes are obvious."

"She may have written, but her letters might not have reached you." Yes, that was surely what had happened! She turned swiftly toward him.

He knew what she was hinting. "If you're suggesting that Imogen would—"

"Newly delivered letters would be easy enough to purloin from the table in the hall."

At the door, Imogen was very still. It was uncanny, almost as if the old crone had watched her do it!

But Patience had now gone too far for Guy. "I don't intend to discuss the matter further, Aunt," he snapped. "My wife has made her wishes plain to all and sundry, and I don't intend to spend the rest of my life tied to a meaningless marriage. Fleur can go to perdition for all I care now."

"No, sirrah, perdition is where Imogen Wakefield can go! It's my bounden duty to make you see sense, and if you will not write to Fleur asking her to return, then I will write to Gerard and ask him to use his influence with her."

Imogen's heart stopped. No!

Guy's green eyes hardened. "Aunt, I cannot prevent you from writing, but it will avail you of nothing. If by any miracle Fleur should return, I will not see her. Is that clear?"

"You'd see her, Guy. You wouldn't be able to help yourself because you still love her. Imogen Wakefield is a very poor substitute, and will never give you the joy you knew with Fleur."

There was a long silence, broken only by the dashing of the rain on the window and another roll of thunder. Then Patience gathered her skirts and limped from the room.

Imogen drew swiftly back out of sight, and her gaze was ugly with malice as she watched the older woman cross the hall and mount the staircase. Lightning scorched the heavens outside, and the downpour became a cloudburst as more thunder growled into the distance. The whole house seemed to drum with rain, and the jagged light exposed Patience in sharp relief as she went awkwardly up the staircase.

Imogen emerged from her hiding place the moment Guy's aunt was out of sight. How foolish of the old witch to announce her intention to write to Gerard Barrymore, especially after she'd already put her finger on the truth by suggesting previous letters might have been intercepted. It wasn't only incoming mail that lay unguarded on the hall table; outgoing mail did, too. Guy's all-important missive to Philadelphia would be posted, for the divorce was vital, but any communication Patience might send would never even leave the house.

A cold smile played on Imogen's lips as she thought of Fleur's distress when she learned there was to be a divorce. Poor Fleur, so cleverly lied about and tricked by the friend she'd never suspected to be her rival. There was no Richard Ashwood; he was invented to blacken Fleur in Guy's eyes. The real reason for her precipitate flight was that she'd been deceived into believing Guy had a mistress and two children in Kensington.

The cold smile spread to Imogen's eyes as she congratulated herself upon her masterly scheme. An actress had been hired to be the mistress, and played the part very well indeed, so well that Fleur had been completely distraught. After that, her hasty departure had been simple enough to achieve, for she couldn't bring herself to face Guy in person. She'd left him a pathetic note, however, and had even caused her enemy a moment's alarm by promising to delay two weeks in Falmouth before sailing. What if she changed her mind during those two weeks and came back to London? It was a risk that had to be taken. The plan had proceeded relentlessly. Fleur's note had been burned and instead Guy had been shown a letter his wife was supposed to have received from Richard Ashwood.

Imogen felt sleek as she recalled forging that damning missive. She'd changed her writing so completely that no one could ever have guessed it was her work, and Guy had been utterly taken in. He'd been left with only one conclusion to make, that his beloved bride had loved another man all along. As for the two-week wait in Falmouth, it passed without event, and at last Fleur had set sail for Philadelphia. Every communication she'd subsequently sent from there had been carefully removed from the hall table, and soon she stopped writing.

Guy's heart had been broken, and his pain had been jealously resented by the poor relation who was responsible for it all. It wasn't fair that he should love Fleur so much, not when a better love craved his attention! But the resentment was soothed by each new lie she told him about his wife. Maligning Fleur had been like applying a balm to her jealousy, and now the ultimate prize was within her grasp at last. But she'd remain vigilant, not resting until Guy's wedding ring was actually on her finger.

She clutched the reticule to her breast and felt the precious diary beneath the black velvet. It was unwise to have written it all down, but she needed to confide her cleverness, if only to a book. Besides, the diary was safe enough, provided she never let it out of her sight.

Taking a deep breath, she turned to go back into the library, but as the door closed behind her, Patience appeared at the top of the staircase, from where she'd been secretly watching the cunning expressions flitting across Imogen's feline face. There was no mistaking the creature's guilt. Her eavesdropping would have warned her of the proposed letter to Gerard, but if she fondly imagined she was going to outwit Patience Fitzallen this time, she was very much mistaken. The letter wouldn't be sent from the house, but from Richmond town, and Imogen wouldn't know anything about it. She'd think her adversary had had second thoughts. And she'd feel safe. All that could be hoped then was that Gerard would prevail upon Fleur to return to England and at least talk to her husband. If they could be brought face to face again, Patience was convinced they wouldn't be able to deny their enduring love for each other, for in her heart she was sure Fleur had never ceased loving Guy.

Patience smiled down at the library door. "Two can play games, Imogen, my dear, and if you ever leave that diary unguarded, I swear it will be your undoing. I'm sure the scales would soon fall from Guy's eyes if he read it."

Turning, she went to her room. Guy wanted it all set in motion by Christmas. Well, his aunt wanted the same, but in Fleur's favor. Come Christmas, Imogen Wakefield had to be turned out of this house and out of Guy's life, and his adored wife had to be back where she belonged.

That evening after dinner, when the storm was over and the sunset a glory of crimson and gold, Guy went out to the terrace to smoke a cigar. Behind him the windows of the house reflected the brilliant sky, and overhead a flock of seagulls flew slowly back to sea on the ebbing Thames tide. It was serenely beautiful, but he couldn't enjoy it because his feelings were so very mixed. Now that his letter was actually on its way to Philadelphia, he wished he hadn't sent it, for whatever else, at this moment Fleur was still his wife.

Smoke curled idly from the cigar as he recalled the first time she'd been here on the terrace with him. He hadn't yet held her close and certainly hadn't kissed her, but suddenly she'd turned to slip her arms around his waist and stretch up on tiptoe to kiss his lips. Her passion had seemed to mirror his own as kiss followed kiss, each one more compellingly seductive than the one before.

If lust could be pure, then that was how it was to him. His desire had been a scorching flame, and from that moment on he could never glance at her without wanting to touch her, or touch her without needing to satisfy the tumultuous emotions burning through him. Fool that he was, he believed she felt the same, for he was still a long way from learning about Richard Ashwood.

Dear God, if there were one decision he could now reverse, it would be the fateful whim that took him to dinner at Grillion's. If it hadn't been for that, he'd never even have met Fleur Barrymore. He dropped the cigar and ground it savagely with his heel.

"Damn you, Fleur," he breathed, and then went back into the house.

2

With a fair wind, ships took approximately thirty days to cross the Atlantic, so it was the beginning of November when the two letters from England arrived at Barrymore Place, Philadelphia. Gerard Barrymore returned to the house in his gig just as they were delivered, and when he read what Patience had written, his brow darkened immediately.

He went into the hall calling for Fleur, but it was her black maid, Martha, who came. She was twenty-seven, the same age as Fleur, and plumply handsome, with a warm smile and gentle nature. She wore blue, and her tightly curled hair was pushed up beneath a starched mobcap. She'd been in Fleur's service for ten years and was very close to her.

"Where is Miss Fleur?" Gerard asked.

"She's out walkin', sir, but she'll be back soon."

He nodded. "Very well, I'll wait on the piazza."

"Sir." Martha bobbed a curtsy and hurried away again.

With a sigh, Gerard pushed the letters into his pocket and then walked through the house to the white-columned piazza at the back. He sat on one of the chairs and lit a cigar before stretching his long legs out. He was a dignified man with a commendable head of gray hair. His features were classical, and he'd never lost his lean shape, which was eminently suited to the stylish clothes he wore. He didn't lack female attention, but in the fifteen years since his dear wife's death there had only been one woman in his life: Patience Fitzallen. Now, quite suddenly, she'd written to him again, and a very interesting letter it was, too. He moved the cigar thoughtfully from one side of his mouth to the other. He knew what had to be done, but could Fleur be persuaded?

He could see her now. She'd crossed the little bridge over the stream and was walking slowly along the avenue of lemon trees toward the house.

Her wonderful chestnut curls were piled up on top of her head, and she wore only a cream muslin gown with a shawl around her shoulders, for the day was unexpectedly warm. He thought how pale she still looked, but then it was to be expected after all she'd gone through over the past year, and, more especially, over the past few months.

She smiled as she reached the piazza. "I didn't expect you back just yet," she said, sitting opposite him.

"A man can only do so much socializing, my dear, and it's a trifle wearisome trying to flatter all the ladies at once."

"You shouldn't be so winning, sir," Fleur replied.

He shrugged. "It's a natural gift, I guess." He surveyed her for a long moment. "How are you feeling?"

"Better, I suppose. I improve each day now, thank goodness."

Martha was singing a lullaby in the bedroom above their heads, and Fleur glanced up with a smile. "She always soothes Christopher, no matter how fractious he is. She thinks he's getting his first tooth already."

Gerard nodded, his gaze still intent upon her. "She's probably right. Your son is a fine baby, my dear."

"Yes." Fleur lowered her eyes.

Gerard was silent for a moment, choosing his next words with great care. "Fleur, have you given thought to the business of telling his father?"

She shifted uncomfortably. "Do we have to talk about Guy now?"

"Yes, my dear, I'm afraid we do. Tell me, are you truly over him?"

"Yes. Of course." But the response lacked conviction, as always it did.

"You still wear your wedding ring."

She immediately took it off and put it on the table. "There, will that do?"

"Oh, a grand gesture, to be sure," he murmured.

"Uncle Gerard, I'm trying hard to forget about Guy, and I wish you'd let me get on with it."

"You can't forget him when you've borne his son, my dear," Gerard pointed out quietly. "I know you had a difficult time all through your pregnancy, and that the birth itself was far from easy, but Christopher's four months old now and on your own admission you're getting better each day. You can't put things off anymore. You have to consider what you intend to do."

"Do?"

"About Guy."

A shadow crossed her eyes. "There's nothing I can do. I left because he kept a mistress and had children by her. I don't know what passes as acceptable to London society, but it certainly wasn't acceptable to me."

"Such things go on here as well, my dear," Gerard pointed out.

"Possibly, but I expect better."

He smiled. "Oh, how like your father you are at times. I look at you and see my brother Pierce looking back at me."

"I wish I could remember him."

"You're doubly unfortunate because a carriage overturn robbed you of both your father and mother. In a perfect world, every child would know its parents," he murmured.

She met his gaze. "Why do I have the strangest feeling we're back to Guy again?"

"Because we *are* back to him."

There was more to this than met the eye, she

thought, sitting forward in concern. "What's all this about, Uncle?"

"I've received a letter from Patience."

"Patience? After all this time?"

"Yes. She wants me to persuade you to go back to England."

Fleur rose to her feet. "Whatever for? I'm sure Guy doesn't want me to return."

"It seems he wishes to divorce you," Gerard said bluntly.

She was shaken, and moved to the edge of the piazza. "Divorce me?" she whispered, her face taking on a new pallor. She was stricken to the heart, for try as she could, she couldn't fall out of love with the English lord she'd married so unwisely

Gerard drew a long breath. "Aren't you interested in *why* he wants a divorce?"

She looked unwillingly at him. "It doesn't take genius to guess he's found someone else."

"You're quite right."

Fleur swallowed, trying not to succumb to the tears stinging her eyes. "I—I can only trust he's more faithful to her than he ever was to me."

"Don't you want to know who she is?" he pressed.

"You make it sound as if I'm acquainted with her."

"You are, my dear; in fact you know her very well. It's Imogen Wakefield."

Fleur stared in disbelief. "There must be some mistake."

"Not according to Patience, whose veracity I'm sure is beyond question."

"But Imogen was my dear friend!"

"That's something upon which you and I will always differ," Gerard replied, thinking back to the demure companion whose dark eyes had had a disconcertingly calculating glitter he'd never taken to. Imogen Wakefield was a snake in the grass, and he'd always suspected her of wanting Guy for herself. This letter from Patience seemed to confirm those fears.

"I still say there must be some mistake. Imogen wasn't in the least interested in Guy; in fact she thought him despicable for keeping that woman in Kensington," Fleur insisted, trying to collect thoughts that had scattered in a thousand directions at once.

"Very well, you may have it that way for the moment, but I suggest you read this second letter that came by the same post." He tossed it on to the table. "It's from Guy, and according to Patience it's very brief and to the point. He wants an uncontested divorce on the grounds of your desertion. Read, Fleur, for you cannot ignore it."

With trembling hands she broke the seal and unfolded the vellum. The date at the top seemed to taunt her. The thirtieth of September. Their wedding anniversary. How doubly cruel of Guy. The letter itself was as Gerard said. A few lines, remote and formal, as if they were strangers. But they'd lain naked together, body to body, flesh to flesh, loving each other passionately night after ecstatic night . . .

Gerard watched sadly. "Fleur?" he prompted at last.

She refolded it. "He wrote it on our wedding anniversary," she whispered.

He drew a long breath. "Be that as it may, what do you intend to do now?"

"Nothing. If he wishes to divorce me, he can do so. After all, technically I did desert him, did I not? I'm sure English law will not give a fig for the deep offense and insult caused to me by my husband having a mistress and illegitimate children. I daresay such conduct doesn't even pass for adultery!"

"It was Imogen who told you about this so-called mistress," Gerard said quietly.

"So-called? Uncle, I met the woman in her villa in Kensington!" Fleur cried.

"Actresses can be hired, my dear, and Patience certainly makes no mention of a mistress in her letter to me." Gerard got up and went to her. "Fleur, must I remind you you didn't face Guy with what you'd learned? Not once did you confront him and ask him outright if it was the truth."

"I—I couldn't. I was too upset. But I wrote to him. I told him I'd wait in Falmouth for two weeks before sailing, and that if he wished to see me, he could do so. I couldn't face him in London, you see, but Falmouth was neutral ..."

"And to whose tender hands did you entrust this vital missive? Why, to Imogen's." Gerard took her by the elbows and made her look at him. "Nothing you wrote has ever been received at Lanham House, my dear. Guy certainly didn't receive your note about Falmouth, and I'm now utterly convinced he has never kept a mistress, let alone had children by her. Patience writes that as far as Guy is concerned, you deserted him to return to a former lover, a planter from Georgia."

Fleur stared at him. "A planter from ... ? But that's nonsense!"

"Not to a man whose wife left him and apparently didn't even see fit to write a note explaining why. According to Patience, Imogen confessed in a flood of pretty tears to having been your unwilling confidante at the time of your departure. She even produced a letter you'd supposedly received from this planter, in which he asked you to return to him."

Fleur was speechless.

"Sit down, my dear." Her uncle steered her back to the chair and then faced her again. "Fleur, Patience specifically says she herself wrote several times, both to you and to me, and she says that nothing was ever received from us. It is her contention that Imogen Wakefield intercepted everything and saw to it that Guy remained isolated in every way. The only reason this letter has reached us now is that she had it sent from Richmond town rather than from the house. Consider how odd it is that the only letter to reach us from Lanham House itself is the one mentioning divorce! I've long believed Imogen Wakefield to be duplicitous, but Patience has only recently begun to suspect her of not being the sweet thing she appears to be. Fleur, if everything Patience says is the truth, and there's no reason why it should not be, it's clear Guy has been as misled about you as I'm sure you were about him. There's hope for your marriage, my dear, and for both your sakes, as well as for Christopher, you *must* go back to England. And if you stubbornly refuse to risk your foolish pride on your own account, you must do it for the sake of your son's heritage. Christopher is Guy's legitimate son and heir, Fleur. He's the future fifth Lord Lanham, and now he's also a future Earl of Danchester."

"Earl of Danchester?"

"It seems Guy's distant cousin is the present earl, and the only other heir died recently in a riding accident. So, you see, Christopher's heritage is considerable."

"Yes, but—"

"There cannot be any argument, Fleur. You owe it to the child to take him back to England. Besides which, you owe it to yourself. You haven't been able to fall out of love with the man you married."

Gerard picked up the wedding ring and pushed it firmly back on her finger before looking sternly into her eyes. "Or do you deny still loving him?"

Fleur gazed at the ring through a blur of tears. "You know I can't deny it," she whispered. But then a new thought struck her and she got up agitatedly. "What if he doesn't believe Christopher is his?"

"The child already has his father's eyes. There have never been green eyes in the Barrymores."

"Possibly, but I'm sure there are planters in Georgia with green eyes. Uncle Gerard, Guy believed me capable of running off to a former lover," she interrupted quietly.

"And you believed he deceived you with a mistress and children, which in my book makes you quits, since both charges appear to me to be contrived by an interested third party. Look, my dear, you and Guy are older and wiser now, and the time has come to face up to things. And remember, whatever you may feel, Christopher still has the undeniable right to know his father, and that father has the equal right to know he has a son. Christopher is as much a British nobleman as he is an American citizen."

He was very persuasive, and Fleur was racked with indecision.

Gerard pressed her. "Go back, Fleur. We both will, for it's time I was honest as well. Patience Fitzallen is a damned fine woman, and I should have insisted she marry me instead of accepting her feeble excuses. I fear there's no fool like an old fool."

Fleur managed a rueful smile. "Yes there is, there's a young one." Then she looked urgently at him. "If we go, it must be soon, so I don't have time to lose my nerve."

"I thought perhaps in the new year."

She shook her head. "Make arrangements now."

"But your health . . ."

"Is strong enough."

"Very well, but it will mean spending Christmas in London."

"I know."

"You must respond to Guy, telling him about your return and about Christopher, and I'll write to Patience, although I doubt either letter will reach the addressee, not when Imogen is bound to read them first. She won't like what they say one little bit, for she wants you to stay obligingly here and allow yourself to be divorced, she certainly doesn't want you back in England together with Guy's child! Still, there's a possibility such letters might escape her attention, and on that premise I'll inform Patience of the so-called mistress and children in Kensington. I'm sure they'll be as much a surprise to Guy as your fictitious planter was to you. Oh, and I'll also write to Grillion's Hotel, for it seems appropriate to stay there again." He paused, remembering the luxurious establishment and its excellent table. "Upon my soul, I hope to find myself eating goose with rum-soaked apples again. Grillion's have a way of cooking it that fair makes my mouth water at the thought."

Fleur glanced up toward the nursery, where the singing had now stopped. "Martha will be glad to see Grillion's again," she murmured.

"She will?" Gerard looked inquiringly at her.

"Yes. There was a black footman there. Thomas, I believe his name was. He and Martha saw a lot of each other during our stay. She missed him greatly when we left."

Gerard smiled. "Then perhaps you should tell her she might see him again."

Fleur nodded and left the piazza to hurry up through the house to Christopher's nursery.

Gerard watched her go, then lowered his eyes sadly. He could only pray that good would come of this second visit to Grillion's Hotel. But there was many a slip 'twixt cup and lip, and fate wasn't always disposed to be kind, as the Barrymores had found out to their cost over the past two years.

Fleur went quietly into the nursery. Martha was seated by the window sewing.

"Mizz Fleur?" she said, rising swiftly to her feet.

"Hello, Martha." Fleur went to the cradle to look at her sleeping son. How perfect he was, with his down of golden hair and cheeks like warm silk. He wore a little robe she'd embroidered herself, and his tiny hands were encased in cotton mittens. When his eyes were open they were exactly the same green as Guy's, just as Uncle Gerard had pointed out earlier, and she knew that when he grew up he would be the image of his father. He was a Fitzallen with scarcely any Barrymore in his looks, and perhaps that was fitting for the future Lord Lanham and Earl of Danchester.

She glanced across at Martha. "We're going back to London for a while."

The maid was startled. "We are?"

Fleur told her what had happened. She and the maid were close, and Martha knew she'd never stopped loving Guy.

When she'd finished, Martha drew herself up indignantly. "That 'Mogen, I never did take to her! All smooth as scald cream. I tell you, I believes Mizz Patience."

"So does Uncle Gerard."

Martha was silent for a moment. "We're really goin' to London again? To Grillion's?" she added hopefully.

"I thought we might try the Pulteney this time," Fleur replied mischievously, and then smiled at the maid's dismay. "Oh, don't look so crestfallen; of course we'll go to Grillion's. You're bound to see Thomas again."

"If he's still there," Martha declared dolefully.

"I'm sure he will be." Fleur looked down at Christopher again, and then nodded at the maid. "You can have a little time to yourself now, if you wish. I'll stay here."

When the door had closed again, Fleur gazed down at Christopher. He was hers, hers and Guy's. Their passion had brought him into the world, a living reminder of the immense love they'd shared for that one magnificent year. He must have been conceived on the night of their first wedding anniversary. She remembered the occasion with the oddest of clarity. Perhaps it was a mother's instinct to know which particular act of love had resulted in a precious child.

That anniversary night had been so very special. They'd dined at Grillion's again, because that was how they first met, and after driving home through the moonlight to Lanham House had gone to their private apartment. She recalled the candlelight as she'd rested naked on the bed, waiting for him to come to her. She'd felt so warm and safe, and so loved and cherished, and so very, very happy ... Then he'd been there with her, his body against hers, his lips to her breasts. Desire had been immediate and intense, as always it was.

They'd found their rhythm, moving sensuously together to draw every last ounce of pleasure from the act. When they'd reached the ultimate peak of joy, she'd become ethereal as wave after wave of ecstasy washed through her. That was the moment this beautiful baby was created; she knew it as surely as day followed night, and spring followed winter.

They'd lain together afterward, with an eternity of happiness stretching before them. Or so she'd thought. But within hours it had all been destroyed when Imogen Wakefield persuaded her she should visit a certain villa in Kensington.

Fleur closed her eyes. What awaited her in England this Christmas? Please let Guy still love her as much as she loved him. Let everything that had driven her from him prove to be lies, and let Imogen's wickedness be exposed and punished . . .

3

Grillion's Hotel received Gerard's letter and made preparations accordingly, but the letters from Barrymore Place to Lanham House, although delivered, were not opened by the correct recipients because they fell into Imogen's hands.

It was a snowy morning in early December, and as usual she made it her business to be crossing the hall as the footman placed the newly delivered mail on the silver salver. The moment he'd withdrawn, she inspected the letters and removed the two from Philadelphia. She'd been expecting a response from Fleur to Guy, and intended to read it and then reseal it, but she hadn't been expecting anything from Gerard to Patience because until that moment she'd been under the impression the latter had changed her mind about writing. Her heart lurched with alarm as she realized this had not been so.

Hiding both letters in her reticule, she hurried up to the safety of her room to read them. It wasn't long before her alarm increased. Patience had evidently done her worst, relaying all the lies Guy had been told about his wife's Georgian lover, and now Gerard had written about the similar lies Fleur had been told about Guy's mistress and children. But worst of all, the Barrymores were returning to England for Christmas, and were bringing Guy's *son* with them!

The letters slipped from Imogen's frozen fingers, and for a few minutes she was so devastated she couldn't move. All her plans were in ruins, and she herself was bound to be exposed in all her villainy. Her stomach was knotted with fear, and her mouth was as dry as parchment. Panic welled inside her, but then her mind began to race. All was not yet lost, and disaster might yet be averted. Precious time had been won because these letters had fallen into her hands. She, Imogen Wakefield, was the only person here at Lanham House to know the Barrymores were on their way back to England, and it was therefore up to her to see their arrival went unheeded. Guy and Fleur had to be kept apart at all costs.

Imogen began to pace, and soon a cunning smile began to curve her lips. What if Gerard and Fleur were to arrive at Grillion's and find a message from Guy waiting for them? What if that message were curt in the extreme, and informed them they were not to contact either Patience or him because his only desire was for a divorce? And what if he also denied Fleur's son?

Imogen paused. She'd have to be careful, for Guy's handwriting was very distinctive and any forgery was certain to be found out. The message would have to be verbal, delivered by a footman in Lanham House livery. She began to smile again, for the actress she'd hired to be Guy's mistress had had a brother who also trod the boards. If his palm were to be crossed with silver, and livery purloined for the purpose, she was sure he would perform the task as efficiently as his sister. And if the message included the information that Guy and Patience had left Lanham House for an unknown destination, surely that would deter any spur-of-the-moment visit.

Such a harsh and cruel snub was bound to have the desired effect. Fleur would believe all was still lost after all, and Gerard would think Patience had bowed to Guy's firmly expressed wishes. With luck they'd spend their Christmas on the high seas, en route back to Philadelphia!

Imogen knew she was only dealing with the immediate problems, without looking further ahead, but if a little time was gained, maybe she could still scheme her way to victory. She would lie and cheat for as long as she could, and only when her back was finally against the wall would she admit defeat. Until then, she had everything to fight for. Guy Fitzallen was everything to her, and nothing, *nothing,* would be allowed to stand in her way.

Ripping both letters into shreds, she flung them on the fire before going to the window and gazing out at the snow-covered countryside. She was calm again now, confident she could still keep Guy and his wife apart. With a sudden surge of optimism she took her diary and pencil from the reticule and sat down on the window seat to write. The lines spilled easily onto the page as she confided everything to her private journal. The written word somehow made it all seem a foregone conclusion. The alarm occasioned by the arrival of the letters from America now faded into oblivion. Suddenly victory was within her grasp.

A week before Christmas Guy spent the day at his club in St. James's Street. After luncheon, he enjoyed an agreeable few hours at the billiard table with a group of friends, and then adjourned to a comfortable leather armchair in the card room to savor a glass of cognac before driving his curricle back to Richmond.

Cigar smoke hung in the stuffy air and numerous gentlemen were seated around the green baize tables. Outside, London was blanketed with snow, and the excitement of Christmas was beginning to be almost tangible. Carts of holly and mistletoe had been brought in from the surrounding countryside, and carols were sung on street corners. The journey into town from Lanham House had been held up by flocks of geese and turkeys being driven to market, and as he sat with his legs stretched toward the fire he could hear the cries of the pieman who strolled the fashionable pavements of St. James's. It wasn't plain meat pies the man hawked now, but fine mince pies, the finest in all England and the tastiest of the season, or so he'd have everyone believe.

Guy's attention drifted around the quiet room, and he noted some particularly intense play at the nearest table, where one of the gentlemen involved was his close friend, Harry Templeford. A little concerned, Guy sat forward. If Harry plunged in much deeper, he'd be over his fool head. But even as this dread prospect hove into view, Harry gave a triumphant cry and casually tossed down a winning trump. There was a good deal of grumbling from the other players, but a trump was a trump. A broad grin lit Harry's amiable face as he gathered his winnings.

Guy leaned back again. Harry's luck was phenomenal. One lost count of the times he slipped from the very jaws of ruin. His wife's nerves were so frayed that from time to time she threatened to leave him. Poor Jane, there were clearly occasions when, much as she loved Harry, she could cheerfully have strangled him.

Guy's thoughts turned inevitably to his own wife, who hadn't merely threatened to leave him, but had actually done so. Fleur hadn't replied to his letter about divorce. A reply could have gone astray, of course, but he doubted it. Fleur was simply ignoring it, just as she'd ignored his very existence since she'd left. He wished she'd responded, for at least then he'd know if she intended to contest a divorce or merely allow things to proceed unchallenged. He'd have to write again, and again if necessary. He'd sworn to Imogen that by Christmas he'd have announced his intentions to society, and Christmas Eve itself was now only a week away, but he was no nearer resolving the situation than he'd been on the last day of September.

"Guy? I'd offer a penny for them, but I doubt they're worth it."

Harry's voice aroused him from his reverie, and he looked up. "Forgive me, I was miles away."

"So I noticed," Harry said, still pushing his gains into his pockets.

"I see you've been disgustingly lucky again."

"Naturally."

"It doesn't do to be too sure of oneself," Guy murmured, putting down his glass and getting up.

Harry searched his face. "What is it, Guy? Your face is as long as a blind man's fiddle. Where's your Christmas spirit?"

"In Philadelphia." The answer slipped from Guy's lips before he realized it was there.

Harry raised an eyebrow. "So, in spite of the Mrs. Wakefield you told me about, you're still not over Fleur?"

"I have to be over her, Harry."

"I'm intrigued about Mrs. Wakefield. Why are you hiding her away?"

"I'm not hiding her anywhere; I'm simply waiting for the right moment to introduce her to our circle."

"Perhaps a convivial dinner followed by a little elegant dancing will provide an ideal opportunity? Not at our place, of course, since the refurbishment appears to be self-perpetuating, and the stench of paint is beginning to choke Park Lane itself! We've had a word with Grillion, and he's going to attend to it for us. There's to be a veritable glut of Christmas goodies, and any overindulgence will be compensated for by the vigor of the subsequent hoofing." Harry paused "In view of your continuing feelings for Fleur, are you sure you should still marry Mrs. Wakefield?"

"Yes." The single word was uttered flatly.

Harry raised an eyebrow. "Is that wise?"

"Is it any of your business?" Guy countered a little tersely.

"Er—no, it isn't. Forgive me." Harry shifted uncomfortably. "Look, Guy, if it's to be Mrs. Wakefield, perhaps the dinner at Grillion's *would* be an appropriate occasion at which to start formally acquainting the *monde* with your plans?"

Guy smiled a little wryly. "Actually, I promised her that by Christmas I'd have begun to properly broadcast her new importance in my life, and that's what I was thinking about when you spoke a few minutes ago. At the end of September I wrote to Fleur about a divorce, but she hasn't replied. I was hoping I'd have received some word by now."

"And what form do you really wish that word to take?" Harry asked quietly.

"I don't know," Guy replied honestly. "Sometimes I want it all to be finished so that I can start anew, but at other times I just want Fleur back again."

"Well, at Christmas one must endeavor to enjoy oneself, so accept my invitation anyway," Harry pressed, determined to jolly him out of the doldrums if he could.

Guy grinned. "Very well, Harry, I accept for both Imogen and myself."

"Excellent."

"When's this great occasion to take place?"

"Didn't I say? Christmas Eve."

"So it's dinner at Grillion's on the twenty-fourth?"

Harry nodded. "It is indeed."

Guy took his leave then, and a few moments later stepped out on to the snowy pavement of St. James's Street. A group of street urchins, boys and girls, were singing carols nearby. Their faces were rosy and their breath silvery as they finished "Good King Wenceslaus" and immediately embarked upon "The Holly and the Ivy." He smiled as a small girl detached herself from her fellows and came toward him with an upturned hat.

"A penny for Christmas, sir?" she asked, bobbing a curtsy.

"Here's some for all of you," he replied generously, dropping coins into the hat.

Her eyes brightened. "Thank you, sir. Merry Christmas."

"Merry Christmas."

He turned then as one of the club's grooms brought his curricle. A breeze swept icily along the street, fluttering a pantomime bill fixed to a lamp-post. Guy shivered and flexed his fingers in his gloves before tugging his top hat on more firmly and then getting on to the curricle seat. Tossing another coin to the obliging groom, he took up the reins and flung the horses away from the curb toward Piccadilly. The light vehicle skimmed over the hard-packed snow covering the cobbles, and as he turned west to drive out of London, he glanced toward Albemarle Street and the elegant doors of Grillion's Hotel. He didn't feel like a convivial Christmas Eve dinner party, least of all at Grillion's, where he'd first met Fleur, but he'd go nevertheless. One's spouse might not remain constant, but one's friends were always there.

Flicking the whip, he brought the team up to a smart pace toward Richmond.

The journey from America had been long and wearying, and it was early on the morning of Christmas Eve that the post-chaise hired in Falmouth at last turned the corner from Piccadilly into Albemarle Street. Gerard had sent word ahead from the Hounslow inn where they'd spent the previous night, so their arrival was expected. It was midmorning, and London was in the throes of one of the busiest days of the year.

Fleur was tired after another restless and uncomfortable night, on top of which her health still wasn't fully restored. The voyage hadn't been an easy one, and she wasn't much of a sailor. Most of her time had been spent lying in her cabin, wishing the swaying would stop, but at least the road journey from Cornwall had been accomplished with ease, in spite of the snow still lying thickly everywhere.

She'd forgotten how small and intimate a country England was. After the wide-open spaces of Pennsylvania it seemed almost parochial. Nor had she expected to feel at home here again, but she did. There was something comfortable and welcoming about the villages, farms, cottages, and mansions lining the broad turnpikes, and something very ordered and reassuring about the gracious parks, with their specimen trees and landscaped lakes. But now she was in London again, arriving at Grillion's just as she had once before, she felt almost sick with nerves.

The hotel had been open for thirteen years, and was one of the most stylish in London. It was decked for Christmas and the windows were bright with lights and garlands. There was a huge holly wreath on the gleaming door, and its red ribbons fluttered softly as Gerard alighted and then handed Fleur down, before carefully assisting Martha, who had Christopher sleeping in her arms.

Traffic rattled to and fro over the fashionable cobbles, and a little further along the snowy pavement a man selling hot chestnuts was doing a brisk trade. The cook at a house opposite was arguing with a poulterer about the price of a turkey, and a donkey cart rumbled past with a load of Yule logs for sale.

There was a bite to the air, and Fleur shivered a little, drawing her fur-lined cloak more closely around her. Gerard put a loving arm around her shoulder. "Come, my dear, the sooner we go inside, the sooner you can rest properly. The journey has been more of an ordeal for you than I would wish."

She nodded, and they walked toward the hotel door, which opened as if by magic as two liveried footmen anticipated their approach. One of them was Martha's former admirer, Thomas, and Fleur couldn't help glancing over her shoulder at the maid, who was all of a fluster at seeing him so swiftly.

Thomas was very tall and striking, with an open countenance that could suddenly crease into a very broad and infectious smile. He suited the hotel's blue and silver livery, and as he bowed there was no mistaking his delight at seeing Martha again.

They entered a splendid hall where pretty holly and ivy decorations had been festooned against the walls. There was a magnificent elliptical staircase, with garlands twined around the handrail and banisters, while from the high ceiling was suspended a huge kissing bough, complete with trailing red ribbons and lighted candles.

There were footmen everywhere, and from the crowded dining room nearby came the sound of refined conversation and the chink of fine porcelain and cutlery. The aroma of coffee hung in the air, as well as the appetizing smell of delicious French food, and the atmosphere was one of elegance and style. Monsieur Grillion no longer deigned to welcome guests in person, unless they were royalty, and so his *maître d'hotel* greeted the new arrivals from America.

"Mr. Barrymore and Lady Lanham?" he guessed correctly, sweeping them a rather officious bow, for he was that sort of man, all puffed up with his own importance.

Gerard nodded, but at that moment another footman appeared at their elbow. A footman in Lanham House livery.

Fleur recognized the maroon and gold uniform, and her heart leapt with hope, only to be plunged into wretchedness a moment later when he delivered his message.

"Mr. Barrymore?" he inquired, bowing low to Gerard.

Gerard turned. "Yes?" he replied.

"I've been sent by Lord Lanham, sir."

Gerard's glance flickered toward Fleur and then back to the footman. "I take it you have a message?"

"Sir." The footman cleared his throat and glanced uneasily at the *maître d'hotel*, who stood with them.

With a rather offended frown, the *maître* removed himself to a discreet distance, and then the footman spoke. "Forgive me, Mr. Barrymore, for I do not like to say what I must say."

Fleur's heart began its plunge.

"Lord Lanham wishes you to know that he does not intend to receive you during your stay here, nor does he intend to call here. His only interest is in obtaining an end to his marriage, and on that count he also denies the child Lady Lanham claims is his."

A small cry slipped from Fleur's lips as she fought back swift tears.

Gerard was incensed, and only just contained himself from taking the footman by the lapels. "Is it the custom in this goddamned country to deliver such personal and uncivil messages through footmen?" he demanded.

The footman swallowed. "I—I'm not very well acquainted with such matters, sir," he stammered. "F—forgive me, but it is my task to tell you."

"I'll go out there right now and take Lanham by his damned throat!" Gerard exclaimed, uttering the threat a little more loudly than he intended, so that a silence fell upon the entrance hall and all eyes turned toward him.

Tears were now wet on Fleur's cheeks. "Please, Uncle Gerard . . ." she whispered, almost overcome with disappointment. So they'd come all this way only to be greeted monstrously. Feeling as tired and unwell as she did, it was almost too much to bear.

The footman was ready for Gerard's threat, however, having been well schooled by Imogen. "It will avail you little to go to Lanham House, sir, for Lord Lanham and Miss Patience are not there."

"Where are they?"

"I—I don't know, sir. They left quite suddenly last night."

"Then I'll go to his damned lawyer," Gerard said.

"Which lawyer, sir?"

"Why, Sir Arthur Dench, of course."

The footman held his gaze. "Sir Arthur passed away a month ago, sir, and his lordship hasn't yet appointed anyone in his place."

"So, you're telling me that Lord Lanham and Miss Patience have simply vanished?"

"I—er—well, yes, sir. Something of the sort."

Gerard looked intently at him. Something didn't ring true here. It was all a little too glib, and the fellow's eyes had a way of sliding away. That was the mark of a liar. "What's your name?" he demanded suddenly.

The footman swallowed. "Alfred, sir."

"Well, Alfred, you may as well know that I don't intend to take your word for anything. I'm going to call at Lanham House, and God help you if I find you've been fibbing."

"Sir?" The footman went pale, and glanced uneasily around. This wasn't going quite as planned.

The *maître d'hotel* perceived that something wasn't as it should be, and now approached again. "Is everything all right, Mr. Barrymore?"

Gerard turned to him. "Everything's just fine," he replied, but when he looked toward the footman again, the fellow had gone, and was just to be seen scurrying out into the street.

Gerard made to chase after him, but Fleur tearfully restrained him. "Please, Uncle, just leave it at that."

"But, my dear, it's clear to me that that message

was no more truthful than that fairy tale about a certain villa in Kensington!''

"But what if it was?"

He stared at her. "You don't believe that."

Fresh tears stung her eyes. "I don't know what to believe. I'm tired, and afraid, and all I want is to rest. Promise me you won't do anything until we've both had time to think," she pleaded.

"I don't need time, I've already thought enough," he replied, but then softened and nodded. "Very well, my dear, if that's the way you want it, that's how it will be."

"Thank you."

The *maître d'hotel* was still waiting patiently. "Do you wish to be conducted to your apartment, sir?" he asked.

"If you please."

They followed a footman, while others carried their luggage in from the chaise. Martha brought up the rear, pausing halfway up to look toward Thomas. His dark eyes were upon her, and he gave a broad wink that made her blush so much she had to hurry on.

The apartment set aside for them was very handsome. Situated directly above the main entrance, one of its bedrooms boasted a fine balcony over the street. Gerard insisted on Fleur having the balcony room because it contained the most comfortable bed, and she went to lie down, suddenly drained of all strength by the shock of what had happened on their arrival. The sobs she'd somehow held in check had their way now, and she hid her face in the pillow as she wept.

A nerve flickered at Gerard's temple as he heard her. Damn Imogen Wakefield for this. If it *were* Imogen's work. There was always the possibility that the footman's message had indeed been from

Guy, just as there was always the possibility that
Guy really was in love with Imogen now . . . Gerard
considered both thoughts and then rejected them.
"Hell, no," he breathed aloud, wishing he hadn't
promised Fleur he'd stay away from Lanham House
for the time being. But a promise was a promise.

The Christmas Eve morning was quiet at Lanham
House. Patience sat on the window seat in her bedroom, gazing down the white-clad hill toward the
Thames. Her face was sad. Gerard hadn't replied
to her letter, and she felt more low-spirited than
she had in years. She'd been so sure he'd persuade
Fleur to come back, and that he'd probably come
too, but there'd been only silence from Philadelphia. There hadn't even been a reply to Guy's letter. Nothing. It was as if the Barrymores had
never been.

There was a movement on the terrace below and
she glanced down to see Guy and Imogen strolling
together. Guy's golden hair shone in the sun, and
his crimson coat made a vivid splash of color
against the snow. He was smiling at Imogen, and
his aunt looked down approvingly at his patrician
profile. How handsome he was, and how charming
when he chose. What a pity he chose to direct it
toward an undeserving adventuress like her
companion!

Patience's displeased gaze came to rest upon Imogen, who wore a blue cloak trimmed with white
fur and carried a huge armful of holly she'd gathered in the park. How fascinating she was being,
tossing her feline head back to reveal her slender
lily-white throat, and affecting not to notice when
some of her glossy dark hair fell loose from its pins.
Patience's gaze became positively sour. The Wakefield creature was going to win, and there was noth-

ing she, Patience Fitzallen, could do about it. Unless, of course . . .

A gleam entered Patience's eyes. Tonight she at last hoped to have a chance to inspect the secret diary. Imogen was accompanying Guy to the Templefords' dinner party, and the old handbag wouldn't be at all the thing with the dainty pink silk gown she intended to wear. Her other reticules were far too small, which meant the diary would have to be left behind. She'd hide it and lock the door, of course, but Patience was determined to breach these defenses. If there were anything incriminating at that wretched book, she'd sniff it out before Imogen Wakefield returned to Lanham House tonight!

On the terrace, Imogen was unaware of the savage gaze to which she was being subjected from the house, just as she was also unaware of the venue of tonight's dinner. She was under the happy impression it was to take place at Templeford House, Park Lane, because Guy had neglected to say anything to the contrary.

A kitchen maid at Grillion's was in her pay, and had sent word to her that the Barrymores had reached Hounslow. They were probably at the hotel by now, and the hired actor would have delivered his message. Oh, how she wished she could have witnessed the scene! It didn't occur to her that Gerard wouldn't believe what he was told. By now she was so carried away by her own cleverness that she believed herself invincible.

That sense of invincibility made her more beautiful, bringing an extra shine to her dark eyes and touching her complexion with a rosy glow. She was overjoyed to be accompanying Guy tonight, and the prospect of arriving at such a function on his arm filled her with excitement. But her excitement was abruptly extinguished as at last the hotel was mentioned.

"I trust Grillion's does us proud tonight," Guy said casually.

"Grillion's?" She halted and turned swiftly toward him. "Why do you say that?"

"Because the dinner is to be held there. Hadn't I said?"

"No." Her heart stopped, and the holly tumbled from her arms. Suddenly she felt less invincible than a moment before.

He saw how pale she'd gone. "Is something wrong?"

"Er—no—of course not."

He thought she was unwell. "Come, we'll go inside, for I'm sure it's too cold out here."

"No, not just yet." Her thoughts were running like wildfire. She had to think of something. Anything. "Guy, do we have to go tonight?"

He was taken aback. "But I thought you were looking forward to it."

She looked seductively as she could into his eyes. "I'd rather spend Christmas Eve here with you," she whispered. "Kiss me, Guy."

He bent his mouth to her lips, but even as she sighed and melted against him, he knew he wasn't aroused. Her body was eager and desirous, her movements knowing and shameless, but the skill of her kiss failed to find a response. He was going through the motions, pretending to return the passion, but his flesh told tales on him. It had never been like that with Fleur. He'd wanted his wife all the time, and to make love to her was to enter the gates of heaven ... Fleur filled his thoughts now, and he drew sharply back from the kiss. "We'll be seen," he murmured.

She was conscious of the reserve in him, and it cut through her like a knife, especially now. "I love you, Guy," she whispered desperately, determined to win a matching reassurance from him, but before he could say anything the head groom suddenly interrupted them from the end of the terrace.

"Begging your pardon, my lord, but there's a problem and I think you should come."

Guy was glad of the diversion. "I'll come now, Johnson."

"My lord."

Guy looked at Imogen. "I must go," he murmured, putting his hand to her cheek for a moment.

Panic still gripped her. "About tonight . . ." she began urgently.

"I've given Harry my word."

"Please let's stay here alone," she begged.

"I can't cry off at this late hour," he replied, knowing that it was an excuse, for the truth was he didn't want to be alone with her.

"Guy—"

"If you don't wish to come, I'll go alone," he interrupted, meeting her eyes.

Go alone to the hotel where his wife and child were staying? That was the last thing she dared risk. She managed a smile. "No, of course I—I won't let you go without me."

With a quick smile he drew her hand to his lips, and then hurried away toward the waiting groom.

When he'd gone, Imogen could barely control her bitterness and dismay. Grillion's! Of all the places in London, it had to be there! Alarm and trepidation pounded through her, and she trembled so much she felt her knees might not support her. Now she could only pray that the actor had played his part as superbly as his sister had before him, and that Fleur's path wouldn't cross Guy's. After all, it was a private dinner party, and was bound to be held in one of the rooms set aside for such functions. Fleur and Gerard would be in the main part of the hotel.

For a long moment she struggled to regain her composure, and at last felt able to return to the house. She left the holly lying in the snow.

4

At Grillion's, Fleur had fallen into a deep exhausted sleep, and Gerard paced the apartment, still mulling the situation over. Fleur might wish to delay matters for the moment because she was overwrought, but an attempt to see Guy was inevitable, and Gerard prayed it would lead to a satisfactory conclusion. If it didn't because Guy *had* sent the footman, then Gerard didn't care to think of his own response. He wouldn't be capable of allowing the matter to lie; a challenge was inescapable, and pistols at dawn was the very last thing Fleur needed.

As a distraction, and to calm his temper as much as possible, Gerard decided to adjourn to the hotel billiard room, where he guessed some agreeable company would be found. Leaving Martha to look after Fleur and Christopher, he made his way downstairs, pausing in the hall to speak to Thomas, whom he recognized.

"And how are you, Thomas?" he asked.

"Very well, sir." The footman bowed.

"Married yet?"

Thomas's eyes widened with surprise. "Married? No, sir!"

Gerard surveyed him. "Good, for it seems a certain young woman by the name of Martha considers you to be quite the thing, Thomas."

"She does?" Thomas brightened visibly.

"So I'm led to believe. I'm fond of Martha, sir, so you'd better be warned I'm watching over her. If you take any liberties—"

"I won't, sir," the footman interrupted hastily.

"Good. Don't misunderstand, for I'm not forbidding you to speak to her, I'm just making sure you and I see eye to eye on this." Gerard nodded at him and then strolled toward the billiard room at the rear of the hotel.

Thomas smiled. Permission had just been given for him to see Martha. But what was the best way to go about it? He was so deep in thought that he didn't hear the *maître d'hotel* crossing the hall toward him.

"Thomas?"

The footman gave a start. "Sir?"

"Daydream in your own time, sir, not Monsieur Grillion's."

"Sir."

"I require to know if the American guests will be taking luncheon and dinner. Be so good as to make inquiries."

Thomas could hardly conceal his delight. "Oh, yes, sir!" He went up to the Barrymore apartment, and straightened his powdered wig before knocking at the door.

After a moment it opened, and Martha stared out at him. "Thomas?" she whispered eagerly, but then lowered her eyes as she remembered it was more becoming to be shy.

"Oh, Martha, it's good to see you again," he began.

But she glanced awkwardly over her shoulder.

"Mizz Fleur's sleepin' in the next room," she warned.

"I'm here on hotel business," he explained. "I'm to find out about luncheon and dinner tonight."

"I—I don't know."

"Let me come in a while, Martha," he pleaded, making so bold as to put his hand to her cheek.

Her breath caught. "Someone might come!"

"Mr. Barrymore's in the billiard room, and your mistress is asleep. We could steal a few minutes," he urged, stroking her cheek with his thumb. "I've often thought about you, Martha."

"You—you have?"

"Have you thought about me?"

She nodded, and before she knew it he'd stepped past her into the apartment, and closed the door behind him.

"We've time to make up, Martha," he said softly, catching her hand and pulling her into his muscular arms.

She knew she should stop him because Fleur might awaken at any moment, but she could no more have spurned him than she could have sprouted wings and flown. She'd tried not to think about him since returning to Philadelphia, but it had been impossible. Now she was actually here with him at Grillion's. It was a wish come true, and at Christmas too! Raising her lips to meet his, she surrendered to the embrace.

Fleur slept on in the adjoining room, but gradually external sounds from the street began to influence her dreams. A military band was marching past the hotel playing "God Rest Ye Merry, Gentlemen," and the tune brought old memories to life again. Suddenly it was Christmas two years before, the only Christmas she and Guy had spent together.

They'd been married nearly three months, and were so happy it seemed they were under a wonderful enchantment.

The Richmond wassailers had come to Lanham House, and the whole household gathered in the hall to listen. She and Guy slipped away to their apartment, and as they crept secretly up the staircase without anyone noticing, the wassailers had been singing this song.

The apartment was firelit, and the warm air released the scent of pine from the evergreens fixed to the walls and mantelpiece. A jug of mulled wine flavored with orange, cloves, and cinnamon waited on the hearth. It soon imparted a comfortable glow as they sat on the floor gazing into the flames that leapt around the Yule log.

Her hair was defying its pins, and Guy reached out to push a stray curl back from her face. "Are you sorry you're not in Philadelphia now?"

"No. I only want to be with you."

"And I with you."

The flames had seemed to dance in his eyes as she looked at him. "I love you, Guy Fitzallen," she whispered, holding out her wine so they could link arms and sip from each other's glass.

Then they kissed. It had been a slow and tender kiss. Their lips tasted of the wine and their skin was warm from the fire. They knew they'd make love right there by the hearth, and the knowledge added a voluptuousness to the kiss, enriching their passion until their bodies seemed to scintillate with desire.

He drew her gently down to the floor, leaning over her so that he could undo her gown and put his lips to her breast. He'd drawn her nipple into his mouth, and she sighed as delicious sensations swept over her. She could feel his virility pressing urgently as he pulled her gown up above her thighs before pushing the iron-hard shaft into her. Oh, how slow and sensuous were his thrusts as he gave and took endless pleasure.

A fierce hunger seized her, a ravenous desire that could not be held back. Their lips were bruised by the passionate craving that raged through them both. Their bodies pulsed together, and gratification almost robbed her of consciousness itself. And from somewhere beyond the erotic waves of pleasure she could still hear the wassailers singing.

They were singing now. No, it was military music she heard. She opened her eyes to see not firelight at Lanham House but the midmorning sun shining through the window at Grillion's. Tears stung her eyes as she realized she'd only been dreaming. But what a wonderful dream. She felt as if she really had been making love with Guy . . .

Then she heard low voices in the next room. Martha was talking to someone, and it wasn't Uncle Gerard. Puzzled, she got up from the bed, smoothing her clothes and patting her hair before going to the door, which stood slightly ajar. There she paused, for she could see the maid with Thomas.

They were standing by the window, and the footman had his arm around Martha's waist as she rested her head on his shoulder. "Oh, Martha, why can't you come tonight?" he was saying. "It's only here in the hotel, and—"

"I've duties to attend to, Thomas. I'd love to come, but I've Master Christopher to look after."

Fleur went into the room. "What's this?" she asked.

They moved hastily apart, and Martha was covered with confusion. "Oh, Mizz Fleur, I didn't know you were awake!"

"So I see." Fleur couldn't help smiling. "Well, what were you discussing?"

Martha lowered her eyes. "Thomas was askin' me if I'd go to the hotel servants' dinner tonight, Mizz Fleur. Only I said I couldn't."

"Because you have to look after Christopher? Yes, so I heard. Don't look so anxious, Martha, for I'm not about to dismiss you."

"I—I know I shouldn't be talkin' to Thomas like this, Mizz Fleur, but—"

"There's no need to explain. When is this dinner to take place, Thomas?"

"From nine o'clock on, my lady. It's a continuous dinner, so everyone can eat as they finish work for the night. I finish at nine."

Fleur nodded and then looked at Martha. "Do you wish to go?"

"Yes, Mizz Fleur."

"Then you can. I'll look after Christopher."

Martha's face lit up. "Are you sure, Mizz Fleur?"

"Quite sure." Fleur looked at Thomas. "I'm also quite sure you have things you should be attending to, sir."

"Yes, my lady." He backed toward the door, but then remembered why he'd been sent to the apartment in the first place. "My lady, I'm to ask if you'll be requiring luncheon and dinner tonight?"

"Er—yes, I'm sure we will." Luncheon and dinner? Food was the last thing on Fleur's mind.

"My lady." With a quick bow, he hurried out.

Fleur looked at Martha's happy face. "Well, at least one of us hasn't had a wasted journey," she murmured.

Martha was instantly all concern. "Oh, Mizz Fleur, you mustn't believe Master Guy sent that footman, for I agree with Master Gerard, it was that 'Mogen."

"I'd like to think you're right, but I fear you're not."

"You mustn't give up, Mizz Fleur."

"I'm trying not to," Fleur said quietly.

At Lanham House, Guy and Patience were drinking chocolate in the conservatory, where the luxuriant tropical foliage seemed at odds with the snow outside. Imogen was supposed to have joined them, but had yet to come down from her room, where she'd been ever since learning where the Templeford dinner was to take place.

Guy was in a quiet mood and had barely touched his cup. Patience glanced at him. "What is it?" she asked at last.

"Mm?"

"Wherever you are, it isn't here with me."

He collected himself. "Forgive me. I was thinking about tonight. It seems Imogen no longer really wishes to go. One moment she was clearly looking forward to it, the next she'd changed completely."

Patience lowered her cup, her eyes quickening with interest. "How strange. What were you talking about when it happened?"

He shrugged. "I can't remember. Oh, yes, I can. It was when I mentioned that the dinner was at Grillion's. I think she thought it was to be at Templeford House. Anyway, suddenly she wanted us to stay here this evening instead, but I told her it wouldn't be the thing to cry off at such a late stage. She's still coming, if reluctantly."

Patience pursed her lips shrewdly. Why would Imogen be upset to that extent by the venue of the dinner?

Guy sighed. "I think she merely felt a little unwell, it was very cold out there." He stared at his chocolate and fell silent.

The moments passed, and Patience set the mystery of Imogen and Grillion's aside to look closely at him again. "Come, sir, tell me what else is on your mind. I know there is, so pray do not attempt to deny it."

"You're too sharp for your own good," he muttered, getting up to go to the nearest window and gaze down the snowy hillside.

"Well?" she pressed.

He glanced back a little ruefully. "You'll only say you told me so."

She studied him. "Which means it is to do with Imogen."

"Yes."

"You're having second thoughts?" she asked hopefully.

"No."

"Then what?" She was puzzled.

"Well, perhaps I should have said I can't have second thoughts. Not now."

Patience was dismayed. The creature was with child? Oh, please, no! "You aren't telling me she's—?"

He shook his head reassuringly. "No, it's nothing like that."

"Thank Heavens," she replied with relief. "What then?"

He looked at her. "You were right; Imogen is a poor substitute for Fleur."

"Ha! I knew it!" Patience declared triumphantly.

"I've felt it all along, but haven't admitted it. I knew it beyond all shadow of doubt today when she wanted me to cry off the dinner and stay here with her. I just didn't want to be alone with her."

"Then finish it."

"It's too late to change things now. Imogen's name has been inextricably linked with mine, and

I've allowed my closest friends to know of my marital intentions toward her. It would be a very shabby act to desert her at this stage."

"Marry her and you'll soon regret it with all your heart," she pointed out swiftly.

"I must proceed. Fleur isn't going to return to me, that's clear enough, and so, if only for the sake of the title, I have to marry again. And I cannot deny having asked Imogen to be my wife."

"You're a fool, Guy Fitzallen."

"Maybe, but I'm an honorable fool." Guy turned and left the conservatory.

Patience blinked back tears of anger. Oh, would that Imogen Wakefield had never set foot in this house! She crossed her fingers tightly. Please let me find the diary tonight, and let it point so clearly to the writer's villainy that Guy no longer feels obligated to marry her!

It was evening and Imogen was ready to leave for Grillion's. She wore geranium gauze over white silk, but her strained expression didn't go well with her fine plumage. The coming hours were fraught with danger, but she saw no way of avoiding it. If she went with him, at least she could do everything possible to prevent an encounter with Fleur or Gerard. And she could plead a headache and oblige him to leave early.

Her gloved hands shook as she adjusted the aigrettes in her hair, and then her glance fell upon her old black reticule. She mustn't forget to hide it. The diary inside felt heavy as she picked it up, and suddenly she wished she'd never committed pen to paper. It was all very well when she could keep the journal close by her, but when she had to leave it like this she knew how much of a threat it posed.

She must burn it! Yes, that was the thing to do! Taking the book she knelt by the fire, but as she seized the first pages to tear them out, suddenly she couldn't do it. This diary was the friend in which she'd confided everything, and she was only afraid tonight because she feared it might fall into Patience's clutches. All she had to do was find a safe hiding place, somewhere the old tabby couldn't possibly find. But where?

She glanced around the room. Where wouldn't Patience think of? For a long moment she couldn't think, but then a smile curved her lips. Of course! Taking a scarf from a drawer, she wrapped it tightly around the diary and then went to open the window. She cleared the powdery snow from the wide outside sill and wedged the diary into place before smoothing snow over it. When she closed the window again, there was no sign of disturbance in the snow. Satisfied she'd concealed it completely, she brushed some snow from her gloves and then put on her evening cloak, but her fingers were still trembling and she tied it too tightly, although she didn't realize it. It was an oversight that was to cost her precious seconds during the evening ahead. After extinguishing the candles, she went down to the hall, where Guy was waiting.

He wore a deep purple velvet coat and white trousers, and the amethyst pin in his neckcloth sparkled as he came to the foot of the stairs. His glance raked her. "You look very lovely," he said truthfully, wishing again that he could love her as much as she loved him.

"Thank you."

The fragrance of her rose scent enveloped him as he raised her hand to his lips, but she suddenly realized her glove was damp with melted snow and drew the hand swiftly away. "I—er—spilled a glass of water," she explained.

"Don't you wish to change your gloves?"

"No, it's quite all right. Besides, these are the only ones that go with this gown." She managed a smile.

"Shall we go, then?" He offered her his arm.

A footman opened the door, and they emerged beneath the lamplit portico to the waiting carriage. She shivered. But it wasn't from the cold of the night.

As the carriage commenced the one and a half-hour drive to Albemarle Street, Patience limped from the shadows at the back of the hall, from where she'd observed their departure. Taking a lighted candle from a table, she made her way up to Imogen's room. She was relieved to find the door unlocked, for she'd been prepared to go so far as to order a footman to break in if necessary.

Shadows leapt over the walls as she glanced thoughtfully around the silent chamber. Now, then, where to begin?

At Grillion's a little later, Fleur also dressed for dinner. She'd chosen ivory silk and Martha had looped fine strings of pearls through her hair.

She'd managed to make a show of eating a little luncheon, but the prospect of dinner made her feel positively ill. But it was Christmas Eve, and she meant to make the best of it. As to how to proceed next where Guy was concerned, she still shrank from any definite decision. She wanted to defer things until after Christmas Day itself, but knew she was stalling because she was afraid Guy had sent the footman. To make that discovery would be to end her secret longings once and for all. For the past year she'd striven to keep Guy Fitzallen out of her thoughts, but Patience's letter had renewed her hope. To have that hope dashed yet again would be more than she could bear.

But if Fleur were low spirited, Martha, on the other hand, could hardly contain her excitement. Things had gone so well for her today that she found it hard to believe Dame Fortune was being so generous. Not only was Thomas still here at Grillion's, but he was as interested in her as she was in him. Knowing how wretched her mistress was, the maid tried not to let her own happiness spill out, but she couldn't help herself, and hummed softly as she put the finishing touches to Fleur's coiffure.

When the maid had finished, Fleur got up and went to look at Christopher. He was awake in his cot, and she picked him up. She loved the little sounds he made, and his sweet baby smell. Smiling, she pushed her finger into his hand so he grasped it tightly, and then she looked at his eyes. How much like Guy would he really be when he grew up? Would he twist her heart with memories each time she saw him? And would he twist the hearts of every woman who fell in love with him?

She hugged him and then put him gently back into the cot. Martha was waiting at the door, and Fleur smiled at her. "I haven't forgotten my promise, Martha. I'll be back in time for you to keep your appointment."

"Thank you, Mizz Fleur."

At that moment Gerard emerged from his room, looking very elegant in evening attire. He toyed with the frill at his cuff and then looked approvingly at his niece. "Upon my soul, my dear, you look particularly beautiful tonight."

"You flatter me, I fancy," she murmured, knowing her face was pale and her eyes tired.

"You should have more confidence in yourself, Fleur. Now then, are we ready?"

"I'm as ready as I'm ever likely to be at the moment."

"We must try to forget the Fitzallens for a few hours, my dear. It's Christmas Eve, we're at one of London's finest hotels, and Monsieur Grillion's roast goose with rum-soaked apples awaits." He offered her his arm, and they left the apartment.

The sound of music drifted up through the hotel, for a fashionable orchestra had been engaged to play seasonal tunes. It was playing "Hark the Herald Angels Sing," but was so restrained and refined that the joy of the carol was lost. The air was very warm and the smell of fine Christmas food was almost heavy in such a stuffy atmosphere.

As they reached the foot of the staircase, Fleur noticed that a door that had been closed earlier was now open to reveal what appeared to be another dining room. A large dinner party was evidently in the offing, for the long table had been laid with a snowy cloth and napkins. Fine crystal sparkled, gold and white porcelain shone, cutlery gleamed, and four elaborate epergnes tumbled with holly, mistletoe, ivy, and scarlet ribbons. Garlands of more seasonal greenery had been looped around the cloth, and it all looked very inviting and expensive.

Gerard saw her looking. "I gather it's a private dinner party. Someone mentioned it in the billiard room earlier."

"It looks extremely exclusive."

"Come, the *maître d'hotel* is waiting to conduct us to our table, and he looks fit to burst if we don't oblige him immediately."

Living up to one's name was sometimes virtually impossible, as Patience was discovering as she searched Imogen's room. She'd looked in every drawer and cupboard, under the bed, under the wardrobe, and even under the carpet, but to no avail. Anger always exaggerated her limp. She felt helpless in the face of adversity. Imogen Wakefield didn't deserve to win Guy, but it seemed she was going to after all.

With a sigh she turned to leave, but then halted as she suddenly recalled something odd. When Imogen had gone down her glove had been damp. Some excuse had been given about a spilled glass, but there wasn't a glass in the room! How then had the glove become wet? Patience looked swiftly around and at last noticed some droplets of water on the floor by the window. She limped over to examine them, and in an instant knew they were melted snow.

With a swift intake of breath, she opened the window and looked out at the sill. At first she saw nothing, but gradually, as her eyes became accustomed to the light, she noticed how the snow had been freshly smoothed. Brushing it away, she found the diary in the scarf. Closing the window again, she sat on the bed to read.

The minutes passed and her eyes darkened with fury and disbelief as she realized how Fleur had been fooled into believing there was a mistress and children, and how the farewell note to Guy had been tossed vindictively into the fire. Poor Fleur had waited two long and wretched weeks in Falmouth, hoping that Guy would come after her! Then there had been the forged letter from the nonexistent Richard Ashwood, and the removal of incoming mail from America, of which there had been a great deal.

But then Patience read further, and suddenly saw why Imogen had been so loath to go to Grillion's tonight. Fleur and Gerard were there right now, with Guy's little son, Christopher.

Patience's hand crept to her throat and she felt weak with shock. Fleur had a child? She closed the book and stared at the fire. She'd suspected Imogen of wrongdoing, but had never guessed the extent of the deceit. Guy had to see this diary right away!

Clutching the book, she limped to the top of the staircase and called down to the footman in the hall. "Henry, have a carriage made ready at once. I'm going to Grillion's."

He gaped. "Grillion's, madam?"

"That's what I said."

"But—"

"But I never leave this house? That's very true. However, tonight I mean to break with that particular tradition! Go now, for I need the carriage as quickly as possible."

"Madam." Bowing, he hurried away.

Patience gathered her skirts and hastened awkwardly toward her own room. Lavender merino was all very well for the seclusion of Lanham House, but one had to look one's best for Grillion's. And that meant the silver pompadour!

A quarter of an hour later, with the vital diary still clutched tightly in her hand, Patience left Lanham House en route for a denouement that she prayed would consign Imogen Wakefield to oblivion, and reunite Fleur and Guy forever.

5

As Patience's carriage drove swiftly through the snow toward Kew Bridge over the Thames, Fleur and Gerard were bringing their dinner to a premature end. They'd proceeded no further than the excellent soup because Fleur wasn't able to muster any appetite at all. She tried to show some enthusiasm, but to no avail, and her wretchedness took the edge off Gerard's appetite as well.

She sat unhappily in her chair, toying with her wedding ring, which she wore over her glove. She took it off and placed it on the table, for intuition told her she wouldn't be wearing it for much longer anyway. Somehow, tonight she felt that Guy really was in love with Imogen now, and that when he asked for a divorce, he meant it.

Without noticing what she'd done with the ring, Gerard got up suddenly. "Let's dispense with this farcical meal. Neither of us has any desire to prolong the agony, so I'll take you back to the apartment. Then I fancy I'll take a stroll along Piccadilly."

The wedding ring slipped her mind as they quitted the dining room. Gerard left her at the apartment door, and she went in to find Martha choosing what to wear for her own dinner engagement. After some deliberation she decided upon a yellow muslin gown. It was some time after that that Fleur suddenly remembered the wedding ring.

"Oh, no! I'll have to go down again."

"Mizz Fleur?" Martha's face fell as she thought there was going to be a long delay.

Fleur put a reassuring hand on her arm. "I won't be any time at all, and you can go to Thomas the moment I return."

"Yes, Mizz Fleur."

Fleur was retrieving the ring from the dining room as Guy's carriage drew up at the hotel, and he and Imogen alighted. Fleur was just about to return to her apartment when she recognized Harry Templeford walking toward the front door. She halted in dismay in the dining room as he spoke to someone out of her view.

"Ah, there you are at last, Guy! We were beginning to think you'd lost your way!"

Fleur's heart began to beat more swiftly. Surely Guy hadn't come here to Grillion's after all? She moved closer to the doorway and looked cautiously out. Her heart ceased its frantic rushing, and seemed to stop altogether as she saw Harry greeting Guy and Imogen. She stared, her eyes stinging with tears. Guy knew she and her uncle were here at this hotel, but he still brought Imogen here! Uncle Gerard and Martha were wrong—he *had* sent the footman. Maybe he didn't intend to come here to call upon his wife, but evidently that didn't preclude him from bringing his new love! How *could* he be so unutterably cruel?

Biting her lip in a vain attempt to stem the flow of tears, she stared at the group in the hall. How little Guy had changed! He was still as arrestingly handsome as ever. Still as beloved as ever ... Oh, was ever there a greater fool than she? Even now, after all he'd done, she still loved him!

It was then that Harry happened to glance in her direction. His smile changed and his lips parted. "Good God," he breathed.

Imogen didn't hear or see anything, for her earlier clumsiness tying her cloak meant that a footman was required to try to undo the knot she'd made, and her attention was diverted. Guy heard Harry's smothered exclamation, however, and turned to see what had startled him. He froze with shock. Fleur? It couldn't possibly be!

But then there was another interruption as Harry's pretty blond wife hastened delightedly across the hall in a flurry of carmine taffeta. "Guy! How good it is to see you again!" she cried, taking his hands and reaching up to kiss his cheek.

Distracted, he had to smile at her. When he looked again, Fleur had gone.

Seizing her opportunity, she'd drawn back into the dining room and fled toward a small door at the far end. It opened into a little-used anteroom, from which another door led to the back staircase to the floors above. With the ring held tightly in her hand, she hurried up to the apartment, pausing at the doorway to compose herself before going in.

Martha had just finished pinning a fresh mobcap on her dark hair, and Fleur managed an admiring smile. "You—you look splendid, Martha," she said, endeavoring to sound light.

"Thank you, Mizz Fleur."

"You—er—can go now, if you wish."

The maid looked curiously at her. "Is everything all right, Mizz Fleur?"

"Quite all right, thank you. Off you go, now. I—er—I think you should use the back stairs." It wouldn't do for Guy to see her.

"Yes, Mizz Fleur." Patting the mobcap more firmly into place, the maid hurried out.

As soon as she'd gone, Fleur locked the door behind her. She doubted if Guy would attempt to speak to her, but if he did she wouldn't respond. She bit her lip again, still trying to hold back the tears, but she couldn't. They welled wretchedly down her cheeks, and she hid her face in her hands. She'd thought many things of Guy Fitzallen over the past months, but never that he'd be so unkind and uncaring as to bring his new love to the very hotel where he knew his wife and child were staying. Oh, how gravely she'd misjudged him. He might masquerade as a gentleman, but he was base through and through.

* * *

Guy was beginning to think he'd imagined seeing Fleur, but when he caught Harry's eye, he knew he hadn't imagined anything, for Harry had seen her, too.

Imogen had at last been divested of her cloak, and turned to smile apologetically. "Forgive me, I was so nervous about tonight that I tightened the ties far too much."

Guy performed the necessary introductions, but his mind was still upon Fleur. He glanced toward the dining room again, willing her to reappear, but she didn't.

Jane Templeford was determined to put Imogen at her ease. "You mustn't be nervous, my dear, for Harry and I are your friends, and we'll do all we can to help. Won't we, Harry?"

"Eh? Er—yes. Of course." Harry shifted uneasily.

Guy gave him an urgent look. "Harry, would you and Jane escort Imogen into dinner? I have something I must attend to."

Imogen was dismayed. "Guy?"

"I'll join you shortly," he replied, and then turned to hurry toward the dining room.

Jane looked after him in surprise. "What's all that about?"

Harry cleared his throat. "I don't know. Come, ladies, one on each arm, if you please," he went on more briskly.

As Imogen accepted, her haunted gaze flitted around the hall, and into the dining room, where she could see Guy speaking earnestly to the *maître d'hotel*. What was he saying? Surely it couldn't concern Fleur? Panic rose within her, but she quelled it immediately, chiding herself for being foolish. How could it possibly be about Fleur when he had no idea she was here? She, Imogen, would know if he'd seen anything already. Composing herself, she walked toward the private dining room with Harry and his wife.

If she had but known it, Imogen could not have been further from Guy's mind at that moment. He faced the *maître d'hotel.* "I wish to know about a lady I saw in this room a few moments ago. Lady Lanham?"

"Your message was delivered, my lord," the *maître* assured him.

"What message?"

"The one you sent with the footman."

"What footman? I sent no footman."

The man was taken aback. "No, my lord? Well, he was in your livery and he spoke to Mr. Barrymore the moment he and Lady Lanham arrived on their visit from America. I was there at the time."

"My livery?"

"Maroon and gold, with your crest embroidered upon the collar. And he *said* he was here on your business, my lord. Oh, dear, are you saying he was an imposter?" The *maître* looked a little faint.

"He certainly was." What was going on? Was his aunt right? Was it Imogen? Guy ran his fingers through his hair, but then realized exactly what the *maître* had said a moment before. When Gerard and Fleur arrived on their *visit*?

Guy was very still. "Am I to understand that Lady Lanham and her uncle are staying here?"

"Yes, my lord."

"Which rooms do they have?"

"The balcony apartment above the main entrance. Shall I—?" The *maître* broke off and stared as Guy almost ran toward the staircase.

Reaching the apartment, Guy knocked urgently. "Fleur?"

She didn't answer.

He knocked again. "Fleur? Open the door, I beg of you!"

She remained silent.

"Please answer, Fleur, for I *must* speak with you!" he cried.

Still she said nothing.

He stepped back, his sharp gaze going to the bottom of the door, where he could see the faint glow of candlelight. She was in there, he knew she was! Very well, if she wouldn't admit him the conventional way, he'd get in unconventionally!

Turning, he ran back along the passage.

In the apartment, she exhaled very slowly. Refusing to admit him had been the hardest thing she'd ever done, but she had to protect herself from further pain. This man had broken her heart; he wasn't going to crush the pieces beneath his boot.

She went through into Christopher's room. He was still awake, cooing and gurgling as he watched the candleshadows on the ceiling. Fresh tears stained Fleur's cheeks.

Gerard was returning to the hotel after his leisurely stroll in Piccadilly. It had begun to snow again, and he turned his collar up for the final yards along crowded Albemarle Street. A carriage drove swiftly up behind him, the horses sweating as the coachman reined them in at the hotel door.

The lady passenger alighted quickly and began to make her way between the people walking along the pavement. Gerard halted incredulously, for there was no mistaking that patrician profile and uneven gait.

"Patience?" The single word was almost jerked from his lips.

She gasped and whirled about to stare at him.

"Gerard?" Her voice was almost drowned by the noise of a passing hackney coach.

He took a hesitant step toward her, not knowing what to say, but then their attention was diverted by a shout of alarm from the hot chestnut man across the road.

" 'Ere look up there! That's cove's breaking in!"

There was a stir on the pavement and everyone followed his pointing finger toward the second floor of the hotel, where a shadowy figure could be plainly seen climbing up a drainpipe toward the balcony above the main entrance.

Transfixed, Patience stared up as she recognized Guy. Gerard saw her incredulity and hurried to join her.

He looked up as well. "Isn't that—?" he began.

Patience nodded. "Yes, it is."

"He's climbing to our apartment balcony," he said quietly.

"Then he knows you're here?" She looked swiftly at him.

"I have no idea, but I would imagine he must. Why else would he climb up?"

"Is Fleur there now?"

"I believe so."

Patience looked swiftly at him. "They belong together, you know."

Gerard met her gaze. "May I ask a question?"

"By all means."

"Did Guy send a footman here today with a message for us?"

Patience's eyes cleared and she drew Imogen's diary from beneath her cloak. "Neither Guy nor I knew you were coming to London, Gerard, and Guy certainly didn't send a message to Grillion's. But I know who did. It's all written here, and I was bringing it to show Guy." She opened the diary to reveal the flyleaf. Imogen's name was clearly visible in the light from a street lamp. "The footman who met you today was the brother of the actress she hired before to play the part of Guy's mistress in Kensington," Patience explained.

Gerard stared at the book and then at Patience. "Are you telling me she actually wrote everything down?"

"Yes, absolutely everything. She has a great deal to answer for, Gerard, for the whole business has been her doing. But for her, Guy and Fleur would never have parted." She closed the diary. "I don't know how Guy has found out about you and Fleur being here, but he certainly didn't know when he left earlier this evening. I only know because I searched Imogen's room when they left and found this wretched journal."

"They? Are you telling me Imogen is here as well?"

"I fear so. They were invited to Harry and Jane Templeford's dinner party. Gerard, Guy doesn't love Imogen; he still loves Fleur. He admitted as much to me just today. He's only proceeding with things because he feels he's compromised Imogen, and because he still believes Fleur left him for someone else. I've come here to expose Imogen for the demon she is, and to see that Guy and Fleur are brought together again. Will you help me?"

"Help you? I'll be at your side every step of the way!"

Patience smiled at him. "I—I'm also here to make amends to you, Gerard," she said quietly.

"I trust that means changing your mind about marrying me?" he observed bluntly.

A warm flush leapt to her cheeks. "You're always so direct," she murmured.

"It's a lovable American trait. You British are

too damned coy by far." He smiled at her. "I came back here to help Fleur, but I came on my own behalf as well. I haven't found anyone who comes even close to matching you, Patience Fitzallen, and I'm damned if I'm going to give up without fighting for you."

She gazed at him through a haze of tears. "Oh, Gerard . . ."

Suddenly everyone on the pavement gasped as Guy almost lost his hold and fell back a foot or two. Patience pressed a hand fearfully to her lips as it seemed he must fall, but then he began to climb again and she exhaled with relief.

In the apartment, Fleur gradually became aware of the disturbance in the street. Putting Christopher back in his cot, she went to the window in time to see someone scrambling over the balcony railings. Her heart almost turned over as she recognized Guy, but at that very same moment she heard frantic knocking at the apartment door. It was the *maître d'hotel,* who'd been alerted that there was an intruder attempting to gain entry.

Guy came to the French windows, looking urgently into her eyes. "Let me in, Fleur, I beg of you!" he cried, his voice muffled through the glass.

Someone down in the crowd shouted as well. "Yes, love, let 'im in, for Gawd's sake, before 'e breaks 'is fool neck!"

There was a ripple of laughter.

Behind her, the *maître d'hotel* hammered anxiously at the door. "Are you all right, Lady Lanham?" he called.

She stared at Guy, not knowing what to do. Her heart bade her let him in; her head told her not to.

"Please, Fleur." He pressed his left hand pleadingly to the pane, and she saw that he wore his wedding ring.

Her heart had its way, and slowly she went to open the window. Then she backed swiftly away to allow him in. There was a roar of approval from outside, but then he'd closed the windows behind him.

The *maître d'hotel* shook the door handle with increasing apprehension. "My lady? Are you all right?" he cried again.

She went to the door and unlocked it to look out at him. "Yes, I'm all right," she said quietly.

"There's a man climbing up to your balcony—"

"It's Lord Lanham, and I've admitted him now. There's no need for further concern."

Lord Lanham? The *maître* couldn't hide his bemusement. "Are you quite sure all is well, my lady?"

"Quite sure. Thank you."

He bowed and withdrew, followed by the two footmen he'd brought with him. Fleur closed the door again and then turned to face Guy.

He stepped closer. "Fleur, I—"

"I don't really think we have much to say to each other, sir," she interrupted a little coolly, but beneath that cool veneer she was in a turmoil of mixed emotions. She wanted to run to him, to fling her arms around him and beg him to say he still loved her. But he'd come here tonight with Imogen, and he'd asked for a divorce . . .

"Why didn't you reply to my letter? Why didn't you say you were coming to London?"

"I did both things, sir, just as I also wrote when I left you. I informed you then that I'd wait in Falmouth for two weeks if you wished to see me. You clearly had no such wish."

"Wait in Falmouth? I didn't know. All I knew was that you'd chosen to return to a former lover."

"And all I knew was that you had a mistress and two children in Kensington," she replied.

He stared at her. "I've never kept a mistress."

"And I've never had a lover from Georgia."

He continued to hold her gaze. "Who told you about my mistress? Was it Imogen?"

"Yes."

"And she was the one who told me about your lover; indeed she even produced a letter supposedly from him." He gave an ironic laugh. "My God, it would seem she has a clever way with letters, whether it be to steal or forge them. She also appears to have a talent for finding excellent actors," he murmured, thinking of the footman he'd just learned about. He looked urgently at her. "Fleur, I didn't send any message here today, you must believe me. I can only think it was Imogen's work. My aunt has been warning me for some time, and now I'm forced to believe her. Imogen has striven from the outset to drive a wedge between you and me. What would you say if I told you I'd never received any word from you from the moment you left Lanham House?"

"That I wrote many times."

His heart turned over with gladness. She'd written. She'd waited for him in Falmouth. There hadn't been a Richard Ashwood ... "And if I told you I still loved you, what would you say then?" he whispered.

She drew back defensively. "What would I say? I'd remind you that you arrived here tonight with Imogen."

"I don't love her, Fleur. I admit to having been taken in by her, and to thinking I felt sufficient attachment to marry her, but my heart has remained with you. My only reason for continuing with her now is that I believe I'd compromised her. My honor wouldn't allow me to desert her."

"Fine words."

"But true. Dear God above, Fleur, why do you think I went to the length of climbing up to you like some latter-day Romeo?" He went to her then, seizing her arms and making her look into his eyes. "I know I came with Imogen tonight, and that I wrote to you about divorce in order to marry her, but neither thing is what I wanted. You are the one I want, the one I've always wanted, and now I have this chance to speak to you again, I mean to use it properly." She felt so good in his hands. Holding her was like rebirth, as if his withered soul were being replenished. This woman, his wife, meant everything in the world to him, and he'd die rather than lose her again.

"I love you with all my heart, Fleur, and if the happiness we once shared means anything to you, you'll be my wife again. Come back to me, let me love and cherish you as I did before."

She hardly dared hope this was really happening. She was asleep, and would suddenly awaken, just as she had earlier this very day. She tried desperately to cling to facts. "I—I want to believe you still love me, Guy, but—"

His fingers tightened desperately. "If there are buts, Fleur, why did you come to London?"

"I had a very good reason, Guy," she said quietly. "You see, there is someone else involved now, someone whose future must be protected."

He drew back slowly. "Someone else? Who?"

Composing herself, she went into Christopher's room and brought him to his father. "Meet our son, Guy. His name is Christopher."

Guy stared at her, and then at the sleeping baby. "Our son?" he repeated in astonishment.

She nodded. "I didn't know I was carrying him when I left you. I—I believe he was conceived on our first wedding anniversary." She looked at him. "He's your child, Guy. You do believe me, don't you?"

He reached out to touch the baby's cheek. "Yes, of course I believe you," he said softly.

"You don't still harbor any secret suspicion about my lover from Georgia?"

"Do you still believe I had a mistress and children?" He met her gaze.

Tears stung her eyes. "No, not now," she whispered. "Do you want to hold him?"

He nodded, and she put Christopher gently into his arms. He looked down as the baby made a little sound and then awoke, revealing large green eyes that were a mirror of his own. Guy smiled at her. "Is he just Christopher, or does he have other names?"

"He's called Christopher Guy Gerard Barrymore Fitzallen."

"Very impressive for such a small being," he murmured.

"If—if you want us, Guy, we'll come to you," she said suddenly.

"Want you? Fleur, it's what I want more than anything in the world." He went to the cot and laid Christopher gently down before returning to take her in his arms.

She raised her mouth to meet his, and joy flooded through them both like a charge of electricity. He crushed her close, his fingers twining desirously in the warmth of her hair. Need coursed wildly through them both and she drew his tongue deep into her mouth, as if she would draw his very essence. This was no dream now, for she was wide awake, and her body ached with arousal.

He lifted her and carried her to the bed.

6

From the outset, the stir on the pavement and in the hotel itself had aroused the guests' interest. Many of them, including those at Harry Templeford's dinner, came out to see what was happening. Imogen was among them, and she looked up just in time to recognize Guy on the balcony before he went into the bedroom. A look of haunted dismay whitened her face, for she knew she'd lost.

Patience saw her and caught Gerard's arm to steer him toward her. Imogen sensed their approach and turned sharply. Her eyes fled guiltily from one face to the other, and then came to rest on the diary.

Patience looked coldly at her. "How very vain and foolish of you to write this, my dear, for it's the instrument of your destruction."

Imogen stared at the book she knew she should have destroyed. But it was too late now. Far too late. "How—how did you find it?" she whispered, her voice almost lost in the noise of the street.

"Damp gloves," Patience replied.

Imogen lowered her eyes. A small mistake, but costly.

Patience was unsparing. "I suggest you remove yourself from this vicinity, madam, for I doubt my nephew will wish to set eyes upon you once he's seen what this book contains. In fact, I suggest you remove yourself entirely. I don't care where you go or what becomes of you, just that you never come near Lanham House or any of my family ever again. You won't be admitted to the house should you return, for I've already issued the necessary instructions. Your belongings will be forwarded once you send your new address."

Imogen's lips parted in alarm. "But I can't possibly find anywhere tonight!"

"Christmas Eve? Why, I'm sure you'll find some tavern or other," Patience murmured unsympathetically. "Have you considered the Halfway House in Kensington? You'll undoubtedly find a welcome there, as I gather it caters to undesirables. Stay one moment more in my sight, and I swear I'll have you arrested for theft."

Imogen's eyes widened. "Theft? But I—"

"I'll invent a stolen necklace, madam, of that you may be sure. Lying isn't exclusively your domain, and I rather fancy I'll prove even better at it than you!"

Imogen's breath caught, and she turned to hurry back into the hotel for her outdoor things. A moment later she emerged again and fled along the pavement toward Piccadilly. Patience felt nothing but contempt for her. The creature deserved to suffer far more than this for what she'd done. Far more.

Now that Guy had gained entry from the balcony and there was nothing more of interest to see, the people on the pavement began to disperse. Soon there were only the Christmas Eve strollers passing to and fro, and across the road the hot chestnut man resumed his calls, shouting as loudly as he could to be heard above the rattle of the traffic.

Gerard took Patience's hand and drew it over his sleeve. "Since the excitement seems to be at an end for the moment, my dear, I think it might be agreeable if you and I took dinner together. I couldn't eat properly earlier, but now I could positively *de-*

vour roast goose with rum-soaked apples. What d'you say?"

"But should we not show Guy and Fleur the diary?" Patience asked a little ingenuously.

Gerard raised an eyebrow. "*Now?* My dear, I rather think that that might be execrable timing."

She went pink. "Oh, yes. Of course."

He put his hand fondly to her cheek. "Oh, Patience, you're quite delightful, truly you are."

"Delightful? Sir, I'm a foolish old maid."

"You're neither foolish nor old, and as to being a maid, well, I intend to do something about that." He bent his head to kiss her on the lips.

She trembled with pleasure, and then drew back smiling.

"My kisses amuse you, madam?" he inquired, smiling as well.

"Indeed not, sir. I was just thinking of the old adage. There's many a good tune played on an old fiddle."

"These two old fiddles might produce a fine duet."

"Yes, so they might." She eyed him. "I trust you don't mean to wait a long time to enjoy the tune?"

"I'm willing to enjoy it tonight, but I'm sure such a thought would offend your principles."

"Tonight will be excellent, sir."

He stared at her. "Madam, are you propositioning me?"

"Yes, sir, I believe I am. Why should the young ones have all the fun?"

"Why indeed." He smiled and drew her hand to his lips. "Very well, Miss Fitzallen, I will allow you to lead me grievously astray."

As Gerard and Patience adjourned to the dining room to order goose and champagne, word spread through the hotel kitchens of Lord Lanham's astonishing method of gaining entry to his estranged wife's apartment.

There was seasonal joviality in the air, and the entire kitchen was decked with greenery, including an immense bunch of mistletoe. Martha and Thomas were seated on a settle by the cavernous fireplace, sipping some of the cook's excellent mulled ale prior to taking their allotted places at the long scrubbed table where the servants' Christmas Eve dinners were to be served.

Thomas heard Guy's name mentioned. Lowering his cup of ale, he looked swiftly at Martha. "Lanham? Isn't that—?"

She'd heard as well and got up quickly. "I—I'd better go to see if everything's all right."

But one of the other footmen pushed her good-humoredly back on to the settle. "Don't bother, for I doubt your presence will be appreciated right now."

"I should go," Martha insisted.

The footman grinned at her. "I was there with the *maître,* and I can tell you your mistress won't be wanting you. She said her husband was with her, and everything was all right. If she wants you, she'll send for you. My advice is to stay here and make merry. It's what you and Thomas want, isn't it?"

She glanced at Thomas and then nodded. "Yes, it is."

The cook rang the small gong on the sideboard. "Dinner is served, ladies and gentlemen," she said grandly, and there was much cheering and clapping as a huge roast turkey was carried ceremoniously in and placed on the table.

Thomas led Martha toward their places, but then halted beneath the mistletoe to pull her into his arms. She went gladly, and there were tears in her eyes as she returned his kiss. Suddenly she knew she'd never return to Philadelphia. London was where she belonged now. With Thomas.

The bells of London rang out joyously at midnight as Christmas Eve gave way to Christmas Day itself. There was cheering and singing in the streets, and in the hotel as everyone raised their glasses to toast the occasion.

Fleur and Guy lay together in the bed, their naked bodies close and tender. They felt warm and sated. It was as if they were newly in love, with all the passion and urgency that accompanies that time.

Hearing the church bells pealing, she leaned over him, her hair tumbling over her shoulders, her breasts brushing his skin. "Merry Christmas, my lord," she whispered.

"Merry Christmas, my lady," he replied, drawing a fingertip across her nipple and then cupping her breast in his palm.

There was a discreet tap at the door, and he looked irritably toward the sound "Yes? What is it?"

"Begging your pardon, my lord," said the *maître d'hotel*, "but the kitchens are about to be closed for the night, and if you will wish to have dinner ..."

Fleur began to laugh, and buried her face against Guy's shoulder for fear the man might hear.

Guy kept a straight face as best he could. "Er— no, I don't think we'll require dinner now, but I fancy a hearty breakfast might prove just the thing."

"Very well, my lord, and—er—the compliments of the season."

"The compliments of the season to you, too," Guy replied.

Fleur was helpless with mirth, and Guy rolled her on to her back and looked sternly at her. "Fie on you, madam, for the poor fellow was only performing his duty."

She overcame her amusement and gave him a playful look. "As I trust you are about to again, Lord Lanham," she murmured.

He lowered his lips to kiss her, and his arms slipped around her, pulling her toward him. They lingered over the kiss, and she felt his body stirring with a desire that matched her own.

They made love again and again that night, and Christopher slept contentedly in his cot, not knowing that his parents were united once more, that his uncle and aunt would soon walk up the aisle, or that his nurse had found happiness as well. If he dreamed at all, it was of the warmth and love that had always surrounded him, and that would now be redoubled.

Snow continued to fall outside, as this most special of nights wove its magic and mystery, but for the six lovers who one way or another had set out to have dinner at Grillion's, no other Christmas would ever be as wonderful as this one.

The Best Gift

❦

Mary Balogh

"Christmas is an unutterable bore," Lady Enid Penn said with an affected sigh. "There is positively no one with whom to amuse oneself except parents and aunts and uncles and cousins by the score and nothing to do except feast and make merry—with one's own family!"

There was a murmur of sympathetic agreement from several other young ladies.

"I shall simply die," the Honorable Miss Elspeth Lynch informed her listeners, "if the Worsleys remain in town for the holiday, as they did last year, instead of returning home. Patricia Worsley is my dearest bosom friend, and Howard Worsley is—well, he is interesting." She looked around archly at her companions, who tittered on cue.

"If one were only sixteen instead of fifteen," the Honorable Miss Deborah Latimer said, adding her sigh to everyone else's. "One's parents and aunts and uncles and all their friends have a wonderful time dancing and partaking of the wassail bowl and staying up almost until dawn while one is banished to the nursery and to bed with the children."

"And what about you, Craggs?" Lady Enid turned her head to look at the lady who had sat silently writing at her desk while they talked. "Do you find Christmas a bore, too? Or do you have wonderfully exciting plans? You are older than six-teen, after all."

The other young ladies tittered again, though there was an edge of cruelty to their laughter this time.

"Do you have dozens of beaux, Craggs? *Do* tell," Miss Lynch said, widening her eyes.

Miss Jane Craggs looked up from the journal in which she was writing. Although it was homework hour and school rules stated quite categorically that it was to be a silent hour, she was not enforcing the rule this evening. It was the last day of school before Christmas. Tomorrow all the girls would be going home, most of them with their parents or with liveried servants in sumptuous carriages.

"I believe it would be something of an exaggera-tion, Elspeth, to count my beaux in the dozens," she said. "Besides, a lady never does tell, you know."

"But you are not a lady, Craggs," one of the younger girls said.

But she won only frowns for her witticism. Every-one knew that Jane Craggs was not a lady, that she had spent most of her life at Miss Phillpotts's school for young ladies, her board and education paid for by an unknown benefactor—undoubtedly her fa-ther—until she was seventeen, that she had stayed on afterward as a teacher, though Miss Phillpotts treated her more as a servant than as an instructor. All the girls took their cue from the headmistress. The names of all their teachers were preceded by "Miss" except for Craggs. They treated her with a condescension bordering sometimes on insolence. But there was an undefined borderline beyond which they would not go. It was unladylike to re-mind Craggs in words that she was no lady.

"I believe," Jane Craggs said, closing her journal

and getting to her feet, "we will make a concession to the approaching holiday and end homework hour five minutes early. Would anyone care to argue the point?"

There was relieved laughter and some enthusiastic cheering from the young ladies, who jumped to their feet and made for the door.

"Happy Christmas, Craggs," Deborah Latimer said as she was leaving the room.

Jane Craggs smiled at her and returned the greeting.

She sat down again when she was alone and began deliberately to clean and mend the pen she had been using. And she tried to ignore the knowledge that Christmas was approaching—an impossibility, of course.

No one with whom to amuse oneself except aunts and uncles and cousins and parents. Nothing to do but feast and make merry with one's family members. Such a Christmas was unutterably boring? Jane felt rather like crying and ruthlessly suppressed the feeling. If only she could once—just once in her life—experience such a Christmas.

She had always hated Christmas. As a child and as a young girl she had also dreaded it. Dreaded the aloneness, with which she had always lived every day of the year but that always assaulted her most cruelly at Christmas. Dreaded the emptiness. Dreaded the excitement of the other girls as they prepared to go home and waited for family members or servants to come and fetch them. Dreaded the departure of Miss Phillpotts and the teachers until she was quite alone in the school with the few servants who were kept on for the holiday—always, it seemed, the most humorless of the servants.

Now she was three-and-twenty years old. The dread had gone. But the aloneness, the loneliness, the emptiness had not. She had heard and read so much about Christmas. For her there had never been family—she understood that she had spent her early years in an orphanage, a rather expensive one. She believed, though she did not know for sure, that her mother had been a nobody, perhaps a whore, while her father had been a wealthy man who had agreed to support her until she was old enough to support herself. And so there had never been family for her and never Christmas gifts or Christmas parties.

Sometimes she had to remind herself that her name was Jane. A rather plain name, it was true, but her own. She heard it so rarely on anyone's lips that she could not remember the last time. It seemed singularly unfortunate to her that some-one—her mother, she supposed—had blessed her with the surname of Craggs.

As a child she had dreamed of Christmas and the dream had lingered even though she had passed the age of dreams. But did one ever pass the age of dreams? Would life be supportable if one could not dream?

She had dreamed of a large house with three stories in which every window blazed with light. It was always twilight and there was snow outside blanketing the ground and making of the trees and their branches magical creations. Inside there was a large hall, three stories high, with two large fire-places crackling with log fires, the hall decked out in greenery and bows for the season. It was a house filled with people. Happy, beautiful people. All of whom loved her. All of whom she loved.

As a child she had even given names and faces and personalities to all those people. And in her imagination she had bought or made special gifts for each of them and had received gifts in return.

In her dream there was always a carved Nativity Scene in the window of the drawing room and it was always the focal point of family celebrations. The family always went to church on Christmas Eve, trudging through the snow to get there, filling a number of the pews. They always ran and laughed and ambushed one another with snowballs and rolled one another in the snow on the way home.

The contrast between dream and reality had been almost unbearable when she was a child. Now it was bearable. Jane tidied the already tidy teacher's desk, picked up her journal, her best friend, and clasped it with both hands against her bosom as she left the study room to climb the stairs to her small attic room. Now she was old enough to know that Christmas Day was just a day on the calendar like all others, that it would pass, that before she knew it the teachers and girls would be returning for the spring term. She had learned to be sensible.

She lit a candle in her room, shivered, and began to undress. Oh, no, she had not—she had not learned to be sensible. And it had not become bearable. It had not, it had not.

But she had learned to pretend to be sensible. And she had learned to pretend that it was bearable. She had learned to hold on to her childish dreams.

To say that he was feeling annoyed was to understate the case. He disliked Christmas. He had disliked it for most of his adult years. It was all just a parcel of nonsense as far as he was concerned. He liked to remove himself from town and all other centers of merriment well before the collective madness set in and take himself off to Cosway, his country seat, where he could wait out the season in quietness and sanity.

The trouble was that his family knew it and saw him as being available to care for unwanted relatives. Not that it had ever happened before, it was true, but it was happening this year and he knew that it would happen again, that he was setting a trend this year that he would regret forever after. His sister and brother-in-law had decided entirely on the spur of the moment to spend Christmas with friends in Italy and had disposed of the minor inconvenience of a fifteen-year-old daughter by informing him—yes, Susannah had told him, not asked him—that she would spend Christmas with him at Cosway.

What, in the name of all that was wonderful, was he going to do with a fifteen-year-old niece for a few weeks? And at Christmas, of all times?

What he would do, he had decided at once, having neglected the obvious solution of telling his elder sister that she must change her plans, that he just would not do it—what he would do was enlist the help of someone else. Some female who had no other plans for Christmas. Someone who would be pleased enough to spend it at Cosway, keeping Deborah out of mischief. And out of his way.

Agatha, in fact. But Agatha, his maiden aunt, had been invited to spend the week of Christmas with her dear friends, the Skinners, in Bath, and while she hated to inconvenience her dear nephew and great-niece, she really could not disappoint the Skinners this close to Christmas.

When Viscount Buckley descended from his carriage outside Miss Phillpotts's school and had himself announced to speak with the headmistress herself, he was scowling. And his mood matched his expression exactly.

"Deborah will be very delighted to learn that her uncle, the viscount, has come in person to convey her home for the holidays, my lord," Miss Phillpotts said to him, smiling graciously.

His lordship sincerely doubted it. Especially when the child discovered that her parents had taken themselves off to Italy without a word to her. He felt sorry for the girl, if the truth were known. But he felt sorrier for himself.

"I suppose, ma'am," he said, without allowing himself to feel even the faintest glimmering of hope, "that there is not another young lady at the school who has nowhere to go for the holiday? Someone who could come with my niece and be company for her over Christmas?"

"I am afraid not, my lord," the headmistress said. "All our girls will be leaving today."

The viscount sighed. "It was a faint hope," he said. "I am not much in practice as far as entertaining very young ladies is concerned, ma'am." Or as far as celebrating Christmas was concerned. And Deborah would doubtless want to celebrate it. Damn!

"It is indeed kind of you to be willing to extend your hospitality to another young lady," Miss Phillpotts said. "But the only person who will be remaining at the school apart from three servants is Miss Craggs."

Miss Craggs sounded like an elderly tyrant. But Viscount Buckley was somewhat desperate. "Miss Craggs?" he said.

"One of my teachers," Miss Phillpotts explained.

Undoubtedly a tyrant. Poor Deborah. She would probably hate him forever for asking the question he was about to ask.

"Is there any possibility," he asked, "that she would be willing to accompany us to Cosway?"

"I believe she would be delighted, my lord," the headmistress told him. "Shall I send her down to you? I see that Sir Humphrey Byrde's carriage has arrived." She glanced toward the window, which looked down onto a cobbled courtyard. "I should go to greet him."

The viscount bowed his acquiescence and wandered to the window while Miss Phillpotts left the room to see another of her pupils on her way. Damn Susannah and Miles! How could they think of going off to Italy for Christmas when they had a young daughter to care for? And how could they think of leaving her with him when they knew he did not celebrate Christmas? But then Susannah had always been the flighty, selfish one, quite different from their other two sisters. She was the youngest of the three and by far the most beautiful.

He had a suspicion that Susannah had never wanted children.

He thought briefly of his own child. Had he reminded his secretary to send her a gift? But then Aubrey would remember without a reminder. Part of his job was to remember what his employer was likely to forget.

He turned when the door opened behind him. She was not elderly and despite her name, she did not look like a tyrant.

"Miss Craggs?" he said.

She inclined her head.

She was not elderly at all. She was probably five or six years younger than he, in fact. She was rather tall, and slender almost to the point of thinness. She had a rather thin, pale face with fair hair smoothed back into a bun at her neck. Her gray dress was of cheap fabric and was high waisted but made no other concession to fashion. Only her eyes saved her from being so nondescript that she might have faded entirely into her surroundings. Her eyes were dark gray and long lashed. And they appeared to have such depth that he had the strange feeling that most of her living must be done very far within herself.

"Miss Craggs." He took a few steps toward her. "I understand that you will be staying here for Christmas?"

"Yes, my lord." Her voice was unexpectedly low and soft.

"You are expecting company?" he asked. "There would be someone to miss you if you were not here?"

Her face did not change expression. And yet he was given the impression that far within herself, where her living was done, she grimaced. "No, my lord," she said.

"I am Deborah Latimer's uncle," he said. "Warren Nash, Viscount Buckley, at your service, ma'am. Would it be possible to persuade you to come with us to my country seat in Hampshire? My sister and her husband, Deborah's parents, have gone to Italy and left her in my care. Frankly, I do not know what I am to do with a fifteen-year-old over Christmas. I need a female companion or chaperone for her. Will you come?"

There was the merest flicker in her eyes. Nothing more. He had never known a woman who was so impassive. He had always thought of women as open books, their emotions as clear to view as the words on a page. He had never had any problem knowing what his various mistresses felt or thought.

"Yes, my lord," she said.

He waited for more, for some questions or conditions. But she said nothing else. Her eyes, he noticed, were focused, not on his, but on his chin or thereabouts.

"I would guess that Deborah is eager to leave,"

he said. "How soon can you be ready, Miss Craggs?"

"Half an hour?" she said.

Half an hour! Good Lord, most women of his acquaintance would have asked for two or three days. He inclined his head to her. "Would you have Deborah sent to me?" he asked as she turned to leave the room.

Damn Susannah, he thought, too irritated to think of an original way mentally to censure his sister. How was he supposed to break the news to his niece?

Miss Craggs looked as if she had about as much joy in her as would half fill a thimble. A thimble for a small finger.

Damn!

She could not remember going farther from the school than could be accomplished on foot. She could not remember riding in a carriage. She could not remember being in company with a gentleman for longer than a minute or two at a time, except the dancing master who came in to teach the girls. She was usually chosen to partner him when he taught them the steps because he was not allowed to touch any of the girls and none of the other teachers were willing to tolerate his lavishly insincere compliments and his moist hands.

She was not sure if she was glad or sorry to be where she was. At first she had been numbed with the strangeness and wonder of it. She was going on a holiday. She was going to spend Christmas at a private home in Hampshire. The home of Viscount Buckley. She was not going to be alone at the school as she always had been for as far back as she could remember. And then she had been excited. Her teeth had chattered and her hands had shaken and her mind had whirled at dizzying speed as she had packed her few belongings into a valise she had had to borrow from Miss Phillpotts.

Now after hours of travel the luxury of a well-sprung, lavishly upholstered carriage was no longer able to mask the discomfort of the near silence that existed among its three occupants. An unnatural, uncomfortable silence. Deborah was sullen and unhappy. Jane did not blame her when she had discovered only this morning that her parents had gone away for Christmas and left her behind. But she feared that part of the sullenness was caused by the fact that she had been appointed the girl's companion. Craggs, the teacher who was not really a lady.

The viscount was merely silent. Jane doubted that he felt uncomfortable. But she did. Dreadfully so. She had had no experience with maleness. Viscount Buckley seemed suffocatingly male to her. He was dark, not much taller than she, elegant. She imagined he was handsome by any standards. She really had not seen many men. He seemed to her more handsome than any man she could possibly imagine. And very male.

She was uncomfortable and terrified.

"We are almost there," he said, turning his head and looking at Deborah. "You will feel better after a cup of tea."

"I will *not* feel better," his niece said sullenly. "I hate Christmas. And I hate Mama and Papa."

Jane looked at the girl. She wanted to take her hand and tell her that at least she had an uncle willing to take her in. At least she had someone to whom she belonged and somewhere to go. But such an assurance would not console, she supposed.

"If it is any consolation," the girl's uncle said,

"they are not exactly my favorite people at this moment either, Deborah."

"Meaning that you do not want to be burdened with me, I suppose," the girl said, misery overlaying the sullenness. "Everyone knows you do not believe in Christmas, Uncle Warren."

"Well," he said with a sigh, "I shall have to see what I can do to exert myself on your behalf this year, Deborah. Ah, the house. It is always a relief to see it at the end of a long journey."

Jane did not hear the rest of the conversation if, indeed, there was more. She had seen the house. Built within the last century, it had a classical symmetry of line combined with a deceptive simplicity of design. Built of light gray stone, it was rectangular in shape, three stories high, with a domed central portion and a pillared portico with wide marble steps leading up to double doors. It was larger and more magnificent than the house of her dream. And there was no snow, only bare trees and flowerbeds and grass of faded green. But it was all like enough to the dream house to catch at her breathing.

This was Cosway? This was where she was to spend the holiday?

She was aware suddenly that she had leaned forward and was gazing rather intently through the window. She was aware of the silence of her two companions. She turned her head and met the viscount's dark eyes. She sat back in her seat again and retreated within herself, into that secret place far inside where it never mattered that no one noticed her or respected her or loved her. A secret place she had discovered as a very young child.

"You admire my home, Miss Craggs?" the viscount asked her.

"Yes, my lord," she said. She felt the uncharac-

teristic urge to babble, to enthuse. She curbed it.
"It is very beautiful."

"I think so, too," he said.

She felt his eyes on her for a few moments
longer. She kept her own eyes firmly on the hands
she had clasped in her lap. And then the carriage
lurched slightly as it stopped, and the door was
being opened and the steps set down. She felt excitement ball in her stomach again.

Was this really happening? To her?

Always as he drove up to the house, and more
especially when he stepped inside the great domed
hall, he wondered why he did not spend more of
his time here. There was always a special feeling of
homecoming when returning to Cosway. He loved
the hall, especially in the winter, when the log fires
in the great twin fireplaces at opposite sides gave
welcome and the illusion of warmth. The hall was
too large and too high, of course, ever to be really
warm in reality.

"Ah, Kemp," he said to his butler, rubbing his
hands together as a footman took his hat and his
gloves and waited for him to remove his greatcoat.
"It is good to be home. I have brought my niece
with me, as you see, and her companion, Miss
Craggs. You will see that Mrs. Dexter assigns rooms
to them? And that their bags are taken up? We will
have tea served in the drawing room immediately."

Kemp cleared his throat. "There was a ah deliv-
ery for you earlier this afternoon, m'lord," he said,
nodding his head significantly to one side. "I did
not know quite what to do with it but knew you
would be arriving yourself before the afternoon
was out."

The viscount turned his head toward one of the
fireplaces. Beside it, seated on a wooden settle,

quite upright and quite still, sat a small child so bundled up inside a large coat and woolen scarf and mittens and so hidden beneath an absurdly large hat that she looked more like a bundle of abandoned laundry than a living child. To the left side of her chest was pinned a square sheet of paper.

"She would not ah remove her gloves or her hat, m'lord, or allow either Mrs. Dexter or myself to remove the label," the butler said. "The name on the label is Miss Veronica Weston, m'lord, care of yourself and this house."

Veronica Weston. Oh, good Lord. Viscount Buckley crossed the hall, his booted feet echoing on the marble tiles, and stopped a few feet in front of the child, who looked up at him with eyes that he supposed were very like his own.

He had never seen her before. He had known of her existence since before her birth and had never tried to deny paternity or to shirk the responsibility of providing for her financially. But he and Nancy had parted company before she discovered the pregnancy and she had moved on to another protector soon after the birth. He himself had never felt any particular human interest in his daughter.

"Veronica?" he asked.

"Yes." She was looking very directly into his eyes. "Are you my papa? I am not to speak to anyone except my papa."

Papa! He had never thought of himself by any such name. He was a father. He had a daughter. He had never been a papa.

"This name is mine." He touched one finger lightly to the label she wore on her chest. "You may speak to me. Your mama sent you here?"

"Mama went away," the child said. "Mrs. Armstrong said I was to come to my papa."

"Mrs. Armstrong?" He raised his eyebrows.

"She looks after me," the child said. "But Mama went away and Mrs. Armstrong said there was no money. I was to come to my papa."

The label was thick. He guessed that there was a letter sealed up within it. Nancy had never neglected the child despite the demands of an acting career. Aubrey had assured him of that. But she had gone away? She had tired of the child?

"Do you have a letter for me, Veronica?" he asked, holding out one hand. He was only just beginning to realize what a coil he was in now. As if things were not bad enough as they were.

The child looked down and laboriously unpinned the label from her coat. She handed it to him. Sure enough, there was a letter. Nancy had been out of town for a weekend party, leaving her daughter with Mrs. Armstrong, a neighbor who frequently cared for the child. Nancy had fallen from an upper gallery in the house she was visiting to the hall below and had died instantly. Mrs. Armstrong, with six children of her own, could not afford to keep the child when there was no chance of payment. She respectfully sent her to her father. She had been to the expense of hiring someone to write the letter for her and of sending the child on the stagecoach. She hoped she would be reimbursed for her pains.

Poor Nancy, he thought. She had been beautiful and a talented actress. And a skilled lover. She had borne his child. And now she was dead. He folded the letter again and looked down at his daughter. She was gazing up at him, quiet and self-contained. And all of four years old.

Lord. Oh, dear Lord. What was he to do?

He turned his head to the two young ladies, who

were still standing there, watching him. His eyes instinctively came to rest on Miss Craggs.

"She is my daughter," he said. "Her mother has d—her mother has gone away and she has been sent here." He looked at her in mute appeal, like a child himself who did not know how to proceed.

"Uncle Warren!" Deborah said, shock in her voice.

Miss Craggs came closer, her eyes on the child. "She will want something to eat and a glass of milk," she said. "She will need to remove her hat and her coat and have them and her bag taken to a room that will be hers."

Of course! How practical and how simple. "Are you hungry, Veronica?" he asked.

"Yes, Papa," the child said.

"Come along, then," he said, clasping his hands awkwardly behind him. Good Lord, his illegitimate child, his by-blow, was in his own home with his niece. His servants would be scandalized. His neighbors would be shocked. "Will you give your hat and your coat to Kemp?"

"Will you let me help you, Veronica?" He watched as Miss Craggs went down on her knees before the child, who stood up and allowed her outer garments to be removed. "What a pretty color your scarf is. There—now you will be more comfortable. But we will need to comb those curls of yours before you sit down for your milk and your food." She touched the backs of two fingers to a tangled curl at the child's cheek and smiled at her.

The viscount felt jolted, first by the sight of his daughter without the heavy outer garments—she was little more than a baby—and then by the smile on the face of his niece's teacher. Good God, he thought, he had not noticed that the woman was beautiful. Though he knew even as he thought it that she was not beautiful, that it was merely something from deep within her that for the moment she had allowed to the surface of her face.

"Would you like to hold my hand?" she asked his daughter.

"Yes, please," the child said, looking up at her and suiting action to words.

"Uncle Warren?" Deborah asked faintly.

"She is my child," he told her. He felt almost as if he were realizing it for the first time. It was one thing to know one had fathered a child and to have accepted financial responsibility for her. It was another thing entirely to see the child, tiny and dainty and quiet, her eyes and her hair the color of his own.

"But—" Deborah said.

"She is my daughter," he said firmly. "Shall we go up for tea and get warm again?" He offered her his arm.

"Is this Papa's very own house?" Veronica was asking Miss Craggs.

Her own awkwardness and awe and even her excitement had been forgotten. Although the great hall was the hall of her dream with the addition of a painted and gilded dome, and although the staircase was wide and magnificent and the drawing room large and splendid, Jane noticed them only with her eyes and not with her heart. And her own bedchamber with a separate dressing room was large and richly furnished and far surpassed anything she might have dreamed for herself. But she merely glanced at it when she hurried in to change her dress for dinner—to change from one drab gray dress to another.

Her time and her attention and her heart were

otherwise engaged than in the perusal of a mere house and in the recognition of a dream come true.

She had never had anything to do with very young children. The girls who came to Miss Phillpotts's school were older and more independent and did not really need her for anything outside her capacity as a teacher.

No one had ever needed her. The thought came without any self-pity. It was simply the truth.

Until today. But today she had seen a small child bewildered and frightened by the loss of her mother and by her arrival at the home of the father she had never seen before. And her heart had lurched with all the love she had never been called upon to give.

She had taken a comb from her own reticule in the drawing room and drawn it gently through the soft baby curls. And she had sat by the child and helped her to food and milk. And then she had taken her to the nursery, where a bed had been made up, and had helped her unpack her little bag, which had been full of surprisingly pretty dresses. She had taken the child down to dinner, although she would probably eat in the nursery on future days, and had helped her wash and change into her nightgown afterward. She had tucked her into bed.

A maid was to stay in the nursery next to the bedchamber and sleep on a truckle bed there.

"Good night, Veronica," Jane said as she was leaving. Her heart ached with the unfamiliar love and happiness. Someone had needed her for almost half a day and would need her again tomorrow.

"Good night, Miss Craggs," the child said, peering at her with wide eyes over the blanket that had been tucked beneath her chin. "When will Mama be coming back?"

Ah, poor child. Poor child. "Mama had to go

away for a long time," she said, walking back to the bed and smoothing her hand over the child's head. "She did not want to leave you, Veronica, but she had to go. She sent you here, where you will be safe."

"Miss Craggs," the child said, "don't leave."

"I'll stay for a while," Jane said, seating herself on the side of the bed. "You are quite safe, dear. My name is Jane. It sounds a little nicer than 'Miss Craggs,' does it not?"

"Miss Jane," the child said and closed her eyes.

There was a rather painful aching around the heart to hear her name spoken aloud by another person. Jane sat quietly on the side of the bed, waiting for the little girl to fall asleep. But after a few moments the child's eyes opened and she lay staring quietly upward.

And then the door opened softly and when Jane turned her head it was to find Viscount Buckley standing there, his hand on the doorknob.

"She is still awake?" he asked after a few moments.

"Yes," Jane said.

He came to stand beside her and gazed down at his daughter. A daughter he had had with a mistress. A child he had never seen until today. And a child he seemed not to know what to do with. What *would* he do with her? Jane felt fear for the defenseless baby who was still staring quietly upward.

"Veronica?" he said. "Is there anything you need?"

"No, thank you," the child said, not moving the direction of her gaze.

"You are tired?" he asked.

"Yes."

"Go to sleep, then." He leaned forward rather

jerkily to lay the backs of his fingers against her cheek for a moment. "You are quite safe now. I will arrange something for you."

The child looked at him finally. "Good night, Papa," she said.

"Are you coming, Miss Craggs?" he asked, looking at Jane

"I will stay until she falls asleep," Jane said.

He inclined his head to her. "Deborah is having an early night," he said. "Will you join me in the library as soon as you may? I need to talk with you."

Veronica was asleep no more than ten minutes later, not having spoken or moved since her father left the room. Jane got carefully to her feet, bent down after a moment's hesitation to kiss the child's forehead, and tiptoed from the room.

How wonderful it must be, she thought, how wonderful beyond imagining, to be a mother.

He sat in the library resisting the urge to refill his brandy glass for the second time. If he drank any more he would be foxed. The thought had its definite appeal, but getting drunk would solve nothing. He had learned that much in his almost thirty years of living.

Deborah was sullen and unhappy—and angry.

"How could you, Uncle Warren?" she had said just before going to bed. "How could you let her stay here and announce for all the world to hear that she is your daughter? Mama will be furious with you. Papa will kill you."

Yes, they would be a trifle annoyed, he conceded. But serve them right for foisting their daughter on him without so much as a by-your-leave.

What was he to do? How did one go about finding a good home for a young child? Aubrey would doubtless know, but Aubrey was in London, about to take a holiday with his family. Perhaps Miss Craggs would have some idea. He hoped so.

He was relieved when she was admitted to the library less than half an hour after he had left her in the nursery. He rose to his feet and motioned her to a chair. She sat straight-backed on the edge of it, he noticed, and clasped her hands in her lap. Her face had the impassive, empty look again now that Veronica was no longer present.

"These things happen, Miss Craggs," he said. He wondered how shocked this prim schoolteacher was beneath the calm exterior.

"Yes, my lord," she said. "I know."

"Can you blame me for taking her into my own home?" he asked. "What was I to do?"

She looked fully into his eyes but did not reply. He shifted uncomfortably. He had never encountered eyes quite like hers.

"Send her back where she came from?" he asked. "I could not do it, ma'am. She is my own flesh and blood."

"Yes, my lord," she said.

"What am I to do, then?" he asked. "How does one find a home for a child? A home in which one can be quite sure she will be well cared for. It is an infernally awkward time of year. Everything will be complicated by the fact that it is Christmas. What am I to do?"

"Perhaps, my lord," she said, "you should celebrate Christmas."

He frowned at her.

"You have a young niece," she said, "who is unhappy at being abandoned by her parents at this of all times. And you have a small child who is bewildered at the disappearance of her mother. Perhaps it is the very best time of year. Let Christmas bring some healing to them both."

He might have known it. For all her drab appearance and seemingly sensible manner and bearing, she was a sentimentalist. Christmas bringing healing, indeed! As if there were something inherently different in that day from all others. Besides, how could Christmas bring any sort of happiness to four such very different people—Deborah, Veronica, Miss Craggs, and himself?

"You believe in miracles, Miss Craggs?" he asked. "Do you have any suggestions as to how this healing can be effected?"

She leaned slightly forward in her chair and there was a suggestion of eagerness in her face. "We could decorate the house," she said. "I have always dreamed of ... There must be greenery outside that we can gather."

"Holly and such?" he asked, still frowning.

"And mistletoe," she said, and interestingly enough she blushed.

"And that will do it?" he asked, a note of sarcasm in his voice. "An instant miracle, Miss Craggs?"

"Deborah needs company," she said. "She is of an age at which it seems that life is passing her by unless she has company of her own age and activities to keep them busy and happy."

He grimaced. "Company of her own age?" he said. "From memory and experience I would say that young people of Deborah's age are usually ignored at Christmastime—and all other times of the year, for that matter. Adults want nothing to do with them, yet they are too old to enjoy being with the children. It is an unfortunate time of life that has to be endured until it passes."

"Perhaps," she said, "there are other young people in the neighborhood who would be only too happy to get together independently of either the adults or the children."

"Are you seriously suggesting that I visit all my neighbors within the next few days seeking out the young and organizing a party here?" he asked, aghast.

"I think that a wonderful suggestion, my lord," she said.

He should have left the woman where she was, he thought. She was definitely dangerous.

"You would doubtless be left to organize and chaperone such an affair," he warned her. "I will be invited to join a sane adult party." And he would accept, too, though he usually sent his excuses.

"I am accustomed to supervising young people, my lord," she reminded him.

"Very well, then," he said. "On your own head be it." He was feeling decidedly annoyed. Except that her suggestion made sense. And it would definitely solve the problem of Deborah. "I will have to postpone making a decision about Veronica until after Christmas. I suppose it will not matter greatly. She is a quiet and well-behaved child."

"She is hiding," Miss Craggs said quietly.

"Hiding?" he frowned.

"She suspects that something dreadful has happened to her mother," she said. "And she knows that you are a stranger although you are her father. She is not at all sure that she is safe, despite your assurances to her and my own. She does not know what is going to happen to her. And so she has found a hiding place. The only one available. She is hiding inside herself."

The notion was thoroughly preposterous. Except that he recalled his impression that morning that

Miss Craggs herself did most of her living far inside herself. What was her own story? he wondered briefly. But there was a topic of more pressing importance on which to focus his mind.

"But she must know," he said, "that I will care for her, that I will find her a good home. I always have cared for her."

"Why must she know any such thing?" Miss Craggs asked. "She is four years old, my lord. A baby. Financial care and the assurances of a good home mean nothing to her. Her world has rested firmly on one person, and that person is now gone."

"Miss Craggs," he asked quietly, though he already knew what her answer was going to be, "you are not suggesting that I keep the child here, are you?"

She looked down at the hands in her lap. "I am suggesting nothing, my lord," she said.

But she was. She obviously knew nothing about life. She knew nothing about the types of relationships that might exist, or not exist, between a man and his illegitimate offspring.

And yet, even as he thought it, he recalled the totally unfamiliar experience of standing in the nursery looking down at his own small child in the bed there, lying still and staring quietly upward, in a most unchildlike way. And he felt now, as he had felt then, an unidentifiable ache about his heart.

She was his child, the product of his own seed. She was his baby.

"Miss Craggs." He heard the irritability in his voice as he got to his feet. "I see clearly that nothing can be done and no decisions can be made until Christmas is over. It is looming ahead of us, a dark and gloomy obstacle, but one that must be lived through. Make of it what you will, then. Load the house with greenery if you must. Do whatever you will. And in the meantime I shall call upon my neighbors and try to organize that unheard-of phenomenon, a preadult party." He felt thoroughly out of sorts.

"Very well, my lord," she said and looked up at him.

He felt almost as if he might fall into her eyes.

"Come," he said, extending an arm to her even though he had brought her here as more of a servant than a guest, "I will escort you to your room, Miss Craggs."

She got to her feet and looked at his arm with some misgiving before linking her own through it. Her arm was trembling quite noticeably though she did not feel cold, and she stood as far from him as their linked arms would allow.

Good Lord, he thought, had she been shut up inside that school for so long?

He stopped outside her dressing room and opened the door for her. "Thank you," he said, "for agreeing to accompany Deborah here. And thank you for showing kindness and gentleness to Veronica. Good night."

"Good night, my lord," she said, her eyes on a level with his neckcloth. And she moved hastily into the dressing room and closed the door behind her even as he prepared to take her hand to raise to his lips.

He was glad then that she had not given him a chance to do it. She was, after all, merely a servant. What was her first name? he wondered. He hoped it was something more fortunate than her surname. Though it was of no concern to him. He would never have reason either to know it or to use it.

Jane helped Veronica get dressed the following morning and brushed her curls into a pretty style while the child sat very still on a stool, her legs dangling over its edge. They were breakfasting together in the nursery when Mrs. Dexter, the viscount's housekeeper, arrived there to ask Miss Craggs what her orders were regarding the Christmas baking and cooking.

"What my orders are?" Jane asked, bewildered. "Should you not be consulting his lordship, Mrs. Dexter?"

"He said I should come to you, miss," the housekeeper said, looking somewhat dubious. "He said that whatever you wanted was to be supplied."

Oh, dear. He really meant what he had said last night, then. She was to do whatever she wanted to celebrate Christmas. The thought was dizzying when at the age of three-and-twenty she never had celebrated the season. She was to have a free hand?

"Where is his lordship?" she asked.

"He has gone visiting with Miss Deborah, miss," the housekeeper said. "He said you were to wait until this afternoon to gather greenery so that he can help you carry it."

"Oh, dear," Jane said. "What is usually cooked for Christmas, Mrs. Dexter?"

The housekeeper raised her eyebrows. "Anything that will not remind his lordship that it is Christmas," she said. "The cook threatens every year to resign, miss, but she stays on. It is unnatural not to have a goose and mince pies at the very least."

Goose and mince pies. The very thought of them was enough to set Jane's mouth to watering. "Perhaps," she said, "I should go down to the kitchen and consult the cook."

"Yes, miss," Mrs. Dexter said. But she paused as she was about to leave the room. "It is time Christmas came back to this house. It has been too long gone. And it needs to be celebrated when there is a child in the house, poor little mite." She nodded in Veronica's direction.

Jane wondered what had happened to banish Christmas from Cosway. She could not imagine anyone's deliberately deciding not to celebrate it. She looked at Veronica and smiled.

"Shall we go down to the kitchen and talk to Cook?" she asked.

The child nodded and got down from her stool to hold out her hand for Jane's. Jane, taking it in hers and feeling its soft smallness, wondered if there could be a greater happiness in life.

The cook was so overjoyed at the prospect of Christmas baking that Jane found she did not need to make any suggestions at all. She merely sat at the kitchen table with a cup of tea and approved every suggestion made. The cook lifted Veronica to the table, placed a large shiny apple in her hand, and clucked over her and talked about the delight of having a child in the house again.

"I do not care what side of the blanket she was born on, if you take my meaning, miss," she said to Jane. "She is a child and children have a right to a home and a right to be loved. Chew carefully, ducky. You do not want to choke on a piece."

Veronica obediently chewed carefully.

"It will do his heart good to have her here," the cook said, jerking her head toward the ceiling. "He does not love easy, miss, and when he do, his heart is easy to break."

Jane could not resist. "Was his heart broken once?" she asked.

The cook clucked her tongue. "By his childhood sweetheart," she said. "You never saw a man so besotted, miss, though she were a flighty piece if you was to ask me. Their betrothal was to be announced on Christmas Day here at a big party. A big secret it was supposed to be, but we all knew it, miss. And then halfway through the evening, just when his lordship were excited enough to burst, a stranger who had come home with her brother a month before stood up and announced *his* betrothal to her. And she smiled at him as sweet as you please without so much as a guilty glance at our boy—or at her papa, who was as weak as water, as far as she was concerned. Six years ago it was, miss. His heart don't heal easy. But this is one to mend any heart."

She nodded at Veronica, who had spotted a cat curled beside the fire and had wriggled off the table to go and kneel beside it and reach out gingerly to pat its fur. The cat purred with contentment.

"A blessed Christmas gift she is for any man," the cook said.

Yes. Jane remembered sitting alone with him in the library last evening. She alone with a man! And talking with him. Being consulted on what he should do with his daughter. And having the temerity to give her opinion and her suggestions. She would have expected to have been quite tongue-tied in a man's presence. But she had made a discovery about this particular man. He was not the infallible figure of authority she had thought all men were. He was an ordinary human being who did not have all of life's answers or even the most obvious of them.

He did not know that all his child needed—all!—was love. The love of her father. And he did not know that good, docile behavior in a child did not necessarily denote a happy child. He had turned to her, Jane, for help. Even a man could need her in some small way for one small moment of time.

It was the thought she had hugged to herself in bed. And also the memory of how it had felt to touch him. To feel his strongly muscled, unmistakably male arm with her own. To smell the unfamiliar odor of male cologne. To feel the body heat of a man only inches away from her own body. And to know that the yearning she had suffered and suppressed in herself for years had a definite cause. It was the yearning for a man, for his approval and his support and companionship. And for something else, too. She did not know quite what that something else was except that outside her dressing room, when he had stopped and thanked her for coming and for giving her attention to Veronica, she had felt suffocated. She had felt that there was no air in the corridor.

She had felt the yearning for—for *him.* She still could not express the need less vaguely than that.

And so she had fled into her room like a frightened rabbit.

"And there." The cook's hand patting her shoulder felt strangely comforting. There had been so few physical touches in her life. "He would be a blessed Christmas gift for some lady too, missy."

But you are not a lady, Craggs. She heard again the words that had been spoken in the homework room just two days before. No, she was no lady. She smiled and got to her feet.

"You are going to be busy if you are to make everything you have suggested," she said. "Oh, I can hardly wait for all the smells and all the tastes. I can hardly wait for Christmas."

The cook chuckled. "It will come, miss, as it always does," she said.

But it had never come before. This would be her first-ever Christmas. She could scarcely wait. At the same time, she wanted to savor every moment as it came. They were to gather greenery during the afternoon, she and Veronica and perhaps Deborah.

And Lord Buckley was to come to help carry the loads.

Veronica was sitting cross-legged on the stone floor, smoothing the cat's fur.

He could not quite believe that this was himself. Himself up a tree, balanced precariously on a branch, feeling hot and disheveled and dusty. His boots, he was sure, though he did not look down at them, must be in a condition to give his valet heart palpitations. Below him Miss Craggs stood with arms partly spread as if to catch him if he fell, Deborah had her hands to her mouth and was alternately squealing and giggling, and Veronica was gazing gravely upward.

"Miss Craggs believes that in addition to all the holly we have gathered and all the pine boughs we have cut down we need some mistletoe," he had said to his daughter a short while before. "What do you think, Veronica? Do we need mistletoe?"

"Yes, please, Papa," she had said.

And Deborah had giggled—she had started giggling during their morning visits and had scarcely stopped since—and had added her voice to everyone else's. It just would not be Christmas, it seemed, unless there was some mistletoe hanging in strategic places so that one might be caught beneath it accidentally on purpose.

So here he was up a tree.

And then down with a sizable armful of mistletoe and a tear on the back of one kid glove and a scrape so deep on the inside of his left boot that it would never be the same again.

And all in the name of Christmas.

"Do you know why I have risked life and limb just to gather this?" he asked Veronica, frowning.

"Because Miss Jane wanted it?" she asked.

Jane. He might have guessed that she would have such a name. And yet it suited her. It was quietly, discreetly pretty.

"Not at all," he said. "This is what it is used for." He held one sprig above the absurd hat, which Nancy had doubtless thought suitably flamboyant for the daughter of an actress, stooped down, and kissed her soft, cold little cheek. And took himself quite by surprise. Now why had he done that?

"Any gentleman has the right to kiss any lady he catches beneath the mistletoe," he said, "without fear of having his face slapped. It is a Christmas custom. You see?" And he straightened up and repeated the action with Deborah, who giggled. "Now we have to carry all this greenery back to the house."

"What about Miss Jane?" a grave little voice asked him.

And he knew he was caught. Caught in the act of maneuvering. For when he had demonstrated the use of mistletoe on his daughter and his niece, he had really wanted to use Miss Craggs as his model. Even though she was prim and gray and every inch the schoolteacher. Though that was not the whole truth this afternoon. Since they had left the house there had been a light in her eyes that had touched him. She was enjoying all this just like a child.

"Oh, it works with Miss Craggs, too," he said, turning to her and raising his sprig of mistletoe again. And he felt suddenly and stupidly breathless. She was standing very still and wide-eyed.

He kissed her lightly and briefly as he had kissed the other two. Except that foolishly he kissed her on the lips. And ended up feeling even hotter than his excursion up the tree had made him.

She turned hurriedly away before their eyes

could meet and began energetically arranging the
heap of holly they had gathered into three bundles.

"Here, Veronica," he said, "you may carry the
mistletoe, since it will not prick you all to pieces.
Deborah, take that bundle of holly. I'll take this
one."

His hand brushed Miss Craggs's as he gathered
up the largest bundle and belatedly their eyes met.
Her own were still large and bright. Brighter. Was
it the cold that had brought the tears there? Or was
it the kiss? Surely she had been kissed before.
Surely that had not been her first kiss.

Had it? Once again he wondered about her past,
about her life. Impoverished parents and the need
to go out and make her own living? But she had
not been planning to go home for Christmas.

"I will send someone back with a wagon for the
pine boughs," he said.

"Deck the halls with boughs of holly," Deborah
sang suddenly with loud enthusiasm and no musical
talent whatsoever.

"Fa la la la la la la la la," Miss Craggs sang with
her in a rather lovely contralto voice.

"'Tis the season to be jolly." He joined his tenor
voice to their singing and looked down at Veronica.

"Fa la la la la la la la la." She piped up with
them, off key.

"Don we now our gay apparel." Three of them
sang out lustily while the fourth continued with the
fa-la-las.

And the damned thing was, Viscount Buckley
thought, that it could grab at one quite unawares.
Christmas, that was.

Jane had never been very assertive, even as a
teacher. She had never been the type who liked to
boss and organize people. And yet over the next

couple of days she seemed to be transformed into a wholly different person.

It was she who directed the decorating of the house—of drawing room, staircase, and hall. The viscount had suggested that the servants could do it, but she had exclaimed in horror and disappointment before she could stop herself, and he had meekly agreed that perhaps they could do it themselves, the four of them.

"But I have no eye for design, Miss Craggs," he had told her. "You will have to tell us what you want."

And she had told them. She stood in the middle of the drawing room giving orders like a sergeant with a company of soldiers. Boughs and sprigs and wreaths were hung exactly where and exactly how she directed, and if she did not like the look of them when the deed was done, then she directed their replacement. And everyone obeyed, even the viscount, who was given all the climbing to do. He balanced on chairs and tables and ladders in his shirtsleeves, decking out pictures and mirrors and doorframes while she stood critically below him, head to one side, examining the effects of his handiwork and criticizing any slight error on his part.

She felt so happy by the time they were finished that she thought she might well burst with it. She was surrounded by Christmas—by the sights and smells of it. She could smell the pine boughs, and there were interesting smells wafting up from the kitchens. Particularly the smell of Christmas puddings.

"Oh, it is so very beautiful," she said, her hands clasped to her bosom when they were all finished and were all standing admiring their efforts. "If only we had some ribbons for bows."

"Oh, yes," Deborah said. "Red ones and green ones."

Viscount Buckley sighed. "Ribbons and bows," he said. "And bells, too, I suppose? Doubtless you will find what you need in the village, Miss Craggs. Go there if you must and purchase whatever you need and have the bill sent to me."

"Oh." She turned to him with glowing eyes. "May I? Oh, thank you, my lord."

He looked at her and made her a little mocking bow. And she remembered the earth-shattering feeling of his lips touching hers and wondered if he realized what an enormous treasure this Christmas was going to be to her in memory. The most precious treasure of her life.

Veronica was tugging at her skirt. "May I come too, Miss Jane?" she asked.

"Of course, sweetheart," she said, hearing in some surprise the unexpected endearment she had used. "I will need you to help me choose."

"And I will come too, Craggs," Deborah said. But she flushed suddenly and added, "*Miss* Craggs." And then she extended both arms and twirled into the steps of a waltz. "Uncle Warren," she said, "do you think we may dance on Christmas Day?"

Deborah had completely changed since the visits she had paid with her uncle during the morning. She had come rushing into the house on their return home to announce to Jane that she was to have a party of her very own on Christmas Day. Fifteen young people were to come during the afternoon for walks and games and were to stay for the evening while their parents—and her uncle—engaged in an adult party at the home of the Oxendens. Even the seventeen-year-old and very dashing George Oxenden had decided to come to Cosway though his parents had agreed to allow him to attend the adult party if he wished.

Jane saw the viscount grimace. "A dance?" he said. "And who is to provide the music, pray?"

But Deborah made it instantly clear that the idea had not come to her on the spur of the moment. "Mr. George Oxenden told me that his aunt plays the pianoforte rather well," she said, "and that she would be only too pleased to be with the young people rather than with the adults on Christmas Day."

Her uncle looked skeptical. "I will have to see what can be arranged," he said.

"Oh, thank you, Uncle Warren," she said, darting back across the room to hug him. "This is going to be the best Christmas ever, after all. I just know it."

The viscount raised his eyebrows and looked at Jane.

Jane could only agree with his niece.

But there was work to be done. The village shop had to be visited and yards of the widest, brightest ribbon to be chosen and measured. Jane felt guilty when she was told the total cost but she did not change her purchases. Viscount Buckley was a wealthy man, was he not? When Veronica gazed admiringly and rather longingly at some porcelain bells, she even added three to her purchases, a dreadful extravagance. But they would look lovely hanging from the holly on the mantel in the drawing room.

And then she discovered during a visit to the kitchen that the servants were murmuring over the fact that there was to be no Yule log. The head gardener was only too delighted to go in search of the largest one he could find when Jane insisted that they must have one. A Yule log! She had not even thought of it. She knew so little about Christmas.

During the same visit she learned that one of the grooms was skilled with his hands and loved to whittle on wood whenever he had a few spare moments. When Jane admired a spoon he was carving for his girl in the village, he offered to carve a small crib for the drawing room. And that other detail of her dream returned to Jane. Time was short, but the groom agreed to try to carve a baby Jesus to go inside the crib and a Mary and Joseph to kneel beside it and perhaps even a shepherd or two and an animal or two to worship and adore.

The decorations would be complete, Jane decided, standing alone in the drawing room after the ribbons and bells had been added to all the greenery, if only there could be a Nativity Scene in the window.

Oh, Christmas would be complete. She twirled around and around rather as Deborah had done and thought of the little bonnet and muff for Veronica and the small bottle of perfume for Deborah she had had set aside in the village shop as Christmas gifts. They would take all the meager hoard of money in her purse, but she could not resist. She had never bought Christmas presents before. She had nothing for Viscount Buckley, but it would be inappropriate anyway to give a gentleman a gift.

For Deborah's sake she was going to make this a wonderful Christmas. And for Veronica's sake. Veronica was quietly obedient, but Jane knew that the child was still hiding inside herself. And she knew from long experience how that felt. She was going to do her very best to see that Christmas brought the child out of herself again, even if it was only to a realization of her grief and her insecurity. At least then she could be properly comforted.

If there could be any meaningful comfort. Jane stopped twirling. Her heart chilled to the memory of the viscount's asking how he was to find his daughter a good home. He intended to send the child away again to be cared for by strangers. They would be strangers, no matter how kindly they might be.

Oh, for the viscount's sake, too, this must be a wonderful Christmas. He must be made to see that love was everything, that family was everything. Why could people who had always had family not see that? Why could he not see that his daughter was his most priceless possession?

And for her own sake she was going to see that this Christmas was celebrated to the limit. It was her first and might well be her last. It was going to be a Christmas to remember for a lifetime.

Yes, it was. Oh, yes, indeed it was.

She twirled again.

Christmas Eve dawned gray and gloomy and Viscount Buckley, surrounded by all the foolish sights of Christmas, his nostrils assailed by all the smells of it, felt his irritation return. Because she—Miss Jane Craggs, the tyrant—had persuaded him into the madness of allowing a party for young people to take place in his home tomorrow, he had been faced with the necessity of absenting himself from that home. And so he was facing the unspeakable monotony of a Christmas gathering at the Oxendens'. He was being forced to enjoy himself.

Well, it could not be done. Just look at the weather. He did just that, standing at the window of his bedchamber, gazing out at raw, cheerless December.

But one hour later he felt foolish. How was it he had recognized none of the signs when they had

been as plain as the nose on his face? For of course
the grayness and the gloom were harbingers of
snow, and before the morning was even half over,
it was falling so thickly that he could scarcely see
six feet beyond the window. And it was settling too,
just like a white blanket being spread.

Good Lord, snow! He could not remember when
it had last fallen at Christmastime. Certainly not
the year Elise had humiliated him and broken his
foolish young heart. It had been raining that year
and blowing a gale. Typical British winter weather.
This was not typical at all. He wondered if Veronica
had seen the snow and was halfway up the stairs
to the nursery before he realized how strange it was
that he had thought of sharing the sight of snow
with a child. But he continued on his way.

They were all in there, Veronica and Deborah
kneeling on the windowseat, their noses pressed
against the glass, Miss Craggs standing behind
them.

"Look, my lord." She was the only one who had
glanced back to see who was coming through the
door. "Snow. We are going to have a white Christmas. Can you conceive of anything more
wonderful?"

Some time before she returned to Miss Phillpotts's school he was going to have to sit down and
have a good talk with Miss Jane Craggs. There was
something deep inside the woman that could occasionally break through to her face and make her
almost incredibly beautiful. She was beautiful now,
flushed and wide eyed and animated. And all over
the fact that it was snowing for Christmas.

He found himself wondering quite inappropriately what her face would look like as he was making love to her. Totally inappropriately! He had a
mistress waiting for him in London with whose ser-

vices he was more than satisfied. He had had her
for only two months. He had not even begun to
tire of her yet.

"I am trying," he said in belated answer to her
question. "And at the moment I can think of
nothing."

She smiled at him and his heart and his stomach
danced a *pas de deux*.

Good Lord, he wanted her, the gray and prim
Miss Craggs.

"Look, Papa," his daughter was saying. "Look at
the trees. They are magic."

He strolled over to the window and stood almost
shoulder to shoulder with Jane Craggs, looking out
on a Christmas wonderland.

"And so they are," he said, setting his hand on
the child's soft curls. "I have just had a thought.
There used to be sleds when I was a boy. I wonder
what happened to them."

"Sleds?" Deborah turned her attention to him.
"Oh, Uncle Warren, we could go sledding tomorrow. A sledding party. Do you think so? How many
are there?"

"Wait a minute," he said, holding up one hand.
"I am not even sure they still exist. I suppose you
are going to insist that I get on my greatcoat and
my topboots and wade out to the stables without
further delay."

Yes. Three pairs of eyes confirmed him in his
suspicions. And then three voices informed him
that they were coming with him and Jane Craggs
was bundling Veronica inside her coat and winding
her inside her scarf and burying her beneath her
hat while Deborah darted out to don her own outdoor clothes.

"I knew," Miss Craggs said, looking up at him

with a face that was still beautiful, "that this was going to be a perfect Christmas. I just knew it."

How could it be perfect for her, he wondered, when she had been brought here merely as a glorified servant to chaperone a sullen girl and then had been saddled with the responsibility of caring for an illegitimate child, whose presence in the house might well have offended her sensibilities? How could it be perfect when she was away from her own family?

But there was that light in her eyes and that beauty in her face, and he knew that she was not lying.

And he knew suddenly that for the first time in many years there was hope in him. The hope that somehow she might be right, that somehow this might be the perfect Christmas.

That somehow the magic might come back.

There were four sleds, three of them somewhat dilapidated. But he was assured that by the morrow they would be in perfect condition.

"Well, Veronica," he said as they were wading back to the house with the snow still falling thickly about them and onto them, "are you going to ride on a sled tomorrow too? Faster than lightning down a hill?"

"No, Papa," she said.

"With me?" he asked her. "If I ride with you and hold you tight?"

"Yes, Papa," she said gravely.

He could not ask for a more docile and obedient child. Nancy had brought her up well. And yet he could not help remembering what Jane Craggs had said about her—that she was hiding inside herself. And wondering how she could know such a thing, if it were so. But he was beginning to believe that perhaps it was true. Over the past few days the child had joined in all the activities and she had made a great friend of the kitchen cat, whom he had found curled impertinently in his favorite chair in the drawing room, of all places, just the day before. But there had been no exuberance in her as there had been in Deborah and even in Miss Craggs.

He was beginning to worry about Veronica. The sooner he found her a good home to go to the better it would be for her. She needed a mother and father to care for her. As soon as Christmas was over he must set Aubrey to work on it. It must take priority over all else.

"Look at me," Deborah shrieked suddenly, and she hurled herself backward into a smooth drift of snow, swished her arms and legs to the sides, and got up carefully. "Look. A perfect angel."

"Which you assuredly are not," he said, looking at the snow caked all over her back.

She giggled at him. "I dare you to try it, Uncle Warren," she said.

"It certainly does not behoove my dignity to be making snow angels," he said.

But he did it anyway because it had never been his way to resist a dare. And then they were all doing it until they had a whole army of angels fast disappearing beneath the still-falling snow. Like a parcel of children, he thought in some disgust, instead of two adults, one young person, and one child.

"This must be the multitude of the heavenly host that sang with the angel Gabriel to Mary," he said. "I do not know about the rest of you, but I have snow trickling down my neck and turning to water. It does not feel comfortable at all. I think hot drinks at the house are called for."

"Veronica has made the best angels," Deborah said generously. "Look how dainty they are."

It was the first time she had mentioned his daughter by name, the viscount thought.

"That is because she is a real little angel," he said, stooping down impulsively and sweeping the child up into his arms. "Are you cold, Veronica?"

"A little, Papa," she admitted.

She weighed almost nothing at all. He tightened his hold on her and realized something suddenly. He was going to miss her when she went away. He was always going to be wondering if she were happy, if she were being loved properly, if she were hiding inside herself.

"Snuggle close," he said. "I shall have you inside where it is warm before you know it."

Miss Craggs, he noticed, was watching him with shining eyes—and shining red nose. She looked more beautiful than ever. Which was a strange thought to have when, really, she was not beautiful at all.

At first she was going to go to church alone. It was something she had always done on Christmas Eve and something she wanted to do more than ever here. She had seen the picturesque stone church on her journeys to the village. And the thought of trudging through snow in order to reach it was somehow appealing. It would bring another part of her dream to life.

She asked Veronica at dinner—the child still ate in the dining room with the adults—if she would mind not being sat with tonight until she slept. Jane explained her reason.

"I promise to look in on you as soon as I return," she said.

But Veronica looked at her rather wistfully. "May I come too, Miss Jane?" she asked.

It would be very late for a child to be up, but Viscount Buckley immediately gave his permission and announced his intention of attending church, too. And then Deborah wondered aloud if Mr. George Oxenden would be at church, blushed, and declared that anyway she always enjoyed a Christmas service.

And so they walked together the mile to the church, the snow being rather too deep for the carriage wheels, Veronica between Jane and the viscount, holding to a hand of each, while Deborah half tripped along beside them. And they sat together in church, Veronica once again between the two adults until after a series of yawns she climbed onto Jane's lap and snuggled close. Jane was unable to stand for the final hymn, but she sat holding the child, thinking about the birth of the Christ Child, and understanding for the first time the ecstasy Mary must have felt to have her baby even though she had had to give birth far from home and inside a stable.

Christmas, Jane thought, was the most wonderful, wonderful time of the year.

They walked home after the viscount had greeted his neighbors and Deborah had chatted with her new friends, the Oxenden sisters, and had been rewarded with a nod and a smile and a Christmas greeting from their elder brother. Jane sat holding the sleeping child on her lap while she waited for them.

And then Viscount Buckley was bending over her in the pew and opening his greatcoat and lifting his daughter into his own arms and wrapping the coat about her. Jane smiled at him. Oh, he felt it too. What a tender paternal gesture! He loved the

child and would keep her with him. Of course he
would. It was something she, Jane, would be able
to console herself with when she was back at Miss
Phillpotts's. Though she would not think of that.
Not yet. She was going to have her one wonderful
Christmas first.

And wonderful it was, too, she thought as they
approached the house in a night that was curiously
bright despite the fact that there were clouds overhead—more snow clouds. It was her dream come
true, even though not every window in the house
blazed with light. But close enough to her dream
to make her believe for once in her life in miracles.

Deborah was yawning and ready for bed by the
time they reached the house. She went straight to
her room. Veronica stirred and grumbled in her
father's arms as he carried her upstairs. Jane followed him and undressed the child in her bedchamber while he waited in the nursery. He came to
stand in the doorway as he always did after Jane
had tucked her up in bed. She was only half-awake.

"Good night, Mama," she said.

Jane could hardly speak past the ache in her
throat. "Good night, sweetheart," she said softly.

"Good night, Papa."

"Good night, Veronica," he said.

Jane sat for a few minutes on the side of the bed,
though it was obvious that the child had slipped back
into sleep. She was too embarrassed to face the viscount. But when she rose and turned to leave the
room, she found that he was still standing in the
doorway.

"I ordered hot cider sent to the library," he said.
"Come with me there?"

She longed to be able to escape to her room. Or
a part of her did, anyway—that part that was flustered and even frightened at the thought of being

alone with him. But the other part of herself, the part that was living and enjoying this Christmas to the full, leapt with gladness. She was going to sit and talk with him again? She only hoped that she would be able to think of something to say, that her mind would not turn blank.

When they reached the library, he motioned her to the chair she had occupied once before. He ladled hot cider into two glasses and handed her one before seating himself at the other side of the fire.

She had never drunk cider before. It was hot and tasted of cinnamon and other unidentified spices. It was delicious. She looked into the glass and concentrated her attention on it. She could not think of anything to say. She wished she had made some excuse after all and gone to bed.

"You were going to spend Christmas alone at the school?" he asked her.

"Yes." She looked up at him unwillingly.

"Where does your family live?" he asked. "Was it too far for you to travel?"

She had never talked about herself. There was nothing to talk about. She could be of no possible interest to anyone except herself.

"I have no family," she said. She was not particularly given to self-pity, either. But the words sounded horribly forlorn. She looked down into her drink again.

"Ah," he said, "I am sorry. Have they been long deceased?"

"I believe," she said after rejecting her first impulse, which was to invent a mythical warm and loving family, "I was the product of a union much like yours and Veronica's mother's. I do not know who my mother was. I believe she must have died when I was very young. Or perhaps she merely did not want to be burdened with me. I do not know my father, either. He put me into an orphanage until I was old enough to go to Miss Phillpotts's school. He supported me there until I was seventeen. I have earned my way there since."

He said nothing for a long time. She kept her eyes on her drink, but she did not lift it to her mouth. She knew her hand would shake if she tried it.

"You have never known a family," he said very quietly at last.

"No." But she did not want him to think that she was trying to enlist his pity. "The orphanage was a good one. The school is an expensive one. He cared enough to make sure that my material needs were catered to and that I had a good enough education to make my way in the world."

"But you stayed at the school," he said. "Why?"

How could she explain that, cold and cheerless as it was, the school was the only home she had known, that it was the only anchor in her existence? How could she explain how the thought of being cast adrift in unfamiliar surroundings, without even the illusion of home and family, terrified her?

"I suppose," she said, "I drifted into staying there."

"In an environment that is wholly female," he said. "Have you never wanted to find yourself a husband and have a family of your own, Miss Craggs?"

Oh, it was a cruel question. How could she find a husband for herself? Even if she left Miss Phillpotts's, what could she hope to do except teach somewhere else or perhaps be someone's governess? There was no hope of matrimony for someone like her. And a family of her own? How could she even dream of a family when there was no possibility of a husband?

To her annoyance, she could think of no answer to make. And in her attempt to cover up her confusion, she lifted her glass to her lips, forgetting that her hand would shake. It did so and she had to lower the glass, the cider untasted. She wondered if he had noticed.

"How did you know," he asked, seeming to change the subject, "that Veronica hides inside herself? I begin to think you must be right, but how did you realize it?"

"She is too quiet, too docile, too obedient for a child," she said.

"Did you know it from experience?" he asked.

"I—" She swallowed. "Is this an interrogation, my lord? I am not accustomed to talking about myself."

"Why not?" he asked. "Does no one ever ask you about yourself? Does Miss Phillpotts believe she does you a favor by keeping you on at the school? And do the teachers and pupils take their cue from her? Do they all call you Craggs, as Deborah did until recently? Does no one call you Jane?"

For some reason she felt as if she had been stabbed to the heart. There was intense pain.

"Teachers are not usually called by their first names," she said.

"But teachers should have identities apart from their career," he said. "Should they not, Jane? For how long have you been in hiding?"

"Please." She set her hardly tasted cider on the small table beside her and got to her feet. "It is late, my lord. It is time for me to say good night."

"Have I been very impertinent, Jane?" He too stood and somehow he possessed himself of both her hands. "No, you do not need to answer. I have been impertinent and it has been unpardonable of me when you are a guest in my home and when you have been very kind to both Deborah and my daughter and when you have brought Christmas to this house for the first time in years. Forgive me?"

"Of course," she said, trying to draw her hands free of his without jerking on them. She felt again as if she were suffocating. His closeness and his maleness were overpowering her. "It is nothing, my lord."

"It is something," he said. "It is just that you have intrigued me during the past few days, Jane. You are like two people. Much of the time you are a disciplined, prim and—forgive me—plain teacher. But sometimes you are eager and warm and quite incredibly beautiful. I have been given the impression that the latter person has come bubbling up from very deep within. Is she the real person, the one you hide from the world, the one you have never had a chance to share with anyone else?"

"Please." She dragged at her hands but was unable to free them. Her voice, she noticed in some dismay, sounded thin and distressed. She sounded on the verge of tears.

"He was a fool, your father," he said. "He had you to love and let opportunity pass him by."

She forgot herself instantly. She looked up into his face, her eyes wide. "And are you going to make the same mistake?" she asked. "You too have a daughter to love."

"But the situation is different," he said. "I am not going to abandon her to an orphanage or a school. I am going to find her the very best parents I can."

"But she is four years old," Jane said. "Do you not think she will remember, however hazily? She will remember that her mother disappeared mysteriously and she will try to persuade herself that she died and did not merely abandon her. You need to tell her the truth. However cruel it seems now, she needs to know. And she will remember that her father was titled and wealthy and that he cared enough to provide for her physical needs but did not care enough to provide for the only need that mattered."

"And that is?" He was frowning and she thought that perhaps he was angry. But so was she. She would answer his question.

"The need for love," she said. "The need to know that to someone she means more than anything else in the world."

"But she is illegitimate." He was almost whispering. "She is the daughter I fathered on a mistress. Do you understand, Jane? Do you know anything about what is acceptable and what is not in polite society?"

"Yes," she said. "Oh, yes, I know, my lord. I am such a daughter too, remember. No one in my memory has ever wanted to know me as a person. No one has ever hugged me. Or kissed me. No one has ever loved me. I am three-and-twenty now, old enough to bear the burdens of life alone, but I would not want another child to have to live the life I have lived. Not Veronica. I hope she will remember that you have kissed her cheek and rubbed your hand in her hair and carried her home from church inside your greatcoat. I am not sure it will help a great deal, but I hope she remembers even so. I wish I had such memories."

"Jane," he said, his voice shaken. "Oh, my poor Jane."

And before she knew what was to happen or could do anything to prevent it, his hands had released hers and grasped her by the shoulders instead, and he had pulled her against him. And before her mind could cope with the shock of feel-

ing a man's warm and firmly muscled body against
her own, his mouth was on hers, warm and firm,
his lips slightly parted.

For a moment—for a fleeting moment after her
mind had recovered from its first shock—she surrendered to the heady physical sensation of being
embraced by a man and to the realization that she
was experiencing her first real kiss. And then she
got her palms against his chest and pushed firmly
away from him.

"No," she said. "No, my lord, it is not poor Jane.
It is poor Veronica. She has a father who could love
her, I believe, but who feels that the conventions of
society are of greater importance than love."

She did not give him a chance to reply though
he reached for her again. She whisked herself about
and out of the room and fled upstairs to her bedchamber as if being pursued by a thousand devils.

It had snowed a little more during the night. The
viscount stood at his window, eager to go downstairs to begin the day, yet wanting at the same
time to stay where he was until he could safely
escape to the Oxendens' house. He wanted to go
downstairs because he had told her the truth last
night. She had brought Christmas to his home for
the first time in many years and he found himself
hungry for it. And yet he dreaded seeing her this
morning after his unpardonable indiscretion of the
night before. And he dreaded seeing Veronica. He
dreaded being confronted with love. He had decided six years ago to the day that he must be inca-
pable of loving enough to satisfy another person.
He had confined his feelings since then to friend-
ships and to lust.

She was wrong. It was not that he put the conventions of society before love as much as that he

did not believe he could love his daughter as well as a carefully chosen couple would. He wanted Veronica to have a happy childhood. Because he loved her. He tested the thought in his mind, but he could not find fault with it. He did love her. The thought of giving her up to another couple was not a pleasant one. And that was an understatement.

He was the first one downstairs. Before going to the breakfast room he went into the drawing room to take the parcels he had bought in a visit to a nearby town two days before and a few he had brought home with him and to set them down beside the rudely carved but curiously lovely Nativity Scene with its Mary and Joseph and babe in a manger and a single shepherd and lamb. They had been set up last night. He was seeing them for the first time.

He looked about the room. And he thought of his irritation at finding himself saddled with his niece for Christmas and of her sullenness at being abandoned by her parents and left to his care. And of the terrible aloneness of Veronica as she had sat in his hall, like a labeled parcel abandoned until someone could find time to open it.

Yes, Jane had transformed his home and the three of them who lived in it with her. Under the most unpromising of circumstances she had brought the warmth and joy of Christmas. He wondered if it was something she was accustomed to doing. But he knew even as he thought it that that was not it at all. If she had been about to spend Christmas alone at the school this year, then surely she must have spent it alone there last year and the year before. His heart chilled. Had she ever spent Christmas in company with others? Had she always been alone?

Was all the love of her heart, all the love of her

life being poured out on this one Christmas she was spending with strangers? With three other waifs like herself? But she was so much stronger than they. Without her, he felt, the rest of them would have wallowed in gloom.

But his thoughts were interrupted. Deborah burst into the room, parcels in her hands. She set them beside his and turned to smile at him.

"Happy Christmas, Uncle Warren," she said. "Veronica is up. Craggs—*Miss* Craggs—is dressing her and brushing her hair. They will be down soon. I wish they would hurry. I have presents for everyone. I bought them in the village shop. And you have presents too. Is there one for me?"

"Yes." He grinned at her. "Happy Christmas, Deborah."

And then they came into the room, hand in hand, Jane and Veronica, and his heart constricted at sight of them. His two ladies. Jane was carrying two parcels. Veronica was saucer-eyed.

And finally it was there again, full grown—the glorious wonder of Christmas in a young child's eyes, which were fixed on the Nativity Scene and on the parcels beside it. He hurried across the room to her and stooped down without thought to lift her into his arms.

"Happy Christmas, Veronica," he said and kissed her on her soft little lips. "Someone brought the baby Jesus with his mama and papa during the night. And someone brought gifts, too. I will wager some of them are yours."

Jane, he saw, had hurried across the room to set down her parcels with the rest.

"For me?" Veronica asked, her eyes growing wider still.

He sat her on his knee close to the gifts, feeling absurdly excited himself, almost as if he were a boy again. And he watched her as she unwrapped the dainty lace-edged handkerchief Deborah had bought for her and held it against her cheek, and the pretty red bonnet and muff Jane had bought her, both of which she had to try on. And then he watched her, his heart beating almost with nervousness, as she unwrapped his exquisitely dressed porcelain doll.

"Oh!" she said after staring at it in silence for a few moments. "Look what I have, Papa. Look what I have, Miss Jane. Look, Deborah."

Viscount Buckley blinked several times, aware of the acute embarrassment of the fact that he had tears in his eyes. And yet when he sneaked a look at Jane, it was to find that her own eyes were brimming with tears.

"She is beautiful, Veronica," she said.

"Lovely," Deborah agreed with enthusiasm.

"Almost as beautiful as you," her father assured her. "What are you going to call her?"

"Jane," his daughter said without hesitation.

And then Deborah opened her gifts and exclaimed with delight over the perfume Jane had given her and with awe over the diamond-studded watch her parents had left for her and with warm appreciation over the evening gloves and fan her uncle had bought for her—because she was as close to being adult as made no difference, he explained. She declared that she would wear them to the dance that evening.

Viscount Buckley unwrapped a linen handkerchief from Deborah and a silver-backed brush and comb from his sister and brother-in-law.

And he watched as Jane unwrapped her own lace-edged handkerchief from Deborah and smiled rather teary-eyed at the girl. And then he watched more keenly as she took out his cashmere shawl from its wrappings and held it up in front of her, its folds falling free. She bit her lip and shut her eyes very tightly for a few moments.

"It is the most beautiful thing I have ever seen," she said before turning to him, her face looking almost agonized. "Thank you. But I have nothing for you. I did not think it would be seemly."

Veronica had wriggled off his lap and was gazing down with Deborah into the manger at the baby Jesus, her doll clutched in both arms. Deborah was explaining to her what swaddling clothes were.

"You have given me a gift beyond price, Jane," he said quietly, for her ears only. "You have opened my eyes to Christmas again and all its meanings. I thank you."

She gazed back at him, the shawl suspended in front of her from her raised arms.

But Deborah had decided it was time for breakfast and was assuring Veronica that she could bring her doll along and they would find it a chair to sit on and a bowl to eat from. His niece seemed to have quite got over her shock at being exposed to the company of his illegitimate daughter.

"Come," he said to Jane, getting to his feet and extending a hand to her, "let us eat and then we must have the servants up here for their gifts. They will doubtless be happy to see that I can do it without a frown this year."

He smiled at her and she smiled rather tremulously back.

Once, when she was seventeen, Miss Phillpotts had given her a porcelain thimble in recognition of her new status as a teacher. It was the only gift she had ever received—until today. Jane set down her handkerchief and her shawl carefully on her bed, as if they too were of porcelain and might break, smoothed a hand over each, and swallowed back her tears so that she would not have to display reddened eyes when she left her room.

But the best gift of all was what he had said to her. *You have given me a gift beyond price, Jane.* And he had smiled at her. And he had held Veronica on his knee and had looked at her with what was surely tenderness.

Going back to Miss Phillpotts's, being alone again, was going to be more painful than ever, she knew, now that she had had a taste of family life, now that she had fallen in—no, that was a silly idea. That she would have fallen in love with him was thoroughly predictable under the circumstances. It was not real love, of course. But however it was, she would put up with all the pain and all the dreariness, she felt, if only she could know that he would keep Veronica with him. She would give up all claim to future Christmases without a murmur if only she could be sure of that.

It was a busy day, a wonderfully busy day. There were the servants to greet in the drawing room while Viscount Buckley gave each of them a gift, and toasts to be drunk with them and rich dainties to eat. And there were gifts from almost all of them for Veronica to open. It was certainly clear that his staff had taken the viscount's young daughter to their hearts. And there were carols to sing.

After the Christmas dinner, taken *en famille* in the dining room very early in the afternoon, there were the young guests to prepare for. There was no containing Deborah's excitement. As soon as they had arrived, all of them bright and merry at the novel prospect of a party all to themselves without adults to spoil it and tell them to quieten down or to stay out of the way, they were whisked out of doors.

They engaged in an unruly snowball fight even before they reached the hill where the sledding was to take place. Deborah, Jane noticed with indulgent interest, was almost elbow to elbow with Mr. George Oxenden, the two of them fighting the common enemy, almost everyone else. But before she knew it, Jane was fighting for her own life, or at least for her own comfort. A soft snowball splattered against her shoulder and she found that Viscount Buckley was grinning smugly at her from a few yards away. She shattered the grin when by some miracle her own snowball collided with the center of his face.

Jane found herself giggling quite as helplessly as Deborah was doing.

The sleds were much in demand when they reached the hill as the young people raced up the slope with reckless energy and then zoomed down two by two. Nobody complained about the cold even though there was a great deal of foot stamping and hand slapping against sides. And even though everyone sported fiery red cheeks and noses.

Veronica stood quietly watching, holding Jane's hand.

"Well, Veronica," her father said, coming to stand beside them, "what do you think? Shall we try it?"

"We will fall," she said, looking gravely up at him.

"What?" he said. "You do not trust my steering skills? If we fall, we will be covered with snow. Is that so bad?"

"No, Papa," she said, looking dubious.

"Well." He held out a hand for hers. "Shall we try?"

"Can Miss Jane come too?" Veronica asked.

Jane grimaced and found the viscount's eyes directed at her. They were twinkling. "It might be something of a squash," he said. "But I am willing if you two ladies are."

"I—I—" Jane said.

"What?" His eyebrows shot up. "Do we have a coward here? Shall we dare Miss Jane to ride on a sled with us, Veronica?"

"Yes, Papa," his daughter said.

And so less than five minutes later Jane found herself at the top of the hill, seating herself gingerly on one of the sleds, which suddenly looked alarmingly narrow and frail, and having to move back to make room for Veronica until her back was snug against the viscount's front. His arms came about her at either side to arrange the steering rope. And suddenly too it no longer seemed like a cold winter day. She was only half aware of the giggles of the young ladies and the whistles and jeers and cheers of the young gentlemen. She set her arms tightly about Veronica.

And then they were off, hurtling down a slope that seemed ten times steeper than it had looked from the bottom, at a speed that seemed more than ten times faster than that of the other sledders when she had watched them. Two people were shrieking, Veronica and—herself. And then they were at the bottom and the sled performed a complete turn, flirted with the idea of tipping over and dumping its load into the snow, and slid safely to a halt.

Veronica's shrieks had turned to laughter—helpless, joyful, childish laughter. The viscount, the first to rise to his feet, scooped her up and held her close and met Jane's eyes over her shoulder. Perhaps it was the wind and the cold that had made his eyes so bright, but Jane did not think so.

Oh, how good it was—it was the best moment so

far of a wonderful Christmas—how very good it
was to hear the child laugh. And beg to be taken
up again. And wriggle to get down and grab at her
father's hand and tug him impatiently in the direction of the slope. And to watch her ride down again
with him, shrieking and laughing once more.

And how good it was—how achingly good—to
see him laughing and happy with the little child he
had fathered almost five years before but had not
even seen until a few days ago.

Chilly as she was—her hands and her feet were
aching with the cold—Jane willed the afternoon to
last forever. He was to go to the Oxendens' for
dinner and he was to spend the evening there and
perhaps half the night too. Once he had gone she
would be the lone chaperone of the group, apart
from the lady who was coming to play the pianoforte. She was going to feel lonely.

But she quelled the thought. She had had so
much, more than she had ever dreamed. She must
not be greedy. This evening was for the young
people.

And then, just before it was mutually agreed that
it was time to return to the house to thaw out and
partake of some of Cook's hot Christmas drinks
and mince pies, Veronica was borne off by Deborah
to ride a sled with her and Mr. Oxenden, and Viscount Buckley took Jane firmly by one hand and
led her toward the slope.

"If you stand there any longer," he said, "you
may well become frozen to the spot. Come and sled
with me now that I have relearned the knack of
doing it safely."

She savored the moment, this final moment of
her very own Christmas. But alas, this time they
were not so fortunate. Perhaps the constant passing
of the sleds had made the surface over which they

sped just too slippery for successful navigation. Or perhaps there was some other cause. However it was, something went very wrong when they were halfway down the slope. The sled went quite out of control, and its two riders were unceremoniously dumped into a bank of soft, cold snow. They rolled into it, arms and legs all tangled together.

They finally came to rest with Jane on the bottom, flat on her back, and Viscount Buckley on top of her. They were both laughing and then both self-conscious. His eyes slid to her mouth at the same moment as hers slid to his. But for a moment only. The delighted laughter of the young people brought them to their senses and their feet, and they both brushed vigorously at themselves and joined in the laughter.

Jane was tingling with warmth again. If only, she thought shamelessly. If only there had been no one else in sight. If only he had kissed her again. Just once more. One more kiss to hug to herself for the rest of her life.

Oh, she really had become greedy, she told herself severely. Would she never be satisfied?

An unwanted inner voice answered her. No, not any longer. She never would.

But it was time to take Veronica by the hand again. It was time to go back to the house.

Viscount Buckley went upstairs to change into his evening clothes while the young people played charades in the drawing room and Jane played unobtrusively in one corner with Veronica and her new doll, the kitchen cat curled beside them, apparently oblivious to the loud mirth proceeding all about it. He had lingered in the room himself, reluctant to leave despite the squeals from the girls and loud laughter from the boys that just a few days before he had welcomed the thought of escaping. But he could delay no longer if he were to arrive at the Oxendens' in good time for dinner.

Yet despite the fact that he was pressed for time, he wandered to the window of his bedchamber after his valet had exercised all his artistic skills on the tying of his neckcloth and had helped him into his blue evening coat, as tight as a second skin, according to fashion. He stood gazing out at twilight and snow, not really seeing either.

He was seeing Veronica in her red Christmas bonnet, her muff on a ribbon about her neck. He was seeing her rosy cheeked with the cold, bright-eyed and laughing, and tugging impatiently at his hand. Looking and sounding like a four-year-old. And he was thinking of her next week or the week after or the week after that, going away to settle with her new family.

He was going to be lonely. He was going to grieve for her for the rest of his life. And if Jane were correct, he was not even doing what was best for Veronica.

Jane! He could see her, too, animated and giggling—yes, giggling!—and beautiful. Ah, so beautiful, his prim, plain Jane. And he thought of her the week after next, returning to Miss Phillpotts's school with Deborah, returning to her life of drudgery and utter aloneness. She had never been hugged or kissed or loved, she had said—not out of self-pity but in an attempt to save Veronica from such a fate.

He was going to be lonely without Jane. He thought of his mistress, waiting for him in London with her luscious, perfumed body, and of the skills she used to match his own in bed. But he could feel no desire, no longing for her. He wanted Jane with her inevitable gray dress and her nondescript figure and her face that was plain except when she stopped hiding inside herself. Jane, who did not even know how to kiss—she pursed her lips and kept them rigidly closed. She probably did not know what happened between a man and a woman in bed.

He wanted her.

And he wanted to keep Veronica.

His valet cleared his throat from the doorway into his dressing room and informed him that the carriage was waiting. The viscount knew it was waiting. He had been aware of it below him on the terrace for at least the past ten minutes. The horses, he saw now when he looked down, were stamping and snorting, impatient to be in motion.

"Have it returned to the carriage house," he heard himself say, "and brought up again after dinner. I had better stay here and help Miss Craggs with the young people at dinner. They are rather exuberant and unruly."

That last word was unfair. And what the devil was he doing explaining himself to his valet?

"Yes, m'lord," the man said and withdrew.

Well, that was the excuse he would give the Oxendens later, he thought, as he hurried from the room and downstairs to the drawing room, lightness in his step. It would seem an eminently believable excuse.

And so he sat at the head of the table during dinner, the second of the day, while Jane sat at the foot, Veronica beside her, and the young people were ranged along the two long sides. And he listened indulgently to all their silly chatter and laughter without once wincing with distaste. And he feasted his stomach on rich foods, which it just did not need, and feasted his eyes on his two ladies, who were both making sure that the doll Jane was having her fair share of each course.

And then it was time for the young people and their chaperone to adjourn to the drawing room. The servants had rolled back the carpet during dinner and Mrs. Carpenter had arrived to provide music for the dancing. Veronica was to be allowed to stay up and watch until she was sleepy. And he was to go to the Oxendens'. The carriage was waiting for him again.

But what if any of the silly children decided to imitate their elders and disappear in couples to more remote locations? What if young George Oxenden, in particular, decided to become amorous with Deborah? They had been flirting quite outrageously with each other all afternoon. He had even spotted the young man kissing her beneath the mistletoe she had deliberately stood under. How could Jane handle all that alone when she had Veronica to look after, too?

No, he could not leave her alone. It would be grossly unfair when he was the master of the house—and when Susannah and Miles had entrusted Deborah to his care.

"Have the carriage sent away," he told his butler. "I will not be needing it this evening after all." He smiled fleetingly in self-mockery. This was the most blatant example of rationalization he had ever been involved in. And he must have windmills in the brain. He was choosing to party with young people rather than with sane adults?

No, actually he was choosing to party with his lady and his daughter.

They had danced a quadrille and numerous country dances. All the young people danced every set. They were clearly enjoying the novelty of being

able to use the skills they had learned from dancing
masters in the setting of a real ball—or what was
almost a real ball.

Jane was feeling wonderfully happy as she
watched and as she played with an increasingly
tired Veronica. The child did not want to give in
to suggestions that she be taken up to bed. At the
moment she was seated cross-legged on the floor
beside the Nativity Scene, rocking her doll to sleep
in her arms and looking as if she was not far from
sleep herself.

But what completed Jane's happiness was the fact
that for some reason Viscount Buckley had not
gone to the Oxendens' after all but had stayed at
the house. He had mingled with the company and
chatted with Mrs. Carpenter between dances and
had not been near Jane and Veronica. But it did
not matter. Just having him in the room, just being
able to feast her eyes on him, was enough. He
looked even more splendidly handsome than usual
in a pale blue evening coat with gray knee breeches
and white linen and lace.

She thought with secret, guilty wonder of the fact
that she had been kissed by this man. And that she
had his gift, the lovely shawl, to hug about her—
literally—for the rest of her life.

He was bending over Mrs. Carpenter, speaking
to her, and she was nodding and smiling. He turned
to his young guests and clapped his hands to gain
their attention.

"This is to be a waltz, ladies and gentlemen," he
said. "Do you all know the steps?"

They all did. But the young ladies in particular
had not expected to be able to dance them in public
for many years, until they had made their come-
outs and had been approved by the patronesses of

Almack's in London. There was a buzz of excitement.

Jane knew the steps of the waltz too. She remembered with an inward shudder demonstrating it for the girls at school with the dancing master, whose hands had always seemed too hot and too moist, and who had always tried to cause her to stumble against him. But it was a wonderful dance. Wonderfully romantic—a couple dancing face to face, their hands touching each other.

"Jane?" Suddenly he was there before her, bowing elegantly as if she were the Duchess of Somewhere, and extending a hand toward her. "Will you do me the honor?"

"Me?" she said foolishly, spreading a hand over her chest.

He smiled at her and something strange happened to her knees and someone had sucked half the air out of the room.

"Thank you." She set her hand in his and he looked down at Veronica.

"Do you mind if I steal Miss Jane for a few minutes?" he asked. "Will you watch us dance?"

Veronica yawned.

Jane had dreamed of happiness and romance and pleasure. But never until this ten-minute period had she had even the glimmering of a notion of what any of the three might really feel like. They were almost an agony. She danced—he was an exquisite dancer—and felt that her feet scarcely touched the floor. She danced and did not even have to think about the steps. She danced and was unaware that the room held anyone else but the two of them and the music. She was too happy even to wish that time would stop so that forever she would be caught up in the waltz with the man she had so foolishly fallen in love with.

To say that it was the happiest ten minutes of her life was so grossly to understate the case that the words would be meaningless.

"Thank you," she said when it was over, coolly, as if it really had not meant a great deal to her at all. "I think I should take Veronica up to bed, my lord. She is very tired."

"Yes," he said, glancing down at his child. "Take her up, then. I will come in ten minutes or so to say good night to her."

And so the magic was gone and the day was almost over. She took the sleepy child by the hand and led her up to the nursery, undressed her and washed her quickly, helped her into her nightgown, and tucked her into bed beside her doll.

"Good night, sweetheart," she said, smoothing back the child's curls with one gentle hand. "Has it been a happy Christmas?"

Veronica nodded, though she did not open her eyes and she did not speak. And then Jane's heart lurched with alarm. Two tears had squeezed themselves from between the child's eyelids and were rolling diagonally across her cheeks.

Jane turned instinctively toward the door. He was standing there, as he did each night. When he saw her face, he looked more closely at his daughter. Jane could tell that he could see the tears. His face paled and he came walking across the room toward the bed.

He did not know what to do for a moment. She had seemed so happy for most of the day. She had been laughing and excited during the afternoon. What had happened to upset her? And how could he cope with whatever it was?

"Veronica?" He touched his fingers to her cheek. "What is it?"

She kept her eyes closed and did not answer him for a while. But more tears followed the first. There was something horrifying about a child crying silently. Jane had got up from the bed to stand behind him.

"Why did Mama not come?" his daughter asked finally. "Why was there no present from Mama?"

Oh, God. Oh, dear Lord God, he could not handle this. He sat down on the bed in the spot just vacated by Jane. "Mama had to go far away," he said, cupping the little face with his hands and wiping the tears away with his thumbs. "She would be here if she could, dear. She loves you dearly." He rejected the idea of telling her that the doll was from her mother. Children were usually more intelligent than adults gave them credit for.

His daughter was looking at him suddenly. "Is she dead?" she asked.

A denial was on his lips. And then Jane's words came back to him. She needed to know. Ultimately it would be worse for her not to know, for her to grow up believing that her mother had just tired of her and abandoned her. He stood up for a moment, drew back the bedclothes, scooped up his daughter in his arms, and sat down again, cradling her against him.

"Yes," he said. "She died, Veronica. But she sent you to Papa. And Papa loves you more than anyone or anything else in this world."

She was sobbing then with all of a child's abandoned woe. And he, rocking her in his arms, was crying too. Crying over his daughter's loss and grief. Crying over the truth of the words he had just spoken and over the treasure he had so very nearly given carelessly away.

She stopped crying eventually and lay quietly in

his arms. "You are not going to send me away, Papa?" she whispered.

"Send you away?" he said. "How could I do that? What would I do without my little girl? Who would there be to make me happy?"

She looked up at him with wet and swollen face so that he was reaching into his pocket for a handkerchief even as she spoke. "Do you really love me, Papa?"

"You are my little Christmas treasure," he said, drying her eyes and her cheeks. "The best gift I ever had. I love you, dear."

She reached up to set one soft little hand against his lips. He held it there and kissed it and smiled at her. She yawned hugely and noisily. "Is Miss Jane going to stay, too?" she asked.

He felt Jane shift position behind him.

"Yes," he said, "if I can persuade her to. Would you like that?"

"Yes, Papa," she said.

And in the way of children she was asleep. Asleep and safe and loved in her father's arms. He held her there for a few minutes until he was quite sure she would not wake and then stood to set her down carefully in her bed. Jane held the bedclothes back for him and then stepped aside again.

By the time he had tucked the blankets snugly about his daughter and bent to kiss her little mouth, Jane had disappeared.

It had been agreed that the young people could stay at Cosway until midnight. It was no surprise to anyone, then, when they did not actually leave until thirty minutes after the hour. After all, there had to be just one more dance to follow the last and then one more to follow that.

It was the best, the very best Christmas she had

ever known, Deborah declared, dancing before her uncle and Jane in the hall after everyone had finally gone.

"But do not tell Mama and Papa," she said to the viscount, giggling, "or they will be hurt."

"It will be our secret," he said dryly. "Upstairs with you, now. It is long past your bedtime."

She pulled a face at him before kissing his cheek and dancing in the direction of the stairs. But she came back again and kissed Jane's cheek, too, a little self-consciously. "I am glad you came here with me, Miss Craggs," she said. "Thank you."

"Good night." Jane smiled at her. And then, when the girl was only halfway up the stairs, Jane turned, fixed her eyes on the diamond pin Viscount Buckley wore in his neckcloth, and wished him a hasty good night too.

She was already on her way to the stairs when she felt her hand caught in his.

"Coward!" he said. "You really are a coward, Jane."

"I am tired," she said.

"And a liar," he said.

She looked at him indignantly. He was smiling.

"Into the library," he said, giving her no chance to protest. He was leading her there by the hand. "I have a job to offer you."

As Veronica's nurse? She was too afraid to hope for it, though he had assured his daughter that he would try to persuade her to stay. Oh, would he offer her the job? Could life have such wonder in store for her? After the child no longer needed a nurse, perhaps he would keep her on as a governess. But it was too soon to dream of the future when she was not even sure of the present.

"Jane." He closed the library door behind him

and leaned against it. He was still holding her hand. Someone had lit the branch of candles in there.

"You really do not have to persuade me to stay," she said breathlessly. "Veronica will not even remember in the morning that you promised to do so. If you think me unsuitable for the job of nurse, I will understand. I have had no experience with young children. But I do love her, and I would do my very best if you would consider hiring me. But you must not feel obliged to do so." She stopped talking abruptly and looked down in some confusion.

"A nurse," he said. "I do indeed consider you unsuitable for the job, Jane. It was not what I had in mind at all."

She bit her upper lip, chagrined and shamed. Why, oh why had she not kept her mouth shut?

"I was hoping you would take on the job of mother," he said. "Mother of Veronica and mother of my other children. My future children, that is."

She looked up at him sharply.

"And wife," he added. "My wife, Jane."

Oh. She gaped at him. "Me?" she said foolishly. "You want *me* to be your wife? But you cannot marry me. You know who and what I am."

"You and my daughter both," he said, smiling. "Two treasures. I love you, Jane. I have Veronica, thanks to your words of admonition and advice, and she is a priceless possession. But you can make my happiness complete by marrying me. Will you? I cannot blame you if you do not trust me. I am new to love. I have not trusted it for a long time. But I—"

"Oh," she said, her eyes wide, her heart beating wildly. "You *love* me? You love *me?* How can that be?"

"Because," he said, still smiling, "I have been

playing hide-and-seek, Jane. I have not yet discovered all of you there is to discover. You have done an admirable job over the years of hiding yourself. But what I have seen dazzles me. You are beautiful, inside and out, and I want you for myself. Yes, I love you. Could you ever feel anything for me?"

"Yes," she said without hesitation. "Oh, yes. Oh, yes, my lord. I love you with all my heart."

Somehow his arms were clasped behind her waist and hers behind his neck. Only a part of her mind had grasped what he was saying to her and what he was asking of her. She knew that it would take a long time before the rest of her brain caught up to the knowledge.

"It is going to have to be Warren," he said. "Say it before I kiss you."

"Warren," she said.

It was a kiss that lasted a scandalous length of time. Before it was over she had allowed him to bend the whole of her body against his and she had responded to the coaxing of his lips and softened her own and even parted them. Before it was over she had allowed his tongue into her mouth and his hands on parts of her body she would have thought horrifyingly embarrassing to have touched. Before it was over she was weak with unfamiliar aches of desire.

"My love," he was saying against her mouth, "forgive me. I would not have you for the first time on the library floor. It will be on my bed upstairs on our wedding night. If—" He drew his head back and gazed at her with eyes that were heavy with passion and love—for her. "If there is to be a wedding night. Is there? Will you marry me?"

"Yes," she said, stunned. Had she not already said it? "Warren—"

But whatever she was about to say was soon forgotten as his mouth covered hers again and they moved perilously close after all to anticipating their wedding night.

After all, it was Christmas and they had both just discovered love and joy and romance. And the treasure of a child to love and nurture together.

It was Christmas. Christmas after a long, long time for him. The first Christmas ever for her.

It was Christmas.

Christmas Knight

❧

Emily Hendrickson

Alisandra Percy peered out of the window at the snow-dusted landscape, trying to see what caused the flurry in the drive below. A groom had come dashing up from the stables to handle the arriving carriage and stood at the ready, stamping his feet in the chilly air.

It was a long way from the main gate to the hall, and even though the oak trees that paraded along the avenue were bare, it was not an easy matter to identify a vehicle at such a distance. She stared at the approaching vehicle.

"Well? You know your eyes are better than mine," her younger sister, Joan, said impatiently at her side.

"It is a familiar carriage," Alisandra murmured to her sister while frowning at the nearing shape. "I should think it might be our dear brother, Thomas, home from Oxford."

"Oh, bother," Joan said, slipping across the room to drop herself on a chair by the fire. High ceilings and drafty windows meant warm woolen dresses and huddling by the fire whenever possible. "I had hoped it might be someone interesting." Which description did not include brothers in their last year of school.

"Well, he might bring a friend. He sometimes

does that, you know," Alisandra admonished, frowning at her thin younger sister. She was so delicate, like a fragile waxen doll with large blue eyes and spun gold angel's hair. It nearly broke Alisandra's heart to see her want for anything, even amusement. If she could just be kept from catching cold this winter.

"Well," Joan said in a considering way, studying her sister with a disconcerting gaze, "I should think he might consider you just once. Would it not be wonderful if he brought home a guest who was just right for you, your Christmas gift, so to speak. It would not cost him a cent."

"Brothers do not do such things, I fear," Alisandra said with a chuckle, strolling across the room to join her sister. Once by the fire she allowed her heavy woolen shawl to slip down while she sat near Joan, hoping to absorb some heat in the drafty Yorkshire hall they called home.

"Papa does not let you go anywhere and forgets entirely about a Season in London," Joan said, refusing to drop the subject that irked her. Her statement was followed by an enormous sigh. "I fear he keeps you here to attend me. I could travel with you. I am much stronger than I look."

"Of course you are, dearest. I truly do not long for a Season in London." This was not precisely the truth, but Alisandra had learned long ago that her father carried strong suspicions about the outside world, that vast area beyond the boundary of the Percy estate. He seemed to feel no one was to be trusted—at least in so far as his precious daughters were concerned. And he seemed to delight in holding court at Braeside Hall much as his ancestors did many years in the past. Papa loved antiquity.

"I believe," Alisandra mused aloud, "that I require a knight in shining armor to come riding along and sweep me away from Papa. He would appreciate that, I think," she added with a grimace. "It would fit right in with his notions about living as a baron of old in this drafty old pile." She tucked a stray wisp of hair beneath the net that captured her long auburn hair. On top of her head a little jeweled cap sat, offering precious little warmth, but great charm. Papa deemed it necessary to dress in the old style, proclaiming them pleasing. Alisandra suspected he really liked not having to follow the dictates of fashion.

"If such a man comes along you must promise me you will not allow any thought of me to stop you from riding off with him," Joan insisted. "I refuse to be a millstone about your neck. How I would hate to think I had kept you from a home and family. I cannot imagine anything more hurtful."

Deeply touched by Joan's fervent declaration, Alisandra stretched out a hand to reassure her sister and said, "I promise. And you must promise me that if such a wildly improbable event should occur you will join me, for if I am to have a knight, he must be from the south of England where it is warmer. And," she added thoughtfully, "I believe he ought to have a snug house that is cozy and warm, and not at all difficult to maintain. Certainly," she said with a wave of her hand to encompass the room all beyond it, "not like this ancient place—although I do love it."

Both girls looked about them at the high-ceilinged room with the ancient bed hangings that clung to the posts, the furniture that seemed so old one wondered how it remained standing, and then considered the remainder of the Hall. Papa admired everything baronial, which extended to the dress and the manners of those in the house.

"If the knight does come, you must admit you will be dressed appropriately," Joan said with a giggle, gesturing to their simple high-waisted gowns of wool kerseymere. Their full skirts spread about them in pools of rich color—hunter green for Alisandra and sapphire for Joan.

Alisandra looked down at her gown, then nodded. The low vee was filled with a becoming pale rose-and-white striped wool. Joan wore a simple gown with a high neck to add warmth. The gowns were styled in the manner of the fifteenth century, and most graceful; both girls wore the period clothes with charm.

The arrival of the carriage interrupted their talk. Stamping of horses and the creak of the vehicle as people left it penetrated the room. The two girls hurried from Alisandra's room and down the drafty hall to the top of the stairs, peering over the baluster with great curiosity. Visitors did not come to Braeside Hall every day.

In the entry far below they could see three men come into the house, greeted warmly by Barford, the elderly butler who had served the family since a young man.

"Thomas is not alone," Joan whispered, resting her chin on the baluster while assessing the strangers with their brother.

"So I see," Alisandra whispered back. "I wonder . . ." Her words faded away as one of them glanced up as though aware he was observed. "Oh, my, would you look at that!" she exclaimed softly, quite awed at what she saw.

"I believe your knight has arrived," Joan agreed with a grin. "Is that Max with him? I hope so, for he is such a comfortable sort of person."

"I must confess the stranger is the most elegant creature Thomas ever brought home," Alisandra whispered. "And I think it must be Max with them, for the fellow looks exceedingly familiar although it must be two years since we last saw him. I believe I will go down to greet them. After all, Papa keeps telling me I am his hostess now that Mama has gone aloft." She shared a warm smile with Joan, then straightened up, adjusting her gown so that it hung neatly in place.

"And Aunt Phoebe has not arrived to take charge," Joan reminded. "Not but that she ever does anything useful."

"Come," Alisandra commanded nicely. She gathered her trailing skirts in one hand, and with her head held high she drifted down the stairs to confront her brother and the unexpected guests. Joan followed in her wake.

Alisandra ought to have anticipated the look of surprise on the elegant gentleman when he saw her antiquated garb. If the dress was not enough, Papa insisted the girls wear their hair captured in intricate nets with caps and veils covering them, depending on the style of gown. She wondered if another traitorous wisp of hair had escaped from her net. One hand crept up to reassure herself.

The girls and the village dressmaker did their best with the aid of the effigies, monuments, and brass plates in various churches they were permitted to visit in search of ideas. It was not a simple matter, for the designing of the garments took a great deal of guessing. Alisandra had altered the designs with an eye to simplicity and practicality and the merest hope of style.

"Welcome to Braeside Hall, gentlemen," she said, then dipped a proper curtsy. Joan remained silent, but curtsied as well, peeping shyly at the exceedingly handsome guest.

"Am I to be treated as a stranger, Sandy?" Maximilian Luttrell said in seeming affront. He stepped forward to place a gentle kiss on Alisandra's cheek, holding her shoulders in a light clasp while he studied her face. "We have known each other since you were an infant. Do not say you put aside one who is nearly a part of your family."

"Oh, Max," Alisandra said, flustered at his kiss, which had had a rather peculiar effect on her sensibilities. She rarely saw a gentleman let alone was kissed by one, even on her cheek. "You know I would not treat you as a stranger, but I have grown up since you last saw me. It is not seemly for me to come dashing up to beg for a kiss as I might when a little girl." She darted a glance at the stranger, who watched the little scene with a tolerant smile.

"Alisandra Percy, may I present Sir William Oldershaw," Thomas said with a brotherly dip of his head in her direction. "He's a friend from Oxford. He usually goes home to his family place in Kent, but his young sisters are all sick with the measles, and so he came with me." To Sir William he added, "Joan is the quiet little one peeping from behind Alisandra. Forgot to explain about my father. He prefers the old customs and ways. I vow you will find it amusing, however."

Sir William stepped forward to take Alisandra's hand, placing a light kiss on it. It was the merest whisper of a touch, warm lips on chilled skin. It was an alien sensation for Alisandra; she felt as though she might drown in those silvery blue eyes Sir William fastened upon her with such potent charm. This was indeed to be a fine holiday. With a touch of gracious charm, Sir William also picked up Joan's hand and saluted her in the same manner.

Quite surprised at this attention, Joan blushed and said, "I am sorry your sisters are ill. I hope you enjoy your Christmas with us."

"Indeed," Max inserted, still standing close to Alisandra. "You may look forward to a goodly size Yule log, a wassail bowl, a harper—if Joan plays as well as she did before—spiced wines, with clusters of mistletoe for good measure. Have I left anything out?" He said this to Alisandra, who had not drawn away, remaining as though transfixed.

"The mumming, carols, and the Morris dancers," Joan dared to add with a faint pinkening of her cheeks at the thought that Max had remembered her harp playing.

"And plenty of food," Thomas chimed in. "We have excellent hunting this time of year. My father raises deer on the estate, and there are wild boar as well to offer challenging sport."

Alisandra at last found her tongue and looked at Max. "You will be careful if you hunt them?" To Sir William she added, "They are rather nasty creatures."

"Must have a boar's head for Christmas dinner," Max said, sounding highly amused and still standing close to Alisandra. One hand remained on her shoulder, feeling oddly right. It gave a sensation of security and warmth.

"Ugh," Joan whispered.

Max turned to give her a brotherly pat on her shoulder. "Cheer up; with any luck we may not find one."

She smiled at his understanding of her feelings regarding the sometimes crude customs of the past.

"Well, I feel certain you will wish to see your rooms and possibly change into something more comfortable. Follow me." Alisandra led them toward the oak stairs with its unusual newel posts. Atop each post sat a carving of a lion rampant, ready to do battle, just as was depicted on the family coat of arms.

"Aunt Phoebe arrived as yet?" Thomas inquired while the group slowly made their way up the broad stairs. Behind them Barford directed the disposition of the baggage brought in from the carriage by the army of footmen.

"I expect her any moment. I suppose it is too much to hope for that she will leave those dogs of hers at home," Alisandra said woefully to Thomas's amusement.

"Not likely," he replied with the cheerfulness of one who does not have to endure a pair of yapping spaniels and their repeated nips at one's ankles. "Any chance she might bring Charlotte along?"

Alisandra was not fooled in the least by his casual question. His interest in their odious cousin Charlotte had puzzled her for years. Cold and aloof, and always wearing the very latest fashion from London, dear cousin Charlotte seemed to adore coming to Braeside Hall for the holidays if for no other reason than to preen before an envious Alisandra and Joan and ensnare Thomas with her beauty.

"I fully expect Charlotte to arrive with Aunt and the dogs. Come along." To Max and Sir William she added, "You are in the east wing with Papa. Charlotte and Aunt Phoebe are in the west wing with Joan and me. I expect Charlotte will entertain us with the latest gossip from London and the current fashions once she arrives."

"As usual," Max muttered while giving Alisandra a look she found distinctly unsettling.

"Well, we will change into riding garb and go

looking for Papa. Best not tell him we came in a carriage," Thomas said, exchanging a look with Max.

Smiling at Sir William's raised brows, Alisandra said, "Papa thinks carriages are only for women. A true man rides on horseback, whatever the weather."

She settled Sir William in a paneled room with cheerful yellow draperies and bed covering. It faced the parterre garden. In summer a riot of color could be found in the flower beds. Now, all that could be seen were neat squares ready for the blooms of the coming season.

A peacock screeched in the distance and Max grimaced.

"Hasn't anyone murdered those birds yet?" he said.

"Papa would take a dim view of such a thing. He prizes 'those birds,' as you call them. Each one has a name. Be careful, or he'll name one after you!" Alisandra said while repressing a smile. Max was the same, amusing as always. It had been a quirk of her imagination to think he had changed, that something was different about him.

Sir William glanced about his elegant room, then began to shrug off his coat.

Alisandra hurried them along to the next room and ushered Max inside. Thomas walked on to his own room, leaving the girls temporarily with Max.

Max looked about the paneled room with its beautiful linen-fold paneling, the dark oak bed that gleamed with polish, and the bed hangings of vibrant red, and sighed. He placed his gloves on a small table next to a massive oak chair all carved with spiral twistings and leaves here and there. It had plump red cushions that invited one to rest, and Max gave it a look of such longing that Joan giggled while edging toward the door.

"You are prepared for all the company, Sandy?" Max said while he strolled along back to the door with the two girls.

"Of course. We have had little else to do but prepare for Christmas all these many weeks. If we are not ready now, we will never be." She bestowed a friendly grin on him, once again comfortable in good old Max's company.

"I wonder," he mused before shooing them out.

"Whatever did he mean by that?" Joan demanded.

"You know Max," Alisandra said smoothly. But in her heart she also wondered what her old friend had meant by his odd comment.

A commotion in the entry captured their attention, and they ran to the top of the stairs, descending sedately as Barford attended the door.

"It can only be Aunt Phoebe," Joan whispered as the sound of yapping dogs reached their ears.

"And Cousin Charlotte. Dear Cousin Charlotte," Alisandra said, followed by a heartfelt sigh.

A woman wrapped in furs that made her look far larger than her actual size entered the hall, followed by the pair of King Charles spaniels who were attempting to nibble Barford's ankles before darting about the entry, their nasty little teeth bared between bites and barks.

Then another woman entered the house, her head crowned with a magnificent bonnet no doubt the last minute in fashion above a pelisse that made Alisandra gnash her teeth. Elegant powder blue velvet was smashingly frogged in black. Charlotte carried a black reticule in her black gloved hands. She looked wonderful, stylish, and Alisandra envied her although she knew it was wrong of her.

She swallowed her envy and ire, hurrying down the last steps to greet the guests. "Aunt Phoebe and dear Cousin Charlotte. How lovely to see you again."

"Of course it is, you poor child," Aunt declared in a surprisingly loud voice for one so thin. "You must long for company in this benighted place. I take it your father is as stubborn as ever and refuses you a Season?"

Alisandra accepted the last of the furs, passing them along to Barford before guiding her relatives in the direction of the drawing room. Here they found a blazing fire and the deep red draperies pulled back to admit the pale winter sun that did little to warm the room this season of the year.

Charlotte removed her pelisse once she stood by the fire. Beneath it she wore a delicate powder blue muslin trimmed with three flounces and bedecked with yards of dainty lace. The gown was far too thin and utterly unsuitable for the northern climate in the middle of winter. It was also much prettier than anything Alisandra possessed in her wardrobe. Charlotte looked graceful and charming.

"How very lovely you look," Alisandra said after admonishing herself to be thankful for a papa who cared and for loved ones about her. She knew that in his own way, Baron Percy, eighth Baron Percy of Braeside, cared deeply for his daughters and his son as well.

"Yes, the dress is pretty," Charlotte said complacently. "It is the latest thing from the newest rage in London mantua-makers. Mama would not have me go to just anyone, you know." She left on the splendid bonnet, allowing the pale blue plumes to float about in the air when she turned her head this way and that while chatting.

A maid brought in a tray with the makings for a

sumptuous tea, the very thing for hungry travelers. Alisandra attended to pouring and offering cakes and bread and butter.

"The gentlemen have arrived and are upstairs changing so you can eat now, Charlotte," Joan said with a twinkle in her pretty blue eyes.

Charlotte flushed and helped herself to several dainty cakes, then said, "Who is here besides Thomas?"

"Dear old Max and a stranger, Sir William Oldershaw," Joan said while Alisandra busied herself with the teapot.

"Oldershaw family goes back to William of Orange as I recall," Aunt Phoebe said. She gave her daughter a significant look that was not missed by that young woman.

Charlotte had munched all her cakes and had consumed a second cup of tea when a stir at the door indicated the gentlemen joining them. Immediately, the cup was replaced and Charlotte checked herself to note that all was perfection.

"Ah, the second arrivals," Max declared as he crossed the room in long strides to bow to Phoebe, Lady Fairfax, and then to Charlotte. He gave Alisandra a questioning look that she quite missed, being far too taken with Sir William's elegance. He entered dressed in the supreme understatement of the London gentleman—a jacket of midnight blue over pale gray breeches with a soft gray waistcoat that sported but a single fob in quiet dignity.

Thomas in his unpolished manner introduced all concerned, then joined them in consuming the tea, helping himself to two currant buns. Finding his father rated somewhere below chatting up Charlotte.

Outside, the sun had disappeared behind gathering gray clouds. He gave an impatient glance out of the window, then turned to Sir William. "I trust you have warm clothing along, but if not, I can supply what you need. We have some capital riding hereabouts."

"Indeed, I look forward to a good jaunt in the fresh air tomorrow," Sir William replied with charming grace and a nod to Charlotte, easily the outstanding woman present.

Alisandra exchanged glances with Joan. Both knew that while Charlotte hated going out in the cold, she also adored the company of gentlemen. It would be interesting to see which emotion was the stronger.

"Well, well," said a hearty bass voice from the doorway. The baron entered the room, his coat flapping about him and his red waistcoat and trim gray breeches neatly adorning a manly figure. There was nothing of the town dandy about him. He was a country man, caring deeply for his lands and his tenants.

Barford entered with a pot of tea to replace the now-empty one that sat on the tray. A maid followed with another plate of buns and biscuits.

After the introductions had been made, the baron looked about the room, then said, "How nice to have all of you here for the holidays." To Sir William he added, "We celebrate in the old style. I trust you will join in our simple festivities." He turned to Joan and inquired, "What is it to be this year, puss?"

"We always do a mumming, a costume play without words. I thought that rather than Robin Hood and Maid Marian, or St. George and his dragon, we would do a medieval play, with a knight in armor rescuing a damsel in distress instead—since there are so many of us."

"Will can play the knight," Thomas offered.
"Max would be good at it as well."

"Actually, we shall have two knights, Sir William
and Max," Joan said hastily. "And there will be
two maidens in distress: Alisandra and Charlotte.
Thomas can be the villain. I will direct," she said
with a tentative smile.

Alisandra stared at her younger sister, who was
usually in charge of the children each year. Had
she taken leave of her senses? They always had a
St. George at Christmas and did Robin Hood on
May Day. Well, the plan had been set forth. Already Charlotte preened about being one of the
maidens in distress. There was little doubt who she
expected her knight to be, the way she cast demure
and inviting glances at Sir William. But, Alisandra
thought with a deal of comfort, he had not kissed
Charlotte's hand when introduced.

Nor, a little thought nudged her, had Max kissed
Charlotte's cheek when they met again. But then,
Max had nurtured a hearty dislike for the girl ever
since the time she pushed Alisandra into the lake
before Max had taught her to swim. He had rescued
her, pounding her back dreadfully before she had
coughed up a pool of water and howled in anger
at the entire disgrace. Dear Max, Alisandra thought
fondly. So many memories, so many ties.

She smiled at the recollection of Max teaching
her how to paddle to safety should she tumble into
the water again. Even then, he had been well-mus-
cled although lean. The thought of that bare chest
and strong arms about her brought the most peculiar feeling deep within her. She hastily set it aside
to concentrate on entertaining her guests.

Folly, one of the spaniels, nipped at her ankle,
then sat back awaiting a treat. "Nasty creature,"
Alisandra muttered while handing it a bit of biscuit.

The dog bared its teeth as though expressing the same feeling for her.

Prudence, the other dog, came trotting over to receive the same treat. Alisandra wished she might ban the nasty dogs from the house, but knew she might never do anything so dreadful.

"Miserable mutts, are they not?" Max said quietly while the others discussed the coming days.

"I firmly believe all dogs should be as well trained as Prince." She glanced over to take note of her father's staghound, who sat unobtrusively at his master's feet, ignoring the nips and yips of the two spaniels as though they were not even present.

"Your father has trained you all well," Max said with a gleam of a smile when Alisandra gave him an indignant look.

"I like being here with Papa," she whispered fiercely. "Although I know that someday I will probably leave. But I will not go unless I may take Joan with me."

"I know that, Sandy. But how many would offer for two?"

"Odious man," she hissed back at him, incensed that he would think Sir William would be anything less than noble. It did not occur to her to think that Sir William would have any other interest in mind. He was her Christmas Knight, a gift—however unknowing—from her brother.

"Well, how about a ride? Max, you will like the new addition I made to the stable." The baron rose from his chair, bowed properly to the ladies, then swept the men along with him all the while chatting about horses.

"Alisandra, I suppose there is nothing to be done with your father," Aunt Phoebe said with a sigh and a grimace at her wayward and peculiar brother.

"Nothing at all, Aunt Phoebe; he insists we prefer the Hall to the city," Alisandra replied with a twinkle. Then she rose as well, standing before her aunt in proper modesty. "I suggest we settle you and Charlotte in your rooms so your maids may assist you to prepare for dinner. I have managed to convince Papa that the meal should be held by London time while you are here."

"Will wonders never cease," Aunt declared while gathering her belongings together. With a gesture to Alisandra, she rose and marched from the room without seeing whether or not her niece followed.

"Which wing are we in?" Charlotte casually inquired.

"The west one—as usual," Joan said with a giggle. "We would not be so lost to propriety as to house you close to the men!"

"I trust you will find matters to your liking this year," Alisandra said, wondering if her cousin would continue to bedevil Thomas with her charms or if she would turn her attention to the London gentleman, Sir William. There was a sinking sensation in the pit of her stomach when she realized that Sir William would likely have more in common with Charlotte than her countrified self.

Once her relatives were settled and requests handed over to the maids assigned to their rooms, Alisandra drew Joan along with her back to the cozy fire still burning in the grate in Joan's room. The servants had orders to keep a fire burning there no matter what time of year it might be.

"Well, what do you think, so far?" she said after settling on a comfortable chair.

"I believe we shall have to find you a love potion in the old family herbal," Joan said with a thoughtful frown.

"What? That is for May Day, not Christmas," Alisandra protested. "Which brings to mind, why the changes in the mumming this year? And do you desert the children?"

"Someone else can manage them. I figured if we had St. George that Charlotte would demand to be the princess while as a guest Sir William would be St. George. I ask you, how else can he rescue you from a villain?"

"I see." Alisandra thought for a bit, then said, "You truly believe a love potion would be necessary and work?"

"Indeed," Joan said.

"I wonder," Alisandra said. "I should not like to think I must capture a man with a potion. Surely I am not such an antidote." She gave Joan a troubled look.

"Of course not, ninny. You are a treasure. I fear Charlotte with her London clothes and fancy manners will outshine you. He will not have a chance to see you for your true worth," Joan declared, most indignant at the thought.

"I do not know ... It seems a dreadful thing to do to anyone." Alisandra gave her sister a dubious smile that fully indicated how torn she was. Both girls knew the effectiveness of the old remedies and potions. They had grown up with them.

"I believe it is fair and the most acceptable way. After all, Charlotte will not hesitate to use her lovely clothes and all at her command."

"Very well, we will go down to the stillroom to compound one immediately. Which one do you think the most useful for this purpose?" Alisandra popped up from her chair, pulling Joan along with her to the door.

Outside they found Charlotte in the act of raising her hand to rap on Joan's door. The girls exchanged looks of dismay, both wondering if their cousin had been snooping.

"I wonder if you might lend me some of that rose lotion you make?" Charlotte asked with a dimpled smile.

With a sigh of relief Joan slipped back to fetch the desired item, then they scurried down the stairs.

Charlotte drifted after them, staring down at her disappearing cousins. How silly they were. Love potions? What utter nonsense. Nothing would counteract the charms she intended to use on Sir William.

"What amuses you, Charlotte?" Max asked from behind her.

"Alisandra intends to make a love potion. I suppose she thinks to use it on Sir William, which is quite pointless." She failed to say why, obviously believing it unnecessary.

Max said nothing to Charlotte. He merely smiled in his quiet way, murmured something about meeting Sir William and Thomas in the library, and ran lightly down the steps.

After giving him a vexed look, Charlotte followed him. It was as natural as breathing for a girl like Charlotte to seek out the unattached males in the vicinity, and in this case there were two excellent targets for her wiles. Ever since Max had made it quite plain that he detested her, Charlotte had ignored his presence when possible. But the other two—well, they had distinct possibilities.

Down in the stillroom Joan and Alisandra pored over the old family books of potions and remedies that had been collected over a number of generations.

"Ah, here it is," Joan declared at last. "Now all you need to do is blend these ingredients"—she grimaced at the proposed contents of the love potion—"and you may offer it to Sir William."

Alisandra peered over her shoulder and made a

face. "I should think that latter bit will prove the more difficult."

Perched atop stools, they worked quietly for some time, Alisandra swiftly taking the bottles of herbs that Joan pulled from the shelves and deftly mixing measured amounts together. She ground them to a fine powder, then added a bit of liquid. Before long she sat back and shared a look of satisfaction with Joan.

"Oh, well done," Joan whispered with a glance at the door. While their housekeeper, Mrs. Faraday, might go along with an ancient potion, neither girl wished to explain why they wanted it or on whom it was to be used.

"What excuse can we use to offer refreshments to the gentlemen?" Joan wondered as the girls strolled along down the arched hallway while her sister concealed the bottle of potion in the folds of her skirt.

Alisandra paused, then turned into the large, high-ceilinged kitchen where the cook and her assistants were busy preparing the dinner. It was to be a festive meal, for company always meant extra dishes and fancy desserts.

Mrs. Faraday entered from the large pantry and paused when she saw the girls. "Yes?" she said in her dignified manner.

"I wonder if there might be a bit of refreshment we could offer to the gentlemen." Joan grinned at the older lady.

"Be you up to something?" Mrs. Faraday asked with a narrow look at Joan. Despite her angelic, fragile appearance, she often tumbled into mischief.

"Well, we do not wish to have Cousin Charlotte criticize us for lack of hospitality," Alisandra said softly. "And Papa scolds us if we neglect the guests, even if they are gentlemen. Charlotte never eats anything, so we need not worry about her."

Joan giggled at this bit, for they all knew how Charlotte crept down to the kitchen when she thought no one was about and stuffed herself with food so that when she was at the table she could nibble and appear to have a delicate appetite. Supposedly, it was to impress a gentleman with the notion that Charlotte would be easy on his budget.

"Aye," Mrs. Faraday replied thoughtfully. "I have a plate of little cakes that go powerfully well with wine. Men like them, they do. Run along and I'll see to them."

"Nonsense," Alisandra scoffed, "we know how busy you are. We shall take the tray for you. I suspect you are about to fix a pudding for supper and Papa would never forgive me if I kept you from that admirable task."

Mrs. Faraday gave the girls a grateful look and hurriedly set out a pretty tray with a fine linen napkin, the splendid little cakes, and the prettiest glasses.

"Lovely," Alisandra said to Joan after they escaped from the kitchen. "I'd not have thought of the colored glasses, but that dark blue will cover up the potion just fine!" She added her tiny bottle of potion to the tray.

Once in a sheltered spot and quite unseen, they stopped. Alisandra poured the potion into the glass on the right, then topped it with wine. Then she poured wine into all the others. Standing back, she studied them carefully.

"It looks quite fine to me. Nothing about that one to the right to tell it's partly a potion." Alisandra gave her sister a considered look. "I trust what we do is not wrong. Somehow it seems a trifle underhanded. The poor chap won't have a chance."

"Remember, it is for both of us," Joan reminded her. "If you remain here, so do I. Think about southern England and a cozy home of your own. Kent is supposed to be lovely."

"And he is handsome, is he not?" Alisandra said, her eyes full of dreams. "He has beautiful manners. How my heart fluttered when he kissed my hand." She picked up the tray, and they continued on to the library, making sure that none of the liquid was spilled along the way.

They were dismayed yet not really surprised to find Charlotte in the library with the gentlemen. She was perched near the fire, paging through a large book well-illustrated with hand-tinted botanical pictures. On the far side of the room the men stood clustered below a collection of firearms that hung on the wall, discussing the merits of new over old.

Alisandra curtsied prettily before them, then offered a glass of wine, the glass on the right, to Sir William. "Dinner is some time off, and we thought you all might wish something to stave off dire hunger."

"I should like that, I've a dreadful thirst," Max said, almost snatching the glass from Alisandra. Before she could say a word he had downed the lot. Then he helped himself to a little cake and ate it with relish while giving Alisandra the most disconcerting look.

The other men joked with Max about his thirstiness while also helping themselves to wine and little cakes.

"One thing about Mrs. Faraday, she makes the best cakes in the world," Thomas said fervently when he had sampled the offering.

"Madeira cake, is it not?" Sir William hazarded.

"Excellent," he concluded with a lift of his glass in Alisandra's direction.

"Yes, even the wine has a certain something, an indefinable extra quality to the flavor," Max said with a tilt of his head and a studied look at Alisandra.

She swallowed carefully and hoped her consternation did not show too much. What in the world was she to do now!

"Ignoring me, Cousin?" Charlotte said with a faint hint of a whine in her voice.

Alisandra turned her head to give her cousin a bemused look. "Umm?"

"Why, 'tis well known you have the barest of appetites," Joan said with a twinkle in her pretty blue eyes. "You subsist on butterfly wings and cucumber slices, I vow."

"Then what do you eat, Sandy?" Max said, coming to stand far too close to her for her comfort. His smooth, rich voice almost purred in her ear. "No, do not tell me, let me guess. I'd venture to say 'tis damson tarts and treacle puddings. You're a very sweet lass."

"Now, Max, you will put her utterly out of countenance, for you know she is not accustomed to flirting of any sort," Charlotte chided, helping herself to one of the little cakes.

"Pity, that," Max murmured in Alisandra's tender ear.

His arm brushed against hers, and she felt a panicky sensation; her senses were doing strange things, and she could not discipline them. She had the oddest feeling Max truly meant that little comment, and she felt stranger yet. She gave Joan a beseeching look, then backed away. "I . . . I ought to take the tray back to the kitchen." Her voice squeaked a trifle, and she suspected she blushed.

"Why, Cousin," Charlotte said in a syrupy voice, "there must be at least one hundred and twenty servants drifting about this vast pile. Surely one of them can wait upon you?" She downed the last cake crumb and smiled sweetly.

"Oh. Of course. How silly of me," Alisandra murmured while wishing the floor might open up and swallow her. She listened to the others chat while setting the tray carefully on a table. Max pushed the last of the little cakes into her hand, gesturing that she eat. Which she did—with mechanical nibbles all the while she eyed him askance, wondering if the potion had already begun weaving its magic on him. He was not behaving like the Max of old.

With splendid resourcefulness Joan said, "Alisandra, come with me. We need to fetch more greenery." Tossing a glance at Charlotte, she added, "I know we could send a footman, but it is much more fun to cut the ivy and snip the holly branches ourselves, the bay laurel as well. Does anyone wish to join us?" She moved toward the door, obviously intent upon leaving at once.

Sir William gave Joan a thoughtful perusal, then set down his empty glass as did Max and Thomas. With a shared look, they all agreed to go along.

"I suppose I can go as well," Charlotte said then, reluctant to go out in the cold, but unwilling to let the eligible gentlemen out of her sight for long.

"We want to weave garlands for the candles, make wreaths for the doors and everywhere, and garlands for the stairs as well," Joan said to Sir William.

"Do not forget the mistletoe," Max said to Alisandra with a meaningful grin that this time set her heart to fluttering. He wasn't supposed to act like this, she wailed inwardly, nor look at her like this.

It was all wrong. Sir William was supposed to have drunk that potion!

They parted ways at the top of the stairs so all could dress warmly for the outing. Max whistled merrily all the way down the hall to his room.

Charlotte paused by Alisandra's door to say, "I trust you do not have your heart set upon arousing Sir William's interest. A sophisticated gentleman like Sir William must be accustomed to the elegant manners of London, not the rustic ways of Yorkshire." With that pithy comment she sashayed across the hall and into her room, shutting her door with a snap.

Joan pushed Alisandra into her room, then took her hands in shared dismay at all that had transpired.

"It is quite dreadful," Alisandra cried softly, so as not to alert Charlotte to anything amiss.

"I could not believe it when Max took the glass from your hand and drank it before we could say a word. However did you manage to remain silent?" Joan said. She frowned. "It is most vexing. Now what do we do?" she concluded, then made a wry grimace while watching her sister cross the room.

"I refuse to make another potion," Alisandra stated, hunting through her clothespress for a warm cloak that looked reasonably fashionable. "It would be frightful to have *two* gentlemen in a passion over me at the same time. Oh, Max! Why did he have to interfere? I know he did not mean to, but it certainly complicates matters. Now I will have to wait until the next time Thomas brings home a gentleman, and who knows when that will be! Or who?"

"I had counted upon your Christmas knight to save us both," Joan murmured as she collected a spare cloak from her sister's pile. "I would dearly love to travel south."

"We will just have to make the best of things." Alisandra paused by her door and whispered fiercely, "And if Charlotte snabbles Sir William, I think I shall have an attack of the vapors."

"They do seem well-suited, you must admit," Joan whispered back.

"Horrors, what you must think of Sir William," Alisandra said with a chuckle.

"Actually, he seems quite nice," replied an exceedingly thoughtful Joan. "I quite like his eyes and smile."

With her warmest red cloak about her shoulders Alisandra whisked down the stairs, followed by a pensive Joan to gather up the baskets for the sprays of ivy and the holly and bay branches.

Barford himself handed Alisandra the *sécateurs*, actually smiling the merest trifle. "The best holly may be found on the east side of the herb garden this year, miss. And I am reliably informed that a fine bit of mistletoe can be located in the old oak not far from the herb garden."

"Now that is a must," Max declared so close to Alisandra that she almost stumbled forward in her surprise.

"Max, you ought not," she began, then paused, utterly frustrated. How could she explain that he might feel attracted to her, but it was all a hum, a false sensation generated by the ancient family herbal potion. It suddenly occurred to her she might hurt Max's feelings were she to reveal a preference for Sir William and reject Max. After all, he had been a part of her life for so long.

"I definitely intend to look for the mistletoe," Max said, smiling down into her confused face with an amber glow in his dark eyes. A lock of his dark brown hair fell over his brow and Alisandra knew the most absurd desire to brush it back and stroke that soft, shining pelt.

"I imagine you wish to catch one of the pretty housemaids beneath it," Joan said with a mischievous giggle. "Shall we pick off most of the berries, Alisandra?" With a twirl of her cape, the seventeen-year-old girl whirled around the door after grabbing up a basket and a knife to cut sprays of ivy.

"Indeed," Alisandra said judiciously. At her advanced age of nineteen she moved more sedately, but a part of her felt the need to run from Max. Which had to be silly, for Max was . . . well, Max was Max, her old friend and dear companion of summers and Christmas holidays gone by. Why she had trailed after him through berry bushes, hunting for the ripest and best, rowed him to a fishing spot—then held her tongue while he hoped for a big one. She had adored him with all her childish heart. And now he had changed and Alisandra felt as though her world had been badly shaken.

The worst of it all was that she suspected it was all her fault. Had she not acquired the stupid notion to give Sir William that love potion, all would be the same. Or would it? Even before he drank from the glass, he had behaved oddly. Or did she imagine that?

Confused, her head all in a muddle, Alisandra gave the others baskets and showed them where to go.

Max took the *sécateurs* from her unexpectedly helpless hand and announced most grandly, "I shall cut the holly. I fancy I know just what you need."

The look in his eyes sent Alisandra's heart racing, and she wondered if there was any breath left in her lungs, for it suddenly became very difficult to breathe.

Charlotte placed her beautifully gloved hand on Sir William's arm and tittered her cultivated laugh. "La, sir, you are very gallant to escort me so carefully."

Sir William looked down at the beautiful face turned up to him and gave Charlotte a somewhat practiced smile—the sort he must use on the girls making their come-outs in London. It seemed to Alisandra there was no warmth in that smile and little interest. She saw his gaze jump to where Joan danced before them, gaily swinging her basket, and his face softened into a true smile of pleasure.

Alisandra led the way with a lighter heart. It seemed not all gentlemen immediately tumbled to Charlotte's wiles.

There was much laughing, especially when the delicate Joan squealed in horror upon seeing a fat slug on a stalk of ivy when it ought to have been in hiding from the cold.

"Ugh, that is nearly as bad as a toad," she exclaimed.

Even Charlotte laughed at that remark. She daintily placed sprays of ivy in her basket, arranging them neatly and artistically so that they cascaded down in a pretty manner.

Max glanced at her when she made a flirtatious remark to Sir William, then turned to Alisandra. "How much holly do you wish?"

"Holly?" she said, quite confused again. "Well," she said, her head still feeling not quite sane, "I expect all the baskets ought to be full, for we usually need all we bring inside."

"That you shall have then." He set to work with a will, pruning the trees with skill and care, not hacking here or there, but shaping the trees so that even after the cutting they looked well.

Before long the baskets were all heaped with greens, enough to turn the hall into a very festive place, as well it should be this time of year. The final matter was to pick the mistletoe.

"Shall we find that oak Barford told us about?" Max asked quietly.

"He told me, and you eavesdropped," she scolded, but only with half her intended ire.

"There are times when eavesdropping serves a very useful purpose," he replied with a watchful eye on the others, who now sauntered about the herb garden, laughing and joking over the intended mumming Joan planned. "Come."

Unable to say no—or perhaps merely curious—she sped along the path at his side until they reached the spreading branches of an oak that must have been planted when the first of the Barons Percy lived in the house.

"I see what Barford meant. That is truly a splendid bunch of mistletoe. Such a grand collection of berries. Have you been out here cultivating them, my dear?" Max teased.

She wanted to be indignant that he would even think such a thing of her, but all she could manage was a chuckle at the absurdity of her climbing up in the tree to encourage the mistletoe to put forth an extra fine crop of berries this year. In her heart she was secretly glad it was so, but refused to admit why.

"Ah, here we are," Max said as he jumped down from the low branch after climbing in a rather hazardous way that had Alisandra shutting her eyes in fear for him. He dropped the cluster on top of her basket of holly, but not before he removed one of the white berries and held it up to her.

"Sandy? You know what this means?" Max said after a glance back to where the others lingered at the far end of the garden. The others paid not the least attention to them.

"Of course I do," she whispered back. Try as she might, she could not persuade her feet to move. She stared up at dear old Max, who probably was not all that old if he was a school chum of Thomas's, and waited.

His kiss was warm, for her lips were chilled from the December air. He was gentle, tenderly caring, and most seductive to a girl who had never in her life been kissed like this before. He was also brief. Long before she was willing for the kiss to end, he released her.

"Oh, Max," she breathed. Then she remembered that this was none of his doing, but the effect of the potion, and she could have burst into tears but for her pride. She shook her head as though she might dispel the charm she had worked in him as well as herself. Perhaps there had been a mistake, she thought with hope. Then she took another look at Max, taking note of that naughty gleam in his eyes, and her heart sank. Max had never looked at her like this before. Never.

They were making their way back to the front of the house when a commotion down the avenue caught their attention. A huge log was being towed along by the most stalwart of the servants. Large hooks fastened into the wood enabled them to pull it along over the light covering of snow with relative ease.

"The Yule log," Joan exclaimed with delight.

"Out of fashion in many places. It is nice to see the old customs surviving here," Max said.

"Yes," Alisandra said, "Papa remembers them all. And at times I believe he invents a few of his own. At least he passes a story along, and before you know it, it returns as a fable of old from some village worthy."

"I see from whom you acquired your sense of mischief making," Max said while ushering her into the house, then handed her cloak to Barford, who hovered about the doorway.

Charlotte walked in behind them, frowning at the sight of Alisandra with Max. Then her brow cleared, for clearly Max intended to keep her little cousin away from Sir William for some obscure reason. Perhaps he felt that fashionable gentleman was too worldly for Alisandra. Max had always been disgustingly protective of the chit. Charlotte turned to offer a witty remark to Sir William with the happy knowledge that her pathway was unimpeded.

Alisandra was still trying to make out what Max had meant by his oblique remark about her mischief making. Since he could not possibly know of the potion, she wondered what other mischief she had been up to and couldn't recall.

Max plucked the mistletoe from the top of Alisandra's basket and picked up a length of the ribbon Joan had collected from the attics earlier. It was red ribbon with pretty shadings on it as though watermarked.

He deftly looped the ribbon about the cluster, then added a length to use for hanging. "Let me see, shall it be the center of the arch?"

He turned to Alisandra for confirmation, and she had to concentrate on her reply, for she had been trying to recall just how he had behaved when last here for a Christmas. She gave Max a nod of agreement, then decided that last time he had pretty much ignored her—and the berries. Indeed, he had changed in two years. But then, so had she.

While the servants dragged the giant Yule log

into the Great Room, her father supervising closely, Alisandra watched Max climb up the ladder and nail the mistletoe in place—a prominent spot in the very center of the arched doorway leading from the entry hall to the vast room where celebrations were normally held.

With a smile she cleverly evaded the dangerous trap. Staying close to the wall, she slipped into the room, her basket over her arm. Soon she was busy arranging sprigs of holly, tucking in sprays of ivy, adding touches of bay laurel greens here and there for fullness and contrast, their dark purple berries shining nicely. Totally absorbed in her work, she jumped when Max handed her a particularly pretty sprig of holly as she was about to decorate the great wax tapers that were lit each holiday season. They stood on the massive oak table that had once served for all the household when communal dining was the standard.

"Did I frighten you, Sandy?"

She stared at him for a moment, then said, "You are the only one who calls me by that name. I wonder why?"

"Why I call you Sandy? Or why no one else does?"

"Why do you call me Sandy?" she dared to ask, for she had long wished to know and been hesitant to ask.

"Because," he said, smiling down at her with a positively wicked gleam in his eyes, "it is my very own name for you. And it does suit you, for there are three or four sandy freckles on your pretty nose, and your hair was a sandy color when you were an infant. I like the lovely shade of auburn it has become, however. But I shall still call you by my own name, Sandy."

"You did not ask permission," she said by way

of reply, although she sensed Max would never seek liberty for such a thing. He had always seemed to run the world by his own rules.

"Where is the brand from last year's log, Alisandra?" Joan demanded, intruding upon the chat with a ruthlessness quite unlike her normal politeness and consideration.

"Is it in the usual place?" Max inquired.

At Alisandra's answering nod, he took himself off.

Joan watched him leave the room, then turned to her older sister. "Do you realize he has scarcely left your side since he drank that potion? I had no idea that it would work so well."

"Nor did I, not having done such a stupid thing before. I do believe we ought to remove that page from the herbal book, Joan," Alisandra said thoughtfully.

"He has not importuned you, has he?" Joan whispered with a hint of militancy in her voice, as though she were ready to do battle for her sister's honor.

Alisandra thought a bit, then shook her head. She truthfully could not complain about that stolen kiss in the herb garden any more than she could scold about the kiss on the cheek when he arrived. He was Max, not some monster. And that was what confused her. He ought not be interested in the brat who had tagged behind him everywhere he went while on his past visits. It had to be the potion.

He had dared her to climb trees, challenged her to ride the mare her father had presented her and which frightened her half to death. He had been her very own Max, far more special than her teasing brother, Thomas. Now, thanks to the potion, all was different. Or would he be the old Max once the potion wore off?

She turned to observe Sir William with regret for what might have been. He hovered over Charlotte, who looked especially pretty with pink cheeks and a lovely gown of the latest style in cream jaconet. He would know that modishness and appreciate it. Whereas Alisandra had nothing more than her antiquated garb in which to attract anyone. Her sigh drew Joan's attention.

"If a knight does not appear soon, I am in dire trouble," Alisandra said, sharing a knowing glance with Joan.

When they finished decorating, the house had assumed the festive air Alisandra loved so much. While the baronial splendor of the place always impressed her, it looked vastly more imposing with the tall tapers lit, the greens sparkling from every nook and across the great carved mantelpiece. She draped the last of the garlands along the stairs just as Max returned with the piece from last year's log, the brand, triumphantly in hand.

"Now may we light it?" he asked of the baron.

"Splendid," the baron said, accepting the brand from Max. "Joan, a little music if you please," he commanded nicely.

Sir William left Charlotte's side to stroll over to the hearth, but he watched Joan at the harp.

She settled on the bench by her harp, and soon the joyful sound of carols filled the room. The baron lit the brand, then with great ceremony advanced to the huge log, now decorated by Charlotte with a garland of holly and ivy, and placed the lit brand close to one side of the log.

Alisandra held her breath, waiting to see if the Yule log would take fire, thus assuring another year of good grace and blessings for the house and lands of the Percy family. It must burn all night to be effective.

Then the log flickered, and a smoky flame leapt upward, bringing a cheer from all assembled, for even the servants believed it important and had come to watch.

"Silly, is it not?" Alisandra said softly to Max, who had rejoined her. "I always feel so much better when the flames leap up and the fire takes hold."

"Will you continue that tradition when you marry and depart from here, I wonder?" .

"Marry?" she said, her breath suddenly leaving her again. "I have not given it a thought."

"There is a little time yet, I expect," he said, bestowing an enigmatic smile on her.

Joan continued to play the harp while the family visited in the hall. Even the yapping of Aunt Phoebe's nasty little spaniels could not dispel the air of cheer and festivity. The servants quickly went about their business when the dogs decided they were fair game and began to nip at various ankles exposed for their pleasure.

Across the room Sir William continued to watch the angelic Joan at the harp, a puzzled expression on his handsome face until an annoyed Charlotte demanded his attention again.

Dinner was as splendid as anyone might hope for on Christmas Eve. There was a fine crown roast of lamb and dozens of side dishes and removes. Mrs. Faraday and Cook had outdone all past efforts, it seemed. Several mince pies were presented for their pleasure, to Max's evident delight.

They all straggled from the table after dinner, Aunt Phoebe insistent upon the gentlemen joining the ladies on this one evening.

"What is to be the theme of the mumming, Joan, and why do you not allow the mummers from the village to perform for us, for I suspect there is a group of enthusiasts there," Charlotte demanded, not quite certain if the part of the damsel in distress was suitable to her talents.

Joan expanded on her impromptu story line.

"Do we need to practice?" Max inquired, leaning against the mantel while staring at the leaping flames below.

"I suppose it would not hurt," Joan said with a frown. "We would not wish to make people laugh if we fumble a great deal. Come, we can arrange ourselves beneath the minstrels gallery and the screen at the far end of the room. Those not on stage, as it were, can conceal themselves behind the screen until it is time to step forward."

Max turned to Alisandra and smiled. "One cannot help but wonder just how much that pierced screen is supposed to hide." He gestured to the elaborately carved wood that depicted a scene from sixteenth-century life.

"It will do," she said. "Bits of color ought not distract, and that is all that is seen from a distance."

"Since Sir William is paired with Charlotte and Joan directs all, it would seem that I am to rescue you, my fair damsel in distress. Are you?"

"Am I what?" she said, looking at him in bewilderment.

"In distress. Sometimes, like now, I sense that you are more than a trifle distraught about something."

"I am fine," she insisted, unwilling to admit anything.

"Good. We can have a go at this bit of pantomime before bed, then sleep with confidence we shan't disgrace ourselves on the morrow."

He strolled off to chat with Thomas, and Joan sidled up to Alisandra.

"He is still at it, I fear," she whispered.

"I know. There is naught I can do about it. Perhaps it will wear off?" Alisandra asked with hope.

The practice went extremely well, if one ignored Sir William's teasing aside about the difficulty of rescuing Charlotte when she was not quite as willowy as Alisandra. "What I need is someone as slight as Joan," he joked.

"Ah, but Sandy and Joan have those antique gowns to wear," Max countered. "While they are authentic, I suspect they constitute a fair amount of weight. Or will Charlotte be dressed in like style?" he added in an aside to Alisandra.

"She may well wear one of my costumes should she please," Alisandra said in a carrying voice.

"Wear one of your gowns?" Charlotte exclaimed.

"I vow you would look most charming in such array," Sir William offered. "The styles are elegant and rich."

Charlotte laughed daintily, then turned to Alisandra. "Perhaps I shall if you can find something that would fit me and go with my hair." She looked a trifle askance at Alisandra's dark auburn braids tucked under the net, then patted her own raven curls with a complacent touch. "It must be so dreadful to suffer from freckles," she said quietly to Alisandra. "Have you tried a blend of lemon juice and elder flower water mixed with glycerin? I have a recipe for the mixture somewhere. I shall copy it out for you. And do try honey and almond oil for your hands. It will help them to stay white and soft." Charlotte was justly proud of her own white and graceful hands.

Alisandra hid her hands in the deep folds of her sleeves, unwilling to bring them forth so Charlotte could see the scratches from the holly branches or the evidence that Alisandra performed tasks that were not kind to hands.

"I trust you are not filling Sandy's ears with a lot of nonsense about doing away with her freckles. I think them charming," Max inserted into what had been a private conversation until then.

"Men!" Charlotte scoffed. "What do you know about it?"

"I know what I like," Max said with a narrow look at Charlotte that had her backing away, then turning instead to Sir William with a comment on the Yule log.

"Max," Alisandra cautioned. "I will have this house a pleasant place with no contrary words, if you please."

"I only said that I know what I like," he replied with a disconcerting look into her eyes again.

Not about to question what that might be, for she feared the potion was affecting him strangely, Alisandra suggested they apply themselves to the mumming, then murmured to Max that she found it odd to be doing it on Christmas evening rather than Twelfth Night.

"Sir William must leave before then, you know," Max said.

"Indeed? I suspect Charlotte will go then, as well," Alisandra observed.

Max chuckled and guided Alisandra over to the screen against which the little drama was to enfold. Again they followed Joan's directions. Sir William balked at the notion the men were to wear suits of armor.

"I think it would be very hot," he declared.

"I think it would be very romantic," Joan countered. "Or are you two so delicate you cannot manage to wear what our ancestors did?"

At that challenge both Sir William and Max groaned, but agreed. Max managed to persuade

Joan they compromise with a partial suit of armor that would be easy to remove.

"There's nothing to it, old chaps," Thomas said with a grin. "I have worn armor any number of times. Just be thankful you are not required to ride a horse while wearing it, for it is dashed difficult. Need more than one pair of helping hands, I tell you."

"You must wear it as well, in that case," Max insisted.

Joan dismissed them all when the baron entered the room followed by Barford, who carried a huge silver tray holding an enormous bowl surrounded by wine bottles and a dish with nutmeg, ginger, and sugar plus a few other ingredients.

"Ah, the wassail bowl," Max murmured to Alisandra. "I believe you are old enough to have a sip this year, are you not?"

"Max, you must know I am nineteen," Alisandra said indignantly. "But Papa has always permitted us the tiniest cup—for tradition, you know." Then words slipped out that she'd not intended to say. "It has been all of two years since you were last here for Christmas." Was there a hint of wistfulness in those words? *Horrors,* she hoped not.

"You had to finish growing up." He grinned down at her and with a provocative tilt to his brows quietly added, "It's a grand age, nineteen—the marrying age."

His words were almost smothered by Thomas's debate with Papa over the correct amount of sugar to add to the mixture.

Alisandra ignored the good-natured argument that occurred every Christmas between Thomas and the baron and concentrated on what Max had said. Mercy! He truly had succumbed to the love potion if such notions could pop into his head. She gave him an anguished look, then turned to Joan as she joined Alisandra.

"I heard what he just said," Joan murmured. "Dear me."

The annual disagreement over the quantity of sugar being solved, to the baron's satisfaction, the ingredients were added, stirred with much ceremony, then portioned out into elegant silver cups chased with the Percy symbol of the peacock and lion.

"To your health, sir," Thomas said to his father with good will.

All toasted such an agreeable thought.

"To the continued good fortune of the Percy family," Sir William added.

When glasses had been raised to these toasts, Max said in a commanding but quiet voice, "To the lovely ladies who grace this house. May they find their heart's content and know great pleasure before another Christmas rolls around."

Charlotte darted a quick sidelong glance at Sir William, then smiled as demurely as a nun. However, Sir William's gaze roamed the room, pausing on Joan a few moments before continuing.

Alisandra blushed a delicate peach that blended nicely with her detested freckles.

Joan laughed and cried, "I will have to think long about that toast. Oh, what is my heart's content and what pleasure may I wish to come before next Christmas?"

"A trip to London, perhaps?" Max offered.

"A fashionable gown," Charlotte added with a defiant look at her uncle.

"Now, niece, it is Christmas. Do not provoke me," the baron said with a smile. Yet there was a hint of steel in his voice that all knew Charlotte dare not ignore.

Aunt Phoebe downed her cup of wassail, then turned to her brother. "No, you'd keep these poor gels here forever if you had your way. I dare you to send them to London for a Season." Her challenge was somewhat spoiled by a resounding hiccup.

"Another cup of the brew, dear Aunt?" Thomas said, holding the silver ladle aloft.

With an intrepid toss of her head, Aunt Phoebe declared, "Don't mind if I do."

"Phoebe . . ." the baron said hesitantly.

"Oh pooh, George, do not be a stuffy old goat." With that, Aunt Phoebe downed another cup of wassail and smiled at everyone, even Max. " 'Tis bad enough you incarcerate those girls far from Society. How do you expect them to make a suitable match, eh?"

Joan exchanged a worried look with Alisandra and drew her away from the others. "What do you suppose will happen to Max when he consumes more of that potent wassail on top of the love potion!"

"Heavens above, I cannot imagine." Alisandra gave Max a worried look and wished again that she had never mixed up that dratted love potion.

Before they might speculate further, the baron commanded attention and toasted the guests one by one. When he came to Max, he said, "To our dear Maximilian, known to us as Max and whom I love as a son, the very best of everything and may all his ambitions be attained."

"Amen," Max said fervently in reply, thus earning the general laughter of the group.

"Now, I shall play the pianoforte, and you children shall dance. Thomas, partner your little sister Joan, for how else will she learn the important things in life such as how to perform a country dance!" Aunt Phoebe declared. To everyone's amazement she marched over to the instrument and began to thump out an old country dance tune with more vigor than accuracy.

What a merry, silly time they had with a Scotch reel. Joan mixed up her steps and ended up crashing into Sir William, who fortunately chuckled at her error. When Charlotte danced lightly down the little line with him, she was the envy of both Joan and Alisandra.

Then Max clasped Alisandra's hand tightly in his, and it was their turn. They wove in and out of the line, then back to the top once again. She looked across to where he stood with not a hair out of place and as calm as could be. Alisandra felt quite out of breath and was certain her composure was in tatters. But, she fervently decided, it was great fun. She wondered what it would be like to attend the parties of the London *ton* and dance like this often. What a delight it must be, and most likely never to be hers.

They tried another, this time with Thomas patiently teaching Joan the steps and Charlotte and Sir William demonstrating the correct pattern of the dance. The baron requested Mrs. Faraday to join the group to be his partner, which she did with good nature. It was a lively romp, and by the time they finished, all were laughing merrily.

"Tell us a story, Papa," Joan said, dancing lightly over to where her father stood as strong and solid as the oaks he so loved.

"A Christmas tale, puss?" The baron looked at his youngest child with a gleam in his eyes. Then he glanced to where Aunt Phoebe now fed tidbits to her spaniels while seated close to the fireside.

"Very well, a tale of a Christmas ghost."

The old familiar custom of regaling the company

with stories of ghosts and strange happenings that occurred on Christmas in past years was strictly observed in the Percy home. It fell to the baron to invent this story, told near the hearth where the Yule log snapped and crackled.

The tall wax candles lent a warm glow to the room, adding to the mellowness of the paneling, the ancient tapestries on the wall, and the colorful garments worn by all. Above the mantel a painting of one of the earliest Percys looked down upon the scene with a benign smile. Greenery had been tucked about this portrait, lending a festive touch to the ancient gentleman. The suits of armor that graced the corners of the room also were whimsically decked in holly and ivy, sprigs of holly sprouting from the top of each helmet and garlands about the necks.

With expectant faces the family and friends gathered around the baron and arranged themselves to listen in comfort.

"Once long ago," the baron began. He wove a familiar tale of a pompous man who denied charity and was destroyed by his own greed.

"Well done, Papa," Alisandra said with a clap of her hands.

"Yes, you tell a tale very well," Max added. "Another toast!" he declared. "To the baron for his gracious hospitality. May he continue to be loved and respected by all!"

"Here, here," Sir William added.

Thomas clapped his father on his shoulder in a gesture of affection.

Aunt Phoebe finished off the last of her third cup of wassail and hiccuped into the silence of the room. She stared down into the empty cup, then said, "I must say, George, you do know how to mix an excellent brew even if you do not trust your daughters to venture from home."

"Mama, it is growing late. Church comes early in the morning," Charlotte said, flustered at this plain speaking.

"Will the dancers be on the green tomorrow?" Max asked of Joan, who had come to stand between him and Alisandra.

"Indeed," she promised, then gave a prodigious yawn.

"There will be no carousing in this house with the wassail, my boys," Aunt Phoebe declared, leaning on Charlotte's arm. All too often the wassail turned into a rather wild night, and the men found it difficult to attend the services come morning.

"Why, Aunt Phoebe, I had no idea you desired our company," Max said, and the older lady turned red in her face at his teasing when all knew how she baited him at every turn.

With a sniff Aunt Phoebe took Charlotte by the arm and left the great room, followed by Alisandra and Joan, each picking up bed candles before ascending the garlanded stairway.

"Those men will doubtless spend hours by the fireside, telling tales and swapping outrageous stories," Aunt Phoebe said in a voice only slightly slurred.

"It is Christmas Eve, Mama," Charlotte said more gently than usual.

Joan and Alisandra bid their relatives good night, then whisked into Alisandra's room for a hasty conference.

"Dear Aunt Phoebe. She means well. I wonder if Charlotte decided she had better be a trifle kinder to others after hearing Papa's tale?" Joan said.

"Bother Charlotte," Alisandra said with a wave

of her hand. "What are we going to do about Max?"

"What *can* we do?" Joan countered. "I know of nothing that will cancel a potion once it is taken."

"Oh, peacock feathers," Alisandra muttered in disgust. "So be it. I will only hope to avoid him come the morrow. The potion ought to wear off before long, should it not?" she said with some optimism.

"Oh, I should think so!" Joan declared before slipping off down the hall to her room.

Come morning they found a fresh dusting of snow on the ground. A peacock sat on the lower step to the main door and screeched, fanning its tail in a magnificent display.

"Mercy, what a racket," Charlotte declared as she entered the breakfast room. She elected to sit near the tall windows of leaded glass where the winter sun beamed in with faint warmth.

"Papa insists the birds must remain here as long as the Percy family exists," Alisandra said, helping herself to more toast. In her long gown of ginger kerseymere trimmed with bands of soft fur she truly looked elegant in spite of being a few hundred years behind current fashion.

"No time to dawdle. Aunt Phoebe insists we are to be off for church within the hour," Max declared when he entered minutes later.

Alisandra examined him to see if he retained any signs of the potion still affecting him. She had about decided that the herbal mixture must have worn off when he crossed the room to stand by her side.

"Good morning, my dear. Happy Christmas. I trust you slept well? No ghosts came to haunt you in the night?" He gazed down at her with the peculiar look that set her pulses racing and made her wonder if there was something wrong with her.

"Happy Christmas," she said while trying to calm her fluttering pulse. Then she replied to his query, "Of course no ghosts came to haunt me, for there really aren't such things, are there?" Alisandra gave him a frowning look, then glanced to where Joan watched them.

"One never knows when a spirit, good or evil, chooses to roam the earth," he answered in an obscure way.

"Well, I do not intend to explore the matter," she said, concluding the topic as far as she was concerned.

"Happy Christmas. Is everyone up and alert?" Aunt Phoebe said upon entering the room, searching to see if her brother was present.

"Papa went out to see about the carriages we will require and to wish all a happy Christmas," Joan said after sipping the last of her hot chocolate.

"Thank heavens George does not serve ale for breakfast," Phoebe said. She selected a light meal, then sat down to eat just as though she did this sort of thing every day in the year. She looked rather muzzy, as though her head might bother her a trifle.

"Up already, Aunt Phoebe?" Thomas exclaimed as he came in from the stables where he had been assisting his father.

"I would never miss divine service, and you know it, my boy," the good lady declared, then bent to feed her spaniels.

Thomas watched her, exchanging thankful glances with his sisters for being spared an assault on his person by the nasty little dogs.

The group entering the holly-decorated carriages was a gay one.

Alisandra tried to avoid sitting near Max with

absolutely no success. He handed her up into the carriage, then, ignoring the baron's dictates that carriages were only for women, joined her. He placed a warm rug across her lap, extending it to cover himself. It was a very cozy arrangement, and Alisandra thought it bordered upon scandalous.

"Max," she began, then stopped. What could she say that would not give him a disgust of her? Max had been a part of her life for so long she couldn't bear for him to detest her, and he surely would if he learned of the potion. What a dreadful dilemma!

They drove along in silence, appreciating the beautiful scenery, bushes decorated and frosted with glittering white, the deer in the forest peeking shyly at the carriages and men on horseback as they clattered past. Pale sunlight sparkled on the crystals of snow.

Then Joan began a pretty carol. "Christians awake, salute the happy morn . . ." she sang, with the others quickly joining in. Sir William rode close to the carriage, adding his splendid baritone to the group.

When they entered the village, the residents were lined up to greet them, smiles and cheers abounding for the Percy family.

The baron handed his horse over to a groom, then shook hands with all those near him before entering the ancient stone church.

Ladies dressed much as Joan and Alisandra followed, smiling and nodding their joy in the day to one and all. The words "Happy Christmas" echoed through the church.

"I would not have believed such a sight had I not seen it. It is like a page from history. They even dress as the baron. Does he command it?" Sir William softly inquired of Max, but loud enough for Alisandra to overhear.

"Never," Max replied, then went on, "they respect him and although it seems a trifle odd to us, wish to dress in the old way to please a man who has been kind and good to them over the years."

"I expect it makes the men happy, for their wives do not beg to follow fashion," Sir William concluded.

"Oh, there were fashions then as well. Note the border of fur on Alisandra's gown, the trim on the hood of her cloak. And Joan is dressed elegantly as well, if you notice. She appears older than her nearly eighteen years."

The musicians—on a harpsichord, flute, and violin—began a Christmas anthem, and the choir joined in, effectively quelling any whispering for the duration of the beautiful festival service of the season. Parson Fyfield preached a fine sermon, and by the time they left the little stone church, a spirit of Christmas cheer permeated the group.

When they reached the village green, they found a splendid sight—a band of country lads wearing no coats in spite of the cold and their shirtsleeves fancifully tied with ribbons. Each wore hats decorated with greenery and carried wooden clubs in their hands. With much clicking and knocking of the wood clubs they went through a series of steps, advancing and retreating, whirling and stamping. In the background wandering musicians with pipes and tambors strolled about playing ancient tunes to which the men performed their strange dance.

For Alisandra and Joan it was a familiar sight. Nor did Charlotte turn up her nose at the dancing, which had to be as old as the village itself. Aunt Phoebe smiled wistfully and spoke quietly with her brother.

"Amazing chaps," Sir William murmured to Max.

"Indeed," Max replied thoughtfully, then made

his way through the throng of people until he reached Alisandra's side. "I see you enjoy the ancient dance. I wonder when it first began?"

"As to that, I could not say," she said, trying to evade that disturbing gaze of his. "I know the dance has been performed before the church on every Christmas that I can recall."

"Is it not done on May Day as well?"

She grew uneasy at his reference to May Day, that day when an unmarried girl tried to find out who her future husband might be. The topic was a little too close to love potions, and that she wanted to avoid at all costs.

"May Day is celebrated here in fine tradition," Joan said, rescuing Alisandra from her dilemma. "We always have a Maypole and a Queen of the May as well."

"I will have to visit you on May Day. I should like to see Sandy, a wreath of hawthorn and daisies in her hair, dancing about the pole with her ribbon in hand. It is a time for lovers, you know," Max said with a sage nod.

"Ah, I believe Papa wishes to head for home," Alisandra cried, eager to change the subject from that of lovers of any sort.

At this point one of Aunt Phoebe's little dogs ran up to bark at Alisandra, unable to find her ankles beneath the volume of fabric that made up her skirt and cloak. Max frustrated the little beast as well, having worn highly polished boots, as did the baron.

Alisandra merely scooped up the pup and marched over to the carriage to hand it to Aunt Phoebe.

In short order the women were back in their carriages and the gentlemen on their mounts, except for Max. Once again he joined Alisandra in the carriage, sharing the warm wool rug with her and causing her no end of confusion.

"Are you prepared for this evening? I trust we will have a little dancing first."

Quite forgetting that she was supposed to help Alisandra instead of Max, Joan giggled, then said, "Of course we shall if you wish. I have no doubt Aunt Phoebe will play again, and there will be pipes and a clarinet. We are very merry, if you recall from the last Christmas you spent with us," she concluded, then gave Alisandra an apologetic look when Joan remembered that she was supposed to discourage Max, not the other way around.

"That will be interesting. I trust your father has not invented some ancient dance you now perform?"

"No," Alisandra said, too worried to parry words with him or tease as she might have two years before. This was becoming a serious matter. Max was *not* losing interest in her. Why, he was positively doting! Not that she didn't find it somewhat enchanting to have a man looking at her as men usually gazed at Charlotte. But it was awkward to have poor Max thinking he loved her when he couldn't, although awkward was not quite the proper word. Dreadful. Disastrous. And rather nice as well, she confessed.

The afternoon was spent in preparation for the coming evening when a number of the local people were to join the party for Christmas dinner. In addition to the parson, the local squire and his good wife, and a goodly number of the gentry were expected. Joan teased Thomas about one of them, the Hardcastle eldest, Mary.

"Last I saw her, she had spots and baby fat," he said with barely disguised repugnance.

"Just you wait," Alisandra teased.

Joan exchanged looks with Alisandra and giggled, dancing off to arrange games for the children.

It seemed that the entire household was infected with the merriment of the season. Housemaids hummed as they went about their duties, and in the courtyard the milkmaid and a groom performed an impromptu jig.

Once the family and guests were served, the servants would have their own Christmas belowstairs. It was an occasion looked forward to for the entire year, relished for months to follow. The baron was a generous and good master, and a servant rarely left the house of his own choosing.

The baron inquired as to the games planned for the evening festivities, then said to Sir William, "It is deplorable to see how the old games and amusements have gone by the wayside. Ever since I was a lad, things have changed a great deal." They strolled into the Great Hall toward the fireplace, then paused, the baron studying the younger man.

"Indeed, sir," Sir William said. "Yet your daughters must live in today's world, seek a future for themselves."

"As Phoebe says, I have become mired in the past." The baron sighed, then added, "I mean to send them south. Joan needs a warmer climate and friends, for I suspect Alisandra may leave us before long. I care deeply about them both."

"That is evident, sir. I believe Miss Joan will find Society welcoming. Certainly I will do all I may to assist her in London. Do you think she might like living in Kent?"

The baron raised his brows at the casual question, then nodded. "Indeed, I believe that would do her nicely."

Sir William smiled, then left the baron when called away. Charlotte had come down to show off the gown lent her by Alisandra. Midnight blue and edged with ermine, it gave her a regal appearance her other clothes lacked.

"I vow I may beg to keep this," she said, whirling about for approval.

"Somehow I cannot see you at Almack's wearing that gown, and they will be the losers," Sir William said in a polite way that made Charlotte blush. He offered her a hand to twirl her about in a make-believe minuet step, and she actually giggled, something rare for a girl with her London polish. She batted her lashes at him quite shamelessly.

Joan dashed down the stairs in a flurry of skirts, careening into Sir William as he retreated in the pattern of the dance. She gazed up at him with dismay, clutching at him for balance. "You are the merest feather," he reassured her with a smile, then turned to an impatient Charlotte.

"Games, Papa," Joan cried when she had collected herself. "Who will handle the games for the children this year? I have done it years past, but if I take charge of the Christmas mummery ... well ... I cannot be two places at once."

"The parson should be the one, for he knows all the old games. I shall consult with him immediately." The baron strode out of the house in the direction of the stables, no doubt to ride to the village and his good friend, the parson.

Joan watched Charlotte and Sir William stroll off in the direction of the picture gallery and sighed. Then she whirled about and whisked herself in the direction of the housekeeper's room. Mrs. Faraday could always be counted to enter into the spirit of the holidays and assist with any special doings that Joan planned for the company.

The house fairly hummed with activity. Joan supervised the costumes for the mummery and, after a few helpful words from Mrs. Faraday to determine which sizes appeared to be best, ordered three partial suits of armor to be polished.

When one suit of armor that usually stood in the corner of the entry hall was carted away by two stalwart footmen to be polished up for the evening's entertainment, Max shook his head in dismay.

"I do not see how a fellow is to survive wearing one of those contraptions while indoors," he complained to Alisandra. "Why, I could not hold your hand in a dance, could I?" He gave her such a warm glance that she felt a thousand butterflies take wing inside her.

"You do *not* dance while wearing armor. It is for performing noble deeds," she reproved, but had to laugh at his doleful face.

"I do not see how a chap even moves while in those metal suits—even the partial ones. I think our Joan has taken leave of her senses. Far better to stick with the old Christmas Mummery of Maid Marian and Robin Hood and all the other characters. If I chanced to be Robin, would you be my Maid Marian, Sandy?" His look was quizzical, but appeared to hold a deeper mystery that pierced her composure.

Once again flustered by his look, she evaded his gaze and turned to stare out the window of the Great Hall where he had somehow managed to guide her when she wasn't paying attention. It said a great deal for his ability to confuse her senses that he could lead her about like this, and she did not know where she was nor what she did.

"Maid Marian is not my favorite character for she defied authority to wed an outlaw," Alisandra finally said when she realized she'd remained silent too long.

"Would you never defy authority to wed where

you loved? Somehow I cannot see your father forbidding you to follow your heart, even if he keeps you from London." Max leaned against the casing of the tall bay window, pale sunlight caressing his hair, lending a glint of gold to it.

"He means well," she replied, distracted when he drew her closer than strict propriety allowed. "Joan says my best hope is for a knight in shining armor to rescue me and carry me off." She was utterly horrified when she realized what she had said. The words had slipped from her mouth, and she blamed the lapse on the feeling of their old camaraderie that had crept up on her.

If Max found her words to be shocking, he gave no indication of it. He simply laughed. "Joan has a delightful imagination. Think of the job some poor chap will have to capture her heart. Doubtless, he will have to leap a drawbridge or swim a moat, then scale a wall just to reach her side."

"Papa filled in our moat, and the drawbridge is always let down nowadays," Alisandra said, a twinkle finding its way back into her eyes. This was her Max of old, teasing about absurd things, not so serious in his flirting.

The servants bustled about the room, whisking enormously long, snowy white linen tablecloths over the wide oak table, then placing beautifully wrought silver candelabrum here and there down its length. Epergnes with dishes holding shiny red apples, bright holly leaves tucked in for contrast, joined the candle holders followed by the special dishes and silver used at Christmas dinner.

Sheltered in the tall window bay, Max and Alisandra could not be seen by most of the servants and were ignored by the prudent remainder.

"Max," she said uneasily, shifting from foot to foot and quite ignoring the gentle clink of cutlery being placed on the table. "I have a million things to do." Yet she did not move and worse yet, did not wonder why she remained at his side.

He studied her a few moments, then reached up to pull the little cap and the net from her head.

Alisandra grabbed for the head covering she had assumed when she reached the age considered adult by her father. While it was out of fashion, she had grown accustomed to its concealing protection and now felt quite naked without it. Her long hair tumbled over her shoulders and down her back, a silken auburn curtain that the winter sun blessed with a golden sheen.

"Why did you do that?" she asked, totally puzzled at this once-again alien Max.

"I remembered the braids you wore as a little girl, and I wondered if you had cut that glorious hair. 'Tis impossible to tell anything about it with that dratted cap on your head. Yet I suppose your father has the right of it. Were any other man to see you in that lovely ginger gown with the beautiful hair about you, he might lose his head and do any number of strange things."

Intrigued—in spite of the impropriety of his action and words—Alisandra remained where she stood, first eyeing the net and cap in his hand, then turning her gaze to Max's face, which gave not the least clue to what was in his mind.

"What do you mean . . . strange things?" She had to know for she was captivated by the notion that any man would be compelled to act boldly at the sight of her hair. Her hair seemed rather ordinary to her, in front of the looking glass.

"Like this." He bent forward and placed a light kiss on her surprised lips. When he withdrew to lean against the window, he tilted his head to study her. His face was somewhat shadowed, whereas she feared hers captured what sunlight there was to reveal all her emotions.

"But you would never do such a treacherous thing, would you," she said in a voice that was a trifle shaken, much to her dismay.

"I might . . ." He paused, then reached out the hand that was free to stroke her hair in a light, gentle touch. He threaded his fingers through the lovely mass, then let the strands cascade to her shoulders in a fall of auburn silk. "Well, I cannot speculate what I might do, for I would never frighten you, would I?" A lazy grin crept across his face, intriguing her more than words possibly could.

"This is highly improper," she said, taking a step away from this fascinating side of dear old Max.

"Have you never longed to be improper since you grew up, Sandy? Do you not miss those days of the past when we tumbled into one disaster after another?" That lazy and highly appealing grin widened into something more familiar, and Alisandra relaxed just a bit.

"Well, I suppose I do, for we did share a number of infamous escapades." She could not recall when she had felt so tense, not even after the moment when Max had snatched the glass holding the love potion from her hands.

"Oh, certainly not infamous. I recall teaching you to swim, and that was surely a noble deed. Was it not, Sandy?" Again he curved his mouth into that handsome and peculiarly intimate grin. His eyes danced with memories that brought a rosy tint to her cheeks.

"Noble deed?" she whispered. She swallowed with more difficulty than normal and hunted for an answer that was oddly difficult to find. She recalled more of the episode, how she had been so conscious of his warm hands about her waist, his gentle commands murmured in her ears, and his firm reassurance that he would never allow her to be hurt or injured again. Suddenly, the depths of his eyes became pools in which she might drown, only he had promised to care for her always and she wondered what that involved now.

"Alisandra, come help me at once," Joan commanded in a sisterly way from the doorway. "I cannot make head nor tail of these costumes."

Grateful for the escape, yet sorry to leave the alluring and quite different Max, Alisandra turned to go.

"I'll bide my time, but I will have my turn," Max said so softly that she wondered if she had heard aright.

"Alisandra," Joan scolded gently, "are you forgetting that poor Max took a love potion that was not intended for him? Why, he behaves like a lover," Joan whispered while she tugged her elder sister along with her to the room where the costumes selected for the mummery were all laid out for inspection.

Something crashed within Alisandra when reality hit her. Max was not truly himself at the moment. He could not possibly feel all those remarkable things for her. His behavior indicated that the heretofore untried recipe in the old family herbal had worked—even when she had doubted it might. Before long Max would depart, the spell gone.

"Of course," she said quietly. "I know that. I just do not know how to deal with this different Max, that is all." She picked up the tall, pointed hennin with a fine gauze veil that Joan had unearthed from the attic and placed it on her head after sweeping her long and unbound hair to the back. A glance at the distant looking glass told her that while the headpiece was dented and a bit tattered, it also was vastly becoming.

"What happened to your cap and hair net?" Joan cried, finally noticing that her sister's hair had come undone.

"It came off," Alisandra said, unwilling to share that moment with Joan. "I expect I will have to completely hide my hair if I wear this. Do you suppose the sight of a woman's hair was considered improper? Or was it merely unfashionable?" she inquired absently while she strolled to better see how she appeared reflected in the tall looking glass at the far end of the room.

"How strangely you are behaving," Joan said with a frown crossing her pretty face. "Come, if you think these costumes will do, we had best change for dinner. The guests could arrive any moment now."

Obediently following her sister from the room, Alisandra glanced back at the tall headdress before leaving the room, wondering how the women of that day felt about removing it for someone special. That she unconsciously lumped Max in with that category failed to register.

By the time both girls had changed into soft velvet gowns edged with fine sable and had gold necklaces set with exquisite jewels about their necks, the sounds of arrivals could be heard along the avenue to the manor house.

Joan wore a glowing russet gown, while Alisandra had selected one of deep, rich gray. Banded with the sable and with the gold of her necklace glinting against it, the gown gave her quiet satisfaction. She would possibly hold her own against the more vivid Charlotte dressed in the deep blue trimmed in ermine.

Hurrying down to the entry hall, they both

greeted the guests with genuine enthusiasm. First the parson came, her father's good friend who held a real interest in the old customs.

Parson Fyfield beamed his approval on the newcomers, unknowingly assisting Alisandra, who had found the sight of Max in ancient garb most unsettling. He looked far too romantic.

"Your father has graciously requested my expertise in the children's games," the plump, balding parson said.

"Thank you, for Joan has set herself the task of guiding us through the mummery, using a different theme this year," Alisandra said. She ushered him over to where a table had been placed by one of the two fireplaces in the entry hall. The splendid Christmas tapers stood here, blazing with light. A glittering array of silver and gold beakers and ewers held wine and ale for the guests. Here he could sip mulled wine and enjoy visiting with those who came for dinner and the evening's festivities.

Thomas joined the girls by his father. Joan giggled and exchanged a knowing look with Alisandra when Mary Hardcastle arrived with her parents. The spotty, plump child had been replaced by a graceful and very pretty young lady who used her remarkable dark eyes to full advantage when she met old neighbor Thomas. Garbed in forest green velvet edged in gold lace, Mary swept Thomas along with her to visit with Parson Fyfield.

The baron bestowed a tolerant smile on his son, then turned to greet the next arrivals. Before long thirty-four people of various ages congregated in the vast hall, mingling their perfumes with the scents of the spices and greenery.

Mrs. Hardcastle accepted the baron's arm into dinner while Alisandra found Max at her side. Thomas abandoned any notion of escorting Joan and positively fawned over Mary Hardcastle to Joan's delight. Sir William turned to Joan, murmuring something about escorting a charming daughter of the house. His smile at Joan was not missed by others. Charlotte, quickly concealing her ire, managed to enlist the arm of a young man who visited the Hardcastle family.

A blazing fire crackled in the hearth, warming the room now buzzing with conversation. Greenery had been added to every conceivable place from the suits of armor to swords that were arrayed on one of the walls.

When all had been seated, the parson said grace, a long, courtly one full of allusions to the past and asking God's blessing on the assembled guests for the coming year.

After this there was a pause, as though something was expected. A pipe sounded in the hall. Joan slipped away from her place to join with her harp. The newcomers gazed about in confusion.

The butler entered the room, bearing an enormous tray attended by a footman on either side. On the tray reposed a huge boar's head decorated with sprigs of rosemary and an apple in its mouth. The parson burst into some sort of Latin verse Alisandra doubted anyone understood, save those who had attended Oxford or Cambridge. The tray was placed with great ceremony at the head of the table where the baron beamed on it with great approval.

This parade was followed by a succession of dishes, each one more enticing than the previous. A magnificent turkey vied with a sirloin of beef for favorite of the table, while roasted onions and other more mundane foods filled in any niches that might occur. In the center of the table a pie elaborately dressed with peacock feathers held pride of place. While the baron found it difficult to part with even one of his peacocks, sensible management indicated a thinning out of the ranks, hence the Christmas peacock pie.

"I shall eat those creatures with relish," Charlotte declared. "They have bothered me no end."

Aunt Phoebe was teased by the distant relative who always tried to see if he could overset her, which he did rather well. She grew flustered and pink-cheeked.

Although Max had ushered Alisandra to the table, he sat opposite her, as was the custom in this house. Now she wished there was another practice, for whenever she raised her eyes, she found his gaze upon her. It was even more unsettling than the sight of Max in courtly dress. She hadn't expected him to look so romantic.

Once the cloth was removed, the arrival of the enormous plum pudding set aflame by Barford was a highlight of the meal. Having been steamed some three months before and allowed to mature all this time, it was to be enjoyed and totally consumed in a matter of minutes. The mince pies brought a smile of satisfaction to Max's face that amused Alisandra. It was most evident which part of the dinner found favor with him. She'd not have been surprised to find out that Mrs. Faraday had baked a few extra pies, knowing Max was here.

Following that, Barford, with great pomp and ceremony, brought the wassail bowl to set before the baron. Since only a very few of the company had been there the previous evening, the ceremony was replayed, enacted with all the drama one might wish.

The contents prepared and mixed by the baron himself—this time without Thomas's teasing interference—were given a final stir. Then Baron Percy raised a large silver goblet chased with a fanciful design and filled to the brim with the potent brew and toasted all assembled. "Happy Christmas and a prosperous New Year," he declared in a ringing voice.

This time instead of individual glasses the massive cup was sent around the table, each person partaking as it reached him or her. Much good humor came forth as the cup circulated about the table. Men tended to grasp it with both hands and drink rather deeply. The ladies were more inclined to daintily sip, barely touching the rim with their lips amid teasing and chuckles from the gentlemen.

When Alisandra held the cup in hand, she glanced across to catch Max's gaze. She sipped from the goblet, then remembered his odd words about taking these customs with her when she married. Another unsettling comment from Max to mull over again and again.

"Parson Fyfield has consented to be our Lord of Misrule this year," the baron said. "It will be his pleasure to take all the children off with him to conduct the old games. "And," the baron added with a twinkle in his eyes, "there is no age limit for the children. A child of any age is welcome to join in the fun."

Amid general laughter, the ladies left the table and strolled in the direction of the drawing room. The children begged to take leave and scampered after the genial and much-loved parson as though he were a pied piper.

That left the men at leisure, scattered along the vast table in quiet and genial conversation.

For a moment or two Max surveyed the length and breadth of the oak surface, then watched Alisandra whisk around the corner, the last of the women to leave the Great Room.

"We shall leave the ladies to take their tea and

allow our meal to settle in peace," the baron said with a smile to the gentlemen who certainly appeared of like mind.

What followed was more than the animated, somewhat warm conversation usually found at after-dinner. There was a hint of the historical, most likely from the atmosphere of the room. After a bit the subject matter became that which would not be suitable for delicate ears, yet amusing to the gentlemen when the baron launched on a particularly funny tale. Max enjoyed the company, but he was restless, barely remaining still.

Along to the rear of the manor house laughter ruled, with the parson in charge. Children played at blindman's buff, scampering about the room with abandon that would horrify their fond parents. Between giggles and shrieks the noise was anything but saintly. It didn't appear to annoy the jolly parson in the least.

At the same time across the vast entry hall Alisandra tended to the tea table in the drawing room. Since her harp remained in the Great Room, Joan assisted her sister with the pouring of tea and coffee and passing of tiny cakes for those who had a corner remaining after the Christmas feast.

"It goes well this year, I believe," Alisandra commented to Joan when they relaxed while the others sedately chatted and sipped their beverages.

"Neither one of Aunt Phoebe's dogs has bitten a single person," Joan said with obvious relief.

As though they had heard her thanks, Folly and Prudence trotted over to sit before Joan, grinning at her with what seemed like an implied threat. She offered them each a little cake. This they consumed in one gulp before trotting off to plead with Aunt Phoebe.

"I vow I shall carry little cakes with me from

now on," Joan declared, softly so as not to offend Aunt Phoebe, "if it means I can pacify those little beasts."

Alisandra swallowed her tea with difficulty, trying not to laugh, then eased back on her chair. It was much easier in here without the presence of Max to disturb her. Occasionally she could catch a wisp of male laughter from the Great Hall and the eruption of merriment from where the parson ruled the children with a kind and jolly hand. The drawing room provided a haven for her.

Joan glanced across at the clock, then turned to give Alisandra a worried look. "It is time, you know. And you had best face being rescued by Max."

Alisandra rose from her chair by the tea table to excuse them. "It is time that those of us in the mummery must prepare for the event."

A general buzz of conversation arose when the girls left the room. It could be noted that Mary Hardcastle looked as though she would dearly love to join them.

With Joan at her side Alisandra walked over to pass instructions along to Barford that it was time for Max, Thomas, and Sir William to leave the group of gentlemen who were no doubt becoming more jolly by the minute.

" 'Tis as well we pull Thomas and the others away from Papa. This is the one day of the year when he seems inclined to indulge." Joan entered the room where the costumes were spread about and put her headdress on, adjusting the scarf carefully. Although Thomas was to more or less partner her, Joan declared, "I want to look my best. One never knows who will take note of my progress in growing up and decide that I am worth a second glance. I do say that I look rather more hardy this evening than normal, agreed? Sir William commented on my pluck while going in to dinner. He even hinted I might do well in Society!"

"Of course, love," Alisandra murmured, having her hands quite full of hair and the hennin. Neither wished to cooperate. Actually, Joan looked more angelic than was the norm, yet Alisandra had no wish to puncture her bubble of illusion, for if Joan felt more hardy, perhaps it would become reality.

"You had best let me help you," Joan urged, "else you will still be at sixes and sevens when the gentlemen join us."

With Charlotte complaining that her head covering was not half as pretty as the hennin worn by Alisandra, and the maid rushing to and fro to cater to Charlotte's whims, Alisandra was thankful when the door opened to admit Thomas followed by Sir William and Max.

"I say, this looks like a tapestry from the gallery walls," Sir William said, coming to a halt some distance into the room, although he first directed his gaze at Joan.

Charlotte ceased her fussing, turning as sweet as honey at his words when he glanced her way.

Max strolled across the room to confront Alisandra. "Your father informed me that the old custom for women to cover their hair denoted a spinster or the married state. It seems long hair marked virginity and a prospective bride. You are much too pretty for such a fate as spinsterhood. I believe you ought to stop wearing that cap." His grin took away any sting that might have been in the words.

She took refuge in adjusting the veil on her headpiece while searching for a light reply to his comment. Yet she admitted that a week ago she would have chuckled and tossed back some blithe denial. Curiously enough, it seemed she had changed. And she also admitted that the sight of Max in the skin-tight hose with his jerkin snugly fitted, and the long, slim doublet of that period scarcely concealing a firm body stirred something within her.

Before she had found a reply, the door opened and several footmen entered bearing the three partial suits of armor. Sir William groaned, and Thomas looked as though he was quite prepared to flee.

"Resigned to your lot, Max?" Alisandra said, pleased to forget the topic of unmarried ladies and virginal hair styles.

"Indeed. Comes a time in every man's life when he must face the facts and prepare to accept his lot in life." Max picked up the first of his armor pieces, but not before offering her a searching look.

"That sounds rather deep for a simple mummery," she replied. Then she retreated while the men were helped into the armor a piece at a time. The doublets were removed and she could see why the hose had been worn back then, for they were undoubtedly more comfortable for the wearer.

Joan, free to flit about and offer advice without having to do a great deal, was in her element. She laughed merrily and in general entered into the spirit of the mummery more than those who were to partake in the offering.

Sir William smiled at her. "Joan is like a golden sprite, a sunbeam to brighten our lives."

Fortunately, Charlotte did not hear him.

"I feel dashed silly in this getup," Thomas complained.

"Cheer up; I have it on good authority that Mary Hardcastle thinks knights must be the most romantic beings ever to roam the earth. And she must have the right of it, for you all look very handsome," Joan said while she scurried about the room inspecting, offering helpful thoughts, and in general poking into everything and doing very little, often darting glances at Sir William.

"Not to mention polished," Max said wryly as he caught sight of himself in the looking glass.

Before long all was in readiness. While the man put finishing touches to their armor, the ladies withdrew to a window seat to go over what they were to do.

Alisandra crossed the room to face Max with the knowledge that before long he should come to his senses and be the old Max of yore. And she realized she'd miss the present Max dreadfully. The worst possible thing had happened. She had fallen in love with Max, and there was no way on earth that he might ever look at her again after tonight, particularly if he found out that he had been under the influence of a love potion from that first evening. She could feel a blush heating her cheeks at the mere thought of the blistering words he'd deliver once he knew the truth.

Or would he ever know? she wondered. Joan would never tell, and she was the only other person who knew a thing about it. Feeling a trifle more composed, Alisandra walked along the hall to the Great Room with improved calm.

The armor had not only been polished but oiled as well, yet the men still made a dreadful racket as they clanked along beside the ladies.

"Seems to me a chap could have frightened a fellow to death in one of these outfits," Sir William commented to Charlotte.

"You seem most handsome, sir," she said, then spoiled her pose with another girlish giggle. Her short curls were covered by a brief heart-shaped headdress that proved most becoming to her face. The kind of hair net she had deplored on Alisandra and Joan draped over her own hair met with no complaint after she saw the effect it gave.

Joan slipped in ahead of them to alert the other musicians. When the group entered the Great Room, they found all in readiness for them. Her harp joined with the pipes and the clarinet to produce a type of music ancient and appropriate. The performers sat a little apart from the old carved wood screen and enhanced the little drama Joan had devised.

To provide a sense of reality to the scene, Charlotte and Alisandra agreed they would perform their part while on the upper minstrels' gallery—seen by all, yet remote. This way Sir William and Max had the advantage of realism when it came time to search for their respective damsels.

Thomas defended his "castle" with vigor, bashing and clanging at his opponents in a way that had Mary Hardcastle nearly swooning. There was much in the way of sword play, and in spite of the clumsy armor far better suited for horseback than hand-to-hand or sword-to-sword combat, the men acquitted themselves well.

Sir William worked his way past Thomas and in short order claimed Charlotte, bearing her off along the hall and out of sight.

Alisandra remained, watching the fight with great curiosity. Why did Max press her brother so? And what on earth was he doing, anyway? Then Thomas fell with a resounding crash, causing Aunt Phoebe and the baron to wince at the thought of the old armor being dented. Max crossed the room in great strides, pausing before the baron to offer the plume that had been on Thomas's helmet. Max bowed to the baron and murmured a few words that no one else could hear, least of all Alisandra.

The music was all that could be heard as Max

climbed the stairs to where Alisandra waited with bated breath. Below, Sir William joined Joan where she sat by her harp.

"You vanquished Thomas just as St. George did the dragon," she whispered when he reached her side. "Why did you alter the mummery?"

Max merely raised his sword in a salute before placing it on a handy table, then picked up Alisandra and marched off with her to the rousing cheers of the assembled group—led by the baron. The hum of merriment followed them.

They were alone in the vaulted hallway. No servants waited to assist Max.

Alisandra gave Max a guarded look, then said, "You may put me down now. We are no longer playing a part."

"True." Max set her down, then removed his helmet and the awkward gloves that had cut into Alisandra when he carried her. "Help me off with the rest of this, will you? It does not contribute in the least to my plan."

She did her best, thinking this was a job for a footman, not a girl and said so. "The footmen ought to have remained."

"No privacy with them flitting about."

"And you want that?" she whispered.

"I want you to know that I am not playing a part when I declare that I love you and wish to marry you," Max said when he had dropped the last piece of armor to the floor. He drew Alisandra into his arms and proceeded to give her another one of those kisses that sent tremors through her.

"But you cannot," she wailed when released. "Oh, Max, this is dreadful! You do not really love me; you only fancy you do, for you swallowed a love potion that was intended for Sir William. Do you see? What you feel is not real. All the devoted looks and romantic sighs have not been true. You only imagine any feeling of love for me."

"Oh, no, my love. I have been waiting for years for you to grow up. That love potion—if indeed it might be effective—was not necessary for me. I'd been in love with you forever. I forced myself to wait, until I saw Sir William and feared he might claim you before I could act. I must say I was relieved when he turned his interest to Joan. With a home in Kent he will be just right for her." Before Alisandra could comment on this turn of events, Max went on, "I stayed away so you might miss me a little. Did it work?"

"Indeed it did. And"—she paused to recall what her sister had said—"you became my Christmas knight to make my dreams come true. Oh, Max, I do love you. I think I always have."

"I knew it," he declared with obvious satisfaction, then set about claiming his little love.

It Came upon a Midnight Clear

❦

Sheila Walsh

The moon sailed high in a black, velvet sky pricked out with many stars. And brightest of all was the Christmas star.

As the coach sped through the sleeping countryside and turned in at the gates of Neasholme Priory, country seat of the Sheringhams since Elizabethan times, the star seemed to hover overhead with a special brilliance, its rays picking out the crumbling cloisters and the spires of the main building. The coach rounded the last curve in the drive and swept on to the forecourt, the powerful horses drawing to a halt with a toss of manes before the great oak doors.

From within the cloisters, where the shadows were deepest, came the breath of a sigh. It had been a long interminable vigil, but this time she knew that the star was with her. This time Nemesis would be hers, and at last she would be able to rest.

There was the usual bustle as doors opened and the steps of the carriage were let down. *He* came first—tall, arrogant, the collar of his greatcoat and the brim of his tall hat shielding his face. But she knew him, knew that the light of conquest would

be in his eyes as he extended a hand to assist the
woman down.

How young she looked—and apprehensive. But
very beautiful. There had been others before her—
flamboyant beauties—but they had no aura of per-
manence. This one was different. This was the one
she had been waiting for.

Once more a sigh escaped her. The cold breath
of it drifted out across the still air of the courtyard,
and she saw the young woman look round, puzzled,
and lift a hand to rub the back of her neck, before
drawing the hood of her cloak closer.

From the comfortable interior of his companion's
traveling coach, Mr. Vyvian Tremaine watched the
swirling snowflakes gradually obscure the bare winter landscape as they gathered pace.

"When you promised me all the festive delights
of a traditional Christmas, dear boy," he drawled,
gathering the sable collar of his caped greatcoat
more closely about him, "you made no mention of
snow. I hope I may not live to regret allowing myself to be persuaded."

"Poseur!" scoffed Sir Timothy Dalton. "When
did a few flakes of snow ever bother you? I have
seen you ride five miles or more in a positive bliz-
zard without a quibble rather than forgo a good
mill or a particularly promising card game."

"True. But one must draw the line somewhere."

Sir Timothy laughed.

The two men had been friends from their days
at Oxford, though they couldn't have been more
different in appearance—Sir Timothy, golden-
haired, a little too plump and rather jolly; and the
dark, enigmatic Mr. Tremaine, a Corinthian from
the tip of his stylish beaver hat to the gleaming
Hessians that he now contemplated with every ap-

pearance of indifference. But Sir Timothy knew,
none better, that Vyvian's languid manner concealed a keen mind and an acute perception of all
that went on around him—and it was woe betide
anyone who took him for a mere fribble.

"Refresh my memory, Timothy. Why are we
going into the wilds of Norfolk?"

"Because my sister, Beatrice, has invited us to
join Brampton and herself, and their family for the
festivities. Charles's mother and sister will be there
also. And you need not shudder so, Vyvian. There's
many a man would sell his soul for the chance to
sample Brampton's claret."

Mr. Tremaine sighed. "Would that I had known
earlier. They might have had my place, and
welcome."

"Enough," Sir Timothy exclaimed. "If you are
minded to be such a killjoy, I shall begin to wish I
had not asked you."

This brought no reply. Sir Timothy watched his
friend's profile for a moment in anxious silence. He
was aware that an appeal to Vyv's sense of chivalry
could well rebound on him, which was why he had
resolved not to reveal the true purpose of Bea's
invitation until they had gone too far for him to cry
enough, and demand that the less sumptuous coach
traveling in their wake should take him back to
London with all speed.

It would concern Vyvian not at all that the said
coach, presently occupied by two gentlemen's gentlemen, and piled high with the considerable quantity of baggage that was deemed the minimum
required for even a brief stay in the country, would
have to be dismantled and reassembled should he
so demand.

"You have the most revealing profile, Timothy."
His friend's gentle voice cut across these musings.

"Now, suppose you tell me why we are really going to Norfolk? And why I have the curious notion that I am being kidnapped?"

Sir Timothy looked rather like a small boy caught in the act of raiding the larder. Then he laughed and shrugged.

"Never could pull the wool with you, could I? Should know better by now than to try." He paused to collect his thoughts. "Very well. I'll explain if you'll promise not to jump down m'throat." This brought a pained look, but no guarantee. But he had now gone too far to pull back. "You will, no doubt, recall the Vicomte de Laroche?"

"The emigre with a dangerous penchant for gambling? Our paths have crossed. Not a particularly likable fellow—liable to turn nasty when he loses. Isn't he rumored to have killed someone close to Bonaparte over the turn of a card, and been forced to flee the country?"

"I heard that, too. A much favored cousin, I believe. It's said that Bonapartist agents are still seeking him."

A faint note of surprise crept into Mr. Tremain's voice. "Shouldn't think he and your sister would have much in common?"

"They haven't. She can't stand the fellow. But the vicomte has a daughter."

Hair like spun silver and an other-world look about her—Mr. Tremaine recalled having seen her with Bea. Not his style at all. He preferred his women dark and voluptuous—like Rosetta. The memory of his present inamorata brought a frown. He would have to do something about Rosetta when he returned to London. She was becoming rather too possessive.

"Are you listening, Vyv?"

"You have my complete and undivided attention,

dear boy. I believe I have seen the daughter—a rather lovely child. Not at all like Laroche. Must take after her mother."

"I wouldn't know," Sir Timothy said patiently. "Never saw the vicomtess—she died some years ago, I believe. And Mercedes is not a child. She is coming up to eighteen and is a devastatingly lovely young woman."

"Ah, I see." Mr. Tremaine quirked an amused eyebrow. "Fancy your chance, do you? Well, I'm sure you don't need me to hold your hand."

His friend blushed. "It ain't like that at all, though if I thought she would have me, I'd ask her like a shot—"

The coach lurched and came to a sudden halt, putting an end, temporarily, to the conversation.

Mr. Tremaine continued to lounge in his corner as though he hadn't a care in the world, but his slate-hard eyes narrowed, and one hand reached into the pocket of his greatcoat to grasp the silver-mounted pistol that lay heavy against his knee. He eased back the hammer, one finger, featherlight, hovering over the trigger.

Sir Timothy, brandishing his own pistol, sprang nervously to his feet and let down the window.

"What's to do, Broughton?"

"Nothing to worry about, Sir Timothy," came the slow, calm voice of the coachman. "A branch come down across the road, Jem says. Couldn't see it for the snow. 'E's clearin' it now."

"Quick as you can, then. And keep y'r eyes peeled. It could be a ruse."

He sat down again on the edge of his seat, red-faced and still nursing his pistol. He grinned awkwardly at his friend. "It don't do to take chances. Highwaymen and footpads are not unknown on these lonely stretches."

"Quite. However, I'd be grateful if you would refrain from pointing that thing at me."

"What? Oh, yes, sorry. Wish I knew how you manage to stay so damnably cool."

"All clear, Sir Timothy," the coachman called, and they felt the coach sway as he clambered back to his place, then lurch and move forward again.

Sir Timothy put away his pistol and relaxed once more. Mr. Tremaine, being of a more vigilant disposition, waited until he was certain all was well.

"Now, where was I? Ah, yes. Thing is, Bea has rather taken Mercedes under her wing these last few months. With a father like hers, the girl don't have many friends."

"I suppose not. Forgive my stupidity, but I don't quite see where this peroration is leading, or what relevance it has to our present situation."

"Well, you might if you would listen instead of interrupting all the time."

With a curt lift of the eyebrow, Mr. Tremaine inclined his head.

"Of recent times," his friend continued, "Laroche has been seen in various gambling hells in the company of Sheringham—"

"The dissolute earl? Not very wise, unless monsieur le vicomte has all his wits about him."

"He don't. That is, he's good, frighteningly good, but he is also reckless. Word has it that he's been dipping much too steep and is now in debt to the earl for a considerable sum, with no immediate means of redeeming himself." Sir Timothy paused, before continuing with a note of bitterness in his voice. "I've also heard that his lordship is willing to write off the debt—or rather to accept it in lieu of a dowry."

"Ah. The plot begins to thicken. Do I take it

that Sheringham lusts after the vicomte's beautiful daughter?"

"It don't bear thinking about! I'm not sure whether she is fully aware of the proposal, or merely senses that something ain't quite right. What I do know is that Sheringham has invited them both to Neasholm Priory for Christmas, and Bea says Mercedes don't want to go."

"That is hardly surprising. Forgive me, but I still don't see the connection between Mademoiselle de Laroche's dilemma and our visit to your sister."

"Should have thought it was obvious—Neasholme Priory, Sheringham's place, is little more than a mile from Brampton Grange," Sir Timothy concluded gloomily. "We are almost certain to meet socially over the festive period, and Bea is determined to rescue mademoiselle from her fate, if at all possible."

"Ah!"

The softly uttered sound spoke volumes. Mr. Tremaine's initial reaction was annoyance. It had always been his policy not to become embroiled in other people's affairs, and he certainly had no intention of aiding Beatrice Brampton in any dubious crusade. He frowned.

"I understood Sheringham was already married?"

"*Was* being the operative word, dear fellow. Surely you must have heard about the wife?"

"My dear Timothy, I have little interest in Sheringham's affairs and even less in his wife's."

Undeterred by what many would regard as a setdown, Sir Timothy continued, "Seems the wife was delicate—couldn't bring a child to full term. After one miscarriage too many, the earl, still desperate for an heir, took her to Italy to recuperate last year, and after some months returned alone. The journey, it seemed, finally did for her." He paused. "So now, Sheringham is in the market for a wife."

When his friend had remained silent for some time, Sir Timothy turned to him, despair in his voice. "You do see how it is, don't you, Vyv? Something will have to be done—we can't have Mercedes at the mercy of that man."

"I see that *you* are set on becoming her knight in shining armor," mused Mr. Tremaine. He sighed. "It is that little word 'we' that troubles me. In what role, I wonder, do you hope to cast me?"

His friend looked sheepish. "I rather thought that between us we might foil the earl's plans."

If the weather was bleak, the welcome at Brampton Grange more than compensated for its short-comings. An air of excitement had prevailed throughout the day, but it was not until the light was failing that, at last, the sound of coach wheels on gravel brought two young children hurtling down the stair, to the despair of their nurse.

"Uncle Timothy's here, Mama! We've seen his coach coming up the drive!"

"Yes, my dears, but do be still! I will not have you appearing so rag-mannered in front of your uncle, or indeed his guest, who is a very particular kind of gentleman." But the reprimand was delivered without any real anger. "Georgie, you are the elder. You must set your sister a good example. Take Jane's hand and stand beside me."

Beatrice Brampton, though no beauty, had a warmth of manner that made one overlook a square jaw in favor of a pair of large gray eyes that sparkled with merriment, and a manner guaranteed to put the most nervous guest at ease. And her husband, Mr. Charles Brampton, was, so his friends declared, good-natured to a fault.

The front door was flung open, letting in a flurry of snow, through which two figures were presently to be seen approaching.

"Well, now, here's a welcome, to be sure!" cried Sir Timothy, stepping across the threshold to kiss his sister, only to be set upon with squeals of joy by his nephew and niece, their mother's remonstrations long forgotten.

"My, how you've grown!" he exclaimed, lifting one in each arm. "Scarcely recognized you, by Jove!"

"I'm five!"

"And I'm six and a half!"

"Children!" Beatrice exclaimed, with no hope of being attended to.

Behind her brother she saw the tall figure of Mr. Tremaine etched against the curtain of fast falling snow, watchful, wary, quietly waiting. She hurried forward, hands outstretched, a rueful expression in her eyes.

"Poor Vyvian! Have you had a horrid journey? We are delighted to see you, of course, but I had not expected Timothy to embroil you in this affair. I daresay you are wishing nothing so much at this moment as to turn and run!"

He smiled in that gentle and enigmatic way he had and protested that nothing could be further from the truth, but she was not deceived. For she had never doubted Timothy's assertion that concealed beneath those exquisite manners was a will of pure steel. To her, however, he was unfailingly kind.

"Well, do come along in and allow Milsom to relieve you of your hat and coat. Charles, take Vyvian along to the library and pour him a large brandy while I make order out of chaos! Timothy, you will have to earn your reward by helping me to pacify the children."

"Oh, I say! Don't I deserve a brandy, too?"

"Later. Grandmother Brampton and Cecily are not due until tomorrow, and until then, they will be a handful."

There was a distinct look of complacence in the smile Mr. Tremaine bestowed upon his friend as he inclined his head and allowed himself to be led away.

"How much did Timothy tell you about my young friend's predicament?" Bea asked later that evening over dinner.

Mr. Tremaine glanced at his friend. "Very little, I fear. And what I do know, I only managed to drag out of him when we were more than halfway here."

"Oh, Timothy!" Bea was reproachful.

But Timothy, made bold by his brother-in-law's claret, which was proving to be all and more than he had claimed for it, was dismissive of her concern.

"You don't know Vyv as well as I do. If I'd primed him any earlier, he'd have run a mile rather than be dragged into a plot to save some slip of a girl he don't even know."

"Can't blame a fellow for that," Charles observed sagely. "It's a damnable situation. I've told Bea she ought not to interfere. Not our business. Sorry as I am for the girl, if Laroche has decided to give his daughter in marriage, I can't imagine what Vyv, or any one of us, for that matter, can hope to do for the poor child."

"That is the philosophy of a coward!" declared his wife. "If it comes to the push, there is always *something* one can do."

Mr. Tremaine regarded Bea with a kind of amused awe. "I seem to remember that, even as a child, you were the champion of lost causes. I now observe that you haven't changed one whit!"

"No, I must protest!" Bea laughed, then leaned forward, her earnest honest gaze resting on each of them in turn. "But we have to try, don't you see?" Frustration lent force to her argument. "It isn't just that Sheringham is more than five and forty and dissolute, and she scarcely eighteen. The truth is, he makes my skin creep. Oh, he is impeccably polite, even charming when he chooses, but there is sometimes a terrible coldness behind his smile—a hint of cruelty, even. The thought of Mercedes being married to him fills me with dread ..."

"Oh, come, m'dear," said her husband. "The fellow's a bit of a profligate, I'll grant you, but—"

"Furthermore, it's my belief he did away with his wife whilst they were in Italy," she concluded defiantly.

"Really, Bea!" Timothy exclaimed. "That's coming it a bit strong!"

Vyvian Tremaine lounged back in his chair, taking no part in the conversation, his long slim fingers curled round the stem of his glass as the arguments ranged back and forth. In the course of this exercise he learned that the earl and his party were already in residence up at the Priory, and that they included, aside from the Laroches, Lord Melvin and his wife, and Sheringham's unmarried sister, Lady Lavinia Truscott. He was further dismayed to learn that not only were they coming to dine on the following evening, but that the Bramptons and their guests were invited to the Priory the following night, Christmas Eve, and were to accompany Sheringham and his party to the adjoining church for a midnight service. Devil take Timothy!

*   *   *

Mercedes de Laroche awoke and lay quite still for a moment, wondering where she was.

The room was still in darkness, though a thread of early morning light was squeezing through a small gap in the curtains. And as her eyes adjusted to the darkness, various shapes became discernible—dark, heavy shadows that loomed over her with menace until at last they resolved themselves into cupboards and tallboys.

She was at Lord Sheringham's house, which was not a house at all, but a priory where once there had been monks. The ruins of the cloisters were here still. She had seen them last evening when they arrived, looming over her in the darkness, causing her imagination to run riot. They were dangerous, the earl had said, and no one was allowed to go near them.

She sat up now, shivering—and not simply with the cold. Suppose the spirits of the monks also lingered to haunt this priory? Her heart beat very fast as she pulled the feathered quilt up round her.

"You are awake, ma'moiselle?"

A figure rose from the pallet in the corner, eased her aching bones, and pattered across the polished floor, muttering to herself. "*Merde!* But how this Norfolk freezes one to the bone!"

"Louise?" There was a trembling in her mistress's voice. "Oh, indeed it is you! For a moment I was so afraid . . . please to draw back the curtains at once!"

The heavy curtains rattled on their pole as the elderly maid dragged them back, letting in soft golden light. "Oh, ma'moiselle!"

Mercedes slid down from the high bed—a slight, almost wraithlike figure, trailing her quilt across the floor.

"Ah!" she breathed.

For as far as the eye could see, the countryside
was blanketed in snow, and even as she watched,
the sun, coming up like a great golden ball, was
gilding the treetops and the distant fields with its
rays.

It was impossible not to be moved by so beautiful
a landscape. A *joyeux Noel*, indeed. If only, she
sighed, all else in her life could be as beautiful. She
began to shiver uncontrollably.

"Come back to your bed, ma'moiselle," pleaded
the maid, struggling with the foreign language
which, during their years of exile in England, she
had never bothered to master. But now this earl,
who would marry her little mademoiselle, had
hinted that unless she spoke English more fluently,
she would be replaced—and that was a fate too
horrible to be contemplated. "If you stay 'ere," she
coaxed now, "your marrow will be chilled. I will
clothe myself this minute and go downstairs to
make you the 'ot drink."

"You are so very good to me, Louise," Mercedes
said, her teeth still chattering. "I do not know what
I should do without you. But you must not overex-
ert yourself."

"I do not exert myself, ma'moiselle," declared
Louise, scrambling into her clothes, her long thick
plait of graying hair bouncing with her efforts. "To
me it is nothing to rise early. And as for doing
without me, you need 'ave no fear, for soon I shall
have ze perfect English—and it will take more than
some fine milord to tear me from your side."

She departed and returned swiftly, bearing a tray
on which stood a small pot, a spoon, and a cup
and saucer.

"Chocolat," she announced triumphantly. "I
make it wiz my own 'ands."

Mercedes bit her lip, anxious that Louise should

do nothing to offend. "I hope the cook did not mind?"

"Mind? Why should she mind that I invade her domain?" Louise drew back her shoulders, a royalist to the backbone. "You should appraise that kitchen, ma'moiselle! Bah, in France, in an 'ouse such as this—before the *canaille* destroyed all our lives—such a kitchen would not be allowed!"

"But we are not in France," Mercedes said sadly.

"This is true. But we shall not repine. Drink your chocolat, petite, while it is 'ot, and trust in le Bon Dieu."

When Mercedes made her way downstairs, a huge woollen shawl almost obscuring her slim white gown to protect her against the coldness of the house, it was to find the earl's sister, a thin-faced, humorless woman of indeterminate years, sitting alone at the breakfast table, drinking tea and toying with the remains of a plate of bacon and kidneys under the impassive gaze of a footman who stood like a sentinel.

"Good morning, Mademoiselle de Laroche. Henry will serve you with whatever you choose from the dishes on the sideboard. Lady Melvin is having a light repast in her room, and the gentlemen have gone out shooting."

Her voice and manner lacked cordiality. Already, after two days, it was clear that the Lady Lavinia did not like her. And now that they were alone, Mercedes felt the waves of dislike emanating from her most distinctly. Her appetite, never hearty so early in the day, all but vanished. She smiled apologetically at Henry, shook her head, and took her place at the table.

"Thank you, madam, but, as yesterday, a little bread and butter with some conserve will suffice me."

"As you wish." Lady Lavinia made no attempt to disguise her disapproval. "Though, if you will be guided by me, I believe you will come to find such meager fare—well enough though it may be in London circles—quite inadequate for this inclement weather. There is tea or coffee," she added abruptly.

Lavinia watched Henry pour coffee, which Mercedes drank black, watched her smile her thanks, disliking such familiarity. Edward is a fool, she thought, as the girl nibbled daintily at her bread like a bird. This one is no better than Catherine with her childish figure and her simpering ways. And she will probably be just as inadequate when it comes to bearing sons to carry on the line.

Why could her brother not choose to wed some stout young woman capable of childbirth, like Lord Mincham's plain, sensible Alice, who, with three younger and prettier sisters to be found husbands, would be so grateful to him that she would expect nothing from him that he did not wish to give, and permit him to have as many mistresses as he chose. But he was besotted with Mademoiselle de Laroche, and she had seen Edward in a rage too often over the years to dare to question his choice.

It was perhaps fortunate that Mercedes could not read Lady Lavinia's thoughts. But she could feel the antagonism emanating from her. I cannot stay another whole morning with this person who so obviously dislikes me, she thought in despair.

And then she remembered Beatrice. Yesterday it would not have been appropriate to suggest that she visit her friend. But now, she decided, it could be attempted. But she would have to be a little devious.

"Is it not a beautiful morning, Lady Lavinia?"

she asked artlessly. "I have always found snow most invigorating. I believe I would like to take a walk."

"A walk?" The child was mad. "That would not be at all wise, mademoiselle. I feel sure your father would disapprove. Also my brother expressly asked me to show you over the house. Yesterday you were too fatigued from the journey."

"But there will surely be time enough to see the house when the sun does not shine," Mercedes said, and her father would have recognized the note of wilfullness in her voice that he had never been wholly able to curb.

Lady Lavinia was not so easily routed, however, though she would have to be circumspect, for Edward would not be best pleased if she upset Mercedes.

"It would be neither wise nor safe for you to walk in the grounds while the guns are out, mademoiselle," she said in more conciliatory tones. "I would never forgive myself, and my brother most certainly would not forgive me, if I permitted you to take such risks."

"But neither, I think, can you forbid me, if it is what I wish to do. And it is. I have quite made up my mind that, as my dear friend Beatrice lives close by, I shall visit her this morning. So you see, it is not necessary for you to worry about me."

"Worry! Of course I shall worry."

"Then I cannot stop you. But I mean to be most careful to keep in the main paths." Mercedes finished her coffee and stood up, a decided sparkle in her eyes, though she said politely, "Thank you for the breakfast. If you will tell me, please, what time is luncheon?"

Lady Lavinia admitted defeat. "You cannot possibly walk to Mrs. Brampton's house. It is the best part of a mile away. I will order the carriage and come with you."

"But no! That would never do! You have your other guests to consider. Only suppose that Lady Melvin should come down and find no one to greet her . . ." Mercedes saw that this argument had much merit and pressed home her point. "If you wish me to go by carriage, I will do so. But it need not wait for me, for I am sure Beatrice will see that I arrive back safely."

It was but a short carriage ride, and Mercedes, in a voluminous cloak of ivory wool, its hood trimmed with swansdown, felt a wonderful sense of freedom as they bowled along the tree-lined drive. As they rounded a bend, she saw a young woman some way ahead of them, standing beneath one of the trees. She, too, wore a hooded cloak and looked somehow hunched and a little pathetic.

Mercedes leaned forward to ask the coachman to stop, but when she looked again, the woman had gone. Snow, loosened by the warmth of the sun, fell from several of the trees in a sudden shower. And then the gates came into view, and she decided she had been mistaken, and that what she had seen was just such a fall of snow and not a girl at all.

And soon they were entering the grounds of Brampton Grange, and she was being greeted by Beatrice with such obvious pleasure that all else was forgotten in the warmth of her welcome.

Mr. Tremaine had enjoyed his morning rather more than he had expected. If one had to be immured in the wilds of the countryside, there were worse ways to pass the time, and he was the first to admit that Charles's keeper had provided some excellent covers to challenge their skill. His guns were also equal to anything he owned himself—

indeed, one fowling piece in particular, a beautifully balanced piece of craftsmanship, had aroused him to something approaching envy.

"Will you wear the new blue coat, sir?" inquired his man, when he had washed and changed his linen.

"Why not, Tibbs? It will suffice as well as any."

The valet stiffened a little at this casual dismissal of a superb garment created for his master by no less a person than Weston.

"And better than most, sir, if I may make so bold."

"I daresay." Mr. Tremaine looked up suddenly and met his valet's reproachful gaze. Amusement flickered in his slate gray eyes. "Cast myself in your black books, have I, Tibbs?"

"I am sure it is not for me to question your opinion, sir. Though it is my belief that few gentlemen can display Mr. Weston's artistry to such effect as yourself—his glance measured the fine breadth of shoulder beneath white linen, the length of a leg displaying his master's buff pantaloons to perfection—"and, of those, very few may do so without any recourse to padding."

"What can I say, Tibbs?" Mr. Tremaine murmured. "I fear you flatter me, but let us have the blue coat by all means."

When he was dressed to Tibbs's liking, Mr. Tremaine made his way downstairs in search of Timothy. The door to the large front parlor stood slightly ajar, and from within came the excited voices of the two children. He was about to move on when a trill of delightful laughter stayed him.

"But no, *mon cher* Georgie, to make a bow, you must first cross over the ribbons, so. See, I will 'old it with my finger—and you will try once more . . ."

Intrigued in spite of himself, he pushed the door wider and glanced in.

Georgie and Jane were sprawled on the floor in front of the fire, surrounded by piles of ribbons and greenery and what he supposed were angels cut from paper. Their companion, dressed all in white, was earnestly engrossed in her task, her delightfully full curving lower lip trapped by even white teeth, her skirt billowing gently as she reached forward to help Georgie tie a bright red ribbon bow.

Jane saw him first. She stared silently back, still a little in awe of their handsome visitor. Then she nudged her brother.

"It's only Mr. Tremaine, silly," he said, and grinned. "Have you come to help, sir? We want to get finished before Grandmama and Aunt Cecily arrive."

The girl also turned at last, sitting back on her heels. Her delicately pointed face, uplifted to him with a kind of candid curiosity, was framed by a cluster of curls more silver than gold, and poised thus, the firelight played across her face and made an aureole of light about her head. He felt a strange tremor run through him as he looked into those wide inquiring eyes still alive with the lingering echoes of laughter—glorious Byzantine eyes, fringed with gold-tipped lashes, where he had expected the more conventional china blue.

"Oh, Dieu!" she exclaimed in comic dismay, scrambling to her feet and endeavoring at the same time to smooth down her skirts as she realized what a picture she must present. "Forgive me, monsieur. Georgie and Jane and I, we are en-grossed"—she brought the word out with a flush of pride—"in making decorations for the celebration of Noël, which is your Christmas, and we did not 'ear you come."

"No apology is necessary, Mademoiselle de Laroche. It is I who intrude."

Her breath caught and those golden eyes opened even wider. "You know me? We have not been introduced, I think." Her head tilted a little to one side, regarding him with a sudden mischievous smile. "Me—I would not forget such a one."

Mr. Tremaine was amused and inclined his head. "You flatter me. No, we have not met, but I have seen you with Beatrice at several functions in Town." He watched her expressive face with interest. "I was drawn by the sounds of merriment." He indicated the colorful jumble of holly and ivy and ribbons. "You have quite a task on, by the look of it."

"But, yes." She regarded him with lively curiosity that took on a hint of mischief as she added, "It is not one you would aid us with, *bien sur*. I expect you wish for Beatrice. She will return at any minute. She 'as gone to look for some silver lace which was used last year."

Mercedes had scarcely finished speaking when the small ormolu clock on the mantelshelf began to strike the hour. She sprang to her feet, the color draining from her cheeks as she stared at it in dismay.

"Dieu!" she exclaimed, a hand to her mouth. "How the time has flown! I must go— *immediatement!"*

"Like Cinderella?" Mr. Tremaine suggested, amused by her penchant for the dramatic.

She tried to respond to his mood, while calming the protests of the children, but he could sense unease beneath her valiant attempts and wondered at it. He picked up her cloak, which had been thrown carelessly across a chair.

"Come," he said, with a gentleness that would

have astonished anyone who did not know him
well. "I will see you safely back."

"Oh, but it is not *convenable* that I should put
you to such trouble!"

Ignoring her protests, he draped the cloak across
her shoulders, fastened the clasp, and lifted up the
hood to cover her silvery curls, drawing it close so
that the swansdown caressed the curve of her
cheek, framing the face uplifted to him.

Her eyes met his in a hesitant, questioning way
and for a moment time had no meaning. He
watched that enchantingly full lower lip tremble
slightly as if with the force of some inner agitation,
and a degree of will power was required on his part
to resist the urge to kiss away its vulnerability.

"It is no trouble, I assure you, mademoiselle,"
he said huskily, loath to release her.

"It is only that the Lady Lavinia will be displeased with me yet again if I do not return within
the hour!" she concluded breathlessly, not taking
her eyes from his.

It was at this precise moment that Beatrice came
on the scene, full of apologies. Mr. Tremaine released Mercedes without any apparent embarrassment and proceeded to explain the situation, so
that Beatrice was obliged to swallow her curiosity
and give her mind to more immediate matters.

"My dear, there is no problem. I shall have the
horses put to the light chaise at once. The journey
takes no time at all, and Charles will be happy to
accompany you to explain to Lady Lavinia why you
have been away so long!"

"No need to trouble Charles, Bea," Mr. Tremaine said smoothly. "I will see Mademoiselle de
Laroche safely home."

Her eyes widened a little, but she wisely made
no comment.

* * *

Mercedes spoke little in the carriage, and Mr. Tremaine did not attempt to force a conversation upon her. He was, in truth, somewhat shaken to discover the extent to which his feelings, in general so carefully controlled, had been disturbed by this young woman. Even now, sitting close to her, he found himself wanting to take Mercedes de Laroche in his arms. It was absurd, of course—a whim of the moment. And it would pass. Except that he did not want it to pass.

While he was still striving to make sense of what was happening, the carriage turned in at the Priory gates.

Almost immediately, he became aware that his companion was leaning toward the window, as though searching for something, or someone. Then she half turned to him, her voice eager.

"I was not mistaken! There she is again ... beneath the tree. Ah, do you not see her eyes? How cold she looks, and so sad. Oh, please to ask the driver to stop!"

Mystified, Mr. Tremaine did as she asked. He could see nothing but snow scattering from the trees as the sun melted it. Yet as he turned to tell her so, the words died on his lips.

Her whole being was intent, her gaze transfixed upon a point somewhere beyond the carriage. It was as though—he felt the hairs on his neck lift—as though she really could see someone. Perhaps she had an overactive imagination, or was a hysteric—he instinctively rejected the latter. Or could it be that she was what he believed the Irish called *fey*?

Whatever the truth of it, the situation would require the most careful handling. As she attempted to open the door, he put out a hand to prevent her.

"My dear mademoiselle, you must not, you will take a chill." And more gently, "You are mistaken, you know. There is no one waiting."

"But yes, can you not see her, beneath that tree? She has waited since—oh, a long time for me. I know it. It is she who will be chilled. How can I abandon her?"

Mr. Tremaine was afraid of very little, but this was a situation quite unknown to him, and something akin to fear took hold of him. The situation would need careful handling. His fingers bit into her arm, holding her back, preventing her from leaving the carriage. As she tugged angrily to release herself, his free hand took both of her slender wrists in a firm clasp, so that he could feel the soft, agitated thud of her pulse.

"Mademoiselle Mercedes, look at me." The authority in his voice commanded her.

Reluctantly, she turned to face him, hostility in her eyes.

He said, firmly but gently, "Do you trust me?"

After a moment she nodded.

"Then, come with me, now. Believe me, I want only your good." It was as if his words were not registering. She had ceased to struggle, but those lovely eyes were still stormy, and her pulse betrayed an inner agitation. He persisted. "If you are late, your father will be anxious about you. Your host, also, and Lady Lavinia. You would not be disrespectful to them?"

For a long moment his eyes continued to hold hers. At last her whole body seemed to sag a little. Without looking out of the window again, she nodded.

"You can release me, now. I shall not do anything foolish."

Mr. Tremaine did so. He told the coachman to

drive on, and for some time an unnatural silence reigned, which he did nothing to break.

At last, without looking at him, she asked in a subdued voice, "Was there really no one there?"

"No one, mademoiselle," he said quietly.

"You are quite sure?"

"Quite sure. I give you my word."

She sighed, and there was another long silence. "Then it is me—there must be a sickness in me," she said in a low, frightened voice. "I am perhaps becoming deranged."

"Nonsense." He was surprised at the anger her words aroused in him. "You are as sane as I am. The answer is probably very simple. I have heard that sunlight on snow can sometimes play strange tricks on the mind."

"Perhaps." She threw him a sad, grateful little smile that did little to reassure him. "That is what I thought the first time."

So it had happened before. But, of course. *There she is again,* she had said. And, if he believed her, which every instinct persuaded him that he did, then there *had* to be a rational explanation.

Neasholme Priory had by now come into view. Even without the ruins of the cloisters, now starkly etched against the skyline, its early religious origins could scarely be in doubt. Sunlight warmed the Elizabethan stonework and made the diamond window panes sparkle in the sunlight, yet for all that, the house had a slightly brooding look. It crossed Mr. Tremaine's mind that it was not the ideal place for someone as susceptible to atmosphere as Mercedes de Laroche.

The gentlemen had returned from their shoot and stood around a blazing fire in the great open fireplace in the stone-flagged entrance hall, drinking wine and discussing the morning's sport, the portly figure of Lord Melvin offset by his darker more elegant companions.

The talking ceased, and they turned as one man to watch Mercedes enter with her escort. Mr. Tremaine felt a tremor run through her, and his hand instinctively tightened on her arm.

The vicomte looked angry, but Lord Sheringham was the first to step forward. He was on the tall side, with something of the dandy in his dress, and though he wore his age well, his handsome, rather fleshy features were tending to become raddled from too much good living.

"My dear Mercedes, thank heaven you are safe. My sister has been most worried," he said, his hands outstretched to greet her with odious familiarity. "We quite thought you must be lost and were on the point of coming to look for you."

She looked up at him as though coming out of a dream. "But, no," she replied, carefully withdrawing her hands from his clasp. "How could I lose myself? The Lady Lavinia was aware that I was visiting my good friend, Beatrice Brampton. And now, Mr. Tremaine 'as been so good as to escort me back."

"So he has." Lord Sheringham acknowledged her companion with every appearance of gratitude, though his eyes were cold. "We are very much obliged to you, Tremaine. Are we not, Laroche? You and Monsieur de Laroche are acquainted?"

"Monsieur."

"Indeed." The sharp-featured Frenchman bowed curtly before turning immediately to address his daughter in a quick, low voice. Mr. Tremaine could not hear what was said, but his displeasure was evident, and Mercedes lowered her head and appeared to shrink a little.

He tried to recall in more detail what he had

heard of the Frenchman. It was rumored that Monsieur de Laroche had not fled France at the height of the terror, but had used every ounce of his gambler's guile to keep the revolutionaries sweet by robbing and betraying many of his fellow aristocrats.

But Lady Luck had finally deserted him following the death of his wife, and he had run up a pile of gambling debts among his Bonapartist cronies. One in particular challenged him to a duel, but was mysteriously killed before the challenge could be honored. Laroche had arrived in England shortly afterward with scarcely a sou to his name, dragging his pretty, young daughter along with him as a possible future asset, and claiming to have brought vital information about disaffection among Bonapartists for the exiled Comte de Lille, heir to the French throne.

The comte, presently living in the Vale of Aylesbury, and known to his supporters as *Louis le Desire* and to his less ardent admirers as *Louis le Gros* on account of his enormous girth, was known for his kindly nature. He was eager to know all that his countryman could tell him, and since he accepted Laroche, others followed. Laroche's fortunes, however, had continued to fluctuate wildly. And all the while, his daughter grew in grace and beauty and was now of marriageable age.

"You will take a drink with us, sir?" Sheringham's words cut across Mr. Tremaine's reflections. "You are, of course, very welcome to stay to luncheon." He paused significantly. "But I daresay Mrs. Brampton will be expecting you back."

"I am sure she will," he replied. "But, thank you."

"And we shall meet again this evening, I believe,

when we are to have the pleasure of dining with the Bramptons?"

"So I believe." Mr. Tremaine bowed. "I look forward to it. Your servant, Sheringham."

He turned to Mercedes, who stood subdued beside her father.

"Mademoiselle."

"Merci bien, monsieur," she said politely.

He thought back—such a short while ago, it seemed—to the scene in the library, and the vibrant young creature surrounded by streamers and laughing with the children. It was hard to believe that this was the same Mercedes. She was not so much chastened—it was rather as if a light had been extinguished inside her, leaving but a shell.

As he left, he retained in his mind's eye a picture of Sheringham with Mercedes's hands held captive in his, his head bent toward her. It was like watching a small helpless bird caught in a trap.

You are deuced dull this afternoon, Vyv," declared Sir Timothy, running him to earth in the library and finding him with his feet stretched out before the fire, reading a book. "Hardly seen you since luncheon. Not sickening for anything, I trust?"

"My dear Timothy, there is nothing at all wrong with me. It may astonish you to learn that we do not all take pleasure in rushing about, building snowmen"—he shuddered—"to say nothing of climbing ladders and being covered in greenery and adorned with silver tissue and fancy ribbons."

"It's a jolly fine snowman."

Timothy grinned and flopped, red-faced, into the chair opposite his friend in the peace and quiet of the library, having spent the better part of the afternoon getting his fingers pricked with holly, and helping his niece and nephew to wind ivy round the banister rails.

The butler, Milsom, followed him in and poured him a large brandy.

"Sir?" he inquired of Mr. Tremaine, who declined.

As the door closed again, Sir Timothy returned to his theme. It'd do you a world of good, m'lad, to let yourself go and have some good simple fun."

"Fun?" Mr. Tremaine winced and laid aside his book. "I think not. How could I possibly face poor Tibbs if, like you, I were to get myself covered in snow, entangled in greenery, and streaked with dirt."

"Gammon! I don't know why you keep that fellow. He's more of a poseur than you."

"Perhaps. But he is devoted to me, you see."

Timothy laughed again. "Ah, well. It takes all sorts, I suppose. Forgot to ask—did you see Sheringham when you were up at the Priory?"

"Briefly." His friend did not expand.

"What did you make of Mademoiselle de Laroche, by the way? *Jeunes filles,* not your style, I know ... In fact, I was surprised you offered to escort her this morning."

Mr. Tremaine was slow to answer. When he did, he was noncommittal. "It was the very least I could do," he said, which was no less than the truth. "Mademoiselle is charming, but we talked very little. She is shy, I think."

"Such a tragedy if her father forces her to wed a fellow like Sheringham. We'll give her a jolly time this evening, what? See how things go."

"Your sister will doubtless be in her confidence."

"Yes, of course. Here in her own house, they can't stop Bea talking to her. Grandmama Brampton and Cecily have arrived, by the way. Came about an hour since."

The party from the Priory arrived that evening in two carriages, and in all the exchange of greetings, Mr. Tremaine and Mercedes did not exchange more than a brief word. She was looking very beautiful in white gauze embroidered with tiny clusters of amber knots that echoed the color of her eyes. To all outward appearances at least, she seemed quite recovered from her earlier distress—except for her eyes. They had a slightly distrait look about them.

Bea had also noticed, but Mercedes seemed determined to avoid being alone with her, and with so much to be done, she did not have a chance to pursue the matter.

"Who is the angelic creature with Beatrice?" demanded the slightly deaf Mrs. Brampton in a voice that could be heard right across the drawing room. "Looks as though she don't quite belong in this world."

"She is Mademoiselle de Laroche, Mama," murmured her son. "A friend of Beatrice. Her father is the gentleman in the pale blue coat."

"Ah, French, are they? Well, I suppose they ain't all tarred with the same brush. Y'r father probably wouldn't have received them, but he's been dead these two years or more, so it don't signify."

"Mama," Charles murmured.

Mr. Tremaine's lips twitched. It was obvious that Laroche had heard—in fact, the whole room heard, but Mrs. Brampton remained impervious to any momentary coolness in the atmosphere.

Cecily Brampton was well used to her mother's indiscretions, and she accepted them for the most part as a cross she was called upon to bear. She was pleasant and easy going like her brother, with the same humorous twinkle in her eyes. At eight and twenty, she had become resigned to spinsterhood, a life spent looking after her parent, and the occasional indulgence of being allowed to spoil her young niece and nephew.

When everyone was assembled, the earl begged a moment of their time before dinner was announced. He was standing to one side of the fireplace, resplendent in a silver brocade coat, an elaborate cravat, and black knee breeches.

"There is something very special that I wish to share with you," he said, and Mr. Tremaine, having glanced swiftly at Mercedes, knew at once what was coming.

"It is with the greatest pleasure that I am able to share with you my joy that Mademoiselle de Laroche has consented to be my wife."

Timothy flushed and swore beneath his breath, while Beatrice, her glance flying to her young friend, was so taken by surprise she was momentarily lost for words.

It was left to Charles to offer the congratulations of the whole party with the best grace that could be managed and to wish the couple well.

Then everyone began to speak at once, crowding round to add their own good wishes. And in their midst Mercedes stood beside her father, who was for once disposed to be amiable, displaying a square-cut diamond that almost dwarfed her hand and struck shafts of brilliance from the chandelier above her head.

"Is it not perfectly splendid?" she was exclaiming with an almost feverish vivacity that struck a false note among those who knew her well. "I am most fortunate, I think."

Mr. Tremaine did not share in the polite congratulations. He stood apart, watching her face which revealed far more than she realized.

Over dinner Bea did her best to ensure that a festive mood prevailed. The wine flowed freely, and by the time the servants carried in a large goose, all crisp and steaming, everyone was sufficiently relaxed to rid themselves of any lingering remnants of reserve.

Mercedes, seated next to Lord Sheringham, pushed her food around her plate, but ate hardly anything, though she appeared to be responding to the possessive familiarity of his remarks with vivacity, and several times her trill of laughter rose above the general conversation. Perhaps, thought Mr. Tremaine, I am allowing myself to be troubled to no good purpose. Even as the thought crossed his mind, she looked up and met his eyes—and just for a moment he glimpsed bleak despair. Then the brilliant smile returned, and she began to talk again, very fast.

Bea tried to speak to Mercedes after dinner while the gentlemen still lingered over their port, but with Lady Lavinia watching her every move, it was impossible to exchange more than generalities.

When the gentlemen joined the ladies in the drawing room, Bea suggested they might like to dance. The suggestion was enthusiastically received by some, though Grandmama Brampton, the vicomte, and Lord Melvin all excused themselves, as did Lady Lavinia, who confessed herself to be no dancer. But she reluctantly agreed to play the pianoforte for a quadrille.

Of the four couples who made up the set, Lord Sheringham was quick to ensure that Mercedes partnered him, and the rest comprised Bea and Mr. Tremaine, and Timothy and Cecily, leaving Charles to gallantly take on the plump, but enthusiastic

Lady Melvin, who proved to be surprisingly light on her feet.

There was laughter as some couples proved less proficient than others. Mercedes had, to all appearances, thrown herself into the spirit of the dance, though as they met and passed during the *tours-demains,* Mr. Tremaine noticed that her hands trembled and were stone cold.

When the set was at an end, Lady Melvin begged for a waltz.

"An excellent suggestion," Lord Sheringham exclaimed and turned again to Mercedes.

But she confessed to feeling faint and begged to be excused. He was at once all solicitude, made her sit down, and begged his hostess for hartshorn.

"It is nothing, *bien sur,*" Mercedes protested, a touch of hysteria in her voice. "I am perhaps overexcited!"

"Allow me, my lord," Bea intervened. "I am not surprised that Mercedes feels faint—too much excitement combined with the warmth of the room. If you will allow her to come with me—a few moments rest in a quiet room ..."

"Of course," he agreed smoothly. "Come, my love. I shall go with you."

"Oh, but no!" Mercedes exclaimed, then bit her lip and looked further distressed. "Forgive me, but I would simply like to be alone—just for a little while?"

He looked momentarily displeased.

"It would be best," Bea insisted and led Mercedes from the room, returning a few moments later to reassure the earl and pacify the scowling vicomte, who demanded to know where his daughter was.

"There is no cause for concern, truly, Monsieur le Vicomte. Mercedes vows she will return very soon and begs that we will continue with the dancing." Bea turned to the earl. "I am a poor substitute, my lord, but if you are agreeable?"

"I shall be charmed, ma'am," he said politely, though his gaze strayed more than once toward the door.

Lady Lavinia did not for one moment believe Mercedes, and were it not that everyone was waiting to dance, she would have pursued her. But in the circumstances she could hardly refuse to play, though she did not in general approve of the waltz.

Mr. Tremaine, not noticeably displeased at being deprived of his partner, watched the turning couples for a few moments before moving unobtrusively toward the door.

"Where is she?" he had asked when Bea passed him on her return to the room.

"The small back parlor," she had murmured, intrigued by his terseness.

The hall was empty as he made his way unerringly past the staircase toward the rear of the house. The door to the parlor stood slightly ajar, the room lit only by firelight and a pair of candles guttering now and then as they burned low. The slight figure by the window stood, unmoving, gazing out over lawns crisp and sparkling beneath a crescent moon.

She heard him come, started nervously, and then, seeing it was him, turned back to the window once more.

"Are you all right?" he demanded abruptly.

"Of course. I am perfectly fine, Monsieur Tremaine," she returned. But the words were muffled, and she would not face him.

"You don't sound perfectly fine."

She stiffened. "That is because I am being very sorry for the snowman. He looks so c-cold."

Her voice rose and cracked. He took her by the shoulders and turned her toward him. With a strangled sob she bent her head, resting it against his chest. Without speaking, he put his arms around her and drew her close.

"How am I to go on when we are ... when I cannot b-bear his touch?"

"Hush," he said.

From the drawing room came the muted strains of the waltz. Slowly, still holding her, he began to move to the music, and after a few moments she relaxed and allowed him to lead her gently into the dance.

Together they began to dip and sway almost mesmerically. Through the gauze of her gown, he could feel the slightness of her, her bones almost birdlike, her waist so slender he could span it with ease. He had loved many women, but never had he felt, as he did now, this overwhelming desire to protect Mercedes—to shield her from Sheringham and from the new trouble that seemed to have come upon her, which he somehow felt was linked to her present situation.

The music ended, but she made no effort to move. Putting her away from him a little, he saw that her eyes were closed. But tears glinted on her lashes and sheened her cheeks.

"Don't!" he said with an intensity quite foreign to him. "Don't be unhappy. I won't let anyone or anything hurt you."

"Oh, Dieu! If only it could be so simple!" Mercedes opened her eyes and saw that his face was full of shadows, though his eyes were fixed on her with an expression that made her say again, but more softly, "Oh!"

He kissed her, very gently at first and then, as she responded, his mouth took possession of hers and he felt her sweet ardor leaping to match his own.

"I had not known one could be so *bien éléve,*" she whispered tremulously when at last he lifted his head.

"Strangely enough, nor had I," he murmured.

She sighed and reluctantly pulled away from him. "It will be a memory always for me to treasure."

"More than a memory, dearest girl," he insisted, retaining his hold of her. "I intend to repeat it many times. You surely don't expect me to let you go now."

"B-but you must! It is all too late, monsieur ... I am betrothed. And there is nothing I can do to change that!"

"Nonsense. For a start, you can learn to call me Vyvian. And then you can give the earl back his exceedingly vulgar diamond, and marry me."

"But, no! It is not possible!" She began to struggle. "Oh, please to let me go! Papa would never consent ... he is so deeply in debt to the earl, and I am the price he asks in settlement ... it is a matter of honor. Oh, you do not understand!"

"I understand very well." His voice hardened. "But such an agreement is medieval! The debt is your father's, not yours. And I have no intention of allowing you to be used in such a scandalous way. You are much too precious to me."

"Oh, *je vous prie!* No, no, you must not!" She suddenly broke free from his clasp and rushed from the room.

The silence in the carriage was oppressive. Mercedes shrank into a corner, head sunk into the folds of her cloak as though she might thus ward off her father's wrath, yet dreading the moment when the journey would end and retribution would be ex-

acted. It was just possible that Lord Sheringham
had believed that she had felt unwell. When at last
she returned to the party, he had seemed genuinely
concerned. But her father was not deceived. And
neither had the Lady Lavinia been convinced.

The sound of the wheels changed, and Mercedes
knew that they had arrived. The carriage stopped,
and with a feeling of fatalism she allowed herself
to be helped down. The moon illuminated the forecourt with its clear, cold light, making the shadows
blacker by comparison.

She turned, half stumbling, feet frozen and,
straightening, found herself facing the cloisters.
Open to the skies and bathed in moonlight, the
crumbling edifice seemed to take on the beauty of
an ancient sculpture, composed of cold light and
deep shadows. And where the shadows were deepest, she was certain that something moved.

Again that breath of a sigh carried to her, dry as
dust, though there was no wind. Only this time it
had acquired a voice.

I am here . . . waiting for you . . . it murmured.

Mercedes felt as if she were being drawn . . .
drawn . . . and this time there was no Vyvian Tremaine to hold her back. She felt perspiration cold on
her skin—felt her feet begin to move without voli-
tion and swayed, praying that she would not faint.

"Mercedes?"

It was her father's voice, coming from a long way
off, taut with anger or perhaps concern—she neither knew nor cared. Lord Sheringham was lifting
her, carrying her into the hall, putting her down on
a settee.

She heard Lady Lavinia say something about mis-
judging her. " . . . but how was I to know that she
was genuinely unwell?" A smelling bottle most foul

was put under her nose, and she began to cough and splutter.

"Ah, at last!" The earl's voice sounded concerned. "No, my dear, don't try to sit up ... take your time."

"I would like to go to my bed," she said when she could draw breath.

"Of course."

In spite of her protests that she could walk, he carried her upstairs where, to her great relief, Louise took her in charge, dismissing all talk of doctors and demanding that her *petite* should be laid on her bed and left to those who know best how to care for her.

"Hold your tongue, woman." The earl's voice crackled with suppressed fury. "I will decide whether or not Mademoiselle de Laroche has need of a doctor."

He bent over Mercedes, his voice soft, almost caressing. "So pale, my little love. Sleep now, and in the morning we will decide what is best for you." He raised her ice-cold hand to his lips, and without acknowledging Louise, he strode from the room.

Only when all sound of his footsteps had died away did Mercedes give way and was immediately enfolded in the plump comforting arms of her old nurse.

At Brampton Grange the evening had taken on a far from festive air following the departure of the earl's party. Grandmama Brampton had gone to bed, declaring herself to be worn out, and Cecily had been admitted to the council of war.

"Well, what are we going to do?" Timothy demanded, his normally cheerful features suffused with anger. "You saw the way that man pawed her."

"I don't wish to play Devil's advocate, old fellow, but however much it may irk you, they are betrothed."

"Humbug, Charles! The betrothal was forced on Mercedes. You know it was! She flinched every time he touched her!"

"That may be so," his sister said, laying a hand on his arm. "And I am every bit as distressed as you, but Charles is right. The earl has stolen a march on us—deliberately, I suspect, though I'm not sure why. It doesn't change the way I feel, but it does make it difficult for us to help her."

"We could kidnap her—spirit her away."

"Now you are being foolish."

Mr. Tremaine, who had so far taken no part in the conversation, said quietly, "She wouldn't agree."

Timothy swung round accusingly. "How would you know?"

"Because the offer has already been made." All eyes turned toward him, their expressions ranging from skepticism to disbelief. He said with a droll smile, "Not my usual style, I agree. But it seems I have fallen head over ears in love with Mercedes de Laroche, and though little has been said, I have every reason to believe she is very far from indifferent to me."

"Oh, my dear Vyvian!" Beatrice exclaimed, momentarily diverted. "So, I was right. I knew there was something . . ."

"But how—when, Vyv?" Timothy demanded. "Yesterday you had barely spoken to her."

"How long does it take?" Mr. Tremaine looked almost embarrassed. "Call it a *coup de foudre* if you like."

He related to them most of what had happened since his first meeting with Mercedes that morning.

"You mean she's been seeing apparitions?" Charles shook his head. "Don't like the sound of that. Wouldn't have thought there was any mental instability in the girl, but—"

"But nothing," Mr. Tremaine said sharply. "I'm convinced that Mercedes is as sane as you or I. I am equally convinced that she saw—or thought she saw—something."

"It's that Priory," Timothy suggested with a shudder. "Wouldn't catch me living there. Enough to give anyone the shivers. Shouldn't wonder if the place isn't crawling with dead monks."

Cecily half smiled and said in a quiet, practical way that made Mr. Tremaine look at her with new eyes, "I believe there are people, often quite young women, who are susceptible to the atmosphere of very old buildings."

"The late countess, poor woman, never liked the Priory," Beatrice said. "The atmosphere depressed her. She was quite a different person when she came to Town. I remember how excited she was about going to Italy." She sighed. "At least one can say that her last days were happy."

"We are not concerned with the countess," said her brother, bringing them all back to the point. "The thing is, how is Mercedes to break free of this wretched betrothal before it's too late?" He looked from one to the other. "Just a thought—couldn't we offer to settle the father's debt?"

Mr. Tremaine said quietly, "It has already been tried." And as they all stared at him, "I managed to corner the vicomte before they left. He wanted the money, no doubt of it. I could see the greed light up his eyes, but then he became surly and admitted that the earl isn't really interested in a monetary settlement. He wants Mercedes, and if he doesn't get her—well, Laroche wouldn't be drawn, but I could smell the fear on him. Sheringham has some other hold over him, I'm sure."

"The man's a monster," Beatrice exclaimed. "I wouldn't put it past him to rush the marriage through before anyone can stop him."

Her words were more prophetic than she knew.

Mercedes slept long and dreamlessly that night, aided by a small amount of laudanum slipped into her hot drink by Louise, and woke late, quieter than usual, but apparently none the worse for her experience.

Even when Lady Lavinia visited her, she exhibited none of her usual agitation.

"You are recovered, I see." The cold voice betrayed no pleasure in the fact. "The doctor will not be needed, after all. My brother will be relieved. He has talked of calling off this evening's celebrations."

"Oh, but he must cancel nothing on my account," Mercedes said swiftly. "You will please to tell my lord that I am quite well again and wish nothing to be changed. It is Christmas, after all, and I have so looked forward to spending it here with all my dearest friends."

Lady Lavinia's pinched expression showed no relief. "Very well. But Edward insists that you take your breakfast in bed and rest until midday."

"That one 'as ice in 'er veins," muttered Louise when the door had closed behind her. "To smile would crack 'er face, I think." She plumped up the pillows with more than usual vigor. "But at least you are spared 'er presence for a while longer."

Mercedes was not, however, to be spared a visit from her father. He came and stood at the bottom of her bed, and she was very much aware of the nervous twitch beneath one eye, which always afflicted him when he was in any way excited.

"I do not know what little game you were playing last evening," he blustered, making no concessions to her delicate state. "But you will not let me down over this match, you understand me?"

"I understand," she said with sudden spirit, "that it matters nothing to you that my heart is breaking and my life ruined. If Mama had lived, you would not treat me so."

Suddenly, unexpectedly, his mouth began to work, and to her horror, he dropped to his knees beside the bed and began to cry.

"You think I wish to see you unhappy, cherie? But, *merde,* that man, he is immovable! You must do as he wishes!"

Mercedes was horrified by his tears. She was also hopelessly embarrassed and ashamed to see her papa groveling in such a fashion.

"So you will not even try to save me," she accused him. "I am to be sold like a sack of potatoes to pay your debts!"

"If it were only money, I would find it somehow," he sobbed. "But it is my life at stake ... there was a man, an important man ... in France. He died—"

"I remember!" she cried. "You killed him! You swore you had nothing to do with it."

"It was an accident! But Sheringham swears he will have me shipped back to France and delivered into Bonaparte's hands ... and he will do it ..." The sobs grew louder. "Would you send your papa to the guillotine?"

A voice in the corner of her mind told her he was not worth saving, for all that he was her father. For a moment the image of Vyvian Tremaine flashed before her mind's eye, so real that she might reach out and touch her lips to it. Her throat swelled with unbearable tears. Then, with a great sigh, she gathered herself.

"Please, Papa," she said coldly, "do not distress yourself so. I will do what you require of me, though the thought of marrying Lord Sheringham is quite odious to me"—here her voice quivered—"and I think that perhaps, if you loved me even a little bit, you would not demand such a sacrifice of me."

For a moment Mercedes thought that he might strike her. Instead, he scrambled to his feet and stumbled from the room.

The news that Mercedes had recovered, and that the evening's celebrations would proceed as arranged, was delivered to Brampton Grange later that morning.

Relief was tempered with anxiety and renewed frustration. Undoubtedly, she had been coerced, but as yet no way had suggested itself that would release Mercedes from her misery.

"My mind is made up," Mr. Tremaine confided to Beatrice, a harshness in his voice that she had never heard before. "I shall abduct her, as Timothy suggested earlier, and carry her away, well out of reach of Sheringham and her father."

"But won't that be dangerous? And for how long before you are found?"

"Who knows? It is a chance I must take, for in the light of all that has happened, I have the distinct feeling that Sheringham will not waste time making Mercedes his wife." He took her hands and smiled wryly into her eyes. "I am sorry, my dear. It seems certain that my actions will embarrass you and Charles, and I would not have you hurt for the world."

Beatrice was not by nature a romantic, but her

heart was stirred to its depths by the nobility of such a gesture.

"Oh, you mustn't consider us, Vyv. It will be a five-day wonder, soon forgotten. And you know how I feel about Mercedes. Her happiness is my prime concern, and I have no doubt you are exactly right for her."

"Bless you." He lifted her hands briefly to his lips. "But what of Timothy? I really do feel bad for him."

Her eyes twinkled. "Well, you know, I rather think Timothy has accepted that what he felt for Mercedes was little more than air-dreaming. In fact, I believe he is beginning to show an interest in Cecily. I am pretending not to notice at present, lest I disturb the tender shoots of love. Ridiculous, really. They have known each other forever." She gently removed her hands. "Have you decided when?"

"As soon as possible. I thought perhaps at the end of the church service, if a diversion of some kind could be arranged. Sheringham would not be expecting anything then. I wonder if Charles would loan me his chaise and a pair of fast horses?"

"My dear, you have but to ask. It might be worth asking his advice about how best to effect your abduction of Mercedes. I suppose you realize that you will be watched? If it becomes impossible for you to speak to her alone, I am very willing to act as a go-between."

Mr. Tremaine's eyebrow lifted quizzically. "Dear Bea. I have always admired your many admirable qualities, but I had not until now appreciated your capacity for intrigue."

Her eyes kindled. "I have often thought I should be rather good at it." She grew serious again. "But we will not tell Timothy, I think—at least not until we have to. The fewer people who know, the better, don't you think?"

By the time the party set out from Brampton Grange for a late dinner, minus Grandmama Brampton, who vowed she preferred her bed, the night looked set to be clear and bright, and very frosty. A perfect Christmas night, in fact, though Mr. Tremaine had hoped that the moon would be obscured by cloud—a moderate amount of fog would have been even more welcome.

The plan was a simple one, the simpler the better as far as he was concerned. Charles, reluctantly recruited, had proved a splendid coconspirator. He was to leave his chaise at the rear of the church, and Bea would, at the appropriate moment, appear to faint, which would distract everyone's attention, at which point Charles, together with Cecily and Sir Timothy, who were now privy to the plan, would create as much distraction as possible to allow Mr. Tremaine time to spirit Mercedes away.

However, when they arrived at the Priory, it was immediately obvious that something dramatic had happened. Lord Sheringham looked odiously complacent; the vicomte was for once in a benevolent mood; and as for Mercedes—it was clear to anyone who knew her that, in spite of her proud carriage and the lovely amber gown that echoed the unnatural brilliance of her eyes, in spite of her rouged cheeks and an almost feverish attempt to appear happy, Mercedes had reached a point beyond despair.

"My dear, what has happened?" Bea whispered as she and Cecily removed their cloaks and tidied their hair. But Lady Lavinia was hovering near, and Mercedes could only murmur in a toneless voice, "I ... cannot ... It is for the Lord Sheringham to announce it to you."

And announce it he did, with full ceremony, at the end of an excellent dinner that few among his guests, watching Mercedes push her food around her plate, really enjoyed.

He stood, looking round at them all, flushed and replete with goose and rib of beef, with syllabubs and sweetmeats, and a generous quantity of claret.

"The midnight ceremony we are to celebrate in our small priory church will this year take on a special significance."

He paused, glanced with triumphant pride at Mercedes, and continued: "It was only last evening that I announced to you that Mercedes de Laroche had done me the great honor of consenting to be my wife. You will all, I am sure, appreciate my eagerness to possess so beautiful a creature ..."

With a feeling of impending catastrophe Mr. Tremaine sat forward, guessing what he was about to say.

"Earlier today, with her father's consent, I consulted with the rector, as a result of which he has granted me permission to forgo the reading of the banns so that we may be married on this very special night—"

"No, by God!" cried Sir Timothy, scrambling unsteadily to his feet. "I'll see you dead first!"

"Timothy, sit down!" commanded Mr. Tremaine, his expression inscrutable, his voice coldly impersonal. "My lord, I cannot believe you have considered Mademoiselle de Laroche's feelings in this matter."

"Then you err in your belief." His voice altered perceptibly. "Mercedes, you will not be too shy to tell our friends, I am sure. You are happy, are you not, my love?"

"I am," she said, almost in a whisper.

"But, dear Mercedes, this cannot be as you would

wish it," Beatrice said gently, sensing the fragility of her friend's emotions. "Every young woman needs time to prepare, to assemble her trousseau ..." She was gabbling, she knew. "Surely there can be no need for such indecent haste?"

She saw the earl flush and knew the last had been indiscreet.

"Well, I for one, think it vastly romantic!" exclaimed Lady Melvin, pink with wine. "To be swept off one's feet in such a gallant manner."

"Quite so," agreed the vicomte with a complacent arrogance. "As to the need for a trousseau, his lordship will take my daughter to Paris almost at once, where she will have the pick of the finest couturieres."

Mr. Tremaine sat silent, his brain working furiously on ways and means of preempting the ceremony. It was already past eleven o'clock. Very soon the party would be leaving for the church, but if he could manage two minutes alone with Charles, they could perhaps put their plan into action before the service rather than after. It was more risky, of course, but if nothing else presented itself, the thing would have to be attempted. He slipped a hand to where, beneath his waistcoat, he had taken the precaution of concealing his pistol.

Beatrice had already tried to talk Mercedes out of going through with the marriage, drawing her aside as they left the table. But the girl seemed to have gone beyond helping. She was in an almost trancelike state that made Beatrice fear for her young friend's sanity.

"Well, I'm damned if I'll attend such an obvious charade!" Sir Timothy exclaimed, loud enough for all to hear. "It's little short of kidnap!"

"Oh, please!" For one moment Mercedes came

to life, her hands outstretched, panic in her voice. "Do not abandon me, my dear friends!"

"We shall not abandon you," Mr. Tremaine said calmly, taking her ice-cold hands in his for one short moment and looking deep into her eyes. "Don't lose hope, dearest girl."

She did not answer, though her mouth trembled piteously as she turned away.

The Priory church was situated about a quarter of a mile away from the house and had in its previous tenure been linked to the house by the cloisters. But the last section, close to the church, had virtually crumbled away so that now only the ones closest to the house remained, and they were mostly in such a fragile state that the servants were forbidden to use them as they had in the past, as a shortcut to the village in bad weather.

It was but a few minutes' drive to the church, and all too soon they had arrived—in a mood of near despair, praying for miracles. Mercedes was closely guarded by Lady Lavinia, who was acting as her attendant, on the one side, and by her father on the other, so that no one could get near.

"I don't think I can bear this," Beatrice whispered to Charles as the rector met them at the door with his acolytes, an elderly man, balding—his manner uneasy, as though he already regretted sanctioning the ceremony about to be performed.

"It's worse for Vyvian," Charles replied, glancing at Mr. Tremaine's stony profile. "I dread to think what he may do."

There were only a few people in the church, most of them tenant farmers from the surrounding countryside, with their wives. They glanced with open curiosity and admiration at the gentry in their fine clothes, making their way to the private family pew, which in earlier days had been the choir stalls.

The rector, surrounded by his acolytes, prefaced the service by informing the assembled congregation that after the opening prayers, they were to have the felicity of seeing Lord Sheringham married to his young bride.

A murmur of surprise and expectation ran round the church, and there was much turning of heads. The rector called the people to remember where they were, and the midnight service opened with "Hark, the Herald Angels Sing," followed by the first familiar readings for Christmas night.

It was then that it began—a sound almost beyond the range of hearing, like shoes shuffling on the wooden floor—the faintest swish, as of woollen robes—a whiff of incense on the air. Slowly, the sound and the swell of incense grew stronger.

Bea turned half fearfully to Charles, who put an arm round her without any conscious decision. They both felt impelled to move farther along the pew and saw others doing the same.

The rector paused as though listening, then hesitantly began his opening address by speaking of the great feast they were all celebrating that night. He stopped again in midsentence as throughout the body of the church, people shook with fear and began to move down the benches, crowding to one end as though pressed for space because more people had entered the church and were attempting to be seated. And yet the benches were empty.

In the breath-holding silence another even louder sound could be heard as if the timbers of the choir stall were cracking and groaning beneath a great weight.

The rector looked toward his patron and saw that Lord Sheringham's face was beaded with perspiration as those around him squeezed ever closer. Then the cleric's glance was drawn to the bride to be, and what he saw made him blanch and cross himself.

She stared down at a point just ahead of her as if she could see something they could not see. There was no fear in her eyes—only a kind of questioning.

Mr. Tremaine was also watching Mercedes from his place behind and a little to one side of her. She appeared to be listening intently, and once she nodded.

Suddenly, somewhere in the church, a woman began to scream, and others followed suit, weeping noisily. It became clear that at any moment there would be pandemonium and people hurt. The rector's voice rose above them, addressing the earl.

"My lord, we cannot proceed. I am afraid the ceremony must be deferred."

Lord Sheringham leaned forward, his hands gripping the bench, his brow beaded with sweat. "No, damn you. I'll not be stopped now." He was trembling. "Get these fools out and proceed."

"I will not, my lord," the priest returned in a loud, clear voice, though his face, too, sheened with perspiration. "There is more at work here tonight than any of us can understand, and to continue would be to court folly."

He turned to the congregation, his voice loud and clear, calming them, his hand upraised in blessing.

"My dear brethren, this service will not proceed. Go now, without fear. Praise the Lord's birth in your own homes this night. And may the peace of God go with you."

Almost imperceptibly the sensation of congestion began to ease as the farmers scrambled for the door, arms protectively around their wives. In the family pew the same exodus was taking place, and

Lord Sheringham, though furious, was obliged to give way.

Outside, all but the Priory party had vanished. Mr. Tremaine was the first to reach Mercedes, driven by the need to assure himself that the happenings in the church had not destroyed the fragile balance of her mind.

He found her standing alone in the shadow of a great pine tree, head uplifted, facing the distant Priory. A curious stillness surrounded her, and she seemed not to be aware of Lord Sheringham's voice uplifted in the background, angrily denouncing the rector for a paltry coward—"Call yourself a man of God! Letting yourself be panicked by a few hysterical villagers!"—while the vicomte, much shaken, sat on a tree stump, bent over with his head in his hands.

Mr. Tremaine knew he must approach Mercedes with the greatest care. She had a distant look about her that made him uneasy.

"Mercedes?"

She appeared not to hear, and his heart turned over as he met the troubled glances of Bea and the others who had joined him.

"Mercedes," he said again, gently, not touching her. "Let me take you back to Brampton Grange. Bea will look after you."

She turned her huge eyes on him then, and he saw that, although they were troubled, there was no hint of her mind having tipped over the edge.

"I cannot come with you," she said with quiet anguish. "There is a thing that I must do—and I am afraid."

He felt his way carefully. "Is this 'thing' connected with what happened in the church?"

She drew in a sharp breath. "The poor lady. I

must not fail her, but it will be hard." Her fingers grasped his arm. "Please, will you come with me?"

"To the ends of the earth, if need be," he replied, deeply moved. "Only tell me where."

She smiled then, a slightly distrait smile.

"To the Priory, naturally."

"Vyvian, you can't take her there!" Timothy exclaimed.

Charles laid a warning hand on his arm. "Let them be, m'boy. There is more here than we can hope to understand, but I'll vow that Vyv knows what he's doing. We'll follow, just to be sure."

Mr. Tremaine wished he were as confident, but he led Mercedes to the chaise in silence and handed her up. As they drove off, Sheringham saw them and began to swear and call for his own carriage.

Soon Mr. Tremaine and Mercedes were being pursued by several vehicles, with Charles holding Sheringham and the rest off. He drove on to the forecourt and stopped where Mercedes told him, some yards short of the cloisters.

As he helped her down, she drew another painfully deep breath, and he felt a shudder run through her.

"Now, you must leave me. I have to go the rest of the way alone, or she will not come."

The mythical "she" again, as in the park the day before. And again Mr. Tremaine felt the hairs lift on the back of his neck.

"Mercedes, I can't let you do this!" he exclaimed.

But she was already moving away from him into the shadow of the cloisters. It took all the courage he possessed to let her go, but he knew that she was already far beyond listening to him. He was joined almost at once by Bea and the others.

"This is madness!" Timothy exclaimed. "Vyv,

you must go after her!" He darted forward. "Or, if you won't, I will!"

"No." Mr. Tremaine held him back. "Timothy, I beg of you. I don't know what's going on this night any more than you do, but I do know that Mercedes is not mad—and that we must trust her. Look!"

She had by now reached the cloisters, where she paused as if waiting, listening—then she nodded and moved slowly forward into the deep shadows and out of their sight.

At the same moment the forecourt erupted into confusion with the arrival of Lord Sheringham, who leaped from his carriage, waving his arms and shouting abuse as he began running toward the cloisters.

"Have you all gone mad, letting her go in there? It's dangerous! It could come down any time!"

"Fool—madman! Come back!" Mr. Tremaine shouted and raced after him.

After that, everything happened very quickly. Within the ruins light and shadow stood in stark contrast, and ahead of him, beyond Sheringham, Mr. Tremaine could see Mercedes moving steadily forward, in and out of his vision, as though being led, toward a kind of circular turret.

"Come away, for God's sake," the earl shouted, and the vibration of his voice brought down a shower of dust and masonry. "That place is closed off—it isn't safe!"

But Mercedes went steadily on until she reached the turret, where she paused, as if hesitant about what to do next. Sheringham had almost caught up to her when a large piece of masonry fell directly on him, leaving him crushed and bleeding on the ground.

Mr. Tremaine sped past him without a glance and

reached Mercedes, who was staring down through a gap in the wall. He saw that there were steps, badly crumbling away, leading down to what had probably been a refectory in earlier times. And as he stood there, his eyes trying to penetrate the choking dust, there came another smell—not incense this time, but the faint dry odor of decay.

"She is down there," Mercedes said quietly, sounding suddenly, unbearably weary. "Poor lady. Now, perhaps, she will have peace."

"She will," he said, gathering her unresisting body into his arms. "Come away now, dearest girl. Your part is done."

Very much later, when Mercedes had slept long and deeply for many hours, the whole grisly story and its conclusion was revealed to her. She was carried downstairs by Mr. Tremaine, and they all sat together in the drawing room on Christmas afternoon, the children having been banished to the nursery for a rest.

And in that place of festive joy, surrounded by all the decorations she had helped to make and presents still scattered around, and wrapped safely in the arms of her beloved Vyvian, Mercedes at last learned that Lord Sheringham was dead, crushed by the masonry that had fallen on him.

"Oh, the poor man! I did not like him, but—"

"Poor be damned!" Timothy exclaimed, to be reproved by Cecily. "The man's a murderer of the worst kind. And deuced clever. Fooled his sister completely, fooled the lot of us."

"I do not understand."

"Before the earl died," Charles explained, "he confessed how he had killed his wife and thrown her body into the ruins of the refectory on the night before he left for Italy, all those long months ago."

"*Dieu!* But how is it possible that no one knew?"

"As Timothy said, he was clever. He bewitched the countess's maid," Bea told her. "A pretty girl. He made her believe he loved her and wished to run away with her."

"She must have been very silly, I think, to love such a one."

Mr. Tremaine laughed softly and kissed the dainty pink lobe of his beloved's ear. "Very silly," he agreed. "But for such a girl, the prospect of untold wealth must have been an irresistible incentive."

"I would like to believe that she did not know about the murder," Bea said. "The earl's confession was a little confused."

"So the lady I saw in the cloisters was the countess?"

Mr. Tremaine's arms tightened round Mercedes. "When I think how close you came to joining her in those damned ruins . . ."

"She would not have allowed that to happen, I think," came the confident reply, and they all looked at one another. "Lord Sheringham was her quarry. But she needed the right person to be the instrument of his downfall. We were, as you say, *sympathetique*—like twin souls, you know?"

"Well, be that as it may," said Timothy gruffly, "the fact remains that you came deuced close—frightened the life out of us!"

"I am sorry, Sir Timothy."

They were all silent, reliving the terrifying moment when it had seemed that the whole edifice would come down, killing everyone inside. A log stirred and settled, sending up a shower of sparks.

Mercedes sighed. "In the church—I think it was the monks, you know, who rose up on the lady's behalf to destroy the earl's plans."

"I wouldn't like to go through an experience like that again." Bea shuddered. "The remains of the countess will have to have a proper burial, and the rector says he will bless the area of the cloisters before they are pulled down for good."

"And what of Papa?" Mercedes asked hesitantly.

"He is upstairs," Charles said. "Very shaken, as you may imagine. And very chastened. He behaved very badly, of course, but I am convinced that he knew nothing of Lord Sheringham's duplicity. You may care to see him later."

"Yes." Mercedes bit her lip. "I must, of course. But you have not finished the story of Lord Sheringham's terrible deed," she continued, like a child deprived of the ending of a story. "How was it that the Lady Lavinia did not know of it?"

"She is still too distressed to offer a coherent explanation," said Bea. "But we know that he had arranged that they would leave very early in the morning, so that all the good-byes were said the night before. Lady Lavinia did watch their departure from her window, but all she saw was a heavily cloaked figure being assisted into the coach by Lord Sheringham, and waving to her."

"She was the maid," Mercedes said triumphantly.

"Undoubtedly, the maid, who, I suppose her ladyship assumed, was already in the second coach with the baggage."

"And what happened to her?"

"No one knows," said Charles tactfully, though he doubted the girl would have been allowed to live long to tell the tale. But he had reckoned without Mercedes's practical mind.

"He would have to kill her also, the poor silly one."

"Probably."

"How sad." A tear rolled down Mercedes's

cheek and was lovingly wiped away by Mr. Tremaine. "I hope he took her to Italy first, for it seems only fair that at least she should have had a little pleasure before he made away with her."

She could not understand why they all laughed suddenly, breaking the tension, or why Vyvian's arms tightened around her.

Bea stood up. "I must go and see if the children are growing restless," she said and looked meaningfully at the others. Charles took the hint at once and stood up. "I'll come with you."

Timothy continued to lounge with his feet stretched out to the fire, until Cecily hauled him to his feet.

"And you can take me for a nice brisk walk before the best of the day goes."

"Oh, I say," he began, and she kicked his ankle. "Oh, I *see*," he said, coming reluctantly to his feet. "Very well."

"We'll have tea in about half an hour."

When the door had closed behind them, it was very quiet in the drawing room. The only sounds were the tick of the clock and the occasional shifting of a log.

"Why has everyone gone?" Mercedes asked, settling herself more comfortably against Mr. Tremaine's chest.

He laughed softly. "I believe they were being tactful—leaving us alone together."

"Oh!" Pink-cheeked, she lifted up her head to look into his eyes, and with a groan he pulled her to him and kissed her, and went on kissing her in the most delightful and ingenious ways, so that she was very sorry when at last he stopped.

"That was very beautiful," she sighed. "Do you know, I find it quite extraordinary that we have known each other only for three days?"

"Three days, it may be," he said with mock anguish, "but after all you've put me through, I feel as though I have aged three years!"

"Ah, but I will make it up to you, you will see," she whispered, leaning close. "And then you will not feel old at all!"